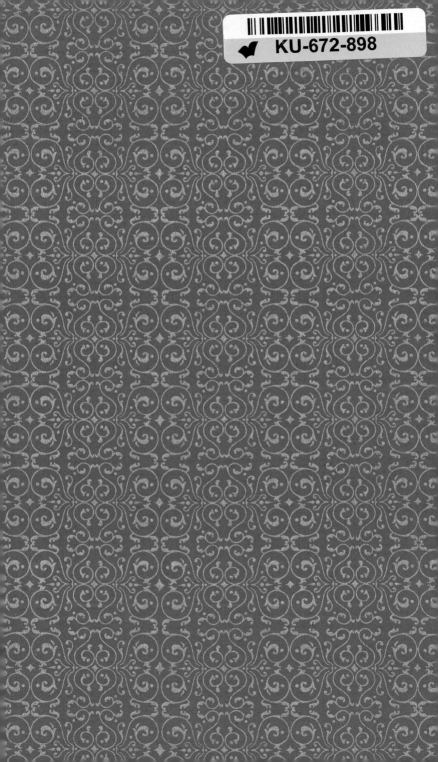

THE
GREATEST MASTERPIECES
OF
RUSSIAN LITERATURE

IVAN S. TURGENEV

VIRGIN SOIL

Translated from the Russian by
Rochelle S. Townsend
with an Introduction by Nikolay Andreyev, Ph.D., M.A.

Original Frontispiece by Marek Rudnicki
Original Illustrations by Sandra Archibald

Distributed by
HERON BOOKS

Published by arrangement with
J. M. Dent & Sons Ltd.

marek Rudnicki

INTRODUCTION

TURGENEV took an exceptionally consistent view of Russia, of her society and of her future. His opinions were founded on a clear-sighted, unsentimental love of his country whose great spaces and rich variety of human types he described so well. But this love of Russia went hand in hand with the conviction that she should be reorganized and re-educated in the spirit of western European traditions and that her future lay along the road of evolution rather than of revolution. Turgenev did not leave out of account the complexity of Russian life in general and the singularity of certain features of Russian manners and customs in particular. He was not a man of spiritual extremes. Perhaps this is the key to his constant disagreements with Tolstoy and Dostoyevsky who, at a period when he was undergoing a wholehearted revulsion from the ideals of the westerners, passionately denounced Turgenev as a 'German bourgeois' and reproached him for his coldness and his aloof detachment from life in Russia. Yet, from the very beginning, Turgenev's works were quite openly bound up with actual current social problems: his *Sportsman's Sketches* (twenty stories from which were first published in 1847, reprinted in 1852 and reappeared in a fuller edition in 1879), his famous novels, *Rudin* (1856), *A Nest of Gentlefolk* (1858), *On the Eve* (1859), *Fathers and Children* (1862), *Smoke* (1867) and *Virgin Soil* (1877), and also the vast majority of his short stories and short novels, dealt with controversial current problems and were to some extent consciously 'sociological' in their aims and inspiration. Naturally Turgenev's presentation and interpretation of public events could not but give rise to clashes with conflicting opinions which were not infrequently extended to the personality of the author. And so Turgenev—so well-intentioned, so moderate, always guided by the desire to be fair to all—became the object of violent discussions, scathing denunciations or ardent praise. Now he was held up as an idol, now cast down to the lowest depths by critics, readers and, to use a phrase which became fashionable in his time, by his 'brother writers'.

Virgin Soil, the last and longest of Turgenev's great novels, was first published in the journal *European Messenger* in the January and February numbers for 1877 at a time when public sympathy for Turgenev happened to be at one of its lowest ebbs. Even today historians of literature tend to dismiss *Virgin Soil* as a failure. This failure is still often explained by the argument that it is the work of 'an already aging writer' (Turgenev was fifty-nine when it was published), who had written it abroad after having lost contact with the genuine emotive forces which swayed Russia at that time—and the author himself admitted in 1874: 'The big thing [*Virgin Soil*] on which I am working is not progressing at all: it is quite impossible to write about Russia when living abroad.' The still more severe judgment of a revolutionary, Lopatin, was also frequently quoted in this context: 'Even a powerful talent is powerless to depict a *milieu* which it knows only from casual hearsay.' The novel was generally considered to be a *roman-à-thèse* and was therefore discredited as a true reflection of the movement 'to the people'. The aim of this movement, which began at the end of the sixties and went on well into the seventies of the last century, was to disseminate propaganda amongst the people by sharing their daily lives with the purpose of inducing them to rise against the régime in the name of 'a better future' rather vaguely envisaged in the rosy tones of —in the majority of cases—Utopian Socialism—and, in a few instances, of anarchism or arbitrary dictatorship. The theoretical foundation of this movement were the exhortations of a Russian *émigré*, the Radical Herzen, to students, who had been sent down from the university for political reasons, to go to the people and to expound to them 'the whole truth', and also the opinions of Bakunin, an anarchist who considered that the position of the Russian peasantry was so miserable and that the peasant himself was so impregnated with hostility to the State that it should be easy to raise 'any single village' against the Government and that local 'rebellions would easily spread and transform themselves into a peasant revolution'. P. L. Lavrov, another political theoretician, contributed to the ideology of the movement in his *Historical Letters* (published 1868–9), when he wrote of 'the unpaid debt to the people' which lay on the conscience of the intelligentsia. This idea was enthusiastically adopted by the radical youth of the country, who found in it a theoretical and moral basis for their usually rather hazy revolutionary aspirations. This was the genesis of the psychology of the 'repentant nobleman', of those 'critically minded individuals' who are the prime movers of all 'human progress'. This psychological atmosphere which led many a young man and woman to give up everything 'to go to the people' reached its culmination in the years 1873–4, when many hundreds of enthusiasts were carried away by this complex of ideas and emotions. But by the end of 1874 the main impetus of the movement was already spent. It broke down because of the retaliatory methods employed by the Government, which arrested more than a thousand people on the charge of spreading 'revolutionary propaganda' and also because of the frequently hostile attitude of the peasants, who regarded the young intellectuals dressed up in workmen's clothing with considerable suspicion, frequentl refused to receive them and quite often actually handed them over to the police. The leading agitators were brought before the courts at the 'Trial of the 193' which, after an inquiry which lasted for more than three years, finally put an end to this episode in the history of the Populist movement.

Turgenev dates the germination of the novel *Virgin Soil* to July 1870: 'I had a passing idea for a new novel.' He sketched a plan with brief characterizations of the heroes. The central idea of the novel was to be the 'romantic revolutionary' (Nezhdanov) contrasted with a Russian revolutionary of a more realistic type—the American-type man of action who goes about his task as calmly as a peasant ploughs and sows (Solomin). In February 1872 the heroes of *Virgin Soil* are delineated in greater detail, to a great extent along lines which the author developed still further when he came to write the novel. In December 1872 he wrote in a letter: 'I have the subject and the plan of a novel all ready for I do not at all believe that there are no more heroes in our epoch, or that there is nothing to write about, but, of the twelve characters who go to make up my *dramatis personae*, there are two who have not been sufficiently studied against their own background, who are not drawn from life, and I do not want to write fiction in that particular sense.' All these facts go to show that Turgenev approached the composition of his new novel with all his usual conscientiousness. He deliberately chose the first attempt to send propagandists among the people which took place at the end of the sixties as the basis for his novel. In the opinion of some scholars the mysterious 'Vassily Nikolayevich' who issues 'the orders' is supposed to suggest the revolutionary Nechayev—the details of whose organization would have been well known to Turgenev from the newspaper reports of their trial. It is an interesting fact that this same Nechayev scandal caught the imagination of Dostoyevsky at much the same time and inspired him to write *The Possessed*, which was published at the end of 1872 (cf. Preface and text, Dostoyevsky, *The Possessed*, Everyman's Library, No. 861, 1960). In this book Dostoyevsky drew a malicious caricature of Turgenev as the ultra-liberal and westernizer, the author Karmazinov. Perhaps, in *Virgin Soil*, there is a kind of answer to Dostoyevsky's condemnation of the underground revolutionary Russia of *The Possessed*. Turgenev's novel gives quite a different picture of the enthusiastic young devotees of the idea of social change. In any case two famous Russian revolutionary leaders, P. A. Lavrov and the theoretician of anarchism, Prince Kropotkin, found words of high praise to describe *Virgin Soil*. Lavrov, writing for the London *Athenaeum* in 1877, noted gratefully: 'In the face of a whole literature dominated by dirty calumniators of youth he has represented this revolutionary youth as the only representative of moral principle.' Kropotkin maintained: 'In *Virgin Soil* Turgenev, with his usual astonishing flair, has observed the most outstanding features of the Populist movement.'

INTRODUCTION

It was only from the beginning of 1876 that Turgenev's plans for *Virgin Soil* began to take on literary flesh quite fast. On 27th July he wrote from his estate, Spasskoye, to his publisher Stassyulevich that the novel was at last finished: 'Its title will be *Virgin Soil*, with the epigraph: "To turn over virgin soil it is necessary to use a deep plough going well into the earth, not a surface plough gliding lightly over the top."' Later Turgenev was to explain: 'The plough in my epigraph does not stand for revolution but for enlightenment.' After this Turgenev returned to France, where he spent several months copying out the novel and changing it constantly as he did so; 'there are some pages on which not one line has remained as it was'. In November the manuscript was dispatched and Turgenev wrote to the poet Polonsky: 'If they beat me with sticks for *Fathers and Children* they will come down on me with tree-trunks for *Virgin Soil* and in exactly the same way from both sides.'

Turgenev himself formulated the central idea of *Virgin Soil* in a letter to his editor in December 1876:

> Up till now the younger generation have either been represented by our literature as a gang of swindlers and rogues, which is false and could only insult the young reader who must regard it as a lie and a libel; or they have been idealized, which again is false and, besides, harmful. I decided to approach the truth along the middle way; to depict young people, most of them good and honest, and to show that notwithstanding their disinterestedness the task which they had set themselves was so artificial and untrue to life that it could only end in complete fiasco.... Whatever happens the young people cannot possibly complain that they have been depicted by an enemy; on the contrary, I think they cannot but feel the sympathy I have if not for their aims then at least for their personalities. It is in this way that a novel written for them and about them can be of use to them.

After the publication of *Virgin Soil* Turgenev did indeed find himself under fire from both camps and the public as a whole were disappointed with the novel. This disappointment had nothing to do with the author's age or with his having lost contact with Russia but was because some sections of the Populist movement had already entered a more dramatic phase than that of the situation depicted in this novel. Turgenev offered a prescription for 'gradual evolution' whereas the radical youth of the country, having passed through the emotional stage of Populism, were already reforming into more organized groups with more sharply defined political aims. They had already established the secret society 'Land and Freedom' and were on the verge of forming the terrorist organization 'The People's Will' which in 1881 organized the assassination of the Emperor Alexander II. At the time of publication *Virgin Soil* was, in effect, already five years out of date. This was bound to affect its immediate success but in no way detracts from the incontrovertibly high literary calibre of Turgenev's work, nor from its importance as a vehicle for Turgenev's opinions. He told his editor that his aim in this novel had been to express everything he felt and thought about the situation in Russia and, as it were, to throw down a last challenge to the forces of reaction and revolution.

As in all Turgenev's novels, the characters of *Virgin Soil* are real people and the psychological motivation of their actions is always convincing, and if, perhaps, he lays particular stress on their helplessness in matters of everyday life and their naïveté, it is probable that this actually corresponded to the facts. Turgenev visited Russia in 1871 with the express purpose of gathering 'impressions' for *Virgin Soil* and he also had many close contacts among the revolutionary-minded *émigrés*. He demonstrated the reason for the failure of the first Populist movement but did not deny the potential usefulness of such a movement for the improvement of life and the establishment of a more just social order. The censor Vedrov was undoubtedly right from his own point of view when, on 29th January 1877, he pointed out to the Committee of Censorship that 'the destructive elements of the Populist movement are not put an end to in *Virgin Soil* by the suicide of Nezhdanov and the retribution which catches up with Markelov—these elements remain in the persistence of Solomin who organizes the factory in Perm on a co-operative basis, the great devotion which Mariana brings to this task, in the intensely secretive nature of Mashurina, a member of the group who is careful not to say too much in front of the chatterbox Paklin, and in the derisive depiction of the civil servant, the representative of law and order. *Virgin Soil* proves only that the Populist movement was ill-timed, not that there is any lack of incendiary material in Russia'. The censor suggested that the end of the novel should not be allowed to be printed, and half the commission agreed with him. The other half, however, which included the chairman, considered that 'to hold up the February number of the *European Messenger*' (in which *Virgin Soil* was first printed) 'would give rise to unbecoming talk and speculation and that this should be avoided'. On 30th January 1877 the Minister for Internal Affairs agreed with the second opinion but added, according to Turgenev, that 'had he read the book all through before he would undoubtedly have forbidden it'.

Turgenev was right when, in August 1877, he wrote in a letter: 'My latest book has cost me much hard work and brought me little joy. It was particularly sad that in writing it so much had to be left unsaid, so many topics avoided.' In the introduction to his Collected Works (1880) Turgenev stated that up to that time there had not been one single well-disposed review of *Virgin Soil* printed in Russia. However, very soon afterwards the book recovered from its initial lack of success and began to be appreciated in Russia as well as in western Europe for the outstanding work of art which it was. Here the novel had met with a happier fate. The trials of the 52 and then of the 103 had created such a sensation that *Virgin Soil* very soon became a best seller in France, England and America. Some critics even hailed Turgenev as a prophet who had forecast the course of history! *Virgin Soil* added still further to Turgenev's formidable literary prestige in western Europe, which received as it were the final accolade when he was chosen to be vice-president of the International Literary Congress in Paris, where he occupied a seat of honour next to Victor Hugo. In 1879, in June, he was honoured by Oxford University with the degree of Doctor of Civil Law and in August he was made an *Officer d'Instruction Publique* by the French Government.

INTRODUCTION

Now that the political passions and curiosity which *Virgin Soil* aroused on its first publication have passed into history, the novel retains its power to hold the interest of the reader. The fascinating historical background; the vivid picture of everyday life in Russia during the seventies of the last century; the authenticity of the psychological portrayal of the characters—sometimes rendered with a certain ironic hyperbole but more often shown simply through the actions of the characters themselves; and, last but by no means least, the sheer beauty and technical mastery of the author's style—all these elements combine to make a classic and immortal work. The novel begins slowly to give the reader the opportunity to get acquainted with the most important personages, and then the action develops at a brisker *tempo* to expound an exciting plot which continues to hold the reader to the last page. As always with Turgenev, human nature finally triumphs over human logic. Turgenev held strong views on the power of nature; it is not fortuitous that Nezhdanov's tragic end harmonizes at the moment when it is accomplished with nature—an overcast sky and a depressing landscape: he had no right to take on a task which was beyond his capacities.

Turgenev's talent is particularly powerful in this immortalization of a curious episode of Russia's history mirrored by his superb art.

Nikolay Andreyev.

1963.

VIRGIN SOIL

" To turn over virgin soil it is necessary to use a deep plough going well into the earth, not a surface plough gliding lightly over the top."— *From a Farmer's Note-book.*

I

AT one o'clock in the afternoon of a spring day in the year 1868, a young man of twenty-seven, carelessly and shabbily dressed, was toiling up the back staircase of a five-storied house in Officers Street in St. Petersburg. Noisily shuffling his down-trodden goloshes and slowly swinging his heavy, clumsy figure, the man at last reached the very top flight and stopped before a half-open door hanging off its hinges. He did not ring the bell, but gave a loud sigh and walked straight into a small, dark passage.

" Is Nejdanov at home? " he called out in a deep, loud voice.

" No, he's not. I'm here. Come in," an equally coarse woman's voice responded from the adjoining room.

" Is that Mashurina? " asked the new-comer.

" Yes, it is I. Are you Ostrodumov? "

Pemien Ostrodumov," he replied, carefully removing his goloshes, and hanging his shabby coat on a nail he went into the room from whence issued the woman's voice.

It was a narrow, untidy room, with dull green coloured walls, badly lighted by two dusty windows. The whole furniture consisted of an iron bedstead standing in a corner, a table in the middle, several chairs, and a bookcase piled up with books. At the table sat a woman of about thirty. She was bareheaded, clad in a black stuff dress, and was

1

smoking a cigarette. On catching sight of Ostrodumov she extended her broad, red hand without a word. He shook it, also without saying anything, dropped into a chair and pulled a half-broken cigar out of a side pocket. Mashurina gave him a light, and without exchanging a single word, or so much as looking at one another, they began sending out long, blue puffs into the stuffy room, already filled with smoke.

There was something similar about these two smokers, although their features were not a bit alike. In these two slovenly figures, with their coarse lips, teeth, and noses (Ostrodumov was even pock-marked), there was something honest and firm and persevering.

" Have you seen Nejdanov? " Ostrodumov asked.

" Yes. He will be back directly. He has gone to the library with some books."

Ostrodumov spat to one side.

" Why is he always rushing about nowadays? One can never get hold of him."

Mashurina took out another cigarette.

" He's bored," she remarked, lighting it carefully.

" Bored! " Ostrodumov repeated reproachfully. " What self-indulgence! One would think we had no work to do. Heaven knows how we shall get through with it, and he complains of being bored! "

" Have you heard from Moscow? " Mashurina asked after a pause.

" Yes. A letter came three days ago."

" Have you read it? "

Ostrodumov nodded his head.

" Well? What news? "

" Some of us must go there soon."

Mashurina took the cigarette out of her mouth.

" But why? " she asked. " They say everything is going on well there."

" Yes, that is so, but one man has turned out unreliable

2

and must be got rid of. Besides that, there are other things. They want you to come too."

" Do they say so in the letter? "

" Yes."

Mashurina shook back her heavy hair, which was twisted into a small plait at the back and fell over her eyebrows in front.

" Well," she remarked; " if the thing is settled, then there is nothing more to be said."

" Of course not. Only one can't do anything without money, and where are we to get it from? "

Mashurina became thoughtful.

" Nejdanov must get the money," she said softly, as if to herself.

" That is precisely what I have come about," Ostrodumov observed.

" Have you got the letter? " Mashurina asked suddenly.

" Yes. Would you like to see it? "

" I should rather. But never mind, we can read it together presently."

" You need not doubt what I say. I am speaking the truth," Ostrodumov grumbled.

" I do not doubt it in the least." They both ceased speaking and, as before, clouds of smoke rose silently from their mouths and curled feebly above their shaggy heads.

A sound of goloshes was heard from the passage.

" There he is," Mashurina whispered.

The door opened slightly and a head was thrust in, but it was not the head of Nejdanov.

It was a round head with rough black hair, a broad wrinkled forehead, bright brown eyes under thick eyebrows, a snub nose and a humorously-set mouth. The head looked round, nodded, smiled, showing a set of tiny white teeth, and came into the room with its feeble body, short arms, and bandy legs, which were a little lame. As soon as

Mashurina and Ostrodumov caught sight of this head an expression of contempt, mixed with condescension, came over their faces, as if each was thinking inwardly, " What a nuisance ! " but neither moved nor uttered a single word. The newly arrived guest was not in the least taken aback by this reception, however; on the contrary it seemed to amuse him.

" What is the meaning of this? " he asked in a squeaky voice. " A duet? Why not a trio? And where's the chief tenor? "

" Do you mean Nejdanov, Mr. Paklin? " Ostrodumov asked solemnly.

" Yes, Mr. Ostrodumov."

" He will be back directly, Mr. Paklin."

" I am glad to hear that, Mr. Ostrodumov."

The little cripple turned to Mashurina. She frowned, and continued leisurely puffing her cigarette.

" How are you, my dear . . . my dear . . . I am so sorry. I always forget your Christian name and your father's name."

Mashurina shrugged her shoulders.

" There is no need for you to know it. I think you know my surname. What more do you want? And why do you always keep on asking how I am? You see that I am still in the land of the living! "

" Of course! " Paklin exclaimed, his face twitching nervously. " If you had been elsewhere, your humble servant would not have had the pleasure of seeing you here, and of talking to you! My curiosity is due to a bad, old-fashioned habit. But with regard to your name, it is awkward, somehow, simply to say Mashurina. I know that even in letters you only sign yourself Bonaparte! I beg pardon, Mashurina, but in conversation, however——"

" And who asks you to talk to me, pray? "

Paklin gave a nervous, gulpy laugh.

" Well, never mind, my dear. Give me your hand.

4

Don't be cross. I know you mean well, and so do I. . . .
Well? "

Paklin extended his hand, Mashurina looked at him
severely and extended her own.

" If you really want to know my name," she said with the
same expression of severity on her face, " I am called
Fiekla."

" And I, Pemien," Ostrodumov added in his bass
voice.

" How very instructive! Then tell me, O Fiekla! and you,
O Pemien! why you are so unfriendly, so persistently
unfriendly to me when I——"

" Mashurina thinks," Ostrodumov interrupted him, " and
not only Mashurina, that you are not to be depended upon,
because you always laugh at everything."

Paklin turned round on his heels.

" That is the usual mistake people make about me, my
dear Pemien! In the first place, I am not always laughing,
and even if I were, that is no reason why you should not
trust me. In the second, I have been flattered with your
confidence on more than one occasion before now, a convincing proof of my trustworthiness. I am an honest man,
my dear Pemien."

Ostrodumov muttered something between his teeth, but
Paklin continued without the slightest trace of a smile on
his face:

" No, I am not always laughing! I am not at all a cheerful person. You have only to look at me! "

Ostrodumov looked at him. And really, when Paklin was
not laughing, when he was silent, his face assumed a dejected, almost scared expression; it became funny and
rather sarcastic only when he opened his lips. Ostrodumov
did not say anything, however, and Paklin turned to Mashurina again.

" Well? And how are your studies getting on? Have
you made any progress in your truly philanthropical art?

5

Is it very hard to help an inexperienced citizen on his first appearance in this world? "

" It is not at all hard if he happens to be no bigger than you are! " Mashurina retorted with a self-satisfied smile. (She had quite recently passed her examination as a mid-wife. Coming from a poor aristocratic family, she had left her home in the south of Russia about two years before, and with about twelve shillings in her pocket had arrived in Moscow, where she had entered a lying-in institution and had worked very hard to gain the necessary certificate. She was unmarried and very chaste. " No wonder! " some sceptics may say, bearing in mind the description of her personal appearance, but we will permit ourselves to say that it was wonderful and rare.)

Paklin laughed at her retort.

" Well done, my dear! I feel quite crushed! But it serves me right for being such a dwarf! I wonder where our host has got to? "

Paklin purposely changed the subject of conversation, which was rather a sore one to him. He could never resign himself to his small stature, nor indeed to the whole of his unprepossessing figure. He felt it the more because he was passionately fond of women and would have given anything to be attractive to them. The consciousness of his pitiful appearance was a much sorer point with him than his low origin and unenviable position in society. His father, a member of the lower middle class, had, through all sorts of dishonest means, attained the rank of titular councillor. He had been fairly successful as an intermediary in legal matters, and managed estates and house property. He had made a moderate fortune, but had taken to drink towards the end of his life and had left nothing after his death. Young Paklin (he was called Sila—Sila Samsonitch,[1] and always regarded this name as a joke against himself) was educated in a commercial school, where he had acquired a

[1] Meaning strength, son of Samson.

6

good knowledge of German. After a great many difficulties he had entered an office, where he received a salary of five hundred roubles a year, out of which he had to keep himself, an invalid aunt, and a humpbacked sister. At the time of our story Paklin was twenty-eight years old. He had a great many acquaintances among students and young people, who liked him for his cynical wit, his harmless, though biting, self-confident speeches, his one-sided, unpedantic, though genuine, learning, but occasionally they sat on him severely. Once, on arriving late at a political meeting, he hastily began excusing himself. "Paklin was afraid!" some one sang out from a corner of the room, and every one laughed. Paklin laughed with them, although it was like a stab in his heart. "He is right, the blackguard!" he thought to himself. Nejdanov he had come across in a little Greek restaurant, where he was in the habit of taking his dinner, and where he sat airing his rather free and audacious views. He assured every one that the main cause of his democratic turn of mind was the bad Greek cooking, which upset his liver.

"I wonder where our host has got to?" he repeated.

"He has been out of sorts lately. Heaven forbid that he should be in love!"

Mashurina scowled.

"He has gone to the library for books. As for falling in love, he has neither the time nor the opportunity."

"Why not with you?" almost escaped Paklin's lips.

"I should like to see him, because I have an important matter to talk over with him," he said aloud.

"What about?" Ostrodumov asked. "Our affairs?"

"Perhaps yours; that is, our common affairs."

Ostrodumov hummed. He did not believe him. "Who knows? He's such a busy body," he thought.

"There he is at last!" Mashurina exclaimed suddenly, and her small unattractive eyes, fixed on the door, bright-

7

ened, as if lit up by an inner ray, making them soft and warm and tender.

The door opened, and this time a young man of twenty-three, with a cap on his head and a bundle of books under his arm, entered the room. It was Nejdanov himself.

II

AT the sight of visitors he stopped in the doorway, took them in at a glance, threw off his cap, dropped the books on to the floor, walked over to the bed, and sat down on the very edge. An expression of annoyance and displeasure passed over his pale handsome face, which seemed even paler than it really was, in contrast to his dark red, wavy hair.

Mashurina turned away and bit her lip; Ostrodumov muttered, "At last!"

Paklin was the first to approach him.

"Why, what is the matter, Alexai Dmitritch, Hamlet of Russia? Has something happened, or are you just simply depressed, without any particular cause?"

"Oh, stop! Mephistopheles of Russia!" Nejdanov exclaimed irritably. "I am not in the mood for fencing with blunt witticisms just now."

Paklin laughed.

"That's not quite correct. If it is wit, then it can't be blunt. If blunt, then it can't be wit."

"All right, all right! We know you are clever!"

"Your nerves are out of order," Paklin remarked hesitatingly. "Or has something really happened?"

"Oh, nothing in particular, only that it is impossible to show one's nose in this hateful town without knocking against some vulgarity, stupidity, tittle tattle, or some horrible injustice. One can't live here any longer!"

"Is that why your advertisement in the papers says that you want a place and have no objection to leaving St. Petersburg?" Ostrodumov asked.

"Yes. I would go away from here with the greatest of

pleasure, if some fool could be found who would offer me a place!"

"You should first fulfil your duties here," Mashurina remarked significantly, her face still turned away.

"What duties?" Nejdanov asked, turning towards her. Mashurina bit her lip. "Ask Ostrodumov."

Nejdanov turned to Ostrodumov. The latter hummed and hawed, as if to say, "Wait a minute."

"But seriously," Paklin broke in, "have you heard any unpleasant news?"

Nejdanov bounced up from the bed like an india-rubber ball. "What more do you want?" he shouted out suddenly, in a ringing voice. Half of Russia is dying of hunger! *The Moscow News* is triumphant! They want to introduce classicism, the students' benefit clubs have been closed, spies everywhere, oppression, lies, betrayals, deceit! And it is not enough for him! He wants some new unpleasantness! He thinks that I am joking. . . . Basanov has been arrested," he added, lowering his voice. "I heard it at the library."

Mashurina and Ostrodumov lifted their heads simultaneously.

"My dear Alexai Dmitritch," Paklin began, "you are upset, and for a very good reason. But have you forgotten in what times and in what country we are living? Amongst us a drowning man must himself create the straw to clutch at. Why be sentimental over it? One must look the devil straight in the face and not get excited like children——"

"Oh, don't, please!" Nejdanov interrupted him desperately, frowning as if in pain. "We know you are energetic and not afraid of anything——"

"I not afraid of anything?" Paklin began.

"I wonder who could have betrayed Basanov?" Nejdanov continued. "I simply can't understand!"

"A friend no doubt. Friends are great at that. One must look alive! I once had a friend, who seemed a good

10

fellow; he was always concerned about me and my reputation. 'I say, what dreadful stories are being circulated about you!' he would greet me one day. 'They say that you poisoned your uncle and that on one occasion, when you were introduced into a certain house, you sat the whole evening with your back to the hostess and that she was so upset that she cried at the insult! What awful nonsense! What fools could possibly believe such things!' Well, and what do you think? A year after I quarrelled with this same friend, and in his farewell letter to me he wrote, 'You who killed your own uncle! You who were not ashamed to insult an honourable lady by sitting with your back to her,' and so on and so on. Here are friends for you!"

Ostrodumov and Mashurina exchanged glances.

"Alexai Dmitritch!" Ostrodumov exclaimed in his heavy bass voice; he was evidently anxious to avoid a useless discussion. "A letter has come from Moscow, from Vassily Nikolaevitch."

Nejdanov trembled slightly and cast down his eyes.

"What does he say?" he asked at last.

"He wants us to go there with her." Ostrodumov indicated Mashurina with his eyebrows.

"Do they want her too?'

"Yes."

"Well, what's the difficulty?

"Why, money, of course."

Nejdanov got up from the bed and walked over to the window.

"How much do you want?"

"Not less than fifty roubles."

Nejdanov was silent.

"I have no money just now," he whispered at last, drumming his fingers on the window pane, "but I could get some. Have you got the letter?"

"Yes, it . . . that is … . certainly. . . ."

"Why are you always trying to keep things from me?"

11

Paklin exclaimed. " Have I not deserved your confidence? Even if I were not fully in sympathy with what you are undertaking, do you think for a moment that I am in a position to turn round or gossip? "

" Without intending to, perhaps," Ostrodumov remarked.

"Neither with nor without intention! Miss Mashurina is looking at me with a smile . . . but I say——"

" I am not smiling! " Mashurina burst out.

" But I say," Paklin went on, " that you have no tact. You are utterly incapable of recognising your real friends. If a man can laugh, then you think that he can't be serious——"

" Is it not so? " Mashurina snapped.

" You are in need of money, for instance," Paklin continued with new force, paying no attenton to Mashurina; " Nejdanov hasn't any. I could get it for you."

Nejdanov wheeled round from the window.

"No, no. It is not necessary. I can get the money. I will draw some of my allowance in advance. Now I recollect, they owe me something. Let us look ' at the letter, Ostrodumov."

Ostrodumov remained motionless for a time, then he looked round, stood up, bent down, turned up one of the legs of his trousers, and carefully pulled a piece of blue paper out of his high boot, blew at it for some reason or another, and handed it to Nejdanov. The latter took the piece of paper, unfolded it, read it carefully, and passed it on to Mashurina. She stood up, also read it, and handed it back to Nejdanov, although Paklin had extended his hand for it. Nejdanov shrugged his shoulders and gave the secret letter to Paklin. The latter scanned the paper in his turn, pressed his lips together significantly, and laid it solemnly on the table. Ostrodumov took it, lit a large match, which exhaled a strong odour of sulphur, lifted the paper high above his head, as if showing it to all present, set fire to it, and, regardless of his fingers, put the ashes into the stove. No one moved or pronounced a word during this proceeding; all had their eyes fixed on the floor. Ostrodumov looked concentrated and business-like, Nejdanov furious, Paklin intense, and Mashurina as if she were present at holy mass.

About two minutes went by in this way, every one feeling uncomfortable. Paklin was the first to break the silence.

" Well? " he began. " Is my sacrifice to be received on the altar of the fatherland? Am I permitted to bring, if not the whole, at any rate twenty-five or thirty roubles for the common cause? "

Nejdanov flared up. He seemed to be boiling over with annoyance, which was not lessened by the solemn burning of the letter—he was only waiting for an opportunity to burst out.

" I tell you that I don't want it, don't want, don't want it! I'll not allow it and I'll not take it! I can get the money. I can get it at once. I am not in need of any one's help! "

" My dear Alexai," Paklin remarked, " I see that you are not a democrat in spite of your being a revolutionist! "

" Why not say straight out that I'm an aristocrat? "

" So you are up to a certain point."

Nejdanov gave a forced laugh.

" I see you are hinting at the fact of my being illegitimate. You can save yourself the trouble, my dear boy. I am not likely to forget it."

Paklin threw up his arms in despair.

" Aliosha! What is the matter with you? How can you twist my words so? I hardly know you to-day."

Nejdanov shrugged his shoulders.

" Basanov's arrest has upset you, but he was so careless——"

" He did not hide his convictions," Mashurina put in gloomily. " It is not for us to sit in judgment upon him! "

" Quite so; only he might have had a little more con-

13

sideration for others, who are likely to be compromised through him now."

"What makes you think so?" Ostrodumov bawled out in his turn. "Basanov has plenty of character, he will not betray any one. Besides, not every one can be cautious you know, Mr. Paklin."

Paklin was offended and was about to say something when Nejdanov interrupted him.

"I vote we leave politics for a time, ladies and gentlemen!" he exclaimed.

A silence ensued.

"I ran across Skoropikin to-day," Paklin was the first to begin. "Our great national critic, æsthetic, and enthusiast! What an insufferable creature! He is for ever boiling and frothing over like a bottle of sour kvas. A waiter runs with it, his finger stuck in the bottle instead of a cork, a fat raisin in the neck, and when it has done frothing and foaming there is nothing left at the bottom but a few drops of some nasty stuff, which far from quenching any one's thirst is enough to make one ill. He's a most dangerous person for young people to come in contact with."

Paklin's true and rather apt comparison raised no smile on his listeners' faces, only Nejdanov remarked that if young people were fools enough to interest themselves in æsthetics, they deserved no pity whatever, even if Skoropikin did lead them astray.

"Of course," Paklin exclaimed with some warmth—the less sympathy he met with, the more heated he became—"I admit that the question is not a political one, but an important one, nevertheless. According to Skoropikin, every ancient work of art is valueless because it is old. If that were true, then art would be reduced to nothing more or less than mere fashion. A preposterous idea, not worth entertaining. If art has no firmer foundation than that, if it is not eternal, then it is utterly useless. Take science, for instance. In mathematics do you look upon Euler,

14

Laplace, or Gauss as fools? Of course not. You accept their authority. Then why question the authority of Raphael and Mozart? I must admit, however, that the laws of art are far more difficult to define than the laws of nature, but they exist just the same, and he who fails to see them is blind, whether he shuts his eyes to them purposely or not."

Paklin ceased, but no one uttered a word. They all sat with tightly closed mouths as if feeling unutterably sorry for him.

" All the same," Ostrodumov remarked, " I am not in the least sorry for the young people who run after Skoropikin."

" You are hopeless," Paklin thought. " I had better be going."

He went up to Nejdanov, intending to ask his opinion about smuggling in the magazine, the *Polar Star*, from abroad (the *Bell* had already ceased to exist), but the conversation took such a turn that it was impossible to raise the question. Paklin had already taken up his hat, when suddenly, without the slightest warning, a wonderfully pleasant, manly baritone was heard from the passage. The very sound of this voice suggested something gentle, fresh, and well-bred.

" Is Mr. Nejdanov at home? "

They all looked at one another in amazement.

" Is Mr. Nejdanov at home? " the baritone repeated.

" Yes, he is," Nejdanov replied at last.

The door opened gently and a man of about forty entered the room and slowly removed his glossy hat from his handsome, closely cropped head. He was tall and well-made, and dressed in a beautiful cloth coat with a gorgeous beaver collar, although it was already the end of April. He impressed Nejdanov and Paklin, and even Mashurina and Ostrodumov, with his elegant, easy carriage and courteous manner. They all rose instinctively on his entrance.

15

III

THE elegantly dressed man went up to Nejdanov with an amiable smile and began: " I have already had the pleasure of meeting you and even speaking to you, Mr. Nejdanov, the day before yesterday, if you remember, at tne theatre." (The visitor paused, as though waiting for Nejdanov to make some remark, but the latter merely bowed slightly and blushed.) " I have come to see you about your advertisement, which I noticed in the paper. I should like us to have a talk if your visitors would not mind. . . ." (He bowed to Mashurina, and waved a grey-gloved hand in the direction of Paklin and Ostrodumov.)

" Not at all," Nejdanov replied awkwardly. " Won't you sit down? "

The visitor bowed from the waist, drew a chair to himself, but did not sit down, as every one else was standing. He merely gazed round the room with his bright though half-closed eyes.

" Good-bye, Alexai Dmitritch," Mashurina exclaimed suddenly. " I will come again presently."

" And I too," Ostrodumov added.

Mashurina did not take the slightest notice of the visitor as she passed him, but went straight up to Nejdanov, gave him a hearty shake of the hand, and left the room without bowing to any one. Ostrodumov followed her, making an unnecessary noise with his boots, and snorting out once or twice contemptuously, " There's a beaver collar for you! "

The visitor accompanied them with a polite though slightly inquisitive look, and then directed his gaze to Paklin, hoping the latter would follow their example, but

Paklin withdrew into a corner and settled down. A peculiarly suppressed smile played on his lips ever since the appearance of the stranger. The visitor and Nejdanov also sat down.

" My name is Sipiagin. You may perhaps have heard of me," the visitor began with modest pride.

We must first relate how Nejdanov had met him at the theatre.

There had been a performance of Ostrovsky's play *Never Sit in Another Man's Sledge*, on the occasion of the great actor Sadovsky's coming from Moscow. Rusakov, one of the characters in the play, was known to be one of his favourite parts. Just before dinner on that day, Nejdanov went down to the theatre to book a ticket, but found a large crowd already waiting there. He walked up to the desk with the intention of getting a ticket for the pit, when an officer, who happened to be standing behind him, thrust a three-rouble note over Nejdanov's head and called out to the man inside: " He " (meaning Nejdanov) " will probably want change. I don't. Give me a ticket for the stalls, please. Make haste, I'm in a hurry! "

" Excuse me, sir, I want a ticket for the stalls myself! " Nejdanov exclaimed, throwing down a three-rouble note, all the ready money he possessed. He got his ticket, and in the evening appeared in the aristocratic part of the Alexandrinsky Theatre.

He was badly dressed, without gloves and in dirty boots. He was uncomfortable and angry with himself for feeling uncomfortable. A general with numerous orders glittering on his breast sat on his right, and on his left this same elegant Sipiagin, whose appearance two days later at Nejdanov's so astonished Mashurina and Ostrodumov. The general stared at Nejdanov every now and again, as though at something indecent, out of place, and offensive. Sipiagin looked at him sideways, but did not seem unfriendly. All the people surrounding him were evidently personages of

17

some importance, and as they all knew one another, they
kept exchanging remarks, exclamations, greetings, occasionally even over Nejdanov's head. He sat there motionless and ill at ease in his spacious armchair, feeling like an
outcast. Ostrovsky's play and Sadovsky's acting afforded
him but little pleasure, and he felt bitter at heart. When
suddenly, Oh wonder! During one of the intervals, his
neighbour on the left, not the glittering general, but the
other with no marks of distinction on his breast, addressed him
politely and kindly, but somewhat timidly. He asked him
what he thought of Ostrovsky's play, wanted to know his
opinion of it as a representative of the new generation.
Nejdanov, overwhelmed and half frightened, his heart
beating fast, answered at first curtly, in monosyllables, but
soon began to be annoyed with his own excitement. "After
all," he thought, "am I not a man like everybody else?"
and began expressing his opinions quite freely, without any
restraint. He got so carried away by his subject, and spoke
so loudly, that he quite alarmed the order-bedecked general.
Nejdanov was a strong admirer of Ostrovsky, but could not
help feeling, in spite of the author's great genius, his evident
desire to throw a slur on modern civilisation in the bur-
lesqued character of Veherov, in *Never Sit in Another Man's
Sledge*.

His polite neighbour listened to him attentively, evidently
interested in what he said. He spoke to him again in the
next interval, not about the play this time, but about various
matters of everyday life, about science, and even touched
upon political questions. He was decidedly interested in
his eloquent young companion. Nejdanov did not feel in
the least constrained as before, but even began to assume
airs, as if saying, "If you really want to know, I can satisfy
your curiosity!" The general's annoyance grew to indignation and even suspicion.

After the play Sipiagin took leave of Nejdanov very
courteously, but did not ask his name, neither did he tell

him his own. Whilst waiting for his carriage he ran against a friend, a certain Prince G., an aide-de-camp.

" I watched you from my box," the latter remarked, through a perfumed moustache. " Do you know whom you were speaking to? "

" No. Do you? A rather clever chap. Who is he? "

The prince whispered in his ear in French. " He is my brother . . . illegitimate. . . . His name is Nejdanov. I will tell you all about it some day. My father did not in the least expect that sort of thing, that was why he called him Nejdanov.[1] But he looked after him all right. *Il lui a fait un sort.* We make him an allowance to live on. He is not stupid. Had quite a good education, thanks to my father. But he has gone quite off the track—I think he's a republican. We refuse to have anything to do with him. *Il est impossible.* Good-bye, I see my carriage is waiting."

The prince separated.

The next day Sipiagin noticed Nejdanov's advertisement in the paper and went to see him.

" My name is Sipiagin," he repeated, as he sat in front of Nejdanov, surveying him with a dignified air. " I see by your advertisement that you are looking for a post, and I should like to know if you would be willing to come to me. I am married and have a boy of eight, a very intelligent child, I may say. We usually spend the summer and autumn in the country, in the province of S., about five miles from the town of that name. I should like you to come to us for the vacation to teach my boy Russian history and grammar. I think those were the subjects you mentioned in your advertisement. I think you will get on with us all right, and I am sure you will like the neighbourhood. We have a large house and garden, the air is excellent, and there is a river close by. Well, would you like to come? We shall only have to come to terms, although I

19

do not think," he added, with a slight grimace, " that there will be any difficulty on that point between us."

Nejdanov watched Sipiagin all the time he was speaking. He gazed at his small head, bent a little to one side, his low, narrow, but intelligent forehead, his fine Roman nose, pleasant eyes, straight lips, out of which his words flowed graciously; he gazed at his drooping whiskers, kept in the English fashion, gazed and wondered. " What does it all mean? " he asked himself. " Why has this man come to seek me out? This aristocrat and I! What have we in common? What does he see in me? "

He was so lost in thought that he did not open his lips when Sipiagin, having finished speaking, evidently awaited an answer. Sipiagin cast a look into the corner where Paklin sat, also watching him. " Perhaps the presence of a third person prevents him from saying what he would like," flashed across Sipiagin's mind. He raised his eyebrows, as if in submission to the strangeness of the surroundings he had come to of his own accord, and repeated his question a second time.

Nejdanov started.

" Of course," he began hurriedly, " I should like to . . . with pleasure . . . only I must confess . . . I am rather surprised . . . having no recommendations . . . and the views I expressed at the theatre were more calculated to prejudice you——"

" There you are quite mistaken Alexai—Alexai Dmitritch —have I got the name right? " Sipiagin asked with a smile. " I may venture to say·that I am well known for my liberal and progressive opinions. On the contrary, what you said the other evening, with the exception perhaps of any youthful characteristics, which are always rather given to exaggeration, if you will excuse my saying so, I fully agreed with, and was even delighted with your enthusiasm."

Sipiagin spoke without the slightest hesitation, his words flowing from him as a stream.

"My wife shares my way of thinking," he continued; "her views are, if anything, more like yours than mine, which is not surprising, considering that she is younger than I am. When I read your name in the paper the day after our meeting—and by the way, you announced your name and address contrary to the usual custom—I was rather struck by the coincidence, having already heard it at the theatre. It seemed to me like the finger of fate. Excuse my being so superstitious. As for recommendations, I do not think they are necessary in this case. I like you, and am accustomed to trusting my intuition. May I hope that you will come?"

"Yes, I will come," Nejdanov replied, "and will try to be worthy of your confidence. But there is one thing I should like to mention. I could undertake to teach your boy, but am not prepared to look after him. I do not wish to undertake anything that would interfere with my freedom."

Sipiagin gave a slight wave of the hand, as if driving away a fly.

"You may be easy on that point. You are not made that way. I only wanted a tutor, and I have found one. Well, now, how about terms? Financial terms, that is. Base metal!"

Nejdanov did not know what to say.

"I think," Sipiagin went on, bending forward and touching Nejdanov with the tips of his fingers, "that decent people can settle such things in two words. I will give you a hundred roubles a month and all travelling expenses. Will you come?"

Nejdanov blushed.

"That is more than I wanted to ask . . . because I——"

"Well," Sipiagin interrupted him, "I look upon the matter as settled, and consider you as a member of our household." He rose from his chair, and became quite gay and expansive, as if he had just received a present. A

21

certain amiable familiarity, verging on the playful, began to show itself in all his gestures. "We shall set out in a day or two," he went on, in an easy tone. "There is nothing I love better than meeting spring in the country, although I am a busy, prosaic sort of person, tied to town. . . . I want you to count your first month as beginning from to-day. My wife and boy have already started, and are probably in Moscow by now. We shall find them in the lap of nature. We will go alone, like two bachelors, ha, ha!" Sipiagin laughed coquettishly, through his nose. "And now——"

He took a black-and-silver pocket-book out of his over-coat pocket and pulled out a card.

"This is my address. Come and see me to-morrow at about twelve o'clock. We can talk things over further. I should like to tell you a few of my views on education. We can also decide when to start."

Sipiagin took Nejdanov's hand. "By the way," he said, lowering his voice and bending his head a little to one side, "if you are in need of money, please do not stand on cere-mony. I can let you have a month's pay in advance."

Nejdanov was at a loss to know what to say. He gazed, with the same puzzled expression, at the kind, bright face, which was so strange yet so close to him, smiling encourag-ingly.

"You are not in need of any?" Sipiagin asked in a whisper.

"I will tell you to-morrow, if I may," Nejdanov said at last.

"Well, good-bye, then. Till to-morrow." Sipiagin dropped Nejdanov's hand and turned to go out.

"I should like to know," Nejdanov asked suddenly, "who told you my name? You said you heard it at the theatre."

"Some one who is very well known to you. A relative of yours, I think. Prince G."

" The aide-de-camp? "

" Yes."

Nejdanov flushed even redder than before, but did not say anything. Sipiagin shook his hand again, without a word this time, then bowing first to him and then to Paklin, put on his hat at the door, and went out with a self-satisfied smile on his lips, denoting the deep impression the visit must have produced on him.

IV

SIPIAGIN had barely crossed the threshold when Paklin jumped up, and rushing across to Nejdanov began showering congratulations upon him.

"What a fine catch!" he exclaimed laughing, scarcely able to stand still. "Do you know who he is? He's quite a celebrity, a chamberlain, one of our pillars of society, a future minister!"

"I have never heard of him," Nejdanov remarked dejectedly.

Paklin threw up his arms in despair.

"That's just where we are mistaken, Alexai Dmitritch! We never know any one. We want to do things, to turn the whole world upside down, and are living outside this very world, amidst two or three friends, jostling each other in our narrow little circle!"

"Excuse me," Nejdanov put in. "I don't think that is quite true. We certainly do not go amongst the enemy, but are constantly mixing with our own kind, and with the masses."

"Just a minute!" Paklin interrupted, in his turn. "Talking of enemies reminds me of Goethe's lines—

> Wer den Dichter will versteh'n
> Muss im Dichter's lande geh'n.

and I say—

> Wer den Feinde will versteh'n
> Muss im Feinde's lande geh'n.

To turn one's back on one's enemies, not to try and understand their manner of life, is utterly stupid! Yes, utterly stu-pid! If I want to shoot a wolf in the forest, I must first find out his haunts. You talked of coming in contact with the people just now. My dear boy! In 1862 the Poles formed their revolutionary bands in the forest; we are just about to enter that same forest, I mean the people, where it is no less dark and dense than in the other."

" Then what would you have us do? "

" The Hindoos cast themselves under the wheels of the Juggernaut," Paklin continued; " they were mangled to pieces and died in ecstasy. We, also, have our Juggernaut —it crushes and mangles us, but there is no ecstasy in it."

" Then what would you have us do? " Nejdanov almost screamed at him. " Would you have us write preachy novels? "

Paklin folded his arms and put his head on one side.

" You, at any rate, could write novels. You have a decidedly literary turn of mind. All right, I won't say anything about it. I know you don't like it being mentioned. I know it is not very exciting to write the sort of stuff wanted, and in the modern style too. " ' Oh, I love you," she bounded——' "

" It's all the same to me," he replied, scratching himself.

" That is precisely why I advise you to get to know all sorts and conditions, beginning from the very highest. We must not be entirely dependent on people like Ostrodumov! They are very honest, worthy folk, but so hopelessly stupid! You need only look at our friend. The very soles of his boots are not like those worn by intelligent people. Why did he hurry away just now? Only because he did not want to be in the same room with an aristocrat, to breathe the same air——"

" Please don't talk like that about Ostrodumov before me! " Nejdanov burst out. " He wears thick boots because they are cheaper! "

" I did not mean it in that sense," Paklin began.

" If he did not wish to remain in the same room with an

aristocrat," Nejdanov continued, raising his voice, " I think it very praiseworthy on his part, and what is more, he is capable of sacrificing himself, will face death, if necessary, which is more than you or I will ever do! "

Paklin made a sad grimace, and pointed to his scraggy, crippled legs.

" Now do I look like a warrior, my dear Alexai Dmitritch? But enough of this. I am delighted that you met this Sipiagin, and can even foresee something useful to our cause as a result of it. You will find yourself in the highest society, will come in contact with those wonderful beauties one hears about, women with velvety bodies on steel springs, as it says in *Letters on Spain*. Get to know them, my dear fellow. If you were at all inclined to be an Epicurean, I should really be afraid to let you go. But those are not the objects with which you are going, are they? "

" I am going away," Nejdanov said, " to earn my living. And to get away from you all," he added to himself.

" Of course, of course! That is why I advise you to learn. Fugh! What a smell this gentleman has left behind him! " Paklin sniffed the air. " The very ambrosia that the governor's wife longed for in Gogol's *Revisor* ! "

" He discussed me with Prince G.," Nejdanov remarked dejectedly. " I suppose he knows my whole history now."

" You need not suppose; you may be quite sure of it! But what does it matter? I wouldn't mind betting that that was the very reason for his wanting to engage you. You will be able to hold your own with the best of them. You are an aristocrat yourself by blood, and consequently an equal. However, I have stayed too long. I must go back to the exploiter's, to my office. Good-bye."

Paklin went to the door, but stopped and turned back.

" I say, Aliosha," he began in a persuasive tone of voice, " you have only just refused me, and I know you will not be short of money now, but, all the same, do allow me to sacrifice just a little for the cause. I can't do anything

26

else, so let me help with my pocket! I have put ten roubles on the table. Will you take them? "

Nejdanov remained motionless, and did not say anything.

" Silence means consent! Thanks! " Paklin exclaimed gaily and vanished.

Nejdanov was left alone. He continued gazing out into the narrow, gloomy court, unpenetrated by the sun even in summer, and he felt sad and gloomy at heart.

We already know that Nejdanov's father was Prince G., a rich adjutant-general. His mother was the daughter of the general's governess, a pretty girl who died on the day of Nejdanov's birth. He received his early education in a boarding school kept by a certain Swiss, a very energetic and severe pedagogue, after which he entered the university. His great ambition was to study law, but his father, who had a violent hatred for nihilists, made him go in for history and philology, or for " æsthetics " as Nejdanov put it with a bitter smile. His father used to see him about four times a year in all, but was, nevertheless, interested in his welfare, and when he died left him a sum of six thousand roubles " in memory of Nastinka " his mother. Nejdanov received the interest on this money from his brothers the Princes G., which they were pleased to call an allowance. Paklin had good reason to call him an aristocrat. Everything about him betokened his origin. His tiny ears, hands, feet, his small but fine features, delicate skin, wavy hair; his very voice was pleasant, although it was slightly guttural. He was highly strung, frightfully conceited, very susceptible, and even capricious. The false position he had been placed in from childhood had made him sensitive and irritable, but his natural generosity had kept him from becoming suspicious and mistrustful. This same false position was the cause of an utter inconsistency, which permeated his whole being. He was fastidiously accurate and horribly squeamish, tried to be cynical and coarse in his speech, but was an idealist by nature. He was passionate and pure-minded,

27

bold and timid at the same time, and, like a repentant sinner ashamed of his sins, he was ashamed alike of his timidity and his purity, and considered it his duty to scoff at all idealism. He had an affectionate heart, but held himself aloof from everybody, was easily exasperated, but never bore ill-will. He was furious with his father for having made him take up " æsthetics," openly interested himself in politics and social questions, professed the most extreme views (which meant more to him than mere words), but secretly took a delight in art, poetry, beauty in all its manifestations, and in his inspired moments wrote verses. It is true that he carefully hid the copy-book in which they were written, and none of his St. Petersburg friends, with the exception of Paklin, and he only by his peculiar intuitiveness, suspected its existence. Nothing hurt or offended Nejdanov more than the smallest allusion to his poetry, which he regarded as an unpardonable weakness in himself. His Swiss schoolmaster had taught him a great many things, and he was not afraid of hard work. He applied himself readily and zealously, but did not work consecutively. All his friends loved him. They were attracted by his natural sense of justice, his kindness, and his pure-mindedness, but Nejdanov was not born under a lucky star, and did not find life an easy matter. He was fully conscious of this fact and felt utterly lonely in spite of the untiring devotion of his friends.

He stood meditating at the window. Sad, oppressive thoughts rose up in his mind one after another about the prospective journey, the new and unexpected change that was coming into his life. He had no regrets at the thought of leaving St. Petersburg, as he would leave nothing behind that was especially dear to him, and he knew that he would be back in the autumn, but he was pervaded by the spirit of indecision, and an involuntary melancholy came over him.

" A fine tutor I shall make ! " flashed across his mind. " Am I cut out for a schoolmaster ? " He was ready to

reproach himself for having undertaken the duties of a
tutor, and would have been unjust in doing so. Nejdanov
was sufficiently cultured, and, in spite of his uncertain temperament, children grew readily fond of him and he of them.
His depression was due to that feeling which takes possession of one before any change of place, a feeling experienced
by all melancholy, dreaming people and unknown to those
of energetic, sanguine temperaments, who always rejoice at
any break in the humdrum of their daily existence and
welcome a change of abode with pleasure. Nejdanov was
so lost in his meditations that his thoughts began quite
unconsciously to take the form of words. His wandering
sensations began to arrange themselves into measured
cadences.

"Damn!" he exclaimed aloud. "I'm wandering off into
poetry!" He shook himself and turned away from the
window. He caught sight of Paklin's ten-rouble note, put
it in his pocket, and began pacing up and down the room.

"I must get some money in advance," he thought to
himself. "What a good thing this gentleman suggested it.
A hundred roubles . . . a hundred from my brothers—
their excellencies. . . . I want fifty to pay my debts, fifty
or seventy for the journey—and the rest Ostrodumov can
have. Then there are Paklin's ten roubles in addition, and
I dare say I can get something from Merkulov——"

In the midst of these calculations the rhythmic cadences
began to reassert themselves. He stood still, as if rooted
to the spot, with fixed gaze. After a while his hands involuntarily found their way to the table drawer, from which
he pulled out a much-used copy-book. He dropped into a
chair with the same fixed look, humming softly to himself
and every now and again shaking back his wavy hair, began
writing line after line, sometimes scratching out and re-
writing.

The door leading into the passage opened slightly and
Mashurina's head appeared. Nejdanov did not notice her

and went on writing. Mashurina stood looking at him intently for some time, shook her head, and drew it back again. Nejdanov sat up straight, and suddenly catching sight of her exclaimed with some annoyance, " Oh, is that you? " and thrust the copy-book into the drawer again.

Mashurina came into the room with a firm step.

" Ostrodumov asked me to come," she began deliberately. " He would like to know when we can have the money. If you could get it to-day, we could start this evening."

" I can't get it to-day," Nejdanov said with a frown. " Please come to-morrow."

" At what time? "

" Two o'clock."

" Very well."

Mashurina was silent for a while and then extended her hand.

" I am afraid I interrupted you. I am so sorry. But then . . . I am going away . . . who knows if we shall ever meet again. . . . I wanted to say good-bye to you."

Nejdanov pressed her cold, red fingers. " You know the man who was here to-day," he began. " I have come to terms with him, and am going with him. His place is down in the province of S., not far from the town itself."

A glad smile lit up Mashurina's face.

" Near S. did you say? Then we may see each other again perhaps. They might send us there! " Mashurina sighed. " Oh, Alexai Dmitritch———"

" What is it? " Nejdanov asked.

Mashurina looked intense.

" Oh, nothing. Good-bye. It's nothing." She squeezed Nejdanov's hand a second time and went out.

" There is not a soul in St. Petersburg who is so attached to me as this eccentric person," he thought. " I wish she had not interrupted me though. However, I suppose it's for the best."

The next morning Nejdanov called at Sipiagin's town

house and was shown into a magnificent study, furnished in a rather severe style, but quite in keeping with the dignity of a statesman of liberal views. The gentleman himself was sitting before an enormous bureau, piled up with all sorts of useless papers, arrayed in the strictest order, and numerous ivory paper-knives, which had never been known to cut anything. During the space of an hour Nejdanov listened to the wise, courteous, patronising speeches of his host, received a hundred roubles, and ten days later was leaning back in the plush seat of a reserved first-class compartment, side by side with this same wise, liberal politician, being borne along to Moscow on the jolting lines of the Nikolaevsky Railway.

V

In the drawing room of a large stone house with a Greek front—built in the twenties of the present century by Sipiagin's father, a well-known landowner, who was distinguished by the free use of his fists—Sipiagin's wife, Valentina Mihailovna, a very beautiful woman, having been informed by telegram of her husband's arrival, sat expecting him every moment. The room was decorated in the best modern taste. Everything in it was charming and inviting, from the walls hung in variegated cretonne and beautiful curtains to the various porcelain, bronze, and crystal knick-knacks, arranged upon the tables and cabinets, the whole blending together into a subdued harmony and brightened by the rays of the May sun, which was streaming in through the wide-open windows. The still air, laden with the scent of lily-of-the-valley (large bunches of these beautiful spring flowers were placed about the room), was stirred from time to time by a slight breeze from without, blowing gently over the richly grown garden.

What a charming picture! And the mistress herself, Valentina Mihailovna Sipiagina, put the finishing touch to it, gave it meaning and life. She was a tall woman of about thirty, with dark brown hair, a fresh dark complexion, resembling the Sistine Madonna, with wonderfully deep, velvety eyes. Her pale lips were somewhat too full, her shoulders perhaps too square, her hands rather too large, but, for all that, any one seeing her as she flitted gracefully about the drawing room, bending from her slender waist to sniff at the flowers with a smile on her lips, or arranging some Chinese vase, or quickly readjusting her glossy hair before the looking-glass, half-closing her wonderful eyes, any one would have declared that there could not be a more fascinating creature.

A pretty curly-haired boy of about nine burst into the room and stopped suddenly on catching sight of her. He was dressed in a Highland costume, his legs bare, and was very much befrizzled and pomaded.

"What do you want, Kolia?" Valentina Mihailovna asked. Her voice was as soft and velvety as her eyes.

"Mamma," the boy began in confusion, "auntie sent me to get some lilies-of-the-valley for her room. . . . She hasn't got any——"

Valentina Mihailovna put her hand under her little boy's chin and raised his pomaded head.

"Tell auntie that she can send to the gardener for flowers. These are mine. I don't want them to be touched. Tell her that I don't like to upset my arrangements. Can you repeat what I said?"

"Yes, I can," the boy whispered.

"Well, repeat it then."

"I will say . . . I will say . . . that you don't wànt."

Valentina Mihailovna laughed, and her laugh, too, was soft.

"I see that one can't give you messages as yet. But never mind, tell her anything you like."

The boy hastily kissed his mother's hand, adorned with rings, and rushed out of the room.

Valentina Mihailovna looked after him, sighed, walked up to a golden wire cage, on one side of which a green parrot was carefully holding on with its beak and claws. She teased it a little with the tip of her finger, then dropped on to a narrow couch, and picking up a number of the *Revue des Deux Mondes* from a round carved table, began turning over its pages.

A respectful cough made her look round. A handsome servant in livery and a white cravat was standing by the door.

33

" What do you want, Agafon? " she asked in the same soft voice.

" Simion Petrovitch Kollomietzev is here. Shall I show him in? "

" Certainly. And tell Mariana Vikentievna to come to the drawing room."

Valentina Mihailovna threw the *Revue des Deux Mondes* on the table, raised her eyes upwards as if thinking—a pose which suited her extremely.

From the languid, though free and easy, way in which Simion Petrovitch Kollomietzev, a young man of thirty-two, entered the room; from the way in which he brightened suddenly, bowed slightly to one side, and drew himself up again gracefully; from the manner in which he spoke, not too harshly, nor too gently; from the respectful way in which he kissed Valentina Mihailovna's hand, one could see that the new-comer was not a mere provincial, an ordinary rich country neighbour, but a St. Petersburg grandee of the highest society. He was dressed in the latest English fashion. A corner of the coloured border of his white cambric pocket handkerchief peeped out of the breast pocket of his tweed coat, a monocle dangled on a wide black ribbon, the pale tint of his suède gloves matched his grey checked trousers. He was clean shaven, and his hair was closely cropped. His features were somewhat effeminate, with his large eyes, set close together, his small flat nose, full red lips, betokening the amiable disposition of a well-bred nobleman. He was effusion itself, but very easily turned spiteful, and even vulgar, when any one dared to annoy him, or to upset his religious, conservative, or patriotic principles. Then he became merciless. All his elegance vanished like smoke, his soft eyes assumed a cruel expression, ugly words would flow from his beautiful mouth, and he usually got the best of an argument by appealing to the authorities.

His family had once been simple gardeners. His great-grandfather was called Kolomientzov after the place in which he was born; his grandfather used to sign himself Kolomietzev; his father added another *l* and wrote himself Kollomietzev, and finally Simion Petrovitch considered himself to be an aristocrat of the bluest blood, with pretensions to having descended from the well-known Barons von Gallenmeier, one of whom had been a field-marshal in the Thirty Years' War. Simion Petrovitch was a chamberlain, and served in the ministerial court. His patriotism had prevented him from entering the diplomatic service, for which he was cut out by his personal appearance, education, knowledge of the world, and his success with women. *Mais quitter la Russie ? Jamais !* Kollomietzev was rich and had a great many influential friends. He passed for a promising, reliable young man *un peu féodal dans ses opinions*, as Prince B. said of him, and Prince B. was one of the leading lights in St. Petersburg official circles. Kollomietzev had come away on a two months' leave to look after his estate, that is, to threaten and oppress his peasants a little more. " You can't yet on without that! " he used to say.

" I thought that your husband would have been here by now," he began, rocking himself from one leg to the other. He suddenly drew himself up and looked down sideways— a very dignified pose.

Valentina Mihailovna made a grimace.

" Would you not have come otherwise? "

Kollomietzev drew back a pace, horrified at the imputation.

" Valentina Mihailovna! " he exclaimed. " How can you possibly say such a thing? "

" Well, never mind. Sit down. My husband will be here soon. I have sent the carriage to the station to meet him. If you wait a little, you will be rewarded by seeing him. What time is it? "

" Half-past two," Kollomietzev replied, taking a large gold enamelled watch out of his waistcoat pocket and

35

showing it to Valentina Mihailovna. " Have you seen this watch? A present from Michael, the Servian Prince Obrenovitch. Look, here are his initials. We are great friends. Go out hunting a lot together. Such a splendid fellow, with an iron hand, just what an administrator ought to be. He will never allow himself to be made a fool of. Not he! Oh dear no! "

Kollomietzev dropped into an armchair, crossed his legs, and began leisurely pulling off his left glove.

" We are badly in need of such a man as Michael in our province here," he remarked.

" Why? Are you dissatisfied with things here? "

Kollomietzev made a wry face.

" It's this abominable county council! What earthly use is it? Only weakens the government and sets people thinking the wrong way." (He gesticulated with his left hand, freed from the pressure of the glove.) " And arouses false hopes." (Kollomietzev blew on his hand.) " I have already mentioned this in St. Petersburg, *mais bah !* they won't listen to me. Even your husband—but then he is known to be a confirmed liberal! "

Valentina Mihailovna sat up straight.

" What do I hear? You opposed to the government, Monsieur Kollomietzev? "

" I. Not in the least! Never! What an idea! *Mais j'ai mon franc parler.* I occasionally allow myself to criticise, but am always obedient."

" And I, on the contrary, never criticise and am never obedient."

" *Ah ! Mais c'est un mot !* Do let me repeat it to my friend *Ladislas. Vous savez,* he is writing a society novel, read me some of it. Charming! *Nous aurons enfin le grand monde russe peint par lui-même.*"

" Where is it to be published? "

" In the *Russian Messenger*, of course. It is our *Revue des Deux Mondes.* I see you take it, by the way."

36

" Yes, but I think it rather dull of late."

" Perhaps, perhaps it is. The *Russian Messenger*, too, has also gone off a bit, using a colloquial expression."

Kollomietzev laughed. It amused him to have said " gone off a bit." " *Mais c'est un journal qui se respecte*," he continued, " and that is the main thing. I am sorry to say that I interest myself very little in Russian literature nowadays. It has grown so horribly vulgar. A cook is now made the heroine of a novel. A mere cook, *parole d'honneur !* Of course, I shall read Ladislas' novel. *Il y aura le petit mot pour rire*, and he writes with a purpose! He will completely crush the nihilists, and I quite agree with him. His ideas *sont très correctes*."

" That is more than can be said of his past," Valentina Mihailovna remarked.

" *Ah ! jeton une voile sur les erreurs de sa jeunesse !* " Kollomietzev exclaimed, pulling off his other glove.

Valentina Mihailovna half-closed her exquisite eyes and looked at him coquettishly.

" Simion Petrovitch! " she exclaimed, " why do you use so many French words when speaking Russian? It seems to me rather old-fashioned, if you will excuse my saying so."

" But, my dear lady, not every one is such a master of our native tongue as you are, for instance. I have a very great respect for the Russian language. There is nothing like it for giving commands or for governmental purposes. I like to keep it pure and uncorrupted by other languages and bow before Karamzin, but as for an every-day language, how can one use Russian? For instance, how would you say, in Russian, *de tout à l'heure, c'est un mot ?* You could not possibly say ' this is a word,' could you? "

" You might say ' a happy expression.' "

Kollomietzev laughed.

" A happy expression! My dear Valentina Mihailovna. Don't you feel that it savours of the schoolroom; that all the salt has gone out of it? "

37

" I am afraid you will not convince me. I wonder where Mariana is? " She rang the bell and a servant entered.

" I asked to have Mariana Vikentievna sent here. Has she not been told? "

The servant had scarcely time to reply when a young girl appeared behind him in the doorway. She had on a loose dark blouse, and her hair was cut short. It was Mariana Vikentievna Sinitska, Sipiagin's niece on the mother's side.

VI

" I am sorry, Valentina Mihailovna," Mariana said, drawing near to her, " I was busy and could not get away."

She bowed to Kollomietzev and withdrew into a corner, where she sat down on a little stool, near the parrot, who began flapping its wings as soon as it caught sight of her.

" Why so far away, Mariana? " Valentina Mihailovna asked, looking after her. " Do you want to be near your little friend? Just think, Simion Petrovitch," she said, turning to Kollomietzev, " our parrot has simply fallen in love with Mariana! "

" I don't wonder at it! "

" But he simply can't bear me! "

" How extraordinary! Perhaps you tease him."

" Oh, no, I never tease him. On the contrary, I feed him with sugar. But he won't take anything out of my hand. It is a case of sympathy and antipathy."

Mariana looked sternly at Valentina Mihailovna and Valentina Mihailovna looked at her. These two women did not love one another.

Compared to her aunt Mariana seemed plain. She had a round face, a large aquiline nose, big bright grey eyes, fine eyebrows, and thin lips. Her thick brown hair was cut short, she seemed retiring, but there was something strong and daring, impetuous and passionate, in the whole of her personality. She had tiny little hands and feet, and her healthy, lithesome little figure reminded one of a Florentine statuette of the sixteenth century. Her movements were free and graceful.

Mariana's position in the Sipiagin's house was a very difficult one. Her father, a brilliant man of Polish extraction, who had attained to the rank of general, was discovered to have embezzled large state funds. He was tried and convicted, deprived of his rank, nobility, and exiled to Siberia. After some time he was pardoned and returned, but was too utterly crushed to begin life anew, and died in extreme poverty. His wife, Sipiagin's sister, did not survive the shock of the disgrace and her husband's death, and died soon after. Uncle Sipiagin gave a home to their only child, Mariana. She loathed her life of dependence and longed for freedom with all the force of her upright soul. There was a constant inner battle between her and her aunt. Valentina Mihailovna looked upon her as a nihilist and freethinker, and Mariana detested her aunt as an unconscious tyrant. She held aloof from her uncle and, indeed, from every one else in the house. She held aloof, but was not afraid of them. She was not timid by nature.

" Antipathy is a strange thing," Kollomietzev repeated. " Everybody knows that I am a deeply religious man, orthodox in the fullest sense of the word, but the sight of a priests' flowing locks drives me nearly mad. It makes me boil over with rage."

" I believe hair in general has an irritating effect upon you, Simion Petrovitch," Mariana remarked. " I feel sure you can't bear to see it cut short like mine."

Valentina Mihailovna lifted her eyebrows slowly, then dropped her head, as if astonished at the freedom with which modern young girls entered into conversation. Kollomietzev smiled condescendingly.

" Of course," he said, " I can't help feeling sorry for beautiful curls such as yours, Mariana Vikentievna, falling under the merciless snip of a pair of scissors, but it doesn't arouse antipathy in me. In any case, your example might even . . . even . . . convert me! "

Kollomietzev could not think of a Russian word, and did not like using a French one, after what his hostess had said.

"Thank heaven," Valentina Mihailovna remarked, "Mariana does not wear glasses and has not yet discarded collars and cuffs, but, unfortunately, she studies natural history, and is even interested in the woman question. Isn't that so, Mariana?"

This was evidently said to make Mariana feel uncomfortable, but Mariana, however, did not feel uncomfortable.

"Yes, auntie," she replied, "I read everything I can get hold of on the subject. I am trying to understand the woman question."

"There is youth for you!" Valentina Mihailovna exclaimed, turning to Kollomietzev. "Now you and I are not at all interested in that sort of thing, are we?"

Kollomietzev smiled good-naturedly; he could not help entering into the playful mood of his amiable hostess.

"Mariana Vikentievna," he began, "is still full of the ideals . . . the romanticism of youth . . . which . . . in time——"

"Heaven, I was unjust to myself," Valentina Mihailovna interrupted him; "I am also interested in these questions. I am not quite an old lady yet."

"Of course. So am I in a way," Kollomietzev put in hastily. "Only I would forbid such things being talked about!"

"Forbid them being talked about?" Mariana asked in astonishment.

"Yes! I would say to the public, ' Interest yourselves in these things as much as you like, but talk about them . . . sh.' " He layed his finger on his lips.

"I would, at any rate, forbid speaking through *the press* under any conditions!"

Valentina Mihailovna laughed.

"What? Would you have a commission appointed by the ministers for settling these questions?"

"Why not? Don't you think we could do it better than these ignorant, hungry loafers who know nothing and imagine themselves to be men of genius? We could appoint Boris Andraevitch as president."

Valentina Mihailovna laughed louder still.

"You had better take care, Boris Andraevitch is some-times such a Jacobin——"

"Jacko, jacko, jacko," the parrot screamed.

Valentina Mihailovna waved her handkerchief at him.

"Don't interrupt an intelligent conversation! Mariana, do teach him manners!"

Mariana turned to the cage and began stroking the parrot's neck with her finger; the parrot stretched towards her.

"Yes," Valentina Mihailovna continued, "Boris Andrae-vitch astonishes me, too, sometimes. There is a certain strain in him . . . a certain strain . . . of the tribune."

"*C'est parce qu'il est orateur!*" Kollomietzev exclaimed enthusiastically in French. "Your husband is a mar-vellous orator and is accustomed to success . . . *ses propres paroles le grisent* . . . and then his desire for popularity. . . . By the way, he is rather annoyed just now, is he not? *Il boude?* Eh?"

Valentina Mihailovna looked at Mariana.

"I haven't noticed it," she said after a pause.

"Yes," Kollomietzev continued pensively, "he was rather overlooked at Easter."

Valentina Mihailovna indicated Mariana with her eyes.

Kollomietzev smiled and screwed up his eyes, conveying to her that he understood. "Mariana Vikentievna," he exclaimed suddenly, in an unnecessarily loud tone of voice, "do you intend teaching at the school again this year?"

Mariana turned round from the cage.

"Are you interested to know, Simion Petrovitch?"

"Certainly. I am very much interested."

"Would you forbid it?"

"I would forbid nihilists even so much as to think of schools. I would put all schools into the hands of the

42

clergy, and with an eye on them I wouldn't mind running one myself!"

"Really! I haven't the slightest idea what I shall do this year. Last year things were not at all successful. Besides, how can you get a school together in the summer?"

Mariana blushed deeply all the time she was speaking, as if it cost her some effort. She was still very self-conscious.

"Are you not sufficiently prepared?" Valentina Mihailovna asked sarcastically.

"Perhaps not."

"Heavens!" Kollomietzev exclaimed. "What do I hear? O ye gods! Is preparation necessary to teach peasants the alphabet?"

At this moment Kolia ran into the drawing room shouting "Mamma! mamma! Papa has come!" And after him, waddling on her stout little legs, appeared an old grey-haired lady in a cap and yellow shawl, and also announced that Boris had come.

This lady was Sipiagin's aunt, and was called Anna Zaharovna. Every one in the drawing room rushed out into the hall, down the stairs, and on to the steps of the portico. A long avenue of chipped yews ran straight from these steps to the high road—a carriage and four was already rolling up the avenue straight towards them. Valentina Mihailovna, standing in front, waved her pocket handkerchief, Kolia shrieked with delight, the coachman adroitly pulled up the steaming horses, a footman came down headlong from the box and almost pulled the carriage door off its hinges in his effort to open it—and then, with a condescending smile on his lips, in his eyes, over the whole of his face, Boris Andraevitch, with one graceful gesture of the shoulders, dropped his cloak and sprang to the ground. Valentina Mihailovna gracefully threw her arms round his neck and they kissed three times. Kolia stamped his little feet and pulled at his father's coat from behind, but Boris Andraevitch first kissed Anna Zaharovna, quickly threw off his uncomfortable, ugly Scotch cap, greeted Mariana and Kollomietzev, who had also come out (he gave Kollomietzev a hearty shake of the hand in the English fashion), and then turned to his little son, lifted him under the arms, and kissed him.

During this scene Nejdanov half guiltily scrambled out of the carriage and, without removing his cap, stood quietly near the front wheel, looking out from under his eyebrows. Valentina Mihailovna, when embracing her husband, had cast a penetrating look over his shoulder at this new figure. Sipiagin had informed her that he was bringing a tutor.

Every one continued exchanging greetings and shaking hands with the newly-arrived host as they all moved up the broad stairs, lined on either side with the principal men and maid servants. They did not come forward to kiss the master's hand (an Asiatic custom they had abandoned long ago), but bowed respectfully. Sipiagin responded to their salutations with a slight movement of the nose and eyebrows, rather than an inclination of the head.

Nejdanov followed the stream up the wide stairs. As soon as they reached the hall, Sipiagin, who had been searching for Nejdanov with his eyes, introduced him to his wife, Anna Zaharovna, and Mariana, and said to Kolia, " This is your tutor. Mind you do as he tells you. Give him your hand." Kolia extended his hand timidly, stared at him fixedly, but finding nothing particularly interesting about his tutor, turned to his " papa " again. Nejdanov felt uncomfortable, just as he had done at the theatre. He wore an old shabby coat, and his face and hands were covered with dust from the journey. Valentina Mihailovna said something kindly to him, but he did not quite catch what it was and did not reply. He noticed that she was very bright, and clung to her husband affectionately. He did not like Kolia's be-frizzled and pomaded head, and when his eye fell on Kollomietzev, thought " What a sleek individual." He paid no attention to the others. Sipiagin turned his head once or twice in a dignified manner, as if looking round at his worldly

44

belongings, a pose that set off to perfection his long drooping whiskers and somewhat small round neck. Then he shouted to one of the servants in a loud resonant voice, not at all husky from the journey, " Ivan! Take this gentleman to the green room and see to his luggage afterwards!" He then told Nejdanov that he could change and rest awhile, and that dinner would be served at five o'clock. Nejdanov bowed and followed Ivan to the " green " room, which was situated on the second floor.

The whole company went into the drawing room. The host was welcomed all over again. An old blind nurse appeared and made him a courtesy. Out of consideration for her years, Sipiagin gave her his hand to kiss. He then begged Kollomietzev to excuse him, and retired to his own room accompanied by his wife.

VII

THE room into which the servant conducted Nejdanov was
beautifully neat and spacious, with wide-open windows
looking on to the garden. A gentle breeze stirred the white
curtains, blowing them out high like sails and letting them
fall again. Golden reflections glided lightly over the ceiling;
the whole room was filled with the moist freshness of spring.
Nejdanov dismissed the servant, unpacked his trunk, washed,
and changed. The journey had thoroughly exhausted him.
The constant presence of a stranger during the last two
days, the many fruitless discussions, had completely upset
his nerves. A certain bitterness, which was neither boredom
nor anger, accumulated mysteriously in the depths of his
being. He was annoyed with himself for his lack of courage,
but his heart ached. He went up to the window and looked
out into the garden. It was an old-fashioned garden, with
rich dark soil, such as one rarely sees around Moscow, laid
out on the slope of a hill into four separate parts. In front
of the house there was a flower garden, with straight gravel
paths, groups of acacias and lilac, and round flower beds.
To the left, past the stable yard, as far down as the barn,
there was an orchard, thickly planted with apples, pears,
plums, currants, and raspberries. Beyond the flower garden,
in front of the house, there was a large square walk, thickly
enterlaced with lime trees. To the right, the view was shut
out by an avenue of silver poplars; a glimpse of an orangery
could be seen through a group of weeping willows. The
whole garden was clothed in its first green leaves; the loud
buzz of summer insects was not yet heard; the leaves rustled
gently, chaffinches twittered everywhere; two doves sat
cooing on a tree; the note of a solitary cuckoo was heard

46

first in one place, then in another; the friendly cawing of rooks was carried from the distance beyond the mill pond, sounding like the creaking of innumerable cart wheels. Light clouds floated dreamily over this gentle stillness, spreading themselves out like the breasts of some huge lazy birds.

Nejdanov gazed and listened, drinking in the cool air through half-parted lips.

His depression left him and a wonderful calmness entered his soul.

Meanwhile he was being discussed in the bedroom below. Sipiagin was telling his wife how he had met him, what Prince G. had said of him, and the gist of their talks on the journey.

"A clever chap!" he repeated, "and well educated, too. It's true he's a revolutionist, but what does it matter? These people are ambitious, at any rate. As for Kolia, he is too young to be spoilt by any of this nonsense."

Valentina Mihailovna listened to her husband affectionately; an amused smile played on her lips, as if he were telling her of some naughty amusing prank. It was pleasant to her to think that her *seigneur et maître,* such a respectable man, of important position, could be as mischievous as a boy of twenty. Standing before the looking-glass in a snow-white shirt and blue silk braces, Sipiagin was brushing his hair in the English fashion with two brushes, whilst Valentina Mihailovna, her feet tucked under her, was sitting on a narrow Turkish couch, telling him various news about the house, the paper mill, which, alas, was not going well, as was to be expected; about the possibilities of changing the cook, about the church, of which the plaster had come off, about Mariana, Kollomietzev. . . .

Between husband and wife there existed the fullest confidence and good understanding; they certainly lived in "love and harmony," as people used to say in olden days. When Sipiagin, after finishing his toilet, asked chivalrously

47

for his wife's hand and she gave him both, and watched him with an affectionate pride as he kissed them in turn, the feeling expressed in their faces was good and true, although in her it shone out of a pair of eyes worthy of Raphael, and in him out of the ordinary eyes of a mere official.

On the stroke of five Nejdanov went down to dinner, which was announced by a Chinese gong, not by a bell. The whole company was already assembled in the dining room. Sipiagin welcomed him again from behind his high cravat, and showed him to a place between Anna Zaharovna and Kolia. Anna Zaharovna was an old maid, a sister of Sipiagin's father; she exhaled a smell of camphor, like a garment that had been put away for a long time, and had a nervous, dejected look. She had acted as Kolia's nurse or governess, and her wrinkled face expressed displeasure when Nejdanov sat down between her and her charge. Kolia looked sideways at his new neighbour; the intelligent boy soon saw that his tutor was shy and uncomfortable, that he did not raise his eyes, and scarcely ate anything. This pleased Kolia, who had been afraid that his tutor would be cross and severe. Valentina Mihailovna also watched Nejdanov.

" He looks like a student," she thought to herself. " He's not accustomed to society, but has a very interesting face, and the colour of his hair is like that of the apostle whose hair the old Italian masters always painted red—and his hands are clean! " Indeed, everybody at the table stared at Nejdanov, but they had mercy on him, and left him in peace for the time being. He was conscious of this, and was pleased and angry about it at the same time.

Sipiagin and Kollomietzev carried on the conversation. They talked about the county council, the governor, the highway-tax, the peasants buying out the land, about mutual Moscow and St. Petersburg acquaintances, Katkov's lyceum, which was just coming into fashion, about the difficulty of getting labour, penalties, and damage caused by cattle, even of Bismarck, the war of 1866, and Napoleon III., whom Kollomietzev called a hero. Kollomietzev gave vent to the most retrograde opinions, going so far as to propose, in jest it is true, a toast given by a certain friend of his on a names-day banquet, " I drink to the only principle I acknowledge, the whip and Roedeger!"

Valentina Mihailovna frowned, and remarked that it was *de très mauvais goût*.

Sipiagin, on the contrary, expressed the most liberal views, refuted Kollomietzev's arguments politely, though with a certain amount of disdain, and even chaffed him a little.

" Your terror of emancipation, my dear Simion Petro-vitch," he said, " puts me in mind of our much respected friend, Alexai Ivanovitch Tveritinov, and the petition he sent in, in the year 1860. He insisted on reading it in every drawing room in St. Petersburg. There was one rather good sentence in it about our liberated serf, who was to march over the face of the fatherland bearing a torch in his hand. You should have seen our dear Alexai Ivano-vitch, blowing out his cheeks and blinking his little eyes, pronounce in his babyish voice, ' T-torch! t-torch! Will march with a t-torch!' Well, the emancipation is now an established fact, but where is the peasant with the torch?"

" Tveritinov was only slightly wrong," Kollomietzev said solemnly. " Not the peasants will march with the torch, but others."

At the words, Nejdanov, who till then had scarcely noticed Mariana, who sat a little to one side, exchanged glances with her, and instantly felt that this solemn girl and he were of the same convictions, of the same stamp. She had made no impression on him whatever when Sipiagin had intro-duced them; then why did he exchange glances with her in particular? He wondered if it was not disgraceful to sit and listen to such views without protesting and by reason of his silence letting others think that he shared them.

Nejdanov looked at Mariana a second time, and her eyes seemed to say, " Wait a while . . . the time is not ripe. . . . It isn't worth it . . . later on . . . there is plenty of time in store."

He was happy to think that she understood him, and began following the conversation again. Valentina Mihailovna supported her husband, and was, if anything, even more radical in her expressions than he. She could not understand, " simply could not un-der-stand, how an educated young man could hold such antiquated views."

" However," she added, " I am convinced that you only say these things for the sake of argument. And you, Alexai Dmitritch," she added to Nejdanov, with a smile (he wondered how she had learnt his Christian name and his father's name), " I know, do not share Simion Petrovitch's fears; my husband told me about your talks on the journey."

Nejdanov blushed, bent over his plate, and mumbled something; he did not feel shy, but was simply unaccustomed to conversing with such brilliant personages. Madame Sipiagin continued smiling to him; her husband nodded his head patronisingly. Kollomietzev stuck his monocle between his eyebrow and nose and stared at the student who dared not to share his " fears." But it was difficult to embarrass Nejdanov in this way; on the contrary, he instantly sat up straight, and in his turn fixed his gaze on the fashionable official. Just as instinctively as he had felt Mariana to be a comrade, so he felt Kollomietzev to be an enemy! Kollomietzev felt it too; he removed his monocle, turned away, and tried to laugh carelessly—but it did not come off somehow. Only Anna Zaharovna, who secretly worshipped him, was on his side, and became even angrier than before with the unwelcome neighbour separating her from Kolia.

Soon after this dinner came to an end. The company went out on the terrace to drink coffee. Sipiagin and Kollomietzev lit up cigars. Sipiagin offered Nejdanov a regalia, but the latter refused.

" Why, of course! " Sipiagin exclaimed; " I've forgotten that you only smoke your own particular cigarettes! "

" A curious taste! " Kollomietzev muttered between his teeth.

Nejdanov very nearly burst out, " I know the difference between a regalia and a cigarette quite well, but I don't want to be under an obligation to any one! " but he contained himself and held his peace. He put down this second piece of insolence to his enemy's account.

" Mariana! " Madame Sipiagin suddenly called, " don't be on ceremony with our new friend . . . smoke your cigarette if you like. All the more so, as I hear," she added, turning to Nejdanov, " that among you all young ladies smoke."

" Yes," Nejdanov remarked dryly. This was the first remark he had made to Madame Sipiagina.

" I don't smoke," she continued, screwing up her velvety eyes caressingly. " I suppose I am behind the times."

Mariana slowly and carefully took out a cigarette, a box of matches, and began to smoke, as if on purpose to spite her aunt. Nejdanov took a light from Mariana and also began smoking.

It was a beautiful evening. Kolia and Anna Zaharovna went into the garden; the others remained for some time longer on the terrace enjoying the fresh air. The conversation was very lively. Kollomietzev condemned modern literature, and on this subject, too, Sipiagin showed himself a liberal. He insisted on the utter freedom and independence of literature, pointed out its uses, instanced Chateaubriand, whom the Emperor Alexander Pavlitch had invested with the order of St. Andrew! Nejdanov did not take part in the discussion; Madame Sipiagina watched him with an expression of approval and surprise at his modesty.

They all went in to drink tea in the drawing room.

" Alexai Dmitritch," Sipiagin said to Nejdanov, " we are addicted to the bad habit of playing cards in the evening,

51

and even play a forbidden game, stukushka. . . . I won't
ask you to join us, but perhaps Mariana will be good enough
to play you something on the piano. You like music, I
hope." And without waiting for an answer Sipiagin took
up a pack of cards. Mariana sat down at the piano and
played, rather indifferently, several of Mendelssohn's " Songs
Without Words." *Charmant! Charmant! quel touché!*
Kollomietzev called out from the other end of the room,
but the exclamation was only due to politeness, and Nejdanov, in spite of Sipiagin's remark, showed no passion for
music.

Meanwhile Sipiagin, his wife, Kollomietzev, and Anna
Zaharovna sat down to cards. Kolia came to say good-night,
and, receiving his parents' blessing and a large glass of milk
instead of tea, went off to bed. His father called after him
to inform him that to-morrow he was to begin his lessons
with Alexai Dmitritch. A little later, seeing Nejdanov
wandering aimlessly about the room and turning over the
photographic albums, apparently without any interest,
Sipiagin begged him not to be on ceremony and retire if
he wished, as he was probably tired after the journey, and
to remember that the ruling principle of their house was
liberty.

Nejdanov took advantage of this and bowing to all present
went out. In the doorway he knocked against Mariana,
and, looking into her eyes, was convinced a second time
that they would be comrades, although she showed no sign
of pleasure at seeing him, but, on the contrary, frowned
heavily.

When he went in, his room was filled with a sweet freshness; the windows had stood wide open all day. In the
garden, opposite his window, a nightingale was trilling out
its sweet song; the evening sky became covered with the
warm glow of the rising moon behind the rounded tops of
the lime trees. Nejdanov lit a candle; a grey moth fluttered
in from the dark garden straight to the flame; she circled

round it, whilst a gentle breeze from without blew on them both, disturbing the yellow-bluish flame of the candle.

" How strange! " Nejdanov thought, lying in bed; " they seem good liberal-minded people, even humane . . . but I feel so troubled in my heart. This chamberlain . . . Kollomietzev. . . . However, morning is wiser than evening. . . . It's no good being sentimental."

At this moment the watchman knocked loudly with his stick and called out, " I say there——"

" Take care," answered another doleful voice.

" Fugh! Heavens! It's like being in prison! " Nejdanov exclaimed.

VIII

Nejdanov awoke early and, without waiting for a servant, dressed and went out into the garden. It was very large and beautiful this garden, and well kept. Hired labourers were scraping the paths with their spades, through the bright green shrubs a glimpse of kerchiefs could be seen on the heads of the peasant girls armed with rakes. Nejdanov wandered down to the pond; the early morning mist had already lifted, only a few curves in its banks still remained in obscurity. The sun, not yet far above the horizon, threw a rosy light over the steely silkiness of its broad surface. Five carpenters were busy about the raft, a newly-painted boat was lightly rocking from side to side, creating a gentle ripple over the water. The men rarely spoke, and then in somewhat preoccupied tones. Everything was submerged in the morning stillness, and every one was occupied with the morning work; the whole gave one a feeling of order and regularity of every-day life. Suddenly, at the other end of the avenue, Nejdanov got a vision of the very incarnation of order and regularity, Sipiagin himself.

He wore a brown coat, something like a dressing gown, and a checkered cap; he was leaning on an English bamboo cane, and his newly-shaven face shone with satisfaction; he was on the round of inspecting his estate. Sipiagin greeted Nejdanov kindly.

"Ah!" he exclaimed, "I see you are one of the early birds!" (He evidently wanted to express his approval by this old saying, which was a little out of place, of the fact that Nejdanov, like himself, did not like lying in bed long.) "At eight o'clock we all take tea in the dining room, and we usually breakfast at twelve. I should like you to give

Kolia his first lesson in Russian grammar at ten o'clock and a lesson in history at two. I don't want him to have any lessons to-morrow, as it will be his name-day, but I would like you to begin to-day."

Nejdanov bowed his head, and Sipiagin took leave of him in the French fashion, quickly lifting his hand several times to his lips and nose, and walked away, whistling and waving his cane energetically, not at all like an important official and state dignitary, but like a jolly Russian country gentleman.

Until eight o'clock Nejdanov stayed in the garden, enjoying the shadows cast by the old trees, the fresh air, the singing of the birds, until the sound of a gong called him to the house. On his entrance he found the whole company already assembled in the dining room. Valentina Mihailovna greeted him in a friendly manner; she seemed to him marvellously beautiful in her morning gown. Mariana looked stern and serious as usual.

Exactly at ten o'clock Nejdanov gave Kolia his first lesson before Valentina Mihailovna, who had asked him if she might be present, and sat very quietly the whole time. Kolia proved an intelligent boy; after the inevitable moments of incertitude and discomfort, the lesson went off very well, and Valentina Mihailovna was evidently satisfied with Nejdanov, and spoke to him several times kindly. He tried to hold aloof a little—but not too much so. Valentina Mihailovna was also present at the second lesson, this time on Russian history. She announced, with a smile, that in this subject she needed instruction almost as much as Kolia. She conducted herself just as quietly as she had done at the first lesson.

Between two and five o'clock Nejdanov stayed in his own room writing letters to his St. Petersburg friends. He was neither bored nor in despair; his overstrained nerves had calmed down somewhat. However, they were set on edge again at dinner, although Kollomietzev was not present, and the kind attention of host and hostess remained unchanged; but it was this very attention that made Nejdanov angry. To make matters worse, the old maiden lady, Anna Zaharovna, was obviously antagonistic, Mariana continued serious, and Kolia rather unceremoniously kicked him under the table. Sipiagin also seemed out of sorts. He was extremely dissatisfied with the manager of his paper mill, a German, to whom he paid a large salary. Sipiagin began by abusing Germans in general, then announced that he was somewhat of a Slavophil, though not a fanatic, and mentioned a certain young Russian, by the name of Solomin, who, it was said, had successfully established another mill belonging to a neighbouring merchant; he was very anxious to meet this Solomin.

Kollomietzev came in the evening; his own estate was only about ten miles away from " Arjanov," the name of Sipiagin's village. There also came a certain justice of the peace, a squire, of the kind so admirably described in the two famous lines of Lermontov—

> Behind a cravat, frock coat to the heels . . .
> Moustache, squeaky voice—and heavy glance.

Another guest arrived, with a dejected look, without a tooth in his head, but very accurately dressed. After him came the local doctor, a very bad doctor, who was fond of coming out with learned expressions. He assured every one, for instance, that he liked Kukolnik better than Pushkin because there was a great deal of " protoplasm " about him. They all sat down to play cards. Nejdanov retired to his own room, and read and wrote until midnight.

The following day, the 9th of May, was Kolia's patron saint's day.

Although the church was not a quarter of a mile off, the whole household drove to mass in three open carriages with footmen at the back. Everything was very festive and gorgeous. Sipiagin decorated himself with his order, Valentina Mihailovna was dressed in a beautiful pale lavender-coloured Parisian gown, and during the service read her prayers out of a tiny little prayer book bound in red velvet. This little book was a matter of great concern among several old peasants, one of whom, unable to contain himself any longer, asked of his neighbour: " What is she doing? Lord have mercy on us! Is she casting a spell? " The sweet scent of the flowers, which filled the whole church, mingled with the smell of the peasant's coats, tarred boots and shoes, the whole being drowned by the delicious, overpowering scent of incense. In the choir the clerks and sacristans tried their very hardest to sing well, and with the help of the men from the factory attempted something like a concert! There was a moment when almost a painful sensation came over the congregation. The tenor's voice (it belonged to one of the men from the factory, who was in the last stages of consumption) rose high above the rest, and without the slightest restraint trilled out long chromatic flat minor notes; they were terrible these notes! but to stop them would have meant the whole concert going to pieces. . . . However, the thing went off without any mishap. Father Kiprian, a priest of the most patriarchal appearance, dressed in the full vestments of the church, delivered his sermon out of a copy-book. Unfortunately, the conscientious father had considered it necessary to introduce the names of several very wise Assyrian kings, which caused him some trouble in pronunciation. He succeeded in showing a certain amount of learning, but perspired very much in the effort!

Nejdanov, who for a long time had not been inside a church, stood in a corner amidst the peasant women, who kept casting sidelong glances at him in between crossing themselves, bowing piously to the ground, and wiping their babies' noses. But the peasant girls in their new coats and beaded head-dresses, and the boys in their embroidered shirts, with girdles round their waists, stared intently at the new worshipper, turning their faces straight towards him.

57

. . . Nejdanov, too, looked at them, and many things rose up in his mind.

After mass, which lasted a very long time—the service of St. Nikolai the Miraculous is well known to be one of the longest in the Orthodox Church—all the clergy, at Sipiagin's invitation, returned to his house, and, after going through several additional ceremonies, such as sprinkling the room with holy water, they all sat down to an abundant breakfast, interspersed with the usual congratulations and rather wearisome talk. The host and hostess, who never took breakfast at such an early hour, broke the rule on this occasion. Sipiagin even went so far as to relate an anecdote, quite proper, of course, but nevertheless amusing, in spite of his dignity and red ribbon, and caused Father Kiprian to be filled with gratitude and amazement. To show that he, too, could tell something worth hearing on occasion, the good father related a conversation he had had with the bishop, when the latter, on a tour round his diocese, had invited all the clergy of the district to come and see him at the monastery in the town. "He is very severe with us," Father Kiprian assured every one. "First he questioned us about our parish, about our arrangements, and then he began to examine us. . . . He turned to me also: 'What is your church's dedication day?' 'The Transfiguration of our Lord,' I replied. 'Do you know the hymn for that day?' 'I think so.' 'Sing it.' 'Thou wert transfigured on the mountain, Christ our Lord,' I began. 'Stop! Do you know the meaning of the Transfiguration?' 'To be quite brief,' I replied, ' our Lord wished to show himself to His disciples in all His glory.' 'Very well,' he said, ' here is a little image in memory of me.' I fell at his feet. 'I thank you, your Holiness. . . .' I did not go away from him empty-handed."

"I have the honour of knowing his Holiness personally," Sipiagin said solemnly. "A most worthy pastor!"

"Most worthy!" Father Kiprian agreed; "only he

puts too much faith in the ecclesiastical superintend-
ents——"

Valentina Mihailovna referred to the peasant school, and
spoke of Mariana as the future schoolmistress; the deacon
(who had been appointed supervisor of the school), a man of
strong athletic build, with long waving hair, bearing a
faint resemblance to the well-groomed tail of an Orlov race
courser, quite forgetting his vocal powers, gave forth such
a volume of sound as to confuse himself and frighten everybody else. Soon after this the clergy took their leave.

Kolia, in his new coat decorated with golden buttons, was
the hero of the day. He was given presents, he was con-
gratulated, his hands were kissed at the front door and at
the back door by servants, workmen from the factory, old
women and young girls and peasants; the latter, in memory
of the days of serfdom, hung around the tables in front of
the house, spread out with pies and small bottles of vodka.
The happy boy was shy and pleased and proud, all at the
same time; he caressed his parents and ran out of the room.
At dinner Sipiagin ordered champagne, and before drinking
his son's health made a speech. He spoke of the significance
of " serving the land," and indicated the road he wished his
Nikolai to follow (he did not use the diminuative of the boy's
name), of the duty he owed, first to his family; secondly to
his class, to society; thirdly to the people—" Yes, my dear
ladies and gentlemen, to the people; and fourthly to the
government! " By degrees Sipiagin became quite eloquent,
with ·his hand under the tail of his coat in imitation of
Robert Peel. He pronounced the word " science " with
emotion, and finished his speech by the Latin exclamation,
laboremus ! which he instantly translated into Russian.
Kolia, with a glass in his hand, went over to thank his
father and be kissed by the others.

Nejdanov exchanged glances with Mariana again. . . .
They no doubt felt the same, but they did not speak to each
other.

However, Nejdanov was more amused than annoyed with the whole proceeding, and the amiable hostess, Valentina Mihailovna, seemed to him to be an intelligent woman, who was aware that she was playing a part, but pleased to think that there was some one else intelligent enough to understand her. Nejdanov probably had no suspicion of the degree in which he was flattered by her attitude towards him.

On the following day lessons were renewed, and life fell back in its ordinary rut.

A week flew by in this way. Nejdanov's thoughts and experiences during that time may be best gathered from an extract of a letter he wrote to a certain Silin, an old school chum and his best friend. Silin did not live in St. Petersburg, but in a distant provincial town, with an old relative on whom he was entirely dependent. His position was such that he could hardly dream of ever getting away from there. He was a man of very poor health, timid, of limited capacity, but of an extraordinarily pure nature. He did not interest himself in politics, but read anything that came in his way, played on the flute as a resource against boredom, and was afraid of young ladies. Silin was passionately fond of Nejdanov—he had an affectionate heart in general. Nejdanov did not express himself to any one as freely as he did to Vladimir Silin; when writing to him he felt as if he were communicating to some dear and intimate soul, dwelling in another world, or to his own conscience. Nejdanov could not for a moment conceive the idea of living together again with Silin, as comrades in the same town. He would probably have lost interest in him, as there was little in common between them, but he wrote him long letters gladly with the fullest confidence. With others, on paper at any rate, he was not himself, but this never happened when writing to Silin. The latter was not a master in the art of writing, and responded only in short clumsy sentences, but Nejdanov had no need of lengthy replies; he knew quite well that his friend swallowed every word of his, as the dust in the road swallows each drop of rain, that he would keep his secrets sacredly, and that in his hopeless solitude he had no other interests but his, Nejdanov's, interests. He had never told any one of his relation with Silin, a relation that was very dear to him.

"Well, my dear friend, my pure-hearted Vladimir!" Thus he wrote to him; he always called him pure-hearted, and not without good cause. "Congratulate me; I have fallen upon green pasture, and can rest awhile and gather strength. I am living in the house of a rich statesman, Sipiagin, as tutor to his little son; I eat well (have never eaten so well in my life!), sleep well, and wander about the beautiful country—but, above all, I have for a time crept out from under the wing of my St. Petersburg friends. At first it was horribly boring, but I feel a bit better now. I shall soon have to go into harness again, that is, put up with the consequences of what I have undertaken (the reason I was allowed to come here). For a time, at any rate, I can enjoy the delights of a purely animal existence, expand in the waist, and write verses if the mood seizes me. I will give you my observations another time. The estate seems to me well managed on the whole, with the exception, perhaps, of the factory, which is not quite right; some of the peasants are unapproachable, and the hired servants have servile faces—but we can talk about these things later on. My host and hostess are courteous, liberal-minded people; the master is for ever condescending, and bursts out from time to time in torrents of eloquence, a most highly cultured person! His lady, a picturesque beauty, who has all her wits about her, keeps such a close watch on one, and is so soft! I should think she has not a bone in her body! I am rather afraid of her, you know what sort of a ladies' man I make! There are neighbours—but uninteresting ones; then there is an old lady in the house who makes me feel uncomfortable. . . . Above all, I am interested in a certain young lady, but whether she is a relative or simply

61

a companion here the Lord only knows! I have scarcely exchanged a couple of words with her, but I feel that we are birds of a feather. . . ."

Here followed a description of Mariana's personal appearance and of all her habits; then he continued:

" That she is unhappy, proud, ambitious, reserved, but above all unhappy, I have not the smallest doubt. But why she is unhappy, I have as yet failed to discover. That she has an upright nature is quite evident, but whether she is good-natured or not remains to be seen. Are there really any good-natured women other than stupid ones? Is goodness essential? However, I know little about women. The lady of the house does not like her, and I believe it is mutual on either side. . . . But which of them is in the right is difficult to say. I think that the mistress is probably in the wrong . . . because she is so awfully polite to her; the *other's* brows twitch nervously when she is speaking to her patroness. She is a most highly-strung individual, like myself, and is just as easily *upset* as I am, although perhaps not in the same way.

" When all this can be disentangled, I will write to you again.

" She hardly ever speaks to me, as I have already told you, but in the few words she has addressed to me (always rather sudden and unexpected) there was a ring of rough sincerity which I liked. By the way, how long is that relative of yours going to bore you to death? When is he going to die?

" Have you read the article in the *European Messenger* about the latest impostors in the province of Orenburg? It happened in 1834, my dear! I don't like the journal, and the writer of the article is a conservative, but the thing is interesting and calculated to give one ideas. . . ."

IX

Mᴀʏ had reached its second half; the first hot summer days had already set in.

After his history lesson one day, Nejdanov wandered out into the garden, and from thence into a birch wood adjoining it on one side. Certain parts of this wood had been cleared by merchants, about fifteen years ago, but these clearings were already densely overgrown by young birches, whose soft silver trunks encircled by grey rings rose as straight as pillars, and whose bright green leaves sparkled as if they had just been washed and polished. The grass shot up in sharp tongues through the even layers of last years' fallen leaves. Little narrow paths ran here and there, from which yellow-beaked blackbirds rose with startled cries, flying close to the earth into the wood as hard as they could go.

After wandering about for half an hour, Nejdanov sat down on the stump of a tree, surrounded by old greyish splinters, lying in heaps, exactly as they had fallen when cut down by the axe. Many a time had these splinters been covered by the winter's snow and been thawed by the spring sun, but nobody had touched them.

Nejdanov leant against a solid wall of young birches casting a heavy though mild shade. He was not thinking of anything in particular, but gave himself up to those peculiar sensations of spring which in the heart of young and old alike are always mixed with a certain degree of sadness—the keen sadness of awaiting in the young and of settled regret in the old.

Nejdanov was suddenly awakened by approaching footsteps.

It did not sound like the footsteps of one person, nor

like a peasant in heavy boots, or a barefooted peasant woman; it seemed as if two people were advancing at a slow, measured pace. The slight rustling of a woman's dress was heard.

Suddenly a deep man's voice was heard to say:

" Is this your last word? Never? "

" Never! " a familiar woman's voice repeated, and a moment later from a bend in the path, hidden from view by a young tree, Mariana appeared, accompanied by a swarthy man with black eyes, an individual whom Nejdanov had never seen before.

They both stood still as if rooted to the spot on catching sight of him, and he was so taken aback that he did not rise from the stump he was sitting on. Mariana blushed to the roots of her hair, but instantly gave a contemptuous smile. It was difficult to say whether the smile was meant for herself, for having blushed, or for Nejdanov. Her companion scowled—a sinister gleam was seen in the yellow-ish whites of his troubled eyes. He exchanged glances with Mariana, and without saying a word they turned their backs on Nejdanov and walked away as slowly as they had come, whilst Nejdanov followed them with a look of amazement.

Half an hour later he returned home to his room, and when, at the sound of the gong, he appeared in the drawing room the dark-eyed stranger whom he had seen in the wood was already there. Sipiagin introduced Nejdanov to him as his *beaufrère'a*, Valentina Mihailovna's brother—Sergai Mihailovitch Markelov.

" I hope you will get to know each other and be friends, gentlemen," Sipiagin exclaimed with the amiable, stately, though absent-minded smile characteristic of him.

Markelov bowed silently; Nejdanov responded in a similar way, and Sipiagin, throwing back his head slightly and shrugging his shoulders, walked away, as much as to say, " I've brought you together, but whether you become friends or not is a matter of equal indifference to me! "

Valentina Mihailovna came up to the silent pair, standing motionless, and introduced them to each other over again; she then turned to her brother with that peculiarly bright, caressing expression which she seemed able to summon at will into her wonderful eyes.

" Why, my dear *Serge*, you've quite forgotten us! You did not even come on Kolia's nameday. Are you so very busy? My brother is making some sort of new arrangement with his peasants," she remarked, turning to Nejdanov. " So very original—three parts of everything for them and one for himself; even then he thinks that he gets more than his share."

" My sister is fond of joking," Markelov said to Nejdanov in his turn, " but I am prepared to agree with her; for *one* man to take a quarter of what belongs to *a hundred*, is certainly too much."

" Do you think that I am fond of joking, Alexai Dmit-ritch? " Madame Sipiagina asked with that same caressing softness in her voice and in her eyes.

Nejdanov was at a loss for a reply, but just then Kollomietzev was announced. The hostess went to meet him, and a few moments later a servant appeared and announced in a sing-song voice that dinner was ready.

At dinner Nejdanov could not keep his eyes off Mariana and Markelov. They sat side by side, both with downcast eyes, compressed lips, and an expression of gloomy severity on their angry faces. Nejdanov wondered how Markelov could possibly be Madame Sipiagina's brother; they were so little like each other. There was only one point of resemblance between them, their dark complexions; but the even colour of Valentina Mihailovna's face, arms, and shoulders constituted one of her charms, whilst in her brother it reached to that shade of swarthiness which polite people call " bronze," but which to the Russian eye suggests a brown leather boot leg.

Markelov had curly hair, a somewhat hooked nose, thick

65

lips, sunken cheeks, a narrow chest, and sinewy hands. He was dry and sinewy all over, and spoke in a curt, harsh, metallic voice. The sleepy look in his eyes, the gloomy expression, denoted a bilious temperament! He ate very little, amused himself by making bread pills, and every now and again would fix his eyes on Kollomietzev. The latter had just returned from town, where he had been to see the governor upon a rather unpleasant matter for himself, upon which he kept a tacit silence, but was very voluble about everything else. Sipiagin sat on him somewhat when he went a little too far, but laughed a good deal at his anecdotes and *bon mots*, although he thought *qu'il est un affreux réactionnaire.* Kollomietzev declared, amongst other things, how he went into raptures at what the peasants, *oui, oui ! les simples mougiks !* call lawyers. " Liars! Liars! " he shouted with delight. " *Ce peuple russe est délicieux !* " He then went on to say how once, when going through a village school, he asked one of the children what a babugnia was, and nobody could tell him, not even the teacher himself. He then asked what a pithecus was, and no one knew even that, although he had quoted the poet Himnitz, ' The weak-witted pithecus that mocks the other beasts.' Such is the deplorable condition of our peasant schools!

" But," Valentina Mihailovna remarked, " I don't know myself what are these animals! "

" Madame! " Kollomietzev exclaimed, " there is no necessity for you to know! "

" Then why should the peasants know? "

" Because it is better for them to know about these animals than about Proudhon or Adam Smith! "

Here Sipiagin again intervened, saying that Adam Smith was one of the leading lights in human thought, and that it would be well to imbibe his principles (he poured himself out a glass of wine) with the (he lifted the glass to his nose and sniffed at it) mother's milk! He swallowed the wine. Kollomietzev also drank a glass and praised it highly.

Markelov payed no special attention to Kollomietzev's talk, but glanced interrogatively at Nejdanov once or twice; he flicked one of his little bread pills, which just missed the nose of the eloquent guest.

Sipiagin left his brother-in-law in peace; neither did Valentina Mihailovna speak to him; it was evident that both husband and wife considered Markelov an eccentric sort of person whom it was better not to provoke.

After dinner Markelov went into the billiard room to smoke a pipe, and Nejdanov withdrew into his own room.

In the corridor he ran against Mariana. He wanted to slip past her, when she stopped him with a quick movement of the hand.

" Mr. Nejdanov," she said in a somewhat unsteady tone of voice, " it ought to be all the same to me what you think of me, but still I find it ... I find it ..."(she could not think of a fitting word) " I find it necessary to tell you that when you met me in the wood to-day with Mr. Markelov . . . you must no doubt have thought, when you saw us both confused, that we had come there by appointment."

" It did seem a little strange to me——" Nejdanov began.

" Mr. Markelov," Mariana interrupted him, " proposed to me . . . and I refused him. That is all I wanted to say to you. Good night. Think what you like of me."

She turned away and walked quickly down the corridor.

Nejdanov entered his own room and sat down by the window musing. " What a strange girl—why this wild issue, this uninvited explanation? Is it a desire to be original, or simply affectation—or pride? Pride, no doubt. She can't endure the idea . . . the faintest suspicion, that any-one should have a wrong opinion of her. What a strange girl! "

Thus Nejdanov pondered, whilst he was being discussed on the terrace below; every word could be heard distinctly.

" I have a feeling," Kollomietzev declared, " a feeling, that he's a revolutionist. When I served on a special com-

67

mission at the governor-general's of Moscow *avec Ladislas*, I learnt to scent these gentlemen as well as nonconformists. I believe in instinct above everything." Here Kollomietzev related how he had once caught an old sectarian by the heel somewhere near Moscow, on whom he had looked in, accompanied by the police, and who nearly jumped out of his cottage window. "He was sitting quite quietly on his bench until that moment, the blackguard!"

Kollomietzev forgot to add that this old man, when put into prison, refused to take any food and starved himself to death.

"And your new tutor," Kollomietzev went on zealously, "is a revolutionist, without a shadow of a doubt! Have you noticed that he is never the first to bow to any one?"

"Why should he?" Madame Sipiagina asked; "on the contrary, that is what I like about him."

"I am a guest in the house in which he serves," Kollomietzev exclaimed, "yes, serves for money, *comme un salarié*. . . . Consequently I am his superior. . . . He *ought* to bow to me first."

"My dear Kollomietzev, you are very particular," Sipiagin put in, laying special stress on the word *dear*. "I thought, if you'll forgive my saying so, that we had outgrown all that. I pay for his services, his work, but he remains a free man."

"He does not feel the bridle, *le frein!* All these revolutionists are like that. I tell you I can smell them from afar! Only *Ladislas* can compare with me in this respect. If this tutor were to fall into my hands wouldn't I give it to him! I would make him sing a very different tune! How he would begin touching his cap to me—it would be a pleasure to see him!"

"Rubbish, you swaggering little braggart!" Nejdanov almost shouted from above, but at this moment the door opened and, to his great astonishment, Markelov entered the room.

68

X

NEJDANOV rose to meet him, and Markelov, coming straight up to him, without any form of greeting, asked him if he was Alexai Dmitritch, a student of the St. Petersburg University.

"Yes," Nejdanov replied.

Markelov took an unsealed letter out of a side pocket.

"In that case, please read this. It is from Vassily Niko-laevitch," he added, lowering his voice significantly.

Nejdanov unfolded and read the letter. It was a semi-official circular in which Sergai Markelov was introduced as one of "us," and absolutely trustworthy; then followed some advice about the urgent necessity of united action in the propaganda of their well-known principles. The circular was addressed to Nejdanov, as being a person worthy of confidence.

Nejdanov extended his hand to Markelov, offered him a chair, and sat down himself.

Markelov, without saying a word, began lighting a cigar-ette; Nejdanov followed his example.

"Have you managed to come in contact with the peasants here?" Markelov asked at last.

"No, I haven't had time as yet."

"How long have you been here?"

"About a fortnight."

"Have you much to do?"

"Not very much."

Markelov gave a severe cough.

"H'm! The people here are stupid enough. A most ignorant lot. They must be enlightened. They're wretchedly poor, but one can't make them understand the cause of their poverty.

" Your brother-in-law's old serfs, as far as one can judge, do not seem to be poor," Nejdanov remarked.

" My brother-in-law knows what he is about; he is a perfect master at humbugging people. His peasants are certainly not so badly off; but he has a factory; that is where we must turn our attention. The slightest dig there will make the ants move. Have you any books with you? "

" Yes, a few."

" I will get you some more. How is it you have so few? "

Nejdanov made no reply. Markelov also ceased, and began sending out puffs of smoke through his nostrils.

" What a pig this Kollomietzev is! " he exclaimed suddenly. " At dinner I could scarcely keep from rushing at him and smashing his impudent face as a warning to others. But no, there are more important things to be done just now. There is no time to waste getting angry with fools for saying stupid things. The time has now come to prevent them *doing* stupid things."

Nejdanov nodded his head and Markelov went on smoking.

" Among the servants here there is only one who is any good," he began again. " Not your man, Ivan, he has no more sense than a fish, but another one, Kirill, the butler." (Kirill was known to be a confirmed drunkard.) " He is a drunken debauchee, but we can't be too particular. What do you think of my sister? " he asked, suddenly fixing his yellowish eyes on Nejdanov. " She is even more artful than my brother-in-law. What do you think of her? "

" I think that she is a very kind and pleasant lady . . . besides, she is very beautiful."

" H'm! With what subtlety you St. Petersburg gentlemen express yourselves! I can only marvel at it. Well, and what about——" he began, but his face darkened suddenly, and he did not finish the sentence. " I see that we must have a good talk," he went on. " It is quite impossible here. Who knows! They may be listening at the door. I have a suggestion. To-day is Saturday; you won't be giving lessons to my nephew to-morrow, will you? "

" I have a rehearsal with him at three o'clock."

" A rehearsal! It sounds like the stage. My sister, no doubt, invented the word. Well, no matter. Would you like to come home with me now? My village is about ten miles off. I have some excellent horses who will get us there in a twinkling. You could stay the night and the morning, and I could bring you back by three o'clock to-morrow. Will you come? "

" With pleasure," Nejdanov replied. Ever since Markelov's appearance he had been in a state of great excitement and embarrassment. This sudden intimacy made him feel ill at ease, but he was nevertheless drawn to him. He felt certain that the man before him was of a sufficiently blunt nature, but for all that honest and full of strength. Moreover, the strange meeting in the wood, Mariana's unexpected explanation. . . .

" Very well! " Markelov exclaimed. " You can get ready whilst I order the carriage to be brought out. By the way, I hope you won't have to ask permission of our host and hostess."

" I must tell them. I don't think it would be wise to go away without doing so."

" I'll tell them," Markelov said. " They are engrossed in their cards just now and will not notice your absence. My brother-in-law aims only at governmental folk, and the only thing he can do well is to play at cards. However, it is said that many succeed in getting what they want through such means. You'll get ready, won't you? I'll make all arrangements immediately."

Markelov withdrew, and an hour later Nejdanov sat by his side on the broad leather-cushioned seat of his comfortable old carriage. The little coachman on the box kept on whistling in wonderfully pleasant bird-like notes; three

71

piebald horses, with plaited manes and tails, flew like the
wind over the smooth even road; and already enveloped
in the first shadows of the night (it was exactly ten o'clock
when they started), trees, bushes, fields, meadows, and ditches,
some in the foreground, others in the background, sailed
swiftly towards them.

Markelov's tiny little village, Borsionkov, consisting of
about two hundred acres in all, and bringing him in an income
of seven hundred roubles a year, was situated about three
miles away from the provincial town, seven miles off from
Sipiagin's village. To get to Borsionkov from Sipiagin's,
one had to go through the town. Our new friends had
scarcely time to exchange a hundred words when glimpses
of the mean little dwellings of shopkeepers on the outskirts
of the town flashed past them, little dwellings with shabby
wooden roofs, from which faint patches of light could be
seen through crooked little windows; the wheels soon rattled
over the town bridge, paved with cobble stones; the carriage
gave a jerk, rocked from side to side, and swaying with every
jolt, rolled past the stupid two-storied stone houses, with
imposing frontals, inhabited by merchants, past the church,
ornamented with pillars, past the shops. . . . It was Saturday
night and the streets were already deserted, only the taverns
were still filled with people. Hoarse drunken voices issued
from them, singing, accompanied by the hideous sounds of
a concertina. Every now and again a door opened suddenly,
letting forth the red reflection of a rush-light and a filthy,
overpowering smell of alcohol. Almost before every tavern
door stood little peasant carts, harnessed with shaggy, big-
bellied, miserable-looking hacks, whose heads were bowed
submissively as if asleep; a tattered, unbelted peasant in
a big winter cap, hanging like a sack at the back of his head,
came out of a tavern door, and leaning his breast against
the shafts, stood there helplessly fumbling at something
with his hands; or a meagre-looking factory worker, his cap
awry, his shirt unfastened, barefooted, his boots having

been left inside, would take a few uncertain steps, stop still, scratch his back, groan suddenly, and turn in again. . . .

"Drink will be the ruin of the Russian!" Markelov remarked gloomily.

"It's from grief, Sergai Mihailovitch," the coachman said without turning round. He ceased whistling on passing each tavern and seemed to sink into his own thoughts.

"Go on! Go on!" Markelov shouted angrily, vigorously tugging at his own coat collar. They drove through the wide market square reeking with the smell of rush mats and cabbages, past the governor's house with coloured sentry boxes standing at the gate, past a private house with turrets, past the boulevard newly planted with trees that were already dying, past the hotel court-yard, filled with the barking of dogs and the clanging of chains, and so on through the town gates, where they overtook a long, long line of waggons, whose drivers had taken advantage of the evening coolness, then out into the open country, where they rolled along more swiftly and evenly over the broad road, planted on either side with willows.

We must now say a few words about Markelov. He was six years older than his sister, Madame Sipiagina, and had been educated at an artillery school, which he left as an ensign, but sent in his resignation when he had reached the rank of lieutenant, owing to a certain unpleasantness that passed between him and his commanding officer, a German. Ever since then he always detested Germans, especially Russian Germans. He quarrelled with his father on account of his resignation, and never saw him again until just before his death, after which he inherited the little property and settled in it. In St. Petersburg he often came in contact with various brilliant people of advanced views, whom he simply worshipped, and who finally brought him round to their way of thinking. Markelov had read little, mostly books relating to the thing that chiefly interested him, and was especially attached to Herzen. He retained his military

73

habits, and lived like a Spartan and a monk. A few years ago he fell passionately in love with a girl who threw him over in a most unceremonious manner and married an adjutant, also a German. He consequently hated adjutants too. He tried to write a series of special articles on the shortcomings of our artillery, but had not the remotest idea of exposition and never finished a single article; he continued, however, covering large sheets of grey paper with his large, awkward, childish handwriting. Markelov was a man obstinate and fearless to desperation, never forgiving or forgetting, with a constant sense of injury done to himself and to all the oppressed, and prepared for anything. His limited mind was for ever knocking against one point; what was beyond his comprehension did not exist, but he loathed and despised all deceit and falsehood. With the upper classes, with the " reactionaries " as he called them, he was severe and even rude, but with the people he was simple, and treated a peasant like a brother. He managed his property fairly well, his head was full of all sorts of socialist schemes, which he could no more put into practice than he could finish his articles on the shortcomings of the artillery. He never succeeded in anything, and was known in his regiment as " the failure." Of a sincere, passionate, and morbid nature, he could at a given moment appear merciless, blood-thirsty, deserving to be called a brute; at another, he would be ready to sacrifice himself without a moment's hesitation and without any idea of reward.

At about two miles away from the town the carriage plunged suddenly into the soft darkness of an aspen wood, amidst the rustling of invisible leaves, the fresh moist odour of the forest, with faint patches of light from above and a mass of tangled shadows below. The moon had already risen above the horizon, broad and red like a copper shield. Emerging from the trees, the carriage came upon a small low farm house. Three illuminated windows stood out sharply on the front of the house, which shut out the moon's disc; the wide, open

74

gate looked as if it was never shut. Two white stage-horses, attached to the back of a high trap, were standing in the court-yard, half in obscurity; two puppies, also white, rushed out from somewhere and gave forth piercing, though harmless, barks. People were seen moving in the house—the carriage rolled up to the doorstep, and Markelov, climbing out and feeling with difficulty for the iron carriage step, put on, as is usually the case, by the domestic blacksmith in the most inconvenient possible place, said to Nejdanov: "Here we are at home. You will find guests here whom you know very well, but little expect to meet. Come in, please."

XI

THE guests turned out to be no other than our old friends Mashurina and Ostrodumov. They were both sitting in the poorly-furnished drawing room of Markelov's house, smoking and drinking beer by the light of a kerosene lamp. Neither of them showed the least astonishment when Nejdanov came in, knowing beforehand that Markelov had intended bringing him back, but Nejdanov was very much surprised on seeing them. On his entrance Ostrodumov merely muttered " Good evening," whilst Mashurina turned scarlet and extended her hand. Markelov began to explain that they had come from St. Petersburg about a week ago, Ostrodumov to remain in the province for some time for propaganda purposes, whilst Mashurina was to go on to K. to meet some one, also in connection with the cause. He then went on to say that the time had now come for them to do something practical, and became suddenly heated, although no one had contradicted him. He bit his lips, and in a hoarse, excited tone of voice began condemning the horrors that were taking place, saying that everything was now in readiness for them to start, that none but cowards could hold back, that a certain amount of violence was just as necessary as the prick of the lancet to the abscess, however ripe it might be! The lancet simile was not original, but one that he had heard somewhere. He seemed to like it, and made use of it on every possible occasion.

Losing all hope of Mariana's love, it seemed that he no longer cared for anything, and was only eager to get to work, to enter the field of action as soon as possible. He spoke harshly, angrily, but straight to the point like the blow of an axe, his words falling from his pale lips mono-

tonously, ponderously, like the savage bark of a grim old
watch dog. He said that he was well acquainted with both
the peasants and factory men of the neighbourhood, and
that there were possible people amongst them. Instanced
a certain Eremy, who, he declared, was prepared to go
anywhere at a moment's notice. This man, Eremy, who
belonged to the village Goloplok, was constantly on his lips.
At nearly every tenth word he thumped his right hand on
the table and waved the left in the air, the forefinger standing
away from the others. This sinewy, hairy hand, the finger,
hoarse voice, flashing eyes, all produced a strong impression
on his hearers.

Markelov had scarcely spoken to Nejdanov on the journey,
and all his accumulated wrath burst forth now. Ostrodumov and Mashurina expressed their approval every now
and again by a look, a smile, a short exclamation, but a
strange feeling came over Nejdanov. He tried to make
some sort of objection at first, pointing out the danger of
hasty action and mentioned certain former premature
attempts. He marvelled at the way in which everything was
settled beyond a shadow of a doubt, without taking into
consideration the special circumstances, or even trying to
find out what the masses really wanted. At last his nerves
became so highly strung that they trembled like the strings
of an instrument, and with a sort of despair, almost with
tears in his eyes, he began speaking at the top of his voice,
in the same strain as Markelov, going even farther than he
had done. What inspired him would be difficult to say;
was it remorse for having been inactive of late, annoyance
with himself and with others, a desire to drown the gnawings
of an inner pain, or merely to show off before his comrades,
whom he had not seen for some time, or had Markelov's
words really had some effect upon him, fired his blood?
They talked until daybreak; Ostrodumov and Mashurina
did not once rise from their seats, whilst Markelov and
Nejdanov remained on their feet all the time. Markelov

stood on the same spot for all the world like a sentinel, and Nejdanov walked up and down the room with nervous strides, now slowly, now hurriedly. They spoke of the necessary means and measures to be employed, of the part each must take upon himself, selected and tied up various bundles of pamphlets and leaflets, mentioned a certain merchant, Golushkin, a nonconformist, as a very possible man, although uneducated, then a young propagandist, Kisliakov, who was very clever, but had an exaggerated idea of his own capabilities, and also spoke of Solomin. . . .

" Is that the man who manages a cotton factory? " Nejdanov asked, recalling what Sipiagin had said of him at table

" Yes, that is the man," Markelov replied. " You should get to know him. We have not sounded him as yet, but I believe he is an extremely capable man."

Eremy of Goloplok was mentioned again, together with Sipiagin's servant, Kirill, and a certain Mendely, known under the name of " Sulks." The latter it seemed was not to be relied upon. He was very bold when sober, but a coward when drunk, and was nearly always drunk.

" And what about your own people? " Nejdanov asked of Markelov. " Are there any reliable men among them? "

Markelov thought there were, but did not mention any one by name, however. He went on to talk of the town tradespeople, of the public-school boys, who they thought might come in useful if matters were to come to fisticuffs. Nejdanov also inquired about the gentry of the neighbourhood, and learnt from Markelov that there were five or six possible young men among them, but, unfortunately, the most radical of them was a German, " and you can't trust a German, you know, he is sure to deceive you sooner or later! " They must wait and see what information Kisliakov would gather. Nejdanov also asked about the military, but Markelov hesitated, tugged at his long whiskers, and announced at last that with regard to them nothing certain

78

was known as yet, unless Kisliakov had made any dis-
coveries.

" Who is this Kisliakov? " Nejdanov asked impatiently.

Markelov smiled significantly.

" He's a wonderful person," he declared. " I know very
little of him, have only met him twice, but you should see
what letters he writes! Marvellous letters! I will show
them to you and you can judge for yourself. He is full of
enthusiasm. And what activity the man is capable of! He
has rushed over the length and breadth of Russia five or
six times, and written a twelve-page letter from every place! "

Nejdanov looked questioningly at Ostrodumov, but the
latter was sitting like a statue, not an eyebrow twitching.
Mashurina was also motionless, a bitter smile playing on
her lips.

Nejdanov went on to ask Markelov if he had made any
socialist experiments on his own estate, but here Ostrodumov
interrupted him.

" What is the good of all that? " he asked. " All the same,
it will have to be altered afterwards."

The conversation turned to political channels again. The
mysterious inner pain again began gnawing at Nejdanov's
heart, but the keener the pain, the more positively and
loudly he spoke. He had drunk only one glass of beer,
but it seemed to him at times that he was quite intoxicated.
His head swam round and his heart beat feverishly.

When the discussion came to an end at last at about
four o'clock in the morning, and they all passed by the servant asleep in the ante-room on their way to their own
rooms, Nejdanov, before retiring to bed, stood for a long
time motionless, gazing straight before him. He was filled
with wonder at the proud, heart-rending note in all that
Markelov had said. The man's vanity must have been
hurt, he must have suffered, but how nobly he forgot his
own personal sorrows for that which he held to be the truth.
" He is a limited soul," Nejdanov thought, " but is it not a

79

thousand times better to be like that than such . . . such as I feel myself to be? "

He immediately became indignant at his own self-depreciation.

" What made me think that? Am I not also capable of self-sacrifice? Just wait, gentlemen, and you too, Paklin. I will show you all that although I am æsthetic and write verses——"

He pushed back his hair with an angry gesture, ground his teeth, undressed hurriedly, and jumped into the cold, damp bed.

" Good night, I am your neighbour," Mashurina's voice was heard from the other side of the door.

" Good night," Nejdanov responded, and remembered suddenly that during the whole evening she had not taken her eyes off him.

" What does she want? " he muttered to himself, and instantly felt ashamed. " If only I could get to sleep! "

But it was difficult for him to calm his overwrought nerves, and the sun was already high when at last he fell into a heavy, troubled sleep.

In the morning he got up late with a bad headache. He dressed, went up to the window of his attic, and looked out upon Markelov's farm. It was practically a mere nothing; the tiny little house was situated in a hollow by the side of a wood. A small barn, the stables, cellar, and a little hut with a half-bare thatched roof, stood on one side; on the other a small pond, a strip of kitchen garden, a hemp field, another hut with a roof like the first one; in the distance yet another barn, a tiny shed, and an empty thrashing floor— this was all the " wealth " that met the eye. It all seemed poor and decaying, not exactly as if it had been allowed to run wild, but as though it had never flourished, like a young tree that had not taken root well.

When Nejdanov went downstairs, Mashurina was sitting in the dining room at the samovar, evidently waiting for him. She told him that Ostrodumov had gone away on business, in connection with the cause, and would not be back for about a fortnight, and that their host had gone to look after his peasants. As it was already at the end of May, and there was no urgent work to be done, Markelov had thought of felling a small birch wood, with such means as he had at his command, and had gone down there to see after it.

Nejdanov felt a strange weariness at heart. So much had been said the night before about the impossibility of holding back any longer, about the necessity of making a beginning. " But how could one begin, now, at once? " he asked himself. It was useless talking it over with Mashurina, there was no hesitation for her. She knew that she had to go to K., and beyond that she did not look ahead. Nejdanov was at a loss to know what to say to her, and as soon as he finished his tea took his hat and went out in the direction of the birch wood. On the way he fell in with some peasants carting manure, a few of Markelov's former serfs. He entered into conversation with them, but was very little the wiser for it. They, too, seemed weary, but with a normal physical weariness, quite unlike the sensation experienced by him. They spoke of their master as a kind-hearted gentleman, but rather odd, and predicted his ruin, because be would go his own way, instead of doing as his forefathers had done before him. " And he's so clever, you know, you can't understand what he says, however hard you may try. But he's a good sort." A little farther on Nejdanov came across Markelov himself.

He was surrounded by a whole crowd of labourers, and one could see from the distance that he was trying to explain something to them as hard as he could, but suddenly threw up his arms in despair, as if it were of no use. His bailiff, a small, short-sighted young man without a trace of authority or firmness in his bearing, was walking beside him, and merely kept on repeating, " Just so, sir," to Markelov's great disgust, who had expected more independence from him. Nejdanov went up to Markelov, and on looking into his face was struck by the same expression of spiritual weariness he was himself suffering from. Soon after greeting one another, Markelov began talking again of last night's " problems " (more briefly this time), about the impending revolution, the weary expression never once leaving his face. He was smothered in perspiration and dust, his voice was hoarse, and his clothes were covered all over with bits of wood shavings and pieces of green moss. The labourers stood by silently, half afraid and half amused. Nejdanov glanced at Markelov, and Ostrodumov's remark, " What is the good of it all? All the same, it will have to be altered afterwards," flashed across his mind. One of the men, who had been fined for some offence, began begging Markelov to let him off. The latter got angry, shouted furiously, but forgave him in the end. " All the same, it will have to be altered afterwards."

Nejdanov asked him for horses and a conveyance to take him home. Markelov seemed surprised at the request, but promised to have everything ready in good time. They turned back to the house together, Markelov staggering as he walked.

" What is the matter with you? " Nejdanov asked.

" I am simply worn out! " Markelov began furiously. " No matter what you do, you simply can't make these people understand anything! They are utterly incapable of carrying out an order, and do not even understand plain Russian. If you talk of ' part,' they know what that means well enough, but the word ' participation ' is utterly beyond their comprehension, just as if it did not belong to the Russian language. They've taken it into their heads that I want to give them a part of the land! "

Markelov had tried to explain to the peasants the principles of co-operation with a view to introducing it on his estate, but they were completely opposed to it. " The pit was deep enough before, but now there's no seeing the bottom of it," one of them remarked, and all the others gave forth a sympathetic sigh, quite crushing poor Markelov. He dismissed the men and went into the house to see about a conveyance and lunch.

The whole of Markelov's household consisted of a man servant, a cook, a coachman, and a very old man with hairy ears, in a long-skirted linen coat, who had once been his grandfather's valet. This old man was for ever gazing at Markelov with a most woe-begone expression on his face. He was too old to do anything, but was always present, huddled together by the door.

After a lunch of hard-boiled eggs, anchovies, and cold hash (the man handing them pepper in an old pomade pot and vinegar in an old eau-de-cologne bottle), Nejdanov took his seat in the same carriage in which he had come the night before. This time it was harnessed to two horses, not three, as the third had been newly shod, and was a little lame.

Markelov had spoken very little during the meal, had eaten nothing whatever, and breathed with difficulty. He let fall a few bitter remarks about his farm and threw up his arms in despair. " All the same, it will have to be altered afterwards!"

Mashurina asked Nejdanov if she might come with him as far as the town, where she had a little shopping to do. " I can walk back afterwards or, if need be, ask the first peasant I meet for a lift in his cart."

Markelov accompanied them to the door, saying that he would soon send for Nejdanov again, and then . . . then (he trembled suddenly, but pulled himself together) they would have to settle things definitely. Solomin must also come. He (Markelov) was only waiting to hear from Vassily Niko-laevitch, and that as soon as he heard from him there would be nothing to hinder them from making a " beginning," as the masses (the same masses who failed to understand the word " participation ") refused to wait any longer!

"Oh, by the way, what about those letters you wanted to show me? What is the fellow's name . . . Kisliakov?" Nejdanov asked.

"Later on . . . I will show them to you later on. We can do it all at the same time."

The carriage moved.

"Hold yourself in readiness!" Markelov's voice was heard again, as he stood on the doorstep. And by his side, with the same hopeless dejection in his face, straightening his bent back, his hands clasped behind him, diffusing an odour of rye bread and mustiness, not hearing a single word that was being said around him, stood the model servant, his grandfather's decrepit old valet.

Mashurina sat smoking silently all the way, but when they reached the town gates she gave a loud sigh.

"I feel so sorry for Sergai Mihailovitch," she remarked, her face darkening.

"He is over-worked, and it seems to me his affairs are in a bad way," Nejdanov said.

"I was not thinking of that."

"What were you thinking of then?"

"He is so unhappy and so unfortunate. It would be difficult to find a better man than he is, but he never seems to get on."

Nejdanov looked at her.

"Do you know anything about him?"

"Nothing whatever, but you can see for yourself. Good-bye, Alexai Dmitritch." Mashurina clambered out of the carriage.

An hour later Nejdanov was rolling up the court-yard leading to Sipiagin's house. He did not feel well after his sleepless night and the numerous discussions and explanations.

A beautiful face smiled to him out of the window. It was Madame Sipiagina welcoming him back home.

"What glorious eyes she has!" he thought.

XII

A GREAT many people came to dinner. When it was over
Nejdanov took advantage of the general bustle and slipped
away to his own room. He wanted to be alone with his
own thoughts, to arrange the impressions he had carried
away from his recent journey. Valentina Mihailovna had
looked at him intently several times during dinner, but
there had been no opportunity of speaking to him. Mariana,
after the unexpected freak which had so bewildered him,
was evidently repenting of it, and seemed to avoid him.
Nejdanov took up a pen to write to his friend Silin, but he
did not know what to say to him. There were so many
conflicting thoughts and sensations crowding in upon him
that he did not attempt to disentangle them, and put them
off for another day.

Kollomietzev had made one of the guests at dinner.
Never before had this worthy shown so much insolence and
snobbish contemptuousness as on this occasion, but Nejdanov
simply ignored him.

He was surrounded by a sort of mist, which seemed to hang
before him like a filmy curtain, separating him from the
rest of the world. And through this film, strange to say,
he perceived only three faces—women's faces—and all three
were gazing at him intently. They were Madame Sipiagina,
Mashurina, and Mariana. What did it mean? Why particularly these three? What had they in common, and what
did they want of him?

He went to bed early, but could not fall asleep. He was
haunted by sad and gloomy reflections about the inevitable
end, death. These thoughts were familiar to him, many
times had he turned them over this way and that, first

shuddering at the probability of annihilation, then welcoming it, almost rejoicing in it. Suddenly a peculiarly familiar agitation took possession of him. . . . He mused awhile, sat down at the table, and wrote down the following lines in his sacred copy-book without a single correction:—

When I die, dear friend, remember
This desire I tell to thee:
Burn thou to the last black ember
All my heart has writ for me.
Let the fairest flowers surround me,
Sunlight laugh about my bed,
Let the sweetest of musicians
To the door of death be led.
Bid them sound no strain of sadness—
Muted string or muffled drum;
Come to me with songs of gladness—
Whirling in the wild waltz come!
I would hear—ere yet I hear not—
Trembling strings their cadence keep,
Chords that quiver: so I also
Tremble as I fall asleep.
Memories of life and laughter,
Memories of earthly glee,
As I go to the hereafter
All my lullaby shall be.

When he wrote the word " friend " he thought of Silin. He read the verses over to himself in an undertone, and was surprised at what had come from his pen. This scepticism, this indifference, this almost frivolous lack of faith—how did it all agree with his principles? How did it agree with what he had said at Markelov's? He thrust the copy-book into the table drawer and went back to bed. But he did not fall asleep until dawn, when the larks had already begun to twitter and the sky was turning paler.

On the following day, soon after he had finished his lesson and was sitting in the billiard room, Madame Sipiagina entered, looked round cautiously, and coming up to him with a smile, invited him to come into her boudoir. She had on a white barege dress, very simple, but extremely pretty. The embroidered frills of her sleeves came down as far as the elbow, a broad ribbon encircled her waist, her hair fell in thick curls about her neck. Everything about

86

her was inviting and caressing, with a sort of restrained, yet encouraging, caressiveness, everything; the subdued lustre of her half-closed eyes, the soft indolence of her voice, her gestures, her very walk. She conducted Nejdanov into her boudoir, a cosy, charming room, filled with the scent of flowers and perfumes, the pure freshness of feminine garments, the constant presence of a woman. She made him sit down in an arm-chair, sat down beside him, and began questioning him about his visit, about Markelov's way of living, with much tact and sweetness. She showed a genuine interest in her brother, although she had not once mentioned him in Nejdanov's presence. One could gather from what she said that the impression Mariana had made on her brother had not escaped her notice. She seemed a little disappointed, but whether it was due to the fact that Mariana did not reciprocate his feelings, or that his choice should have fallen upon a girl so utterly unlike him, was not quite clear. But most of all she evidently strove to soften Nejdanov, to arouse his confidence towards her, break down his shyness; she even went so far as to reproach him a little for having a false idea of her.

Nejdanov listened to her, gazed at her arms, her shoulders, and from time to time cast a look at her rosy lips and her unruly, massive curls. His replies were brief at first; he felt a curious pressure in his throat and chest, but by degrees this sensation gave way to another, just as disturbing, but not devoid of a certain sweetness. . . . He was surprised that such a beautiful aristocratic lady of important position should take the trouble to interest herself in him, a simple student, and not only interest herself, but flirt with him a little besides. He wondered, but could not make out her object in doing so. To tell the truth, he was little concerned about the object. Madame Sipiagina went on to speak of Kolia, and assured Nejdanov that she wished to become better acquainted with him only so that she might talk to him seriously about her son, get to know his views on the education of Russian children. It might have seemed a little curious that such a wish should have come upon her so suddenly, but the root of the matter did not lie in what Valentina Mihailovna had said. She had been seized by a wave of sensuousness, a desire to conquer and bring to her feet this rebellious young man.

Here it is necessary to go back a little. Valentina Mihailovna was the daughter of a general who had been neither over-wise nor over-industrious in his life. He had received only one star and a buckle as a reward for fifty years' service. She was a Little Russian, intriguing and sly, endowed, like many of her countrywomen, with a very simple and even stupid exterior, from which she knew how to extract the maximum of advantage. Valentina Mihailovna's parents were not rich, but they had managed to educate her at the Smolny Convent, where, although considered a republican, she was always in the foreground and very well treated on account of her excellent behaviour and industriousness. On leaving the convent she settled with her mother (her brother had gone into the country, and her father, the general with the star and buckle, had died) in a very clean, but extremely chilly, apartment, in which you could see your own breath as you talked. Valentina Mihailovna used to make fun of it and declare it was like being in church. She was very brave in bearing with all the discomforts of a poor, pinched existence, having a wonderfully sweet temper. With her mother's help, she managed both to keep up and make new connections and acquaintances, and was even spoken of in the highest circles as a very nice well-bred girl. She had several suitors, had fixed upon Sipiagin from them all, and had very quickly and ingeniously made him fall in love with her. However, he was soon convinced that he could not have made a better choice. She was intelligent, rather good than ill natured, at bottom cold and indifferent, but unable to endure the idea that any one should be indifferent to her. Valentina

Mihailovna was possessed of that peculiar charm, the characteristic of all " charming " egoists, in which there is neither poetry nor real sensitiveness, but which is often full of superficial gentleness, sympathy, sometimes even tenderness. But these charming egoists must not be thwarted. They are very domineering and cannot endure independence in others. Women like Madame Sipiagina excite and disturb people of inexperienced and passionate natures, but are fond of a quiet and peaceful life themselves. Virtue comes easy to them, they are placid of temperament, but a constant desire to command, to attract, and to please gives them mobility and brilliance. They have an iron will, and a good deal of their fascination is due to this will. It is difficult for a man to hold his ground when the mysterious sparks of tenderness begin to kindle, as if involuntarily, in one of these unstirred creatures; he waits for the hour to come when the ice will melt, but the rays only play over the transparent surface, and never does he see it melt or its smoothness disturbed!

It cost Madame Sipiagina very little to flirt, knowing full well that it involved no danger for herself, but to take the lustre out of another's eyes and see them sparkle again, to see another's cheeks become flushed with desire and dread, to hear another's voice tremble and break down, to disturb another's soul—oh, how sweet it was to her soul! How delightful it was late at night, when she lay down in her snow-white bed to an untroubled sleep, to remember all these agitated words and looks and sighs. With what a self-satisfied smile she retired into herself, into the consciousness of her inaccessibility, her invulnerability, and with what condescension she abandoned herself to the lawful embrace of her well-bred husband! It was so pleasant that for a little time she was filled with emotion, ready to do some kind deed, to help a fellow creature. . . . Once, after a secretary of legation who was madly in love with her had attempted to cut his throat, she founded a small alms-house!

She had prayed for him fervently, although her religious feelings from earliest childhood had not been strongly developed.

And so she talked to Nejdanov, doing everything she could to bring him to her feet. She allowed him to come near her, she revealed herself to him, as it were, and with a sweet curiosity, with a half-maternal tenderness, she watched this handsome, interesting, stern radical softening towards her quietly and awkwardly. A day, an hour, a minute later and all this would have vanished without leaving a trace, but for the time being it was pleasant, amusing, rather pathetic, and even a little sad. Forgetting his origin, and knowing that such interest is always appreciated by lonely people happening to fall among strangers, she began questioning him about his youth, about his family. . . . But guessing from his curt replies that she had made a mistake, Valentina Mihailovna tried to smooth things over and began to unfold herself still more before him; as a rose unfolds its fragrant petals on a hot summer's noon, closing them again tightly at the first approach of the evening coolness.

She could not fully smooth over her blunder, however. Having been touched on a sensitive spot, Nejdanov could not regain his former confidence. That bitterness which he always carried, always felt at the bottom of his heart, stirred again, awakening all his democratic suspicions and reproaches. " That is not what I've come here for," he thought, recalling Paklin's admonition. He took advantage of a pause in the conversation, got up, bowed slightly, and went out " very foolishly " as he could not help saying to himself afterwards.

His confusion did not escape Valentina Mihailovna's notice, and judging by the smile with which she accompanied him, she had put it down to her own advantage.

In the billiard room Nejdanov came across Mariana. She was standing with her back to the window, not far from the door of Madame Sipiagina's boudoir, with her arms tightly folded. Her face was almost in complete shadow, but she fixed her fearless eyes on Nejdanov so penetratingly, and her tightly closed lips expressed so much contempt and insulting pity, that he stood still in amazement. . . .

"Have you anything to say to me?" he asked involuntarily.

Mariana did not reply for a time.

"No . . . yes I have though, but not now."

"When?"

"You must wait awhile. Perhaps—to-morrow, perhaps—never. I know so little—what are you really like?"

"But," Nejdanov began, "I sometimes feel . . . that between us——"

"But you hardly know me at all," Mariana interrupted him. "Well, wait a little. To-morrow, perhaps. Now I have to go to . . . my mistress. Good-bye, till to-morrow."

Nejdanov took a step or two in advance, but turned back suddenly.

"By the way, Mariana Vikentievna . . . may I come to school with you one day before it closes? I should like to see what you do there."

"With pleasure. . . . But it was not the school about which I wished to speak to you."

"What was it then?"

"To-morrow," Mariana repeated.

But she did not wait until the next day, and the conversation between her and Nejdanov took place on that same evening in one of the linden avenues not far from the terrace.

XIII

She came up to him first.

"Mr. Nejdanov," she began, "it seems that you are quite enchanted with Valentina Mihailovna."

She turned down the avenue without waiting for a reply; he walked by her side.

"What makes you think so?"

"Is it not a fact? In that case she behaved very foolishly to-day. I can imagine how concerned she must have been, and how she tried to cast her wary nets!"

Nejdanov did not utter a word, but looked at his companion sideways.

"Listen," she continued, "it's no use pretending; I don't like Valentina Mihailovna, and you know that well enough. I may seem unjust . . . but I want you to hear me first——"

Mariana's voice gave way. She suddenly flushed 'with emotion; under emotion she always gave one the impression of being angry.

"You are no doubt asking yourself, 'Why does this tiresome young lady tell me all this?' just as you must have done when I spoke to you . . . about Mr. Markelov."

She bent down, tore off a small mushroom, broke it to pieces, and threw it away.

"You are quite mistaken, Mariana Vikentievna," Nejdanov remarked. "On the contrary, I am pleased to think that I inspire you with confidence."

This was not true, the idea had only just occurred to him.

Mariana glanced at him for a moment. Until then she had persistently looked away from him.

"It is not that you inspire me with confidence exactly," she went on pensively; "you are quite a stranger to me.

92

But your position—and mine—are very similar. We are both alike unhappy; that is a bond between us."

" Are you unhappy? " Nejdanov asked.

" And you, are you not? " Mariana asked in her turn. Nejdanov did not say anything.

" Do you know my story? " she asked quickly. " The story of my father's exile? Don't you? Well, here it is: He was arrested, tried, convicted, deprived of his rank . . . and everything . . . and sent to Siberia, where he died. . . . My mother died too. My uncle, Mr. Sipiagin, my mother's brother, brought me up. . . . I am dependent on him—he is my benefactor and—Valentina Mihailovna is my benefactress. . . . I pay them back with base ingratitude because I have an unfeeling heart. . . . But the bread of charity is bitter—and I can't bear insulting condescensions —and can't endure to be patronised. I can't hide things, and when I'm constantly being hurt I only keep from crying out because I'm too proud to do so."

As she uttered these disjointed sentences, Mariana walked faster and faster. Suddenly she stopped. " Do you know that my aunt, in order to get rid of me, wants to marry me to that hateful Kollomietzev? She knows my ideas . . . in her eyes I'm almost a nihilist—and he! It's true he doesn't care for me . . . I'm not good-looking enough, but it's possible to sell me. That would also be considered charity."

"Why didn't you——" Nejdanov began, but stopped short. Mariana looked at him for an instant.

" You wanted to ask why I didn't accept Mr. Markelov, isn't that so? Well, what could I do? He's a good man, but it's not my fault that I don't love him."

Mariana walked on ahead, as if she wished to save her companion the necessity of saying anything to this unexpected confession.

They both reached the end of the avenue. Mariana turned quickly down a narrow path leading into a dense fir grove; Nejdanov followed her. He was under the influence

93

of a twofold astonishment; first, it puzzled him that this shy girl should suddenly become so open and frank with him, and secondly, that he was not in the least surprised at this frankness, that he looked upon it, in fact, as quite natural.

Mariana turned round suddenly, stopped in the middle of the path with her face about a yard from Nejdanov's, and looked straight into his eyes.

"Alexai Dmitritch," she said, "please don't think my aunt is a bad woman. She is not. She is deceitful all over, she's an actress, a poser—she wants every one to bow down before her as a beauty and worship her as a saint! She will invent a pretty speech, say it to one person, repeat it to a second, a third, with an air as if it had only just come to her by inspiration, emphasising it by the use of her wonderful eyes! She understands herself very well—she is fully conscious of looking like a Madonna, and knows that she does not love a living soul! She pretends to be for ever worrying over Kolia, when in reality does nothing but talk about him with clever people. She does not wish harm to any one . . . is all kindness, but let every bone in your body be broken before her very eyes . . . and she wouldn't care a straw! She would not move a finger to save you, and if by any chance it should happen to be necessary or useful to her . . . then heaven have mercy on you. . . ."

Mariana ceased. Her wrath was choking her. She could not contain herself, and had resolved on giving full vent to it, but words failed her. Mariana belonged to a particular class of unfortunate beings, very plentiful in Russia, whom justice satisfies, but does not rejoice, whilst injustice, against which they are very sensitive, revolts them to their innermost being. All the time she was speaking, Nejdanov watched her intently. Her flushed face, her short, untidy hair, the tremulous twitching of her thin lips, struck him as menacing, significant, and beautiful. A ray of sunlight, broken by a net of branches, lay across her forehead like a patch of gold. And this tongue of fire seemed to be in keeping with the keen expression of her face; her fixed wide-open eyes, the earnest sound of her voice.

" Tell me why you think me unhappy," Nejdanov observed at last. " Do you know anything about me? "

" Yes."

" What do you know? Has any one been talking to you about me? "

" I know about your birth."

" Who told you? "

" Why, Valentina Mihailovna, of course, whom you admire so much. She mentioned in my presence, just in passing you know, but quite intentionally, that there was a very interesting incident in your life. She was not condoling the fact, but merely mentioned it as a person of advanced views who is above prejudice. You need not be surprised; in the same way she tells every visitor that comes that my father was sent to Siberia for taking bribes. However much she may think herself an aristocrat, she is nothing more than a mere scandal-monger and a poser. That is your Sistine Madonna! "

" Why is she mine in particular? "

Mariana turned away and resumed her walk down the path.

" Because you had such a long conversation together," she said, a lump rising in her throat.

" I scarcely said a word the whole time," Nejdanov observed. " It was she who did the talking."

Mariana walked on in silence. A turn in the path brought them to the end of the grove in front of which lay a small lawn; a weeping silver birch stood in the middle, its hollow trunk encircled by a round seat. Mariana sat down on this seat and Nejdanov seated himself at her side. The long hanging branches covered with tiny green leaves were waving gently over their heads. Around them masses of lily-of-the-valley could be seen peeping out from amidst the fine grass. The whole place was filled with a sweet scent, re-

95

freshing after the very heavy resinous smell of the pine trees.

" So you want to see the school," Mariana began; " I must warn you that you will not find it very exciting. You have heard that our principal master is the deacon. He is not a bad fellow, but you can't imagine what nonsense he talks to the children. There is a certain boy among them, called Garacy, an orphan of nine years old, and, would you believe it, he learns better than any of the others!"

With the change of conversation, Mariana herself seemed to change. She turned paler, became more composed, and her face assumed an expression of embarrassment, as if she were repenting of her outburst. She evidently wished to lead Nejdanov into discussing some " question " or other, about the school, the peasants, anything, so as not to continue in the former strain. But he was far from " questions " at this moment.

" Mariana Vikentievna," he began; " to be quite frank with you, I little expected all that has happened between us." (At the word " happened " she drew herself up.) " It seems to me that we have suddenly become very . . . very intimate. That is as it should be. We have for some time past been getting closer to one another, only we have not expressed it in words. And so I will also speak to you frankly. It is no doubt wretched for you here, but surely your uncle, although he is limited, seems a kind man, as far as one can judge. Doesn't he understand your position and take your part?"

" My uncle, in the first place, is not a man, he's an official. A senator, or a minister, I forget which . . . and in the second, I don't want to complain and speak badly of people for nothing. It is not at all hard for me here, that is, nobody interferes with me; my aunt's petty pin-pricks are in reality nothing to me. . . . I am quite free."

Nejdanov looked at her in amazement.

" In that case . . . everything that you have just told me——"

"You may laugh at me if you like," she said. " If I am unhappy—it is not as a result of my own sorrows. It sometimes seems to me that I suffer for the miserable, poor and oppressed in the whole of Russia. . . . No, it's not exactly that. I suffer—I am indignant for them, I rebel for them. . . . I am ready to go to the stake for them. I am unhappy because I am a ' young lady,' a parasite, that I am completely unable to do anything . . . anything! When my father was sent to Siberia and I remained with my mother in Moscow, how I longed to go to him! It was not that I loved or respected him very much, but I wanted to know, to see with my own eyes, how the exiled and banished live. . . . How I loathed myself and all these placid, rich, well-fed people! And afterwards, when he returned home, broken in body and soul, and began humbly busying himself, trying to work . . . oh . . . how terrible it was! It was a good thing that he died . . . and my poor mother too. But, unfortunately, I was left behind. . . . What for? Only to feel that I have a bad nature, that I am ungrateful, that there is no peace for me, that I can do nothing, nothing for anything or anybody! "

Mariana turned away—her hand slid on to the seat. Nejdanov felt sorry for her; he touched the drooping hand. Mariana pulled it away quickly; not that Nejdanov's action seemed unsuitable to her, but that he should on no account think that she was asking for sympathy.

Through the branches of the pines a glimpse of a woman's dress could be seen. Mariana drew herself up.

" Look, your Madonna has sent her spy. That maid has to keep a watch on me and inform her mistress where I am and with whom. My aunt very likely guessed that I was with you, and thought it improper, especially after the sentimental scene she acted before you this afternoon. Anyhow, it's time we were back. Let us go."

97

Mariana got up. Nejdanov rose also. She glanced at him over her shoulder, and suddenly there passed over her face an almost childish expression, making her embarrassment seem charming.

" You are not angry with me, are you? You don't think I have been trying to win your sympathy, do you? No, I'm sure you don't," she went on before Nejdanov had time to make any reply; " you are like me, just as unhappy, and your nature . . . is bad, like mine. We can go to the school together to-morrow. We are excellent friends now, aren't we? "

When Mariana and Nejdanov drew near to the house Valentina Mihailovna looked at them from the balcony through her lorgnette, shook her head slowly with a smile on her lips, then returning through the open glass door into the drawing-room, where Sipiagin was already seated at preferences with their toothless neighbour, who had dropped in to tea, she drawled out, laying stress on each syllable: " How damp the air is! It's not good for one's health! "

Mariana and Nejdanov exchanged glances; Sipiagin, who had just scored a trick from his partner, cast a truly ministerial glance at his wife, looking her over from top to toe, then transferred this same cold, sleepy, but penetrating glance to the young couple coming in from the dark garden.

XIV

Two more weeks went by; everything in its accustomed order. Sipiagin fixed every one's daily occupation, if not like a minister, at any rate like the director of a department, and was, as usual, haughty, humane, and somewhat fastidious. Kolia continued taking lessons; Anna Zaharovna, still full of spite, worried about him constantly; visitors came and went, talked, played at cards, and did not seem bored. Valentina Mihailovna continued amusing herself with Nejdanov, although her customary affability had become mixed with a certain amount of good-natured sarcasm. Nejdanov had become very intimate with Mariana, and discovered that her temper was even enough and that one could discuss most things with her without hitting against any violent opposition. He had been to the school with her once or twice, but with the first visit had become convinced that he could do nothing there. It was under the entire control of the deacon, with Sipiagin's full consent. The good father did not teach grammar badly, although his method was rather old-fashioned, but at examinations he would put the most absurd questions. For instance, he once asked Garacy how he would explain the expression, " The waters are dark under the firmament," to which Garacy had to answer, by the deacon's own order, " It cannot be explained." However, the school was soon closed for the summer, not to be opened again until the autumn.

Bearing in mind the suggestion of Paklin and others, Nejdanov did all he could to come in contact with the peasants, but soon found that he was only learning to understand them, in so far as he could make any observation and doing no propaganda whatever! Nejdanov had lived in a town all his life and, consequently, between him and the country people there existed a gulf that could not be crossed. He once happened to exchange a few words with the drunken Kirill, and even with Mendely the Sulky, but besides abuse about things in general he got nothing out of them. Another peasant, called Fituvy, completely nonplussed him. This peasant had an unusually energetic countenance, almost like some brigand. "Well, this one seems hopeful at any rate," Nejdanov thought. But it turned out that Fituvy was a miserable wretch, from whom the mir had taken away his land, because he, a strong healthy man, *would not* work. "I can't," he sobbed out, with deep inward groans, "I can't work! Kill me or I'll lay hands on myself!" And he ended by begging alms in the streets! with a face out of a canvas of Rinaldo Rinaldini! As for the factory men, Nejdanov could not get hold of them at all; these fellows were either too sharp or too gloomy. He wrote a long letter to his friend Silin about the whole thing, in which he bitterly regretted his incapacity, putting it down to the vile education he had received and to his hopelessly æsthetic nature! He suddenly came to the conclusion that his vocation in the field of propaganda lay not in speaking, but in writing. But all the pamphlets he planned did not work out somehow. Whatever he attempted to put down on paper, according to him, was too drawn out, artificial in tone and style, and once or twice—oh horror! he actually found himself wandering off into verse, or on a sceptical, personal effusion. He even decided to speak about this difficulty to Mariana, a very sure sign of confidence and intimacy! He was again surprised to find her sympathetic, not towards his literary attempts, certainly, but to the moral weakness he was suffering from, a weakness with which she, too, was somewhat familiar. Mariana's contempt for æstheticism was no less strong than his, but for all that the main reason why she did not accept Markelov was because there was not the slightest trace of the æsthetic in his nature!

She did not for a moment admit this to herself. It is often the case that what is strongest in us remains only a half suspected secret.

Thus the days went by slowly, with little variety, but with sufficient interest.

A curious change was taking place in Nejdanov. He felt dissatisfied with himself, that is, with his inactivity, and his words had a constant ring of bitter self-reproach. But in the innermost depths of his being there lurked a sense of happiness very soothing to his soul. Was it a result of the peaceful country life, the summer, the fresh air, dainty food, beautiful home, or was it due to the fact that for the first time in his life he was tasting the sweetness of contact with a woman's soul? It would be difficult to say. But he felt happy, although he complained, and quite sincerely, to his friend Silin.

The mood, however, was abruptly destroyed in a single day.

On the morning of this day Nejdanov received a letter from Vassily Nikolaevitch, instructing him, together with Markelov, to lose no time in coming to an understanding with Solomin and a certain merchant Golushkin, an Old Believer, living at S. This letter upset Nejdanov very much; it contained a note of reproach at his inactivity. The bitterness which had shown itself only in his words now rose with full force from the depths of his soul.

Kollomietzev came to dinner, disturbed and agitated. " Would you believe it! " he shouted almost in tears, " what horrors I've read in the papers! My friend, my beloved Michael, the Servian prince, has been assassinated by some blackguards in Belgrade. This is what these Jacobins and revolutionists will bring us to if a firm stop is not put to them all! " Sipiagin permitted himself to remark that this horrible murder was probably not the work of Jacobins, " of whom there could hardly be any in Servia," but might have been committed by some of the followers of the Karageorgievsky party, enemies of Obrenovitch. Kollomietzev would not hear of this, and began to relate, in the same tearful voice, how the late prince had loved him and what a beautiful gun he had given him! Having spent himself somewhat and got rather irritable, he at last turned from foreign Jacobins to home-bred nihilists and socialists, and ended by flying into a passion. He seized a large roll, and breaking it in half over his soup plate, in the manner of the stylish Parisian in the "Café-Riche," announced that he would like to tear limb from limb, reduce to ashes, all those who objected to anybody or to anything! These were his very words. "It is high time! High time!" he announced, raising the spoon to his mouth; "yes, high time!" he repeated, giving his glass to the servant, who was pouring out sherry. He spoke reverentially about the great Moscow publishers, and *Ladislas, notre bon et cher Ladislas*, did not leave his lips. At this point, he fixed his eyes on Nejdanov, seeming to say: "There, this is for you! Make what you like of it! I mean this for you! And there's a lot more to come yet!" The latter, no longer able to contain himself, objected at last, and began in a slightly unsteady tone of voice (not due to fear, of course) defending the ideals, the hopes, the principles of the modern generation. Kollomietzev soon went into a squeak—his anger always expressed itself in falsetto—and became abusive. Sipiagin, with a stately air, began taking Nejdanov's part; Valentina Mihailovna, of course, sided with her husband; Anna Zaharovna tried to distract Kolia's attention, looking furiously at everybody; Mariana did not move, she seemed turned to stone.

Nejdanov, hearing the name of *Ladislas* pronounced at least for the twentieth time, suddenly flared up and thumping the palm of his hand on the table burst out:

"What an authority! As if we do not know who this Ladislas is! A born spy, nothing more!"

"W-w-w-what—what—did you say?" Kollomietzev stammered out, choking with rage. "How dare you express your-

102

self like that of a man who is respected by such people as Prince Blasenkramf and Prince Kovrishkin!"

Nejdanov shrugged his shoulders.

"A very nice recommendation! Prince Kovrishkin, that enthusiastic flunky——"

"Ladislas is my friend," Kollomietzev screamed, "my comrade—and I——"

"So much the worse for you," Nejdanov interrupted him. "It means that you share his way of thinking, in which case my words apply to you too."

Kollomietzev turned deadly pale with passion.

"W-what? How? You—ought to be—on the spot——"

"What would you like to do with me *on the spot*?" Nejdanov asked with sarcastic politeness. Heaven only knows what this skirmish between these two enemies might have led to, had not Sipiagin himself put a stop to it at the very outset. Raising his voice and putting on a serious air, in which it was difficult to say what predominated most, the gravity of an important statesman or the dignity of a host, he announced firmly that he did not wish to hear at his table such immoderate expressions, that he had long ago made it a rule, a sacred rule, he added, to respect every sort of conviction, so long as (at this point he raised his forefinger ornamented with a signet ring) it came within the limits of decent behaviour; that if he could not help, on the one hand, condemning Mr. Nejdanov's intemperate words, for which only his extreme youth could be blamed, he could not, on the other, agree with Mr. Kollomietzev's embittered attack on people of an opposite camp, an attack, he felt sure, that was only due to an over-amount of zeal for the general welfare of society.

"Under my roof," he wound up, "under the Sipiagin's roof, there are no Jacobins and no spies, only honest, well-meaning people, who, once learning to understand one another, would most certainly clasp each other by the hand!"

Neither Nejdanov nor Kollomeitzev ventured on another word, but they did not, however, clasp each other's hands. Their moment for a mutual understanding had not arrived. On the contrary, they had never yet experienced such a strong antipathy to one another.

Dinner ended in an awkward, unpleasant silence. Sipiagin attempted to relate some diplomatic anecdote, but stopped half-way through. Mariana kept looking down at her plate persistently, not wishing to betray her sympathy with what Nejdanov had said. She was by no means afraid, but did not wish to give herself away before Madame Sipiagina. She felt the latter's keen, penetrating glance fixed on her. And, indeed, Madame Sipiagina did not take her eyes either off her or Nejdanov. His unexpected outburst at first came as a surprise to the intelligent lady, but the next moment a light suddenly dawned upon her, so that she involuntarily murmured, " Ah! " She suddenly divined that Nejdanov was slipping away from her, this same Nejdanov who, a short time ago, was ready to come to her arms. " Something has happened. . . . Is it Mariana? Of course it's Mariana. . . . She likes him . . . and he——"

" Something must be done." Thus she concluded her reflections, whilst Kollomietzev was choking with indignation. Even when playing preference two hours later, he pronounced the word " Pass! " or " I buy! " with an aching heart. A hoarse tremulo of wounded pride could be detected in his voice, although he pretended to scorn such things! Sipiagin was the only one really pleased with the scene. It had afforded him an opportunity of showing off the power of his eloquence and of calming the rising storm. He knew Latin, and Virgil's *Quos ego* was not unfamiliar to him. He did not consciously compare himself to Neptune, but thought of him with a kind of sympathetic feeling.

XV

As soon as it was convenient for him to do so, Nejdanov retired to his own room and locked himself in. He did not want to see any one, any one except Mariana. Her room was situated at the very end of a long corridor, intersecting the whole of the upper story. Nejdanov had only once been there for a few moments, but it seemed to him that she would not mind if he knocked at her door, now that she even wished to speak to him herself. It was already fairly late, about ten o'clock. The host and hostess had not considered it necessary to disturb him after what had taken place at the dinner table. Valentina Mihailovna inquired once or twice about Mariana, as she too had disappeared soon after dinner. "Where is Mariana Vikentievna?" she asked first in Russian, then in French, addressing herself to no one in particular, but rather to the walls, as people often do when greatly astonished, but she soon became absorbed in the game.

Nejdanov paced up and down the room several times, then turned down the corridor and knocked gently at Mariana's door. There was no response. He knocked again—then he turned the handle of the door. It was locked. But he had hardly got back to his own room and sat down, when the door creaked softly and Mariana's voice was heard: "Alexai Dmitritch, was that *you* came to me?"

He jumped up instantly and rushed out into the corridor.

Mariana was standing at his door with a candle in her hand, pale and motionless.

"Yes . . . I——" he murmured.

"Come," she said, turning down the corridor, but before

reaching the end she stopped and pushed open a low door. Nejdanov looked into a small, almost bare room.

" We had better go in here, Alexai Dmitritch, no one will disturb us here."

Nejdanov obeyed. Mariana put the candlestick on a window-sill and turned to him.

" I understand why you wanted to see me," she began. " It is wretched for you to live in this house, and for me too."

" Yes, I wanted to see you, Mariana Vikentievna," Nejdanov replied, " but I do not feel wretched here since I've come to know you."

Mariana smiled pensively.

" Thank you, Alexai Dmitritch. But tell me, do you really intend stopping here after all that has happened? "

" I don't think they will keep me—I shall be dismissed," Nejdanov replied.

" But don't you intend going away of your own accord? "

" I . . . No! "

" Why not? "

" Do you want to know the truth? Because *you* are here."

Mariana lowered her head and moved a little further down the room.

" Besides," Nejdanov continued, " *I must* stay here. You know nothing—but I want—I feel that I must tell you everything." He approached Mariana and seized her hand; she did not take it away, but only looked straight into his face. " Listen! " he exclaimed with sudden force, " Listen! " And instantly, without stopping to sit down, although there were two or three chairs in the room, still standing before her and holding her hand, with heated enthusiasm and with an eloquence, surprising even to himself, he began telling her all his plans, his intentions, his reason for having accepted Sipiagin's offer, about all his connections, acquaintances, about his past, things that he had always kept hidden from everybody. He told her about Vassily Nikolaevitch's letters, everything—even about Silin! He spoke hurriedly, without

106

a single pause or the smallest hesitation, as if he were reproaching himself for not having entrusted her with all his secrets before—as if he were begging her pardon. She listened to him attentively, greedily; she was bewildered at first, but this feeling soon wore off. Her heart was overflowing with gratitude, pride, devotion, resoluteness. Her face and eyes shone; she laid her other hand on Nejdanov's—her lips parted in ecstasy. She became marvellously beautiful!

He ceased at last, and suddenly seemed to see *this* face for the first time, although it was so dear and so familiar to him. He gave a deep sigh.

"Ah! how well I did to tell you everything!" He was scarcely able to articulate the words.

"Yes, how well—how well! she repeated, also in a whisper. She imitated him unconsciously—her voice, too, gave way. "And it means," she continued, "that I am at your disposal, that I want to be useful to your cause, that I am ready to do anything that may be necessary, go wherever you may want me to, that I have always longed with my whole soul for all the things that you want——"

She also ceased. Another word—and her emotion would have dissolved into tears. All the strength and force of her nature suddenly softened as wax. She was consumed with a thirst for activity, for self-sacrifice, for immediate self-sacrifice.

A sound of footsteps was heard from the other side of the door—light, rapid, cautious footsteps.

Mariana suddenly drew herself up and disengaged her hands; her mood changed, she became quite cheerful, a certain audacious, scornful expression flitted across her face.

"I know who is listening behind the door at this moment," she remarked, so loudly that every word could be heard distinctly in the corridor; "Madame Sipiagina is listening to us . . . but it makes no difference to me."

The footsteps ceased.

" Well? " Mariana asked, turning to Nejdanov. " What shall I do? How shall I help you? Tell me. . . tell me quickly! What shall I do? "

" I don't know yet," Nejdanov replied. " I have received a note from Markelov——"

" When did you receive it? When? "

" This evening. He and I must go and see Solomin at the factory to-morrow."

" Yes . . . yes. . . . What a splendid man Markelov is! Now he's a real friend! "

" Like me? "

" No—not like you."

" How? "

She turned away suddenly.

" Oh! Don't you understand what you have become for me, and what I am feeling at this moment? "

Nejdanov's heart beat violently; he looked down. This girl who loved him—a poor, homeless wretch, who trusted him, who was ready to follow him, pursue the same cause together with him—this wonderful girl—Mariana—became for Nejdanov at this moment the incarnation of all earthly truth and goodness—the incarnation of the love of mother, sister, wife, all the things he had never known; the incarnation of his country, happiness, struggle, freedom!

He raised his head and encountered her eyes fixed on him again.

Oh, how this sweet, bright glance penetrated to his very soul!

" And so," he began in an unsteady voice, " I am going away to-morrow. . . . And when I come back, I will tell . . . you——" (he suddenly felt it awkward to address Mariana as " you ") " tell you everything that is decided upon. From now everything that I do and think, everything, I will tell thee first."

" Oh, my dear! " Mariana exclaimed, seizing his hand again. " I promise thee the same! "

108

The word " thee " escaped her lips just as simply and easily as if they had been old comrades.

" Have you got the letter? "

" Here it is."

Mariana scanned the letter and looked up at him almost reverently.

" Do they entrust you with such important commissions? "

He smiled in reply and put the letter back in his pocket.

" How curious," he said, " we have come to know of our love, we love one another—and yet we have not said a single word about it."

" There is no need," Mariana whispered, and suddenly threw her arms around his neck and pressed her head closely against his breast. They did not kiss—it would have seemed to them too commonplace and rather terrible—but instantly took leave of one another, tightly clasping each other's hands.

Mariana returned for the candle which she had left on the window-sill of the empty room. Only then a sort of bewilderment came over her; she extinguished the candle and, gliding quickly along the dark corridor, entered her own room, undressed and went to bed in the soothing darkness.

XVI

On awakening the following morning, Nejdanov did not feel the slightest embarrassment at what had taken place the previous night, but was, on the contrary, filled with a sort of quiet joy, as if he had fulfilled something which ought to have been done long ago. Asking for two days' leave from Sipiagin, who consented readily, though with a certain amount of severity, Nejdanov set out for Markelov's. Before his departure he managed to see Mariana. She was also not in the least abashed, looked at him calmly and resolutely, and called him " dear " quite naturally. She was very much concerned about what he might hear at Markelov's, and begged him to tell her everything.

" Of course! " he replied. " After all," he thought, " why should we be disturbed? In our friendship personal feeling played only . . . a secondary part, and we are united for ever. In the name of the cause? Yes, in the name of the cause! "

Thus Nejdanov thought, and he did not himself suspect how much truth and how much falsehood there lay in his reflections.

He found Markelov in the same weary, sullen frame of mind. After a very impromptu dinner they set out in the well-known carriage to the merchant Falyeva's cotton factory where Solomin lived. (The second side horse harnessed to the carriage was a young colt that had never been in harness before. Markelov's own horse was still a little lame.)

Nejdanov's curiosity had been aroused. He very much wanted to become closer acquainted with a man about whom he had heard so much of late. Solomin had been informed of their coming, so that as soon as the two travellers stopped at the gates of the factory and announced who they were, they were immediately conducted into the hideous little wing occupied by the " engineering manager." He was at that time in the main body of the building, and whilst one of the workmen ran to fetch him, Nejdanov and Markelov managed to go up to the window and look around. The factory was apparently in a very flourishing condition and over-loaded with work. From every corner came the quick buzzing sound of unceasing activity; the puffing and rattling of machines, the creaking of looms, the humming of wheels, the whirling of straps, whilst trolleys, barrels, and loaded carts were rolling in and out. Orders were shouted out at the top of the voice amidst the sound of bells and whistles; workmen in blouses with girdles round their waists, their hair fastened with straps, work girls in print dresses, hurried quickly to and fro, harnessed horses were led about. . . . It represented the hum of a thousand human beings working with all their might. Everything went at full speed in fairly regular order, but not only was there an absence of smartness and neatness, but there was not the smallest trace or cleanliness to be seen anywhere. On the contrary, in every corner one was struck by neglect, dirt, grime; here a pane of glass was broken, there the plaster was coming off; in another place the boards were loose; in a third, a door gaped wide open. A large filthy puddle covered with a coating of rainbow-coloured slime stood in the middle of the main yard; farther on lay a heap of discarded bricks; scraps of mats and matting, boxes, and pieces of rope lay scattered here and there; shaggy hungry-looking dogs wandered to and fro, too listless to bark; in a corner, under the fence, sat a grimy little boy of about four, with an enormous belly and dishevelled head, crying hopelessly, as if he had been forsaken by the whole world; close by a sow likewise besmeared in soot and surrounded by a medley of little sucking-pigs was devouring some cabbage stalks; some ragged clothes were stretched on a line—and such stuffiness

111

and stench! in a word, just like a Russian factory—not like a French or a German one.

Nejdanov looked at Markelov.

" I have heard so much about Solomin's superior capabilities," he began, " that I confess all this disorder surprises me. I did not expect it."

" This is not disorder, but the usual Russian slovenliness," Markelov replied gloomily. " But all the same, they are turning over millions. Solomin has to adjust himself to the old ways, to practical things, and to the owner himself. Have you any idea what Falyeva is like? "

" Not in the least."

" He is the biggest skinflint in Moscow. A regular bourgeois."

At this moment Solomin entered the room. Nejdanov was just as disillusioned about him as he had been about the factory. At the first glance he gave one the impression of being a Finn or a Swede. He was tall, lean, broad-shouldered, with colourless eyebrows and eyelashes; had a long sallow face, a short, rather broad nose, small greenish eyes, a placid expression, coarse thick lips, large teeth, and a divided chin covered with a suggestion of down. He was dressed like a mechanic or a stoker in an old pea-jacket with baggy pockets, with an oil-skin cap on his head, a woollen scarf round his neck, and tarred boots on his feet. He was accompanied by a man of about forty in a peasant coat, who had an extraordinarily lively gipsy-like face, coal-black piercing eyes, with which he scanned Nejdanov as soon as he entered the room. Markelov was already known to him. This was Pavel, Solomin's *factotum*.

Solomin approached the two visitors slowly and without a word, pressed the hand of each in turn in his own hard bony one. He opened a drawer, pulled out a sealed letter, which he handed to Pavel, also without a word, and the latter immediately left the room. Then he stretched himself, threw away his cap with one wave of the hand, sat down on a painted wooden stool and, pointing to a couch, begged Nejdanov and Markelov to be seated.

Markelov first introduced Nejdanov, whom Solomin again shook by the hand, then he went on to " business," mentioning Vassily Nikolaevitch's letter, which Nejdanov handed to Solomin. And whilst the latter was reading it carefully, his eyes moving from line to line, Nejdanov sat watching him. Solomin was near the window and the sun, already low in the horizon, was shining full on his tanned face covered with perspiration, on his fair hair covered with dust, making it sparkle like a mass of gold. His nostrils quivered and distended as he read, and his lips moved as though he were forming every word. He held the letter raised tightly in both hands, and when he had finished returned it to Nejdanov and began listening to Markelov again. The latter talked until he had exhausted himself.

" I am afraid," Solomin began (his hoarse voice, full of youth and strength, was pleasing to Nejdanov's ear), " it will be rather inconvenient to talk here. Why not go to your place? It is only a question of seven miles. You came in your carriage, did you not? "

" Yes."

" Well, I suppose you can make room for me. I shall have finished my work in about an hour, and will be quite free. We can talk things over thoroughly. You are also free, are you not? " he asked, turning to Nejdanov.

" Until the day after to-morrow."

" That's all right. We can stay the night at your place, Sergai Mihailovitch, I suppose? "

" Of course you may! "

" Good. I shall be ready in a minute. I'll just make myself a little more presentable."

" And how are things at your factory? " Nejdanov asked significantly.

Solomin looked away.

" We can talk things over thoroughly," he remarked a

second time. "Please excuse me a moment. . . . I'll be back directly. . . . I've forgotten something."

He went out. Had he not already produced a good impression on Nejdanov, the latter would have thought that he was backing out, but such an idea did not occur to him.

An hour later, when from every story, every staircase and door of the enormous building, a noisy crowd of workpeople came streaming out, the carriage containing Markelov, Nejdanov, and Solomin drove out of the gates on to the road.

"Vassily Fedotitch! Is it to be done?" Pavel shouted after Solomin, whom he had accompanied to the gate.

"No, not now," Solomin replied. "He wanted to know about some night work," he explained, turning to his companions.

When they reached Borsionkov they had some supper, merely for the sake of politeness, and afterwards lighted cigars and began a discussion, one of those interminable, midnight Russian discussions which in degree and length are only peculiar to Russians and unequalled by people of any other nationality. During the discussion, too, Solomin did not come up to Nejdanov's expectation. He spoke little—so little that one might almost have said that he was quite silent. But he listened attentively, and whenever he made any remark or gave an opinion, did so briefly, seriously, showing a considerable amount of common-sense. Solomin did not believe that the Russian revolution was so near at hand, but not wishing to act as a wet blanket on others, he did not intrude his opinions or hinder others from making attempts. He looked on from a distance as it were, but was still a comrade by their side. He knew the St. Petersburg revolutionists and agreed with their ideas up to a certain point. He himself belonged to the people, and fully realised that the great bulk of them, without whom one can do nothing, were still quite indifferent, that they must first be prepared, by quite different means and for entirely different ends than the upper classes. So he held aloof, not from a sense of superiority, but as an ordinary man with a few independent ideas, who did not wish to ruin himself or others in vain. But as for listening, there was no harm in that.

Solomin was the only son of a deacon and had five sisters, who were all married to priests or deacons. He was also destined for the church, but with his father's consent threw it up and began to study mathematics, as he had taken a special liking to mechanics. He entered a factory of which the owner was an Englishman, who got to love him like his own son. This man supplied him with the means of going to Manchester, where he stayed for two years, acquiring an excellent knowledge of the English language. With the Moscow merchant he had fallen in but a short time ago. He was exacting with his subordinates, a manner he had acquired in England, but they liked him nevertheless, and treated him as one of themselves. His father was very proud of him, and used to speak of him as a steady sort of man, but was very grieved that he did not marry and settle down.

During the discussion, as we have already said, Solomin sat silent the whole time; but when Markelov began enlarging upon the hopes they put on the factory workers, Solomin remarked, in his usual laconic way, that they must not depend too much on them, as factory workers in Russia were not what they were abroad. " They are an extremely mild set of people here."

" And what about the peasants? "

" The peasants? There are a good many sweaters and money-lenders among them now, and there are likely to be more in time. This kind only look to their own interests, and as for the others, they are as ignorant as sheep."

" Then where are we to turn to? "

Solomin smiled.

" Seek and ye shall find."

There was a constant smile on his lips, but the smile was

as full of meaning as the man himself. With Nejdanov he behaved in a very peculiar manner. He was attracted to the young student and felt an almost tender sympathy for him. At one part of the discussion, where Nejdanov broke out into a perfect torrent of words, Solomin got up quietly, moved across the room with long strides, and shut a window that was standing open just above Nejdanov's head.

" You might catch cold," he observed, in answer to the orator's look of amazement.

Nejdanov began to question him about his factory, asking if any co-operative experiments had been made, if anything had been done so that the workers might come in for a share of the profits.

" My dear fellow! " Solomin exclaimed, " I instituted a school and a tiny hospital, and even then the owner struggled like a bear! "

Solomin lost his temper once in real earnest on hearing of some legal injustice about the suppression of a workman's association. He banged his powerful fist on the table so that everything on it trembled, including a forty-pound weight, which happened to be lying near the ink pot.

When Markelov and Nejdanov began discussing ways and means of executing their plans, Solomin listened with respectful curiosity, but did not pronounce a single word. Their talk lasted until four o'clock in the morning, when they had touched upon almost everything under the sun. Markelov again spoke mysteriously of Kisliakov's untiring journeys and his letters, which were becoming more interesting than ever. He promised to show them to Nejdanov, saying that he would probably have to take them away with him, as they were rather lengthy and written in an illegible handwriting. He assured him that there was a great deal of learning in them and even poetry, not of the frivolous kind, but poetry with a socialistic tendency!

From Kisliakov, Markelov went on to the military, to adjutants, Germans, even got so far as his articles on the

116

shortcomings of the artillery, whilst Nejdanov spoke about the antagonism between Heine and Borne, Proudhon, and realism in art. Solomin alone sat listening and reflecting, the smile never leaving his lips. Without having uttered a single word, he seemed to understand better than the others where the essential difficulty lay.

The hour struck four. Nejdanov and Markelov could scarcely stand on their legs from exhaustion, whilst Solomin was as fresh as could be. They parted for the night, having agreed to go to town the next day to see the merchant Golushkin, an Old Believer, who was said to be very zealous and promised proselytes.

Solomin doubted whether it was worth while going, but agreed to go in the end.

XVII

MARKELOV'S guests were still asleep when a messenger with
a letter came to him from his sister, Madame Sipiagina.
In this letter Valentina Mihailovna spoke about various little
domestic details, asked him to return a book he had bor-
rowed, and added, by the way, in a postscript, the very
" amusing " piece of news that his old flame Mariana was
in love with the tutor Nejdanov and he with her. This
was not merely gossip, but she, Valentina Mihailovna, had
seen with her own eyes and heard with her own ears.
Markelov's face grew blacker than night, but he did not
utter a word. He ordered the book to be returned, and
when he caught sight of Nejdanov coming downstairs greeted
him just as usual and did not even forget to give him the
promised packet of Kisliakov's letters. He did not stay
with him however, but went out to see to the farm.

Nejdanov returned to his own room and glanced through the
letters. The young propagandist spoke mostly about himself, about his unsparing activity. According to him, during
the last month, he had been in no less than eleven provinces,
in nine towns, in twenty-nine villages, fifty-three hamlets,
in one farmhouse, and in seven factories. Sixteen nights he
had slept in hay-lofts, one in a stable, another even in a
cow-shed (here he wrote, in parenthesis, that fleas did not
worry him); he had wheedled himself into mud-huts, workmen's barracks, had preached, taught, distributed pamphlets,
and collected information; some things he had made a note
of on the spot; others he carried in his memory by the
very latest method of mnemonics. He had written fourteen
long letters, twenty-eight shorter ones, and eighteen notes,
four of which were written in pencil, one in blood, and

another in soot and water. All this he had managed to do because he had learnt how to divide his time systematically, according to the examples set by men such as Quintin Johnson, Karrelius, Sverlitskov, and other writers and statisticians. Then he went on to talk of himself again, of his guiding star, saying how he had supplemented Fourier's passions by being the first to discover the " fundaments, the root principle," and how he would not go out of this world without leaving some trace behind him; how he was filled with wonder that he, a youth of twenty-four, should have solved all the problems of life and science; that he would turn the whole of Russia up-side-down, that he would " skake her up ! " " Dixi ! ! " he added at the end of the paragraph. This word " Dixi " appeared very frequently in Kisliakov's letters, and always with a double exclamation mark. In one of the letters there were some verses with a socialist tendency, written to a certain young lady, beginning with the words—

Love not me, but the idea!

Nejdanov marvelled inwardly, not so much at Kisliakov's conceit, as at Markelov's honest simplicity. " Bother æstheticism ! Mr. Kisliakov may be even useful," he thought to himself instantly.

The three friends gathered together for tea in the dining-room, but last night's conversation was not renewed between them. Not one of them wished to talk, but Solomin was the only one who sat silent peacefully. Both Nejdanov and Markelov seemed inwardly agitated.

After tea they set out for the town. Markelov's old servant, who was sitting on the doorstep, accompanied his former master with his habitual dejected glance.

The merchant Golushkin, with whom it was necessary to acquaint Nejdanov, was the son of a wealthy merchant in drugs, an Old Believer, of the Thedosian sect. He had not increased the fortune left to him by his father, being, as the

119

saying goes, a *joneur*, an Epicurean in the Russian fashion, with absolutely no business abilities. He was a man of forty, rather stout and ugly, pock-marked, with small eyes like a pig's. He spoke hurriedly, swallowing his words as it were, gesticulated with his hands, threw his legs about and went into roars of laughter at everything. On the whole, he gave one the impression of being a stupid, spoilt, conceited bounder. He considered himself a man of culture because he dressed in the German fashion, kept an open house (though it was not over-clean), frequented the theatre, and had many protégées among variety actresses, with whom he conversed in some extraordinary jargon meant to be French. His principal passion was a thirst for popularity. " Let the name of Golushkin thunder through the world! As once Suvorov or Potyomkin, then why not now Kapiton Golushkin? " It was this very passion, conquering even his innate meanness, which had thrown him, as he himself expressed it not without a touch of pride, " into the arms of the opposition " (formerly he used to say " position," but had learnt better since then) and brought him in contact with the nihilists. He gave expression to the most extreme views, scoffed at his own Old Believer's faith, ate meat in Lent, played at cards, and drank champagne like water. He never got into difficulties, because he said, " Whereever necessary I have bribed the authorities. All holes are stitched up, all mouths are closed, all ears are stopped."

He was a widower without children. His sister's sons fawned round him continuously, but he called them a lot of ignorant louts, barbarians, and would hardly look at them. He lived in a large, stone house, kept in rather a slovenly manner. Some of the rooms were furnished with foreign furniture, others contained nothing but a few painted wooden chairs and a couch covered with American cloth. There were pictures everywhere of an indifferent variety. Fiery landscapes, purple seascapes, fat naked women with pink-coloured knees and elbows, and " The Kiss " by Moller.

In spite of the fact that Golushkin had no family, there were a great many menials and hangers-on collected under his roof. He did not receive them from any feeling of generosity, but simply from a desire to be popular and to have some one at his beck and call. " My clients," he used to say when he wished to throw dust in one's eyes. He read very little, but had an excellent memory for learned expressions.

The young people found Golushkin in his study, where he was sitting comfortably wrapped up in a long dressing-gown, with a cigar between his lips, pretending to be reading a newspaper. On their entrance he jumped up, rushed up to them, went red in the face, shouted for some refreshments to be brought quickly, asked them some questions, laughed for no reason in particular, and all this in or e breath. He knew Markelov and Solomin, but had not yet met Nejdanov. On hearing that the latter was a student, he broke into another laugh, pressed his hand a second time, exclaiming: " Splendid! Splendid! We are gathering forces! Learning is light, ignorance is darkness—I had a wretched education myself, but I understand things; that's how I've got on! "

It semed to Nejdanov that Golushkin was shy and embarrassed—and indeed it really was so. " Take care, brother Kapiton! Mind what you are about! " was his first thought on meeting a new person. He soon recovered himself however, and began in the same hurried, lisping, confused tone of voice, talking about Vassily Nikolaevitch, about his temperament, about the necessity of pro-pa-ganda (he knew this word quite well, but articulated it slowly), saying that he, Golushkin, had discovered a certain promising young chap, that the time had now come, that the time was now ripe for . . . for the lancet (at this word he glanced at Markelov, but the latter did not stir). He then turned to Nejdanov and began speaking of himself in no less glowing terms than the distinguished correspondent Kisliakov, saying that he had long ago ceased being a fool, that he fully recognised

121

the rights of the proletariat (he remembered this word splendidly), that although he had actually given up commerce and taken to banking instead with a view to increasing his capital, yet only so that this same capital could at any given moment be called upon for the use . . . for the use of the cause, that is to say, for the use of the people, and that he, Golushkin, in reality, despised wealth! At this point a servant entered with some refreshment; Golushkin cleared his throat significantly, asked if they would not partake of something, and was the first to gulp down a glass of strong pepper-brandy. The guests partook of refreshments. Golushkin thrust huge pieces of caviare into his mouth and drank incessantly, saying every now and again, "Come, gentlemen, come, some splendid Maçon, please!" Turning to Nejdanov, he began asking him where he had come from, where he was staying and for how long, and on hearing that he was staying at Sipiagin's, exclaimed: "I know this gentleman! Nothing in him whatever!" and instantly began abusing all the landowners in the province because, he said, not only were they void of public spirit, but they did not even understand their own interests.

But, strange to say, in spite of his being so abusive, his eyes wandered about uneasily. Nejdanov could not make him out at all, and wondered what possible use he could be to them. Solomin was silent as usual and Markelov wore such a gloomy expression that Nejdanov could not help asking what was the matter with him. Markelov declared that it was nothing in a tone in which people commonly let you understand that there is something wrong, but that it does not concern you. Golushkin again started abusing some one or other and then went on to praising the new generation. "Such clever chaps they are nowadays! Clever chaps!" Solomin interrupted him by asking about the hopeful young man whom he had mentioned and where he had discovered him. Golushkin laughed, repeating once or twice, "Just wait, you will see! You will see!" and began questioning him about his factory and its " rogue " of an owner, to which Solomin replied in monosyllables. Then Golushkin poured them all out champagne, and bending over to Nejdanov, whispered in his ear, " To the republic! " and drank off his glass at a gulp. Nejdanov merely put his lips to the glass, Solomin said that he did not take wine in the morning, and Markelov angrily and resolutely drank his glass to the last drop. He was torn by impatience. " Here we are coolly wasting our time and not tackling the real matter in hand." He struck a blow on the table, exclaiming severely, " Gentlemen! " and began to speak.

But at this moment there entered a sleek, consumptive-looking man with a long neck, in a merchant's coat of nankeen, and arms outstretched like a bird. He bowed to the whole company and, approaching Golushkin, communicated something to him in a whisper.

" In a minute! In a minute! " the latter exclaimed, hurriedly. " Gentlemen," he added, " I must ask you to excuse me. Vasia, my clerk, has just told me of such a little piece of news " (Golushkin expressed himself thus purposely by way of a joke) " which absolutely necessitates my leaving you for a while. But I hope, gentlemen, that you will come and have dinner with me at three o'clock. Then we shall be more free! "

Neither Solomin nor Nejdanov knew what to say, but Markelov replied instantly, with that same severity in his face and voice:

" Of course we will come."

" Thanks very much," Golushkin said hastily, and bending down to Markelov, added, " I will give a thousand roubles for the cause in any case. . . . Don't be afraid of that! "

And so saying, he waved his right hand three times, with the thumb and little finger sticking out. " You may rely on me! " he added.

He accompanied his guests to the door, shouting, " I shall expect you at three! "

"Very well," Markelov was the only one to reply.

"Gentlemen!" Solomin exclaimed as soon as they found themselves in the street, "I am going to take a cab and go straight back to the factory. What can we do here until dinner-time? A sheer waste of time, kicking our heels about, and I am afraid our worthy merchant is like the well-known goat, neither good for milk nor for wool."

"The wool is there right enough," Markelov observed gloomily. "He promised to give us some money. Don't you like him? Unfortunately we can't pick and choose. People do not run after us exactly."

"I am not fastidious," Solomin said calmly. "I merely thought that my presence would not do much good. However," he added, glancing at Nejdanov with a smile, "I will stay if you like. Even death is bearable in good company."

Markelov raised his head.

"Supposing we go into the public garden. The weather is lovely. We can sit and look at the people."

"Come along."

They moved on; Markelov and Solomin in front, Nejdanov in the rear.

XVIII

STRANGE was the state of Nejdanov's soul. In the last two days so many new sensations, new faces. . . . For the first time in his life he had come in close contact with a girl whom in all probability he loved. He was present at the beginning of the movement for which in all probability he was to devote his whole life. . . . Well? Was he glad? No. . . . Was he wavering? Was he afraid? Confused? Oh, certainly not! Did he at any rate feel that straining of the whole being, that longing to be amongst the first ranks, which is always inspired by the first approach of the battle? Again, No. Did he really believe in this cause? Did he believe in his love? " Oh, cursed æsthetic! Sceptic! " his lips murmured inaudibly. Why this weariness, this disinclination to speak, unless it be shouting or raving? What is this inner voice that he wishes to drown by his shrieking? But Mariana, this delightful, faithful comrade, this pure, passionate soul, this wonderful girl, does she not love him indeed? And these two beings in front of him, this Markelov and Solomin, whom he as yet knew but little, but to whom he was attracted so much, were they not excellent types of the Russian people—of Russian life—and was it not a happiness in itself to be closely connected with them? Then why this vague, uneasy, gnawing sensation? Why this sadness? If you're such a melancholy dreamer, his lips murmured again, what sort of a revolutionist will you make? You ought to write verses, languish, nurse your own insignificant thoughts and sensations, amuse yourself with psychological fancies and subtleties of all sorts, but don't at any rate mistake your sickly, nervous irritability and caprices for the manly wrath, the honest anger, of a man of convictions! O Hamlet!

Hamlet! thou Prince of Denmark! How escape from the shadow of thy spirit? How cease to imitate thee in everything, even to revelling shamelessly in one's own self-depreciation? Just then, as the echo of his own thoughts, he heard a familiar squeaky voice exclaim, " Alexai! Alexai! Hamlet of Russia! Is it you I behold? " and raising his eyes, to his great astonishment, saw Paklin standing before him! Paklin, in Arcadian attire, consisting of a summer suit of flesh-colour, without a tie, a large straw hat, trimmed with pale blue ribbon, pushed to the back of his head, and patent shoes!

He limped up to Nejdanov quickly and seized his hand.

" In the first place," he began, " although we are in the public garden, we must for the sake of old times embrace and kiss. . . . One! two! three! Secondly, I must tell you, that had I not run across you to-day you would most certainly have seen me to-morrow. I know where you live and have come to this town expressly to see you . . . how and why I will tell you later. Thirdly, introduce me to your friends. Tell me briefly who they are, and tell them who I am, and then let us proceed to enjoy ourselves! "

Nejdanov responded to his friend's request, introduced them to each other, explaining who each was, where he lived, his profession, and so on.

" Splendid! " Paklin exclaimed. " And now let me lead you all far from the crowd, though there is not much of it here, certainly, to a secluded seat, where I sit in hours of contemplation enjoying nature. We will get a magnificent view of the governor's house, two striped sentry boxes, three gendarmes, and not a single dog! Don't be too much surprised at the volubility of my remarks with which I am trying so hard to amuse you. According to my friends, I am the representative of Russian wit . . . probably that is why I am lame."

Paklin conducted the friends to the " secluded seat " and made them sit down, after having first got rid of two beggar

women installed on it. Then the young people proceeded to " exchange ideas," a rather dull occupation mostly, particularly at the beginning, and a fruitless one generally.

" Stop a moment! " Paklin exclaimed, turning to Nejdanov, " I must first tell you why I've come here. You know that I usually take my sister away somewhere every summer, and when I heard that you were coming to this neighbourhood I remembered there were two wonderful creatures living in this very town, husband and wife, distant relations of ours . . . on our mother's side. My father came from the lower middle class and my mother was of noble blood." (Nejdanov knew this, but Paklin mentioned the fact for the benefit of the others.) " These people have for a long time been asking us to come and see them. Why not? I thought. It's just what I want. They're the kindest creatures and it will do my sister no end of good. What could be better? And so here we are. And really I can't tell you how jolly it is for us here! They're such dears! Such original types! You must certainly get to know them! What are you doing here? Where are you going to dine˙ And why did you come here of all places? "

" We are going to dine with a certain Golushkin—a merchant here," Nejdanov replied.

" At what time? "

" At three o'clock."

" Are you going to see him on account . . . on account——"
Paklin looked at Solomin who was smiling and at Markelov who sat enveloped in his gloom.

" Come, Aliosha, tell them—make some sort of Masonic sign . . . tell them not to be on ceremony with me . . . I am one of you—of your party."

" Golushkin is also one of us," Nejdanov observed.

" Why, that's splendid! It is still a long way off three o'clock. Suppose we go and see my relatives! "

" What an idea! How can we——"

" Don't be alarmed, I take all the responsibility upon

127

myself. Imagine, it's an oasis! Neither politics, literature, nor anything modern ever penetrates there. The little house is such a squat one, such as one rarely sees nowadays; the very smell in it is antique; the people antique, the air antique . . . whatever you touch is antique, Catherine II. powder, crinolines, eighteenth century! And the host and hostess . . . imagine a husband and wife both very old, of the same age, without a wrinkle, chubby, round, neat little people, just like two poll-parrots; and kind to stupidity, to saintliness, there is no end to their kindness! I am told that excessive kindness is often a sign of moral weakness. . . . I cannot enter into these subtleties, but I know that my dear old people are goodness itself. They never had any children, the blessed ones! That is what they call them here in the town; blessed ones! They both dress alike, in a sort of loose striped gown, of such good material, also a rarity, not to be found nowadays. They are exactly like one another, except that one wears a mob-cap, the other a skull-cap, which is trimmed with the same kind of frill, only without ribbons. If it were not for these ribbons you would not know one from the other, as the husband is clean-shaven. One is called Fomishka, the other Fimishka. I tell you one ought to pay to go and look at them! They love one another in the most impossible way; and if you ever go to see them, they welcome you with open arms. And so gracious; will show off all their little parlour tricks to amuse you. But there is only one thing they can't stand, and that is smoking, not because they are nonconformists, but because it doesn't agree with them. . . . Of course, nobody smoked in their time. However, to make up for that, they don't keep canaries—this bird was also very little known in their day. I'm sure you'll agree that that's a comfort at any rate! Well? Will you come?"

" I really don't know," Nejdanov began.

" Wait a moment! I forgot to tell you; their voices, too, are exactly alike; close your eyes and you can hardly tell which is speaking. Fomishka, perhaps, speaks just a little more expressively. You are about to enter on a great undertaking, my dear friends; may be on a terrible conflict. . . . Why not, before plunging into the stormy deep, take a dip into——"

" Stagnant water," Markelov put in.

" Stagnant if you like, but not putrid. There are ponds in the steppes which never get putrid, although there is no stream flowing through them, because they have springs at the bottom. My old people have their springs flowing in the depths of their hearts, as pure and as fresh as can be. The question is this: do you want to see how people lived a hundred or a hundred and fifty years ago? If so, then make haste and follow me. Or soon the day, the hour will come—it's bound to be the same hour for them both –when my little parrots will be thrown off their little perches— and everything antique will end with them. The squat little house will tumble down and the place where it stood will be overgrown with that which, according to my grandmother, always grows over the spot where man's handiwork has been—that is, nettles, burdock, thistles, wormwood, dock leaves. The very street will cease to be—other people will come and never will they see anything like it again, never, through all the long ages! "

" Well," Nejdanov exclaimed, " let us go at once! "

" With the greatest of pleasure," Solomin added. " That sort of thing is not in my line, still it will be interesting, and if Mr. Paklin really thinks that we shall not be putting any one out by our visit . . . then . . . why not——"

" You may be at ease on that score! " Paklin exclaimed in his turn. " They will be delighted to see you—and nothing more. You need not be on ceremony. I told you —they were blessed ones. We will get them to sing to us! Will you come too, Mr. Markelov? "

Markelov shrugged his shoulders impatiently.

" You can hardly leave me here alone! We may as well go, I suppose." The young people rose from the seat.

"What a forbidding individual that is you have with you," Paklin whispered to Nejdanov, indicating Markelov. "The very image of John the Baptist eating locusts . . . only locusts, without the honey! But the other is splendid!" he added, with a nod of the head in Solomin's direction. "What a delightful smile he has! I've noticed that people smile like that only when they are far above others, but without knowing it themselves."

"Are there really such people?" Nejdanov asked.

"They are scarce, but there are," Paklin replied.

XIX

Fomishka and Fimishka, otherwise Foma Lavrentievitch and Efimia Pavlovna Subotchev, belonged to one of the oldest and purest branches of the Russian nobility, and were considered to be the oldest inhabitants in the town of S. They married when very young and settled, a long time ago, in the little wooden ancestral house at the very end of the town. Time seemed to have stood still for them, and nothing " modern " ever crossed the boundaries of their " oasis." Their means were not great, but their peasants supplied them several times a year with all the live stock and provisions they needed, just as in the days of serfdom, and their bailiff appeared once a year with the rents and a couple of woodcocks, supposed to have been shot in the master's forests, of which, in reality, not a trace remained. They regaled him with tea at the drawing-room door, made him a present of a sheep-skin cap, a pair of green leather mittens, and sent him away with a blessing. The Subotchevs' house was filled with domestics and menials just as in days gone by. The old man-servant Kalliopitch, clad in a jacket of extraordinarily stout cloth with a stand-up collar and small steel buttons, announced, in a sing-song voice, " Dinner is on the table," and stood dozing behind his mistress's chair as in days of old. The sideboard was under his charge, and so were all the groceries and pickles. To the question, had he not heard of the emancipation, he invariably replied: " How can one take notice of every idle piece of gossip? To be sure the Turks were emancipated, but such a dreadful thing had not happened to him, thank the Lord! " A girl, Pufka, was kept in the house for entertainment, and the old nurse Vassilievna used to come in during dinner with a dark kerchief

131

on her head, and would relate all the news in her deep voice
—about Napoleon, about the war of 1812, about Antichrist
and white niggers—or else, her chin propped on her hand,
with a most woeful expression on her face, she would tell
of a dream she had had, explaining what it meant, or perhaps how she had last read her fortune at cards. The
Subotchevs' house was different from all other houses in
the town. It was built entirely of oak, with perfectly square
windows, the double casements for winter use were never
removed all the year round. It contained numerous little
ante-rooms, garrets, closets, and box-rooms, little landings
with balustrades, little statues on carved wooden pillars,
and all kinds of back passages and sculleries. There was a
hedge right in front and a garden at the back, in which there
was a perfect nest of out-buildings: store rooms and cold-
store rooms, barns, cellars and ice-cellars; not that there
were many goods stored in them—some of them, in fact, were
in an extremely delapidated condition—but they had been
there in olden days and were consequently allowed to
remain. The Subotchevs had only two ancient shaggy
saddle horses, one of which, called the Immovable, had
turned grey from old age. They were harnessed several
times a month to an extraordinary carriage, known to the
whole town, which bore a faint resemblance to a terrestrial
globe with a quarter of it cut away in front, and was upholstered inside with some foreign, yellowish stuff, covered
with a pattern of huge dots, looking for all the world like
warts. The last yard of this stuff must have been woven
in Utrecht or Lyons in the time of the Empress Elisabeth!
The Subotchev's coachman, too, was old—an ancient, ancient
old man with a constant smell of tar and cart-oil about him.
His beard began just below the eyes, while the eyebrows
fell in little cascades to meet it. He was called Perfishka,
and was extremely slow in his movements. It took him at
least five minutes to take a pinch of snuff, two minutes to
fasten the whip in his girdle, and two whole hours to harness

the Immovable alone. If when out driving in their carriage the Subotchevs were ever compelled to go the least bit up or down hill, they would become quite terrified, would cling to the straps, and both cry aloud, " Oh Lord . . . give . . . the horses . . . the horses . . . the strength of Samson . . . and make us . . . as light as a feather! "

The Subotchevs were regarded by every one in the town as very eccentric, almost mad, and indeed they too felt that they were not in keeping with modern times. This, however, did not grieve them very much, and they quietly continued to follow the manner of life in which they had been born and bred and married. One custom of that time, however, did not cling to them; from their earliest childhood they had never punished any of their servants. If one of them turned out to be a thief or a drunkard, then they bore with him for a long time, as one bears with bad weather, and when their patience was quite exhausted they would get rid of him by passing him on to some one else. " Let others bear with him a little," they would say. But any such misfortune rarely happened to them, so rarely that it became an epoch in their lives. They would say, for instance, " Oh, it was long ago; it happened when we had that impudent Aldoshka with us," or " When grandfather's fur cap with the fox's tail was stolen! " Such caps were still to be found at the Subotchevs'. Another distinguishing characteristic of the old world was missing in them; neither Fomishka nor Fimishka were very religious. Fomishka was even a follower of Voltaire, whilst Fimishka had a mortal dread of the clergy and believed them to be possessed of the evil eye. " As soon as a priest comes into my house the cream turns sour! " she used to say. They rarely went to church and fasted in the Catholic fashion, that is, ate eggs, butter, and milk. This was known in the town and did not, of course, add to their reputation. But their kindness conquered everybody; and although the Subotchevs were laughed at and called cranks and blessed ones, still they were respected by every one. No one cared to visit them, however, but they were little concerned about this, too. They were never dull when in each other's company, were never apart, and never desired any other society.

Neither Fomishka nor Fimishka had ever been ill, and if one or the other ever felt the slightest indisposition they would both drink some concoction made of lime-flower, rub warm oil on their stomachs, or drop hot candle grease on the soles of their feet and the little ailment would soon pass over. They spent their days exactly alike. They got up late, drank chocolate in tiny cups shaped like small mortars (tea, they declared, came into fashion after their time), and sat opposite one another chatting (they were never at a loss for a subject of conversation!), or read out of *Pleasant Recreations*, *The World's Mirror*, or *Aonides*, or turned over the leaves of an old album, bound in red morocco, with gilt edges. This album had once belonged, as the inscription showed, to a certain Madame Barbe de Kabyline. How and why it had come into their possession they did not know. It contained several French and a great many Russian poems and prose extracts, of which the following reflections on Cicero form a fair example—

" The disposition in which Cicero undertook the office of quæstor may be gathered from the following. Calling upon the gods to testify to the purity of his sentiments in every rank with which he had hitherto been honoured, he considered himself bound by the most sacred bonds to the fulfilment of this one, and denied himself the indulgence, not only of such pleasures as are forbidden by law, but refrained even from such light amusements which are considered indispensable by all." Below was written, " Composed in Siberia in hunger and cold." An equally good specimen was a poem entitled " Tirsis," which ran like this—

The universe is steeped in calm,
The delightful sparkling dew
Soothing nature like a balm
Gives to her, her life anew.

134

Tersis alone with aching heart,
Is torn by sadness and dismay,
When dear Aneta doth depart
What is there to make him gay?

And the impromptu composition of a certain captain who
had visited the place in the year 1790, dated May 6th—

N'er shall I forget thee,
Village that to love I've grown,
But I ever shall regret thee
And the hours so quickly flown,
Hours which I was honoured in
Spending with your owner's kin,
The five dearest days of my life will hold
Passed amongst most worthy people,
Merry ladies, young and old,
And other interesting people.

On the last page of the album, instead of verses, there
were various recipes for remedies against stomach troubles,
spasms, and worms. The Subotchevs dined exactly at
twelve o'clock and only ate old-fashioned dishes: curd
fritters, pickled cabbage, soups, fruit jellies, minced chicken
with saffron, stews, custards, and honey. They took an
after-dinner nap for an hour, not longer, and on waking up
would sit opposite one another again, drinking bilberry wine
or an effervescent drink called " forty-minds," which nearly
always squirted out of the bottle, affording them great
amusement, much to the disgust of Kalliopitch, who had to
wipe up the mess afterwards. He grumbled at the cook and
housekeeper as if they had invented this dreadful drink on
purpose. " What pleasure does it give one? " he asked;
" it only spoils the furniture." Then the old people again
read something, or got the dwarf Pufka to entertain them,
or sang old-fashioned duets. Their voices were exactly
alike, rather high-pitched, not very strong or steady, and
somewhat husky, especially after their nap, but not without
a certain amount of charm. Or, if need be, they played at
cards, always the same old games, cribbage, écarté, or double
dummy whist. Then the samovar made its appearance.
The only concession they made to the spirit of the age was
to drink tea in the evening, though they always considered

135

it an indulgence, and were convinced that the nation was deteriorating, owing to the use of this "Chinese herb." On the whole, they refrained from criticising modern times or from exulting their own. They had lived like this all their lives, but that others might live in a different and even better way they were quite willing to admit, so long as they were not compelled to conform to it. At seven o'clock Kalliopitch produced the inevitable supper of cold hash, and at nine the high striped feather-bed received their rotund little bodies in its soft embrace, and a calm, untroubled sleep soon descended upon their eyelids. Everything in the little house became hushed; the little lamp before the icon glowed and glimmered, the funny innocent little pair slept the sound sleep of the just, amidst the fragrant scent of musk and the chirping of the cricket.

To these two odd little people, or poll-parrots as Paklin called them, who were taking care of his sister, he now conducted his friends.

Paklin's sister was a clever girl with a fairly attractive face. She had wonderfully beautiful eyes, but her unfortunate deformity had completely broken her spirit, deprived her of self-confidence, joyousness, made her mistrustful and even spiteful. She had been given the unfortunate name of Snandulia, and to Paklin's request that she should be re-christened Sophia, she replied that it was just as it should be; a hunchback ought to be called Snandulia; so she stuck to her strange name. She was an excellent musician and played the piano very well. "Thanks to my long fingers," she would say, not without a touch of bitterness. "Hunchbacks always have fingers like that."

The visitors came upon Fomishka and Fimishka at the very minute when they had awakened from their afternoon nap and were drinking bilberry wine.

"We are going into the eighteenth century!" Paklin exclaimed as they crossed the threshold of the Subotchevs' house.

136

And really they were confronted by the eighteenth century in the very hall, with its low bluish screens, ornamented with black silhouettes cut out of paper, of powdered ladies and gentlemen. Silhouettes, first introduced by Lavater, were much in vogue in the eighties of last century.

The sudden appearance of such a large number of guests—four all at once—produced quite a sensation in the usually quiet house. A hurried sound of feet, both shod and unshod, was heard, several women thrust their heads through the door and instantly drew them back again, some one was pushed, another groaned, a third giggled, some one whispered excitedly, " Be quiet, do ! "

At last Kalliopitch made his appearance in his old coat, and opening the drawing-room door announced in a loud voice:

" Sila Samsonitch with some other gentlemen, sir ! "

The Subotchevs were less disturbed than their servants, although the irruption of four full-sized men into their drawing-room, spacious though it was, did in fact surprise them somewhat. But Paklin soon reassured them, introducing Nejdanov, Solomin, and Markelov in turn, as good quiet people, not " governmental."

Fomishka and Fimishka had a horror of governmental, that is to say, official people.

Snandulia, who appeared at her brother's request, was far more disturbed and agitated than the old couple.

They asked, both together and in exactly the same words, if their guests would be pleased to partake of some tea, chocolate, or an effervescent drink with jam, but learning that they did not require anything, having just lunched with the merchant Golushkin and that they were returning there to dinner, they ceased pressing them, and, folding their arms in exactly the same manner across their stomachs, they entered into conversation. It was a little slow at first, but soon grew livelier.

Paklin amused them very much by relating the well

known Gogol anecdote about a superintendent of police, who managed to push his way into a church already so packed with people that a pin could scarcely drop, and about a pie which turned out to be no other than this same superintendent himself. The old people laughed till the tears rolled down their cheeks. They had exactly the same shrill laugh and both went red in the face from the effort. Paklin noticed that people of the Subotchev type usually went into fits of laughter over quotations from Gogol, but as his object at the present moment was not so much in amusing them as in showing them off to his friends, he changed his tactics and soon managed to put them in an excellent humour.

Fomishka produced a very ancient carved wooden snuff-box and showed it to the visitors with great pride. At one time one could have discerned about thirty-six little human figures in various attitudes carved on its lid, but they were so erased as to be scarcely visible now. Fomishka, however, still saw them and could even count them. He would point to one and say, " Just look! this one is staring out of the window. . . . He has thrust his head out! " but the place indicated by his fat little finger with the nail raised was just as smooth as the rest of the box. He then turned their attention to an oil painting hanging on the wall just above his head. It represented a hunter in profile, galloping at full speed on a bay horse, also in profile, over a snow plain. The hunter was clad in a tall white sheep-skin hat with a pale blue point, a tunic of camel's hair edged with velvet, and a girdle wrought in gold. A glove embroidered in silk was gracefully tucked into the girdle, and a dagger chased in black and silver hung at the side. In one hand the plump, youthful hunter carried an enormous horn, ornamented with red tassels, and the reins and whip in the other. The horse's four legs were all suspended in the air, and on every one of them the artist had carefully painted a horse-shoe and even indicated the nails. " Look," Fomishka observed, pointing with the same fat little finger to four semi-circular spots on the white ground, close to the horse's legs, " he has even put the snow prints in! " Why there were only four of these prints and not any to be seen further back, on this point Fomishka was silent.

" This was I! " he added after a pause, with a modest smile.

" Really! " Nejdanov exclaimed, " were you ever a hunting man? "

" Yes. I was for a time. Once the horse threw me at full gallop and I injured my *kurpey*. Fimishka got frightened and forbade me; so I have given it up since then."

" What did you injure? " Nejdanov asked.

" My *kurpey*," Fomishka repeated, lowering his voice.

The visitors looked at one another. No one knew what *kurpey* meant; at least, Markelov knew that the tassel on a Cossack or Circassian cap was called a *kurpey*, but then how could Fomishka have injured that? But no one dared to question him further.

" Well, now that you have shown off," Fimishka remarked suddenly, " I will show off too." And going up to a small *bonheur du jour*, as they used to call an old-fashioned bureau, on tiny, crooked legs, with a round lid which fitted into the back of it somewhere when opened, she took out a miniature in water colour, in an oval bronze frame, of a perfectly naked little child of four years old with a quiver over her shoulders fastened across the chest with pale blue ribbons, trying the points of the arrows with the tip of her little finger. The child was all smiles and curls and had a slight squint.

" And that was I," she said.

" Really? "

" Yes, as a child. When my father was alive a Frenchman used to come and see him, such a nice Frenchman too! He painted that for my father's birthday. Such a nice man! He used to come and see us often. He would come

139

in, make such a pretty courtesy and kiss your hand, and when going away would kiss the tips of his own fingers so prettily, and bow to the right, to the left, backwards and forwards! He was such a nice Frenchman!"

The guests praised his work; Paklin even declared that he saw a certain likeness.

Here Fomishka began to express his views on the modern French, saying that they had become very wicked nowadays!

"What makes you think so, Foma Lavrentievitch?"

"Look at the awful names they give themselves nowadays!"

"What, for instance?"

"Nogent Saint Lorraine, for instance! A regular brigand's name!"

Fomishka asked incidentally who reigned in Paris now, and when told that it was Napoleon, was surprised and pained at the information.

"How? . . . Such an old man——" he began and stopped, looking round in confusion.

Fomishka had but a poor knowledge of French and read Voltaire in a translation; he always kept a translated manuscript of *Candide* in the bible box at the head of his bed. He used to come out with expressions like: "This, my dear, is *fausse parquet*," meaning suspicious, untrue. He was very much laughed at for this, until a certain learned Frenchman told him that it was an old parliamentary expression employed in his country until the year 1789.

As the conversation turned upon France and the French, Fimishka resolved to ask something that had been very much on her mind. She first thought of addressing herself to Markelov, but he looked too forbidding, so she turned to Solomin, but no! He seemed to her such a plain sort of person, not likely to know French at all, so she turned to Nejdanov.

"I should like to ask you something, if I may," she began;

140

" excuse me, my kinsman Sila Samsonitch makes fun of me and my woman's ignorance."

" What is it? "

" Supposing one wants to ask in French, ' What is it? ' must one say ' Kese-kese-kese-la? ' "

" Yes."

" And can one also say ' Kese-kese-la? ' "

" Yes."

" And simply ' Kese-la? "

" Yes, that's right."

" And does it mean the same thing? "

" Yes, it does."

Fimishka thought awhile, then threw up her arms.

" Well, Silushka," she exclaimed; " I am wrong and you are right. But these Frenchmen. . . . How smart they are! "

Paklin began begging the old people to sing them some ballad. They were both surprised and amused at the idea, but consented readily on condition that Snandulia accompanied them on the harpsichord. In a corner of the room there stood a little spinet, which not one of them had noticed before. Snandulia sat down to it and struck several chords. Nejdanov had never heard such sour, toneless, tingling, jangling notes, but the old people promptly struck up the ballad, " Was it to Mourn."

Fomisha began—

> " In love God gave a heart
> Of burning passion to inspire
> That loving heart with warm desire."

> " But there is agony in bliss "

Fimishka chimed in.

> " And passion free from pain there is,
> Ah! where, where? tell me, tell me this,"

> " Ah! where, where? Tell me, tell me this,"

Fomisha put in.

141

> "Ah! where, where? tell me, tell me this,"

Fimishka repeated.

> "Nowhere in all the world, nowhere,
>   Love bringeth grief and black despair,"

they sang together,

> "And that, love's gift is everywhere,"

Fomisha sang out alone.

"Bravo!" Paklin exclaimed. "We have had the first verse, now please sing us the second."

"With the greatest of pleasure," Fomishka said, "but what about the trill, Snandulia Samsonovna? After my verse there must be a trill."

"Very well, I will play your trill," Snandulia replied.

Fomishka began again—

> "Has ever lover lovéd true
>   And kept his heart from grief and rue?
>   He loveth but to weep anew"

and then Fimishka—

> "Yea- -hearts that love at last are riven
>   As ships that hopelessly have striven
>   For life. To what end were they given?"

> "To what end were they given?"

Fomishka warbled out and waited for Snandulia to play the trill.

> "To what end were they given?"

he repeated, and then they struck up together—

> "Then take, O God, the heart away,
>   Away, away, take hearts away,
>   Away, away, away to-day."

"Bravo! Bravo!" the company exclaimed, all with exception of Markelov.

"I wonder they don't feel like clowns?" Nejdanov thought. "Perhaps they do, who knows? They no doubt think there is no harm in it and may be even amusing to some people. If one looks at it in that light, they are quite right! A thousand times right!"

Under the influence of these reflections he began paying compliments to the host and hostess, which they acknowledged with a courtesy, performed whilst sitting in their chairs. At this moment Pufka the dwarf and Nurse Vassilievna made their appearance from the adjoining room (a bedroom or perhaps the maids' room) from whence a great bustle and whispering had been going on for some time. Pufka began squealing and making hideous grimaces, whilst the nurse first quietened her, then egged her on.

Solomin's habitual smile became even broader, whilst Markelov, who had been for some time showing signs of impatience, suddenly turned to Fomishka:

"I did not expect that you," he began in his severe manner, "with your enlightened mind—I've heard that you are a follower of Voltaire—could be amused with what ought to be an object for compassion—with deformity!" Here he remembered Paklin's sister and could have bitten his tongue off.

Fomishka went red in the face and muttered: "You see . . . it is not my fault . . . she herself——"

Pufka simply flew at Markelov.

"How dare you insult our masters?" she screamed out in her lisping voice. "What is it to you that they took me in, brought me up, and gave me meat and drink? Can't you bear to see another's good fortune, eh? Who asked you to come here? You fusty, musty, black-faced villain with a moustache like a beetle's!" Here Pufka indicated with her thick short fingers what his moustache was like; whilst Nurse Vassilievna's toothless mouth was convulsed with laughter, re-echoed in the adjoining room.

"I am not in a position to judge you," Markelov went on. "To protect the homeless and deformed is a very praiseworthy work, but I must say that to live in ease and luxury, even though without injury to others, not lifting a finger to help a fellow-creature, does not require a great deal of goodness. I, for one, do not attach much importance to that sort of virtue!"

Here Pufka gave forth a deafening howl. She did not understand a word of what Markelov had said, but she felt that the "black one" was scolding, and how dared he! Vassilievna also muttered something, whilst Fomishka folded his hands across his breast and turned to his wife. "Fimishka, my darling," he began, almost in tears; "do you hear what the gentleman is saying? We are both wicked sinners, Pharisees. . . . We are living on the fat of the land, oh! oh! oh! We ought to be turned out into the street . . . with a broom in our hands to work for our living! Oh! oh!"

At these mournful words Pufka howled louder than ever, whilst Fimishka screwed up her eyes, opened her lips, drew in a deep breath, ready to retaliate, to speak.

God knows how it would have ended had not Paklin intervened.

"What is the matter?" he began, gesticulating with his hands and laughing loudly. "I wonder you are not ashamed of yourselves! Mr. Markelov only meant it as a joke. He has such a solemn face that it sounded a little severe and you took him seriously! Calm yourself! Efimia Pavlovna, darling, we are just going, won't you tell us our fortunes at cards? You are such a good hand at it. Snandulia, do get the cards, please!"

Fimishka glanced at her husband, who seemed completely reassured, so she too quieted down.

"I have quite forgotten how to tell fortunes, my dear. It is such a long time since I held the cards in my hand."

But quite of her own accord she took an extraordinary, ancient pack of cards out of Snandalia's hand.

"Whose fortune shall I tell?"

"Why everybody's, of course!" Paklin exclaimed. "What a dear old thing she is. . . . You can do what you like with her," he thought. "Tell us all our fortunes, granny dear," he said aloud. "Tell us our fates, our characters, our futures, everything!"

She began shuffling the cards, but threw them down suddenly.

"I don't need cards!" she exclaimed. "I know all your characters without that, and as the character so is the fate. This one," she said, pointing to Solomin, "is a cool, steady sort of man. That one," she said, pointing threateningly at Markelov, "is a fiery, disastrous man." (Pufka put her tongue out at him.) "And as for you," she looked at Paklin, "there is no need to tell you—you know quite well that you're nothing but a giddy goose! And that one——"

She pointed to Nejdanov, but hesitated.

"Well?" he asked; "do please tell me what sort of a man I am."

"What sort of a man are you," Fimishka repeated slowly. You are pitiable—that is all!"

"Pitiable! But why?"

"Just so. I pity you—that is all I can say."

"But why do you pity me?"

"Because my eyes tell me so. Do you think I am a fool? I am cleverer than you, in spite of your red hair. I pity you—that is all!"

There was a brief silence—they all looked at one another, but did not utter a word.

"Well, good-bye, dear friends," Paklin exclaimed. "We must have bored you to death with our long visit. It is time for these gentlemen to be going, and I am going with them. Good-bye, thanks for your kindness."

"Good-bye, good-bye, come again. Don't be on ceremony," Fomishka and Fimishka exclaimed together. Then Fomishka suddenly drawled out:

"Many, many, many years of life. Many——"

"Many, many," Kalliopitch chimed in quite unexpectedly, when opening the door for the young men to pass out.

The whole four suddenly found themselves in the street before the squat little house, whilst Pufka's voice was heard from within:

" You fools! " she cried.   " You fools! "

Paklin laughed aloud, but no one responded.

Markelov looked at each in turn, as though he expected to hear some expression of indignation. Solomin alone smiled his habitual smile.

XX

"Well," Paklin was the first to begin, "we have been to the eighteenth century, now let us fly to the twentieth! Golushkin is such a go-ahead man that one can hardly count him as belonging to the nineteenth."

"Why, do you know him?"

"What a question! Did you know my poll-parrots?"

"No, but you introduced us."

"Well, then, introduce me. I don't suppose you have any secrets to talk over, and Golushkin is a hospitable man. You will see; he will be delighted to see a new face. We are not very formal here in S."

"Yes," Markelov muttered, "I have certainly noticed an absence of formality about the people here."

Paklin shook his head.

"I suppose that was a hit for me. . . I can't help it. . . I deserve it, no doubt. But may I suggest, my new friend, that you throw off those sad, oppressive thoughts, no doubt due to your bilious temperament . . . and chiefly——"

"And you sir, my new friend," Markelov interrupted him angrily, "allow me to tell you, by way of a warning, that I have never in my life been given to joking, least of all to-day! And what do you know about my temperament, I should like to know? It strikes me that it is not so very long since we first set eyes on one another."

"There, there, don't get angry and don't swear. I believe you without that," Paklin exclaimed. "O you," he said, turning to Solomin, "you, whom the wise Fimishka called a cool sort of man, and there certainly is something restful about you—do you think I had the slightest intention of saying anything unpleasant to any one or of joking out of place? I only suggested going with you to Golushkin's.

147

Besides, I'm such a harmless person; it's not my fault that Mr. Markelov has a bilious complexion."

Solomin first shrugged one shoulder, then the other. It was a habit of his when he did not quite know what to say.

" I don't think," he said at last, " that you could offend any one, Mr. Paklin, or that you wished to—and why should you not come with us to Mr. Golushkin? We shall, no doubt, spend our time there just as pleasantly as we did at your kinsman's—and just as profitably most likely."

Paklin threatened him with his finger.

" Oh! I see, you can be wicked too if you like! However, you are also coming to Golushkin's, are you not? "

" Of course I am. I have wasted the day as it is."

" Well then, *en avant, marchons!* To the twentieth century! To the twentieth century! Nejdanov, you are an advanced man, lead the way! "

" Very well, come along; only don't keep on repeating the same jokes lest we should think you are running short."

" I have still enough left for you, my dear friends," Paklin said gaily and went on ahead, not by leaping, but by limping, as he said.

" What an amusing man! " Solomin remarked as he was walking along arm-in-arm with Nejdanov; " if we should ever be sent to Siberia, which Heaven forbid, there will be some one to entertain us at any rate."

Markelov walked in silence behind the others.

Meanwhile great preparations were going on at Golushkin's to produce a " chic " dinner. (Golushkin, as a man of the highest European culture, kept a French cook, who had formerly been dismissed from a club for dirtiness.) A nasty, greasy fish soup was prepared, various *pâtés chauds* and fricassés and, most important of all, several bottles of champagne had been procured and put into ice.

The host met the young people with his characteristic awkwardness, bustle, and much giggling. He was delighted to see Paklin as the latter had predicted and asked of him,

" Is he one of us? Of course he is! I need not have asked,"
he said, without waiting for a reply. He began telling them
how he had just come from that " old fogey " the governor,
and how the latter worried him to death about some sort of
charity institution. It was difficult to say what satisfied
Golushkin most, the fact that he was received at the governor's or that he was able to abuse that worthy before
these advanced young men. Then he introduced them to
the promised proselyte, who turned out to be no other than
the sleek consumptive individual with the long neck whom
they had seen in the morning, Vasia, Golushkin's clerk.
" He hasn't much to say," Golushkin declared, " but is
devoted heart and soul to our cause." To this Vasia bowed,
blushed, blinked his eyes, and grinned in such a manner
that it was impossible to say whether he was merely a
vulgar fool or an out-and-out knave and blackguard.

" Well, gentlemen, let us go to dinner," Golushkin exclaimed.

They partook of various kinds of salt fish to give them
an appetite and sat down to the table. Directly after the
soup, Golushkin ordered the champagne to be brought up,
which came out in frozen little lumps as he poured it into
the glasses. " For our . . . our enterprise!" Golushkin
exclaimed, winking at the servant, as much as to say, " One
must be careful in the presence of strangers." The proselyte
Vasia continued silent, and though he sat on the very edge
of his chair and conducted himself generally with a servility
quite out of keeping with the convictions to which, according
to his master, he was devoted body and soul, yet gulped
down the wine with an amazing greediness. The others
made up for his silence, however, that is, Golushkin and
Paklin, especially Paklin. Nejdanov was inwardly annoyed,
Markelov angry and indignant, just as indignant, though
in a different way, as he had been at the Subotchevs';
Solomin was observant.

Paklin was in high spirits and delighted Golushkin with

his sharp, ready wit. The latter had not the slightest suspicion that the " little cripple " every now and again whispered to Nejdanov, who happened to be sitting beside him, the most unflattering remarks at his, Golushkin's, expense. He thought him " a simple sort of fellow " who might be patronised; that was probably why he liked him. Had Paklin been sitting next him he would no doubt have poked him in the ribs or slapped him on the shoulder, but as it was, he merely contented himself by nodding and winking in his direction. Between him and Nejdanov sat Markelov, like a dark cloud, and then Solomin. Golushkin went into convulsions at every word Paklin said, laughed on trust in advance, holding his sides and showing his bluish gums. Paklin soon saw what was expected of him and began abusing everything (it being an easy thing for him), everything and everybody; conservatives, liberals, officials, lawyers, administrators, landlords, county councils and district councils, Moscow and St. Petersburg. " Yes, yes, yes," Golushkin put in, " that's just how it is! For instance, our mayor here is a perfect ass! A hopeless blockhead! I tell him one thing after another, but he doesn't understand a single word; just like our governor! "

" Is your governor a fool then? " Paklin asked.

" I told you he was an ass! "

" By the way, does he speak in a hoarse voice or through his nose? "

" What do you mean? " Golushkin asked somewhat bewildered.

" Why, don't you know? In Russia all our important civilians speak in a hoarse voice and our great army men speak through the nose. Only our very highest dignitaries do both at the same time."

Golushkin roared with laughter till the tears rolled down his cheeks.

" Yes, yes," he spluttered, " if he talks through his nose . . . then he's an army man! "

150

"You idiot!" Paklin thought to himself.

"Everything is rotten in this country, wherever you may turn!" he bawled out after a pause. "Everything is rotten, everything!"

"My dear Kapiton Andraitch," Paklin began suggestively (he had just asked Nejdanov in an undertone, "Why does he throw his arms about as if his coat were too tight for him?"), "my dear Kapiton Andraitch, believe me, half measures are of no use!"

"Who talks of half measures!" Golushkin shouted furiously (he had suddenly ceased laughing), "there's only one thing to be done; it must all be pulled up by the roots! Vasia, drink!"

"I am drinking, Kapiton Andraitch," the clerk observed, emptying a glass down his throat.

Golushkin followed his suit.

"I wonder he doesn't burst!" Paklin whispered to Nejdanov.

"He's used to it!" the latter replied.

But the clerk was not the only one who drank. Little by little the wine affected them all. Nejdanov, Markelov, and even Solomin began taking part in the conversation.

At first disdainfully, as if annoyed with himself for doing so, for not keeping up his character, Nejdanov began to hold forth. He maintained that the time had now come to leave off playing with words; that the time had come for "action," that they were now on sure ground! And then, quite unconscious of the fact that he was contradicting himself, he began to demand of them to show him what real existing elements they had to rely on, saying that as far as he could see society was utterly unsympathetic towards them, and the people were as ignorant as could be. Nobody made any objection to what he said, not because there was nothing to object to, but because every one was talking on his own account. Markelov hammered out obstinately in his hoarse, angry, monotonous voice (" just

151

as if he were chopping cabbage," Paklin remarked). Pre-cisely what he was talking about no one could make out, but the word "artillery" could be heard in a momentary hush. He was no doubt referring to the defects he had discovered in its organisation. Germans and adjutants were also brought in. Solomin remarked that there were two ways of waiting, waiting and doing nothing and waiting while pushing things ahead at the same time.

"We don't want moderates," Markelov said angrily.

"The moderates have so far been working among the upper classes," Solomin remarked, "and we must go for the lower."

"We don't want it! damnation! We don't want it!" Golushkin bawled out furiously. "We must do everything with one blow! With one blow, I say!"

"What is the use of extreme measures? It's like jumping out of the window."

"And I'll jump too, if necessary!" Golushkin shouted. "I'll jump! and so will Vasia! I've only to tell him and he'll jump! eh, Vasia? You'll jump, eh?"

The clerk finished his glass of champagne.

"Where you go, Kapiton Andraitch, there I follow. I shouldn't dare do otherwise."

"You had better not, or I'll make mincemeat of you!"

Soon a perfect babel followed.

Like the first flakes of snow whirling round and round in the mild autumn air, so words began flying in all directions in Golushkin's hot, stuffy dining-room; all kinds of words, rolling and tumbling over one another: progress, govern-ment, literature, the taxation question, the church question, the woman question, the law-court question, realism, nihilism, communism, international, clerical, liberal, capital, adminis-tration, organisation, association, and even crystallisation! It was just what Golushkin wanted; this uproar seemed to him the real thing. He was triumphant. "Look at us! out of the way or I'll knock you on the head! Kapiton

Golushkin is coming!" At last the clerk Vasia became so tipsy that he began to giggle and talk to his plate. All at once he jumped up shouting wildly, "What sort of devil is this *progymnasium*?"

Golushkin sprang up too, and throwing back his hot, flushed face, on which an expression of vulgar self-satisfaction was curiously mingled with a feeling of terror, a secret misgiving, he bawled out, "I'll sacrifice another thousand! Get it for me, Vasia!" To which Vasia replied, "All right!"

Just then Paklin, pale and perspiring (he had been drinking no less than the clerk during the last quarter of an hour), jumped up from his seat and, waving both his arms above his head, shouted brokenly, "Sacrifice! Sacrifice! What pollution of such a holy word! Sacrifice! No one dares live up to thee, no one can fulfil thy commands, certainly not one of us here—and this fool, this miserable money-bag opens its belly, lets forth a few of its miserable roubles, and shouts 'Sacrifice!' And wants to be thanked, expects a wreath of laurels, the mean scoundrel!"

Golushkin either did not hear or did not understand what Paklin was saying, or perhaps took it only as a joke, because he shouted again, "Yes, a thousand roubles! Kapiton Golushkin keeps his word!" And so saying he thrust his hand into a side pocket. "Here is the money, take it! Tear it to pieces! Remember Kapiton!" When under excitement Golushkin invariably talked of himself in the third person, as children often do. Nejdanov picked up the notes which Golushkin had flung on the table covered with wine stains. Since there was nothing more to wait for, and the hour was getting late, they rose, took their hats, and departed.

They all felt giddy as soon as they got out into the fresh air, especially Paklin.

"Well, where are we going to now?" he asked with an effort.

"I don't know were you are going, but I'm going home," Solomin replied.

153

" Back to the factory? "

" Yes."

" Now, at night, and on foot? "

" Why not? I don't think there are any wolves or robbers here and my legs are quite strong enough to carry me. It's cooler walking at night."

" But hang it all, it's four miles! "

" I wouldn't mind if it were more. Good-bye, gentlemen."

Solomin buttoned his coat, pulled his cap over his forehead, lighted a cigar, and walked down the street with long strides.

" And where are you going to? " Paklin asked, turning to Nejdanov.

" I'm going home with him." He pointed to Markelov, who was standing motionless, his hands crossed on his breast. " We have horses and a conveyance."

" Very well. . . . And I'm going to Fomishka's and Fimishka's oasis. And do you know what I should like to say? There's twaddle here and twaddle there, only that twaddle, the twaddle of the eighteenth century, is nearer to the Russian character than the twaddle of the twentieth century. Good-bye, gentlemen. I'm drunk, so don't be offended at what I say, only a better woman than my sister Snandulia . . . is not to be found on God's earth, although she is a hunchback and called Snandulia. That's how things are arranged in this world! She ought to have such a name. Do you know who Saint Snandulia was? She was a virtuous woman who used to visit prisons and heal the wounds of the sick. But . . . good-bye! good-bye, Nejdanov, thou man to be pitied! And you, officer . . . ugh! misanthrope! good-bye!"

He dragged himself away, limping and swaying from side to side, towards the oasis, whilst Markelov and Nejdanov sought out the posting inn where they had left their conveyance, ordered the horses to be harnessed, and half an hour later were driving along the high road.

XXI

THE sky was overcast with low-hanging clouds, and though it was light enough to see the cart-ruts winding along the road, still to the right and left no separate object could be distinguished, everything blending together into dark, heavy masses. It was a dim, unsettled kind of night; the wind blew in terrific gusts, bringing with it the scent of rain and wheat, which covered the broad fields. When they passed the oak which served as a sign-post and turned down a bye-road, driving became more difficult, the narrow track being quite lost at times. The coach moved along at a slower pace.

" I hope we're not going to lose our way!" Nejdanov remarked; he had been quite silent until then.

" I don't think so," Markelov responded. " Two misfortunes never happen in one day."

" But what was the first misfortune? "

" A day wasted for nothing. Is that of no importance? "

" Yes . . . certainly . . . and then this Golushkin! We shouldn't have drank so much wine. My head is simply splitting."

" I wasn't thinking of Golushkin. We got some money from him at any rate, so our visit wasn't altogether wasted."

" But surely you're not really sorry that Paklin took us to his . . . what did he call them . . . poll-parrots? "

" As for that, there's nothing to be either sorry or glad about. I'm not interested in such people. That wasn't the misfortune I was referring to."

" What was it then? "

Markelov made no reply, but withdrew himself a little

further into his corner, as if he were muffling himself up. Nejdanov could not see his face very clearly, only his moustache stood out in a straight black line, but he had felt ever since the morning that there was something in Markelov that was best left alone, some mysteriously unknown worry.

" I say, Sergai Mihailovitch," Nejdanov began, " do you really attach any importance to Mr. Kisliakov's letters that you gave me to-day? They are utter nonsense, if you'll excuse my saying so."

Markelov drew himself up.

" In the first place," he began angrily, " I don't agree with you about these letters—I find them extremely interesting . . . and conscientious! In the second place, Kisliakov works very hard and, what is more, he is in earnest; he *believes* in our cause, believes in the revolution! And I must say that *you*, Alexai Dmitritch, are very luke-warm—*you* don't believe in our cause! "

" What makes you think so? " Nejdanov asked slowly.

" It is easy to see from your very words, from your whole behaviour. To-day, for instance, at Golushkin's, who said that he failed to see any elements that we could rely on? You! Who demanded to have them pointed out to him? You again! And when that friend of yours, that grinning buffoon, Mr. Paklin, stood up and declared with his eyes raised to heaven that not one of us was capable of self-sacrifice, who approved of it and nodded to him encouragingly? Wasn't it you? Say what you like of yourself . . . think what you like of yourself, you know best . . . that is your affair, but I know people who could give up everything that is beautiful in life—even love itself—to serve their convictions, to be true to them! Well, *you* . . . couldn't have done that, to-day at any rate! "

" To-day? Why not to-day in particular? "

" Oh, don't pretend, for heaven's sake, you happy Don Juan, you myrtle-crowned lover! " Markelov shouted, quite forgetting the coachman, who, though he did not turn round on the box, must have heard every word. It is true the coachman was at that moment more occupied with the road than with what the gentlemen were saying behind him. He loosened the shaft-horse carefully, though somewhat nervously, she shook her head, backed a little, and went down a slope which had no business there at all.

"I'm afraid I don't quite understand you," Nejdanov observed.

Markelov gave a forced, malicious laugh.

"So you don't understand me! ha, ha, ha! I know everything, my dear sir! I know whom you made love to yesterday, whom you've completely conquered with your good looks and honeyed words! I know who lets you into her room . . . after ten o'clock at night!"

"Sir!" the coachman exclaimed suddenly, turning to Markelov, "hold the reins, please. I'll get down and have a look. I think we've gone off the track. There seems a sort of ravine here."

The carriage was, in fact, standing almost on one side. Markel seized the reins which the coachman handed to him and continued just as loudly:

"I don't blame you in the least, Alexai Dmitritch! You took advantage of. . . . You were quite right. No wonder that you're not so keen about our cause now . . . as I said before, you have something else on your mind. And, really, who can tell beforehand what will please a girl's heart or what man can achieve what she may desire?"

"I understand now," Nejdanov began; "I understand your vexation and can guess . . . who spied on us and lost no time in letting you know——"

"It does not seem to depend on merit," Markelov continued, pretending not to have heard Nejdanov, and purposely drawling out each word in a sing-song voice, "no extraordinary spiritual or physical attractions. . . . Oh no! It's only the damned luck of all . . . bastards!'

The last sentence Markelov pronounced abruptly and hurriedly, but suddenly stopped as if turned to stone.

Nejdanov felt himself grow pale in the darkness and tingled all over. He could scarcely restrain himself from flying at Markelov and seizing him by the throat. " Only blood will wipe out this insult," he thought.

" I've found the road!" the coachman cried, making his appearance at the right front wheel, " I turned to the left by mistake—but it doesn't matter, we'll soon be home. It's not much farther. Sit still, please!"

He got on to the box, took the reins from Markelov, pulled the shaft-horse a little to one side, and the carriage, after one or two jerks, rolled along more smoothly and evenly. The darkness seemed to part and lift itself, a cloud of smoke could be seen curling out of a chimney, ahead some sort of hillock, a light twinkled, vanished, then another. . . . A dog barked.

" That's our place," the coachman observed. " Gee up, my pretties!"

The lights became more and more numerous as they drove on.

" After the way in which you insulted me," Nejdanov said at last, " you will quite understand that I couldn't spend the night under your roof, and I must ask you, however unpleasant it may be for me to do so, to be kind enough to lend me your carriage as soon as we get to your house to take me back to the town. To-morrow I shall find some means of getting home, and will then communicate with you in a way which you doubtless expect.

Markelov did not reply at once.

" Nejdanov," he exclaimed suddenly, in a soft, despairing tone of voice, " Nejdanov! For Heaven's sake come into the house if only to let me beg for your forgiveness on my knees! Nejdanov! forget . . . forget my senseless words! Oh, if some one only knew how wretched I feel!" Markelov struck himself on the breast with his fist, a groan seemed

158

to come from him. " Nejdanov. Be generous. . . . Give me your hand. . . . Say that you forgive me!"

Nejdanov held out his hand irresolutely—Markelov squeezed it so hard that he could almost have cried out.

The carriage stopped at the door of the house.

" Listen to me, Nejdanov," Markelov said to him a quarter of an hour later in his study, " listen." (He addressed him as " thou," and in this unexpected " *thou* " addressed to a man whom he knew to be a successful rival, whom he had only just cruelly insulted, wished to kill, to tear to pieces, in this familiar word " thou " there was a ring of irrevocable renunciation, sad, humble supplication, and a kind of claim. . . . Nejdanov recognised this claim and responded to it by addressing him in the same way. " Listen! I've only just told you that I've refused the happiness of love, renounced everything to serve my convictions. . . . It wasn't true, I was only bragging! Love has never been offered to me, I've had nothing to renounce! I was born unlucky and will continue so for the rest of my days . . . and perhaps it's for the best. Since I can't get that, I must turn my attention to something else! If you can combine the one with the other . . . love and be loved . . . and serve the cause at the same time, you're lucky! I envy you . . . but as for myself . . . I can't. You happy man! You happy man! I can't."

Markelov said all this softly, sitting on a low stool, his head bent and arms hanging loose at his sides. Nejdanov stood before him lost in a sort of dreamy attentiveness, and though Markelov had called him a happy man, he neither looked happy nor did he feel himself to be so.

" I was deceived in my youth," Markelov went on; " she was a remarkable girl, but she threw me over . . . and for whom? For a German! for an adjutant! And Mariana——"

He stopped. It was the first time he had pronounced her name and it seemed to burn his lips.

" Mariana did not deceive me. She told me plainly that

she did not care for me. . . . There is nothing in me she could care for, so she gave herself to you. Of course, she was quite free to do so."

" Stop a minute! " Nejdanov exclaimed. " What are you saying? What do you imply by the words ' gave herself '? I don't know what your sister told you, but I assure you——"

" I didn't mean physically, but morally, that is, with the heart and soul," Markelov interrupted him. He was obviously displeased with Nejdanov's exclamation. " She couldn't have done better. As for my sister, she didn't, of course, wish to hurt me. It can make no difference to her, but she no doubt hates you and Mariana too. She did not tell me anything untrue . . . but enough of her! "

" Yes," Nejdanov thought to himself, " she does hate us."

" It's all for the best," Markelov continued, still sitting in the same position. " The last fetters have been broken; there is nothing to hinder me now! It doesn't matter that Golushkin is an ass, and as for Kisliakov's letters, they may perhaps be absurd, but we must consider the most important thing. Kisliakov says that everything is ready. Perhaps you don't believe that too."

Nejdanov did not reply.

" You may be right, but if we've to wait until everything, absolutely everything, is ready, we shall never make a beginning. If we weigh *all* the consequences beforehand we're sure to find some bad ones among them. For instance, when our forefathers emancipated the serfs, do you think they could foresee that a whole class of money-lending landlords would spring up as a result of the emancipation? Landlords who sell a peasant eight bushels of rotten rye for six roubles and in return for it get labour for the whole six roubles, then the same quantity of good sound rye and interest on top of that! Which means that they drain the peasants to the last drop of blood! You'll agree that our emancipators could hardly have foreseen that. Even if

160

they had foreseen it, they would still have been quite right in freeing the serfs without weighing all the consequences beforehand! That is why I have decided!"

Nejdanov looked at Markelov with amazement, but the latter turned to one side and directed his gaze into a corner of the room. He sat with his eyes closed, biting his lips and chewing his moustache.

"Yes, I've decided!" he repeated, striking his knee with his brown hairy hand. "I'm very obstinate. . . . It's not for nothing that I'm half a Little Russian."

He got up, dragged himself into his bedroom, and came back with a small portrait of Mariana in a glazed frame.

"Take this," he said in a sad, though steady voice. "I drew it some time ago. I don't draw well, but I think it's like her." (It was a pencil sketch in profile and was certainly like Mariana.) "Take it, Alexai; it is my bequest, and with this portrait I give you all my rights. . . . I know I never had any . . . but you know what I mean! I give you up everything, and her. . . . She is very good, Alexai——"

Markelov ceased; his chest heaved visibly.

"Take it. You are not angry with me, are you? Well, take it then. It's no use to me . . . now."

Nejdanov took the portrait, but a strange sensation oppressed his heart. It seemed to him that he had no right to take this gift; that if Markelov knew what was in his, Nejdanov's, heart, he would not have given it him. He stood holding the round piece of cardboard, carefully set in a black frame with a mount of gold paper, not knowing what to do with it. "Why, this is a man's whole life I'm holding in my hand," he thought. He fully realised the sacrifice Markelov was making, but why, why especially to him? Should he give back the portrait? No! that would be the grossest insult. And after all, was not the face dear to him? Did he not love her?

161

Nejdanov turned his gaze on Markelov not without some inward misgiving. "Was he not looking at him, trying to guess his thoughts?" But Markelov was standing in a corner biting his moustache.

The old servant came into the room carrying a candle. Markelov started.

"It's time we were in bed, Alexai," he said. "Morning is wiser than evening. You shall have the horses to-morrow. Good-bye."

"And good-bye to you too, old fellow," he added turning to the servant and slapping him on the shoulder. "Don't be angry with me!"

The old man was so astonished that he nearly dropped the candle, and as he fixed his eyes on his master there was an expression in them of something other, something more, than his habitual dejection.

Nejdanov retired to his room. He was feeling wretched. His head was aching from the wine he had drunk, there were ringing noises in his ears and stars jumping about in front of his eyes, even though he shut them. Golushkin, Vasia the clerk, Fomishka and Fimishka, were dancing about before him, with Mariana's form in the distance, as if distrustful and afraid to come near. Everything that he had said or done during the day now seemed to him so utterly false, such useless nonsense, and the thing that ought to be done, ought to be striven for, was nowhere to be found, unattainable, under lock and key, in the depths of a bottomless pit.

He was filled with a desire to go to Markelov and say to him, "Here, take back your gift, take it back!"

"Ugh! What a miserable thing life is!" he exclaimed.

He departed early on the following morning. Markelov was already standing at the door surrounded by peasants, but whether he had asked them to come, or they had come of their own accord, Nejdanov did not know. Markelov said very little and parted with him coldly, but it seemed to Nejdanov that he had something of importance to communicate to him.

The old servant made his appearance with his usual melancholy expression.

The carriage soon left the town behind it, and coming out into the open country began flying at a furious rate. The horses were the same, but the driver counted on a good tip, as Nejdanov lived in a rich house. And as is usually the case, when the driver has either had a drink, or expects to get one, the horses go at a good pace.

It was an ordinary June day, though the air was rather keen. A steady high wind was blowing, but raising no dust in the road, owing to last night's rain. The laburnums glistened, rustling to and fro in the breeze; a ripple ran over everything. From afar the cry of the quail was carried over the hills, over the grassy ravines, as if the very cry was possessed of wings; the rooks were bathing in the sunshine; along the straight, bare line of the horizon little specks no bigger than flies could be distinguished moving about. These were some peasants re-ploughing a fallow field.

Nejdanov was so lost in thought that he did not see all this. He went on and on and did not even notice when they drove through Sipiagin's village.

He trembled suddenly as he caught sight of the house, the first story and Mariana's window. "Yes," he said to himself, a warm glow entering his heart, "Markelov was right. She is a good girl and I love her."

XXII

NEJDANOV changed his clothes hurriedly and went in to
give Kolia his lesson. On the way he ran across Sipiagin
in the dining-room. He bowed to him with chilling politeness, muttered through his teeth, " Got back all right? " and
went into his study. The great statesman had already
decided in his ministerial mind that as soon as the vacation
came to an end he would lose no time in packing off to
St. Petersburg " this extremely revolutionary young tutor,"
but meanwhile would keep an eye on him. *Je n'ai pas eu
la main heureuse cette fois-ci*, he thought to himself, still
j'aurais pu tomber pire. Valentina Mihailovna's sentiments
towards Nejdanov however, were not quite so negative;
she simply could not endure the idea that he, " a mere boy,"
had slighted her! Mariana had not been mistaken, Valentina Mihailovna had listened at the door in the corridor;
the illustrious lady was not above such proceedings. Although she had said nothing to her " flighty " niece during
Nejdanov's absence, still she had let her plainly understand
that everything was known to her, and that if she had not
been so painfully sorry for her, and did not despise her
from the bottom of her heart, she would have been most
frightfully angry at the whole thing.

An expression of restrained inward contempt played over
her face. She raised her eyebrows in scorn and pity when
she looked at or spoke to Mariana, and she would fix her
wonderful eyes, full of tender remonstrance and painful
disgust, on the wilful girl, who, after all her " fancies and
eccentricities," had ended by kissing an insignificant under-
graduate . . . in a dark room!

Poor Mariana! Her severe, proud lips had never tasted
any man's kisses.

Valentina Mihailovna had not told her husband of the discovery she had made. She merely contented herself by addressing a few words to Mariana in his presence, accompanied by a significant smile, quite irrelevant to the occasion. She regretted having written to her brother, but was, on the whole, more pleased that the thing was done than be spared the regret and the letter not written.

Nejdanov got a glimpse of Mariana at lunch in the dining-room. It seemed to him that she had grown thinner and paler. She was not looking her best on that day, but the penetrating glance she turned on him directly he entered the room went straight to his heart. Valentina Mihailovna looked at him constantly, as though she were inwardly congratulating him. "Splendid! Very smart!" he read on her face, whilst she was studying his to find out if Markelov had shown him the letter. She decided in the end that he had.

On hearing that Nejdanov had been to the factory of which Solomin was the manager, Sipiagin began asking him various questions about it, but was soon convinced from the young man's replies that he had seen nothing there and dropped into a majestic silence, as if reproaching himself for having expected any practical knowledge from such an inexperienced individual! On going out of the room Mariana managed to whisper to Nejdanov: "Wait for me in the birch grove at the end of the garden. I'll be there as soon as possible."

"She is just as familiar with me as Markelov was," he thought to himself, and a strange, pleasant sensation came over him. How strange it would have seemed to him if she had suddenly become distant and formal again, if she had turned away from him. He felt that such a thing would have made him utterly wretched, but was not sure in his own mind whether he loved her or not. She was dear to him and he felt the need of her above everything—this he acknowledged from the bottom of his heart.

165

The grove Mariana mentioned consisted of some hundreds of big old weeping-birches. The wind had not fallen and the long tangled branches were tossing hither and thither like loosened tresses. The clouds, still high, flew quickly over the sky, every now and again obscuring the sun and making everything of an even hue. Suddenly it would make its appearance again and brilliant patches of light would flash out once more through the branches, crossing and recrossing, a tangled pattern of light and shade. The roar of the trees seemed to be filled with a kind of festive joy, like to the violent joy with which passion breaks into a sad, troubled heart. It was just such a heart that Nejdanov carried in his bosom. He leant against the trunk of a tree and waited. He did not really know what he was feeling and had no desire to know, but it seemed to him more awful, and at the same time easier, than at Markelov's. Above everything he wanted to see her, to speak to her. The knot that suddenly binds two separate existences already had him in its grasp. Nejdanov thought of the rope that is flung to the quay to make fast a ship. Now it is twisted about the post and the ship stops. . . . Safe in port! Thank God!

He trembled suddenly. A woman's dress could be seen in the distance coming along the path. It was Mariana. But whether she was coming towards him or going away from him he could not tell until he noticed that the patches of light and shade glided over her figure from below upwards. So she was coming towards him; they would have glided from above downwards had she been going away from him. A few moments longer and she was standing before him with her bright face full of welcome and a caressing light in her eyes. A glad smile played about her lips. He seized the hand she held out to him, but could not say a single word; she also was silent. She had walked very quickly and was somewhat out of breath, but seemed glad that he was pleased to see her. She was the first to speak.

" Well," she began, " tell me quickly what you've decided."

166

Nejdanov was surprised.

"Decided? Why, was it necessary to decide anything just now?"

"Oh, you know what I mean. Tell me what you talked about, whom you've seen—if you've met Solomin. Tell me everything, everything. But wait a moment; let us go on a little further. I know a spot not quite so conspicuous as this."

She made him come with her. He followed her obediently over the tall thin grass.

She led him to the place she mentioned, and they sat down on the trunk of a birch that had been blown down in a storm.

"Now begin!" she said, and added directly afterwards, "I am so glad to see you again! I thought these two days would never come to an end! Do you know, I'm convinced that Valentina Mihailovna listened to us."

"She wrote to Markelov about it," Nejdanov remarked.

"Did she?"

Mariana was silent for a while. She blushed all over, not from shame, but from another, deeper feeling.

"She is a wicked, spiteful woman!" she said slowly and quietly. "She had no right to do such a thing! But it doesn't matter. Now tell me your news."

Nejdanov began talking and Mariana listened to him with a sort of stony attention, only stopping him when she thought he was hurrying over things, not giving her sufficient details. However, not all the details of his visit were of equal interest to her; she laughed over Fomishka and Fimishka, but they did not interest her. Their life was too remote from hers.

"It's just like hearing about Nebuchadnezzar," she remarked.

But she was very keen to know what Markelov had said, what Golushkin had thought (though she soon realised what sort of a bird he was), and above all wanted to know Solo-

167

min's opinion and what sort of a man he was. These were the things that interested her. " But when? when? " was a question constantly in her mind and on her lips the whole time Nejdanov was talking, while he, on the other hand, seemed to try and avoid everything that might give a definite answer to that question. He began to notice himself that he laid special stress on those details that were of least interest to Mariana. He pulled himself up, but returned to them again involuntarily. Humorous descriptions made her impatient, a sceptic or dejected tone hurt her. It was necessary to keep strictly to everything concerning the " cause," and however much he said on the subject did not seem to weary her. It brought back to Nejdanov's mind how once, before he had entered the university, when he was staying with some friends of his in the country one summer, he had undertaken to tell the children some stories; they had also paid no attention to descriptions, personal expressions, personal sensations, they had also demanded nothing but facts and figures. Mariana was not a child, but she was like a child in the directness and simplicity of her feelings.

Nejdanov was sincerely enthusiastic in his praise of Markelov and expressed himself with particular warmth about Solomin. Whilst uttering the most enthusiastic expressions about him, he kept asking himself continually why he had such a high opinion of this man. He had not said anything very brilliant and, in fact, some of his words were in direct opposition to his (Nejdanov's) own convictions. " His head is screwed on the right way," he thought. " A cool, steady man, as Fimishka said; a powerful man, of calm, firm strength. He knows what he wants, has confidence in himself and arouses confidence in others. He has no anxieties and is well-balanced! That is the main thing; he has balance, just what is lacking in me! " Nejdanov ceased speaking and became lost in meditation. Suddenly he felt a hand on his shoulder.

"Alexai! What is the matter with you?" Mariana asked.

He took her tiny, strong hand from his shoulder and kissed it for the first time. Mariana laughed softly, surprised that such a thing should have occurred to him. She in her turn became pensive.

"Did Markelov show you Valentina Mihailovna's letter?" she asked at last.

"Yes, he did."

"Well, and how is he?"

"Markelov? He is the most honourable, most unselfish man in existence! He——"

Nejdanov wanted to tell Mariana about the portrait, but pulled himself up and added, "He is the soul of honour!"

"Oh yes, I know."

Mariana became pensive again. She suddenly turned to Nejdanov on the trunk they were both sitting on and asked quickly:

"Well? What have you decided on?"

Nejdanov shrugged his shoulders.

"I've already told you, dear, that we've decided nothing as yet; we must wait a little longer."

"But why?"

"Those were our last instructions." ("I'm lying," Nejdanov thought to himself.)

"From whom?"

"Why, you know . . . from Vassily Nikolaevitch. And then we must wait until Ostrodumov comes back."

Mariana looked questioningly at Nejdanov.

"But tell me, have you ever seen this Vassily Nikolae-vitch?"

"Yes. I've seen him twice . . . for a minute or two."

"What is he like? Is he an extraordinary man?"

"I don't quite know how to tell you. He is our leader now and directs everything. We couldn't get on without

discipline in our movement; we must obey some one."
(" What nonsense I'm talking! " Nejdanov thought.)

" What is he like to look at? "

" Oh, he's short, thick-set, dark, with high cheek-bones
like a Kalmick . . . a rather coarse face, only he has very
bright, intelligent eyes."

" And what does he talk like? "

" He does not talk, he commands."

" Why did they make him leader? "

" He is a man of strong character. Won't give in to
any one. Would sooner kill if necessary. People are afraid
of him."

" And what is Solomin like? " Mariana asked after a
pause.

" Solomin is also not good-looking, but has a nice, simple,
honest face. Such faces are to be found among schoolboys
of the right sort."

Nejdanov had described Solomin accurately.

Mariana gazed at him for a long, long time, then said, as
if to herself:

" You have also a nice face. I think it would be easy
to get on with you."

Nejdanov was touched; he took her hand again and raised
it to his lips.

" No more gallantries! " she said laughing. Mariana
always laughed when her hand was kissed. " I've done
something very naughty and must ask you to forgive
me."

" What have you done? "

" Well, when you were away, I went into your room and
saw a copy-book of verses lying on your table " (Nejdanov
shuddered; he remembered having left it there), " and I
must confess to you that I couldn't overcome my curiosity
and read the contents. Are they your verses? "

" Yes, they are. And do you know, Mariana, that one of
the strongest proofs that I care for you and have the fullest

confidence in you is that I am hardly angry at what you have done? "

" Hardly! Then you are just a tiny bit. I'm so glad you call me Mariana. I can't call you Nejdanov, so I shall call you Alexai. There is a poem which begins, ' When I die, dear friend, remember,' is that also yours? "

" Yes. Only please don't talk about this any more. . . . Don't torture me."

Mariana shook her head.

" It's a very sad poem. . . . I hope you wrote it before we became intimate. The verses are good though . . . as far as I can judge. I think you have the making of a literary man in you, but you have chosen a better and higher calling than literature. It was good to do that kind of work when it was impossible to do anything else."

Nejdanov looked at her quickly.

" Do you think so? I agree with you. Better ruin there, than success here."

Mariana stood up with difficulty.

" Yes, my dear, you are right! " she exclaimed, her whole face beaming with triumph and emotion, " you are right! But perhaps it may not mean ruin for us yet. We shall succeed, you will see, we'll be useful, our life won't be wasted. We'll go among the people. . . . Do you know any sort of handicraft? No? Never mind, we'll work just the same. We'll bring them, our brothers, everything that we know. . . . If necessary, I can cook, wash, sew. . . . You'll see, you'll see. . . . And there won't be any kind of merit in it, only happiness, happiness——"

Mariana ceased and fixed her eyes eagerly in the distance, not that which lay before her, but another distance as yet unknown to her, which she seemed to see. . . . She was all aglow.

Nejdanov bent down to her waist.

" Oh, Mariana! " he whispered. " I am not worthy of you! "

She trembled all over.

"It's time to go home!" she exclaimed, "or Valentina Mihailovna will be looking for us again. However, I think she's given me up as a bad job. I'm quite a black sheep in her eyes."

Mariana pronounced the last words with such a bright joyful expression that Nejdanov could not help laughing as he looked at her and repeating, "black sheep!"

"She is awfully hurt," Mariana went on, "that you are not at her feet. But that is nothing. The most important thing is that I can't stay here any longer. I must run away."

"Run away?" Nejdanov asked.

"Yes. . . . You are not going to stay here, are you? We'll go away together. . . . We must work together. . . . You'll come with me, won't you?"

"To the ends of the earth!" Nejdanov exclaimed, his voice ringing with sudden emotion in a transport of gratitude. "To the ends of the earth!" At that moment he would have gone with her wherever she wanted, without so much as looking back.

Mariana understood him and gave a gentle, blissful sigh.

"Then take my hand, dearest—only don't kiss it—press it firmly, like a comrade, like a friend—like this!"

They walked home together, pensive, happy. The young grass caressed their feet, the young leaves rustled about them, patches of light and shade played over their garments —and they both smiled at the wild play of the light, at the merry gusts of wind, at the fresh, sparkling leaves, at their own youth, and at one another.

XXIII

THE dawn was already approaching on the night after Golushkin's dinner when Solomin, after a brisk walk of about five miles, knocked at the gate in the high wall surrounding the factory. The watchman let him in at once and, followed by three house-dogs wagging their tails with great delight, accompanied him respectfully to his own dwelling. He seemed to be very pleased that the chief had got back safely.

" How did you manage to get here at night, Vassily Fedotitch? We didn't expect you till to-morrow."

" Oh, that's all right, Gavrilla. It's much nicer walking at night."

The most unusually friendly relations existed between Solomin and his workpeople. They respected him as a superior, treated him as one of themselves, and considered him to be very learned. " Whatever Vassily Fedotitch says," they declared, " is sacred! Because he has learnt everything there is to be learnt, and there isn't an Englishman who can get round him! " And in fact a certain well-known English manufacturer had once visited the factory, but whether it was that Solomin could speak to him in his own tongue or that he was really impressed by his knowledge is uncertain; he had laughed, slapped him on the shoulder, and invited him to come to Liverpool with him, saying to the workmen, in his broken Russian, " Oh, he's all right, your man here! " At which the men laughed a great deal, not without a touch of pride. " So that's what he is! Our man! "

And he really was theirs and one of them. Early the next morning his favourite Pavel woke him, prepared his things for washing, told him various news, and asked him various questions. They partook of some tea together hastily, after which Solomin put on his grey, greasy working-jacket and set out for the factory; and his life began to go round again like some huge fly-wheel.

But the thread had to be broken again. Five days after Solomin's return home there drove into the court-yard a smart little phaeton, harnessed to four splendid horses and a footman in pale green livery, whom Pavel conducted to the little wing, where he solemnly handed Solomin a letter sealed with an armorial crest, from " His Excellency Boris Andraevitch Sipiagin." In this letter, which exhaled an odour, not of perfume, but of some extraordinarily respectable English smell and was written in the third person, not by a secretary, but by the gentleman himself, the cultured owner of the village Arjanov, he begged to be excused for addressing himself to a man with whom he had not the honour of being personally acquainted, but of whom he, Sipiagin, had heard so many flattering accounts, and ventured to invite Mr. Solomin to come and see him at his house, as he very much wanted to ask his valuable advice about a manufacturing enterprise of some importance he had embarked upon. In the hope that Mr. Solomin would be kind enough to come, he, Sipiagin, had sent him his carriage, but in the event of his being unable to do so on that day, would he be kind enough to choose any other day that might be convenient for him and the same carriage would be gladly put at his disposal. Then followed the usual polite signature and a postscript written in the first person: " I hope that you will not refuse to take dinner with us *quite simply*. No dress clothes." (The words " quite simply " were underlined.) Together with this letter the footman (not without a certain amount of embarrassment) gave Solomin another letter from Nejdanov. It was just a simple note, not sealed with wax but merely stuck down, containing the following lines: " Do please come. You're wanted badly and may be extremely useful. I need hardly say not to Mr. Sipiagin."

On finishing Sipiagin's letter Solomin thought, "How else can I go if not simply? I haven't any dress clothes at the factory. . . . And what the devil should I drag myself over there for? It's just a waste of time!" But after reading Nejdanov's note, he scratched the back of his neck and walked over to the window, irresolute.

"What answer am I to take back, sir?" the footman in green livery asked slowly.

Solomin stood for some seconds longer at the window.

"I am coming with you," he announced, shaking back his hair and passing his hand over his forehead; "just let me get dressed."

The footman left the room respectfully and Solomin sent for Pavel, had a talk with him, ran across to the factory once more, then putting on a black coat with a very long waist, which had been made by a provincial tailor, and a shabby top-hat which instantly gave his face a wooden expression, took his seat in the phaeton. He suddenly remembered that he had forgotten his gloves, and called out to the "never-failing" Pavel, who brought him a pair of newly-washed white kid ones, the fingers of which were so stretched at the tips that they looked like long biscuits. Solomin thrust the gloves into his pocket and gave the order to start. Then the footman jumped on to the box with an unnecessary amount of alacrity, the well-bred coachman sang out in a falsetto voice, and the horses started off at a gallop.

While the horses were bearing Solomin along to Sipiagin's, that gentleman was sitting in his drawing-room with a half-cut political pamphlet on his knee, discussing him with his wife. He confided to her that he had written to him with the express purpose of trying to get him away from the merchant's factory to his own, which was in a very bad way and needed reorganising. Sipiagin would not for a

175

moment entertain the idea that Solomin would refuse to come, or even so much as appoint another day, though he had himself suggested it.

" But ours is a paper-mill, not a spinning-mill," Valentina Mihailovna remarked.

" It's all the same, my dear, machines are used in both, and he's a mechanic."

" But supposing he turns out to be a specialist! "

" My dear! In the first place there are no such things as specialists in Russia, in the second, I've told you that he's a mechanic! "

Valentina Mihailovna smiled.

" Do be careful, my dear. You've been unfortunate once already with young men, mind you don't make a second mistake."

" Are you referring to Nejdanov? I don't think I've been altogether mistaken with regard to him. He has been a good tutor to Kolia. And then you know *non bis in idem !* Excuse my being pedantic. . . . It means, things don't repeat themselves! "

" Don't you think so? Well, *I* think that everything in the world repeats itself . . . especially what's in the nature of things . . . and particularly among young people."

" *Que voulez-vous dire ?* " asked Sipiagin, flinging the pamphlet on the table with a graceful gesture of the hand.

" *Ouvrez les yeux, et vous verrez !* " Madame Sipiagina replied. They always spoke to one another in French.

" H'm! " Sipiagin grunted. " Are you referring to that student? "

" Yes, I'm referring to him."

" H'm! Has he got anything on here, eh? " (He passed his hand over his forehead.)

" Open your eyes! "

" Is it Mariana, eh? " (The second " eh " was pronounced more through the nose than the first one.)

" Open your eyes, I tell you! "

Sipiagin frowned.

"We must talk about this later on. I should just like to say now that this Solomin may feel rather uncomfortable. . . . You see, he is not used to society. We must be nice to him so as to make him feel at his ease. Of course, I don't mean this for you, you're such a dear, that I think you could fascinate any one if you chose. *J'en sais quelque chose, madame!* I mean this for the others, if only for——"

He pointed to a fashionable grey hat lying on a shelf. It belonged to Mr. Kollomietzev, who had been in Arjanov since the morning.

"*Il est très cassant* you know. He has far too great a contempt for the people for my liking. And he has been so frightfully quarrelsome and irritable of late. Is his little affair *there* not getting on well?"

Sipiagin nodded his head in some indefinite direction, but his wife understood him.

"Open your eyes, I tell you again!"

Sipiagin stood up.

"Eh?" (This "eh" was pronounced in a quite different tone, much lower.) "Is that how the land lies? They had better take care I don't open them too wide!"

"That is your own affair, my dear. But as for that new young man of yours, you may be quite easy about him. I will see that everything is all right. Every precaution will be taken."

It turned out that no precautions were necessary, however. Solomin was not in the least alarmed or embarrassed.

As soon as he was announced Sipiagin jumped up, exclaiming in a voice loud enough to be heard in the hall, "Show him in, of course show him in!" he then went up to the drawing-room door and stood waiting. No sooner had Solomin crossed the threshold, almost knocking against Sipiagin, when the latter extended both his hands, saying with an amiable smile and a friendly shake of the head,

177

" How very nice of you to come. . . . I can hardly thank you enough." Then he led him up to Valentina Mihailovna.

" Allow me to introduce you to my wife," he said, gently pressing his hand against Solomin's back, pushing him towards her as it were. " My dear, here is our best local engineer and manufacturer, Vassily . . . Fedosaitch Solomin."

Madame Sipiagina stood up, raised her wonderful eye-lashes, smiled sweetly as to an acquaintance, extended her hand with the palm upwards, her elbow pressed against her waist, her head bent a little to the right, in the attitude of a suppliant. Solomin let the husband and wife go through their little comedy, shook hands with them both, and sat down at the first invitation to do so. Sipiagin began to fuss about him, asking if he would like anything, but Solomin assured him that he wanted nothing and was not in the least bit tired from the journey.

" Then may we go to the factory? " Sipiagin asked, a little shame-faced, not daring to believe in so much con-descension on the part of his guest.

" As soon as you like, I'm quite ready," Solomin replied.

" How awfully good of you! Shall we drive or would you like to walk? "

" Is it a long way? "

" About half a mile."

" It's hardly worth while bringing out the carriage."

" Very well. Ivan! my hat and stick! Make haste! And you'll see about some dinner, little one, won't you? My hat, quick! "

Sipiagin was far more excited than his visitor, and calling out once more, " Why don't they give me my hat," he, the stately dignitary, rushed out like a frolicsome schoolboy. Whilst her husband was talking to Solomin, Valentina Mihailovna looked at him stealthily, trying to make out this new " young man." He was sitting in an arm-chair, quite at his ease, his bare hands laid on his knee (he had not put on the gloves after all), calmly, although not without a certain

178

amount of curiosity, looking round at the furniture and pictures. "I don't understand," she thought, "he's a plebeian—quite a plebeian—and yet behaves so naturally!" Solomin did indeed carry himself naturally, not with any view to effect, as much as to say "Look what a splendid fellow I am!" but as a man whose thoughts and feelings are simple, direct, and strong at the same time. Madame Sipiagina wanted to say something to him, but was surprised to find that she did not quite know how to begin.

"Heavens!" she thought. "This mechanic is making me quite nervous!"

"My husband must be very grateful to you," she remarked at last. "It was so good of you to sacrifice a few hours of your valuable time——"

"My time is not so very valuable, madame," he observed. "Besides, I've not come here for long."

"*Voilà où l'ours a montré sa patte*," she thought in French, but at this moment her husband appeared in the doorway, his hat on his head and a walking stick in his hand.

"Are you ready, Vassily Fedosaitch?" he asked in a free and easy tone, half turned towards him.

Solomin rose, bowed to Valentina Mihailovna, and walked out behind Sipiagin.

"This way, this way, Vassily Fedosaitch!" Sipiagin called out, just as if they were groping their way through a tangled forest and Solomin needed a guide. "This way! Do be careful, there are some steps here, Vassily Fedosaitch!"

"If you want to call me by my father's Christian name," Solomin said slowly, "then it isn't Fedosaitch, but Fedotitch."

Sipiagin was taken aback and looked at him over his shoulder.

"I'm so sorry, Vassily Fedotitch."

"Please don't mention it."

As soon as they got outside they ran against Kollomietzev. "Where are you off to?" the latter asked, looking

179

askance at Solomin. "Are you going to the factory? *C'est là l'individu en question ?* "

Sipiagin opened his eyes wide and shook his head slightly by way of warning.

" Yes, we're going to the factory. I want to show all my sins and transgressions to this gentleman who is an engineer. Allow me to introduce you. Mr. Kollomietzev, a neighbouring landowner, Mr. Solomin.

Kollomietzev nodded his head twice in an off-hand manner without looking at Solomin, but the latter looked at him and there was a sinister gleam in his half-closed eyes.

" May I come with you? " Kollomietzev asked. " You know I'm always ready to learn."

" Certainly, if you like."

They went out of the court-yard into the road and had scarcely taken twenty steps when they ran across a priest in a woven cassock, who was wending his way homeward. Kollomietzev left his two companions and, going up to him with long, firm strides, asked for his blessing and gave him a sounding smack on his moist, red hand, much to the discomfiture of the priest, who did not in the least expect this sort of outburst. He then turned to Solomin and gave him a defiant look. He had evidently heard something about him and wanted to show off and get some fun out of this learned scoundrel.

" *C'est une manifestation, mon cher ?* " Sipiagin muttered through his teeth.

Kollomietzev giggled.

" *Oui, mon cher, une manifestation nécessaire par temps qui court !* "

They got to the factory and were met by a Little Russian with an enormous beard and false teeth, who had taken the place of the former manager, a German, whom Sipiagin had dismissed. This man was there in a temporary capacity and understood absolutely nothing; he merely kept on saying " Just so ... yes ... that's it," and sighing all the time. They began inspecting the place. Several of the workmen knew Solomin by sight and bowed to him. He even called out to one of them, " Hallo, Gregory! You here? " Solomin was soon convinced that the place was going badly. Money was simply thrown away for no reason whatever. The machines turned out to be of a very poor kind; many of them were quite superfluous and a great many necessary ones were lacking. Sipiagin kept looking into Solomin's face, trying to guess his opinion, asked a few timid questions, wanted to know if he was at any rate satisfied with the order of the place.

" Oh, the order is all right," Solomin replied, " but I doubt if you can get anything out of it."

Not only Sipiagin, but even Kollomietzev felt, that in the factory Solomin was quite at home, was familiar with every little detail, was master there in fact. He laid his hand on a machine as a rider on his horse's neck; he poked a wheel with his finger and it either stood still or began whirling round; he took some paper pulp out of a vat and it instantly revealed all its defects.

Solomin said very little, took no notice of the Little Russian at all, and went out without saying anything. Sipiagin and Kollomietzev followed him.

Sipiagin was so upset that he did not let any one accompany him. He stamped and ground his teeth with rage.

" I can see by your face," he said turning to Solomin, " that you are not pleased with the place. Of course, I know that it's not in a very excellent condition and doesn't pay as yet. But please . . . give me your candid opinion as to what you consider to be the principal failings and as to what one could do to improve matters."

" Paper-manufacturing is not in my line," Solomin began, " but I can tell you one thing. I doubt if the aristocracy is cut out for industrial enterprises."

" Do you consider it degrading for the aristocracy? " Kollomeitzev asked.

Solomin smiled his habitual broad smile.

" Oh dear no! What is there degrading about it? And even if there were, I don't think the aristocracy would be over-particular."

" What do you mean? "

" I only meant," Solomin continued, calmly, " that the gentry are not used to that kind of business. A knowledge of commerce is needed for that; everything has to be put on a different footing, you want technical training for it. The gentry don't understand this. We see them starting woollen, cotton, and other factories all over the place, but they nearly always fall into the hands of the merchants in the end. It's a pity, because the merchants are even worse sweaters. But it can't be helped, I suppose."

" To listen to you one would think that all questions of finance were above our nobility! " Kollomietzev exclaimed.

" Oh no! On the other hand the nobility are masters at it. For getting concessions for railways, founding banks, exempting themselves from some tax, or anything like that, there is no one to beat them! They make huge fortunes. I hinted at that just now, but it seemed to offend you. I had regular industrial enterprises in my mind when I spoke; I say *regular*, because founding private public houses, petty little grocers' shops, or lending the peasants corn or money at a hundred or a hundred and fifty per cent., as many of our landed gentry are now doing, I cannot consider as genuine financial enterprises."

Kollomietzev did not say anything. He belonged to that new species of money-lending landlord whom Markelov had mentioned in his last talk with Nejdanov, and was the more inhuman in his demands that he had no personal dealings with the peasants themselves. He never allowed them into his perfumed European study, and conducted all his business with them through his manager. He was boiling with rage whilst listening to Solomin's slow, impartial speech, but he held his peace; only the working of the muscles of his face betrayed what was passing within him.

"But allow me, Vassily Fedotitch," Sipiagin began; "what you have just said may have been quite true in former days, when the nobility had quite different privileges and were altogether in a different position; but now, after all the beneficial reforms in our present industrial age, why should not the nobility turn their attention and bring their abilities into enterprises of this nature? Why shouldn't they be able to understand what is understood by a simple illiterate merchant? They are not suffering from lack of education and one might even claim, without any exaggeration, that they are, in a certain sense, the representatives of enlightenment and progress."

Boris Andraevitch spoke very well; his eloquence would have made a great stir in St. Petersburg, in his department, or may be in higher quarters, but it produced no effect whatever on Solomin.

"The nobility cannot manage these things," Solomin repeated.

"But why, I should like to know? Why?" Kollomietzev almost shouted.

"Because there is too much of the bureaucrat about them."

"Bureaucrat?" Kollomietzev laughed maliciously. "I don't think you quite realise what you're saying, Mr. Solomin."

Solomin continued smiling.

"What makes you think so, Mr. Kolomentzev?" (Kollomietzev shuddered at hearing his name thus mutilated.) "I assure you that I always realise what I am saying."

"Then please explain what you meant just now!"

"With pleasure. I think that every bureaucrat is an outsider and was always such. The nobility have now become 'outsiders.'"

Kollomietzev laughed louder than ever.

183

"But, my dear sir, I really don't understand what you mean!"

"So much the worse for you. Perhaps you will if you try hard enough."

"Sir!"

"Gentlemen, gentlemen," Sipiagin interposed hastily, trying to catch some one's eye, "please, please . . . *Kallo-meitzeff, je vous prie de vous calmer.* I suppose dinner will soon be ready. Come along, gentlemen!"

"Valentina Mihailovna!" Kollomietzev cried out five minutes later, rushing into her boudoir. "I really don't know what your husband is doing! He has brought us one nihilist and now he's bringing us another! Only this one is much worse!"

"But why?"

"He is advocating the most awful things, and what do you think? He has been talking to your husband for a whole hour, and not once, *not once*, did he address him as Your Excellency! *Le vagabond!*"

XXIV

JUST before dinner Sipiagin called his wife into the library.
He wanted to have a talk with her alone. He seemed
worried. He told her that the factory was really in a bad
way, that Solomin struck him as a capable man, although
a little stiff, and thought it was necessary to continue being
aux petits soins with him.

"How I should like to get hold of him!" he repeated
once or twice. Sipiagin was very much annoyed at Kollomietzev's being there. "Devil take the man! He sees
nihilists everywhere and is always wanting to suppress
them! Let him do it at his own house! He simply can't
hold his tongue!"

Valentina Mihailovna said that she would be delighted to
be *aux petits soins* with the new visitor, but it seemed to her
that he had no need of these *petits soins* and took no notice
of them; not rudely in any way, but he was quite indifferent;
very remarkable in a man *du commun*.

"Never mind. . . . Be nice to him just the same!"
Sipiagin begged of her.

Valentina Mihailovna promised to do what he wanted and
fulfilled her promise conscientiously. She began by having
a *tête-à-tête* with Kollomietzev. What she said to him
remains a secret, but he came to the table with the air of
a man who had made up his mind to be discreet and submissive at all costs. This "resignation" gave his whole
bearing a slight touch of melancholy; and what dignity . . .
oh, what dignity there was in every one of his movements!
Valentina Mihailovna introduced Solomin to everybody (he
looked more attentively at Mariana than at any of the
others), and made him sit beside her on her right at table.

185

Kollomietzev sat on her left, and as he unfolded his serviette screwed up his face and smiled, as much as to say, " Well, now let us begin our little comedy! " Sipiagin sat on the opposite side and watched him with some anxiety. By a new arrangement of Madame Sipiagina, Nejdanov was not put next to Mariana as usual, but between Anna Zaharovna and Sipiagin. Mariana found her card (as the dinner was a stately one) on her serviette between Kollomietzev and Kolia. The dinner was excellently served; there was even a " menu "—a painted card lay before each person. Directly soup was finished, Sipiagin again brought the conversation round to his factory, and from there went on to Russian manufacture in general. Solomin, as usual, replied very briefly. As soon as he began speaking Mariana fixed her eyes upon him. Kollomietzev, who was sitting beside her, turned to her with various compliments (he had been asked not to start a dispute), but she did not listen to him; and indeed he pronounced all his pleasantries in a half-hearted manner, merely to satisfy his own conscience. He realised that there was something between himself and this young girl that could not be crossed.

As for Nejdanov, something even worse had come to pass between him and the master of the house. For Sipiagin, Nejdanov had become simply a piece of furniture, or an empty space that he quite ignored. These new relations had taken place so quickly and unmistakably that when Nejdanov pronounced a few words in answer to a remark of Anna Zaharovna's, Sipiagin looked round in amazement, as if wondering where the sound came from.

Sipiagin evidently possessed some of the characteristics for which certain of the great Russian bureaucrats are celebrated for.

After the fish, Valentina Mihailovna, who had been lavishing all her charms on Solomin, said to her husband in English that she noticed their visitor did not drink wine and might perhaps like some beer. Sipiagin called aloud for ale, whilst Solomin calmly turned towards Valentina Mihailovna, saying, " You may not be aware, madame, that I spent over two years in England and can understand and speak English. I only mentioned it in case you should wish to say anything private before me." Valentina Mihailovna laughed and assured him that this precaution was altogether unnecessary, since he would hear nothing but good of himself; inwardly she thought Solomin's action rather strange, but delicate in its own way.

At this point Kollomietzev could no longer contain himself.

" And so you've been in England," he began, " and no doubt studied the manners and customs there. Do you think them worth imitating? "

" Some yes, others no."

" Brief but not clear," Kollomietzev remarked, trying not to notice the signs Sipiagin was making to him. " You were speaking of the nobility this morning. . . . No doubt you've had the opportunity of studying the English landed gentry, as they call them there."

" No, I had no such opportunity. I moved in quite a different sphere. But I formed my own ideas about these gentlemen."

" Well, do you think that such a landed gentry is impossible among us? Or that we ought not to want it in any case? "

" In the first place, I certainly do think it impossible, and in the second, it's hardly worth while wanting such a thing."

" But why, my dear sir? " Kollomietzev asked; the polite tone was intended to soothe Sipiagin, who sat very uneasily on his chair.

" Because in twenty or thirty years your landed gentry won't be here in any case."

" What makes you think so? "

" Because by that time the land will fall into the hands of people in no way distinguished by their origin."

" Do you mean the merchants? "

" For the most part probably the merchants."

" But how will it happen? "

" They'll buy it, of course."

" From the gentry? "

" Yes; from the gentry."

Kollomietzev smiled condescendingly. " If you recollect you said the very same thing about factories that you're now saying about the land."

" And it's quite true."

" You will no doubt be very pleased about it! "

" Not at all. I've already told you that the people won't be any the better off for the change."

Kollomietzev raised his hand slightly. " What solicitude on the part of the people, imagine! "

" Vassily Fedotitch! " Sipiagin called out as loudly as he could, " they have brought you some beer! *Voyons, siméon !* " he added in an undertone.

But Kollomietzev would not be suppressed.

" I see you haven't a very high opinion of the merchant class," he began again, turning to Solomin, " but they've sprung from the people."

" So they have."

" I thought that you considered everything about the people, or relating to the people, as above criticism! "

" Not at all! You are quite mistaken. The masses can be condemned for a great many things, though they are not always to blame. Our merchant is an exploiter and uses his capital for that purpose. He thinks that people are always trying to get the better of him, so he tries to get the better of them. But the people——"

" Well, what about the people? " Kollomietzev asked in falsetto.

" The people are asleep."

" And would you like to wake them? "

" That would not be a bad thing to do."

" Aha! aha! So that's what——"

" Gentlemen, gentlemen!" Sipiagin exclaimed impera-
tively. He felt that the moment had come to put an end
to the discussion, and he did put an end to it. With a slight
gesture of his right hand, while the elbow remained propped
on the table, he delivered a long and detailed speech. He
praised the conservatives on the one hand and approved
of the liberals on the other, giving the preference to the
latter as he counted himself of their numbers. He spoke
highly of the people, but drew attention to some of their
weaknesses; expressed his full confidence in the g vernment,
but asked himself whether *all* its officials were faithfully
fulfilling its benevolent designs. He acknowledged the
importance of literature, but declared that without the
utmost caution it was dangerous. He turned to the West
with hope, then became doubtful; he turned to the East,
first sighed, then became enthusiastic. Finally he proposed
a toast in honour of the trinity: Religion, Agriculture, and
Industry!

" Under the wing of authority!" Kollomietzev added
sternly.

" Under the wing of wise and benevolent authority,"
Sipiagin corrected him.

The toast was drunk in silence. The empty space on
Sipiagin's left, in the form of Nejdanov, did certainly make
several sounds of disapproval; but arousing not the least
attention became quiet again, and the dinner, without any
further controversy, reached a happy conclusion.

Valentina Mihailovna, with a most charming smile, handed
Solomin a cup of coffee; he drank it and was already looking
round for his hat when Sipiagin took him gently by the
arm and led him into his study. There he first gave him
an excellent cigar and then made him a proposal to enter
his factory on the most advantageous terms. " You will
be absolute master there, Vassily Fedotitch, I assure you!"
Solomin accepted the cigar and declined the offer about the

189

factory. He stuck to his refusal, however much Sipiagin insisted.

" Please don't say 'no' at once, my dear Vassily Fedotitch! Say, at least, that you'll think it over until to-morrow! "

" It would make no difference. I wouldn't accept your proposal."

" Do think it over till to-morrow, Vassily Fedotitch! It won't cost you anything."

Solomin agreed, came out of the study, and began looking for his hat again. But Nejdanov, who until that moment had had no opportunity of exchanging a word with him, came up to him and whispered hurriedly:

" For heaven's sake don't go yet, or else we won't be able to have a talk! "

Solomin left his hat alone, the more readily as Sipiagin, who had observed his irresoluteness, exclaimed:

" Won't you stay the night with us? "

" As you wish."

The grateful glance Mariana fixed on him as she stood at the drawing-room window set him thinking.

XXV

UNTIL his visit Mariana had pictured Solomin to herself as quite different. At first sight he had struck her as undefined, characterless. She had seen many such fair, lean, sinewy men in her day, but the more she watched him, the longer she listened to him, the stronger grew her feeling of confidence in him—for it was confidence he inspired her with. This calm, not exactly clumsy, but heavy man, was not only incapable of lying or bragging, but one could rely on him as on a stone wall. He would not betray one; more than that, he would understand and help one. It seemed to Mariana that he aroused such a feeling, not only in herself alone, but in every one present. The things he spoke about had no particular interest for her. She attached very little significance to all this talk about factories and merchants, but the way in which he spoke, the manner in which he looked round and smiled, pleased her immensely.

A straightforward man . . . at any rate! this was what appealed to her. It is a well-known fact, though not very easy to understand, that Russians are the greatest liars on the face of the earth, yet there is nothing they respect more than truth, nothing they sympathise with more. And then Solomin, in Mariana's eyes, was surrounded by a particular halo, as a man who had been recommended by Vassily Nikolaevitch himself. During dinner she had exchanged glances with Nejdanov several times on his account, and in the end found herself involuntarily comparing the two, not to Nejdanov's advantage. Nejdanov's face was, it is true, handsomer and pleasanter to look at than Solomin's, but the very face expressed a medley of troubled sensations: embarrassment, annoyance, impatience, and even dejection.

191

He seemed to be sitting on hot coals; tried to speak, but did not, and laughed nervously. Solomin, on the other hand, seemed a little bored, but looked quite at home and utterly independent of what was going on around him. "We must certainly ask advice of this man," Mariana thought, "he is sure to tell us something useful." It was she who had sent Nejdanov to him after dinner.

The evening went very slowly; fortunately dinner was not over until late and not very long remained before bed-time. Kollomietzev was sulky and said nothing.

"What is the matter with you?" Madame Sipiagina asked half-jestingly. "Have you lost anything?"

"Yes, I have," Kollomietzev replied. "There is a story about a certain officer in the life-guards who was very much grieved that his soldiers had lost a sock of his. 'Find me my sock!' he would say to them, and I say, find me the word 'sir!' The word 'sir' is lost, and with it every sense of respect towards rank!"

Madame Sipiagina informed Kollomietzev that she would not help him in the search.

Emboldened by the success of his speech at dinner, Sipiagin delivered two others, in which he let fly various statesman-like reflections about indispensable measures and various words—*des mots*—not so much witty as weighty, which he had especially prepared for St. Petersburg. He even repeated one of these words, saying beforehand, " If you will allow the expression." Above all, he declared that a certain minister had an " idle, unconcentrated mind," and was given " to dreaming." And not forgetting that one of his listeners was a man of the people, he lost no opportunity in trying to show that he too was a Russian through and through, and steeped in the very root of the national life! For instance, to Kollomietzev's remark that the rain might interfere with the haymaking, he replied, " If the hay is black, then the buckwheat will be white;" then he made use of various proverbs like: " A store without a master is an orphan,"

192

" Look before you leap," " When there's bread then there's economy," "If the birch leaves are as big as farthings by St. Yegor's day, the dough can he put into tubs by the feast of Our Lady of Kazan." He sometimes went wrong, however, and would get his proverbs very much mixed; but the society in which these little slips occurred did not even suspect that *notre bon Russe* had made a mistake, and, thanks to Prince Kovrishkin, it had got used to such little blunders. Sipiagin pronounced all these proverbs in a peculiarly powerful, gruff voice—*d'une voix rustique.* Similar sayings let loose at the proper time and place in St. Petersburg would cause influential high-society ladies to exclaim, " *Comme il connait bien les moeurs de notre peuple !* " and great statesmen would add, " *Les moeurs et les besoins !* "

Valentina Mihailovna fussed about Solomin as much as she could, but her failure to arouse him disheartened her. On passing Kollomietzev she said involuntarily, in an undertone: " *Mon Dieu, que je me sens fatiguée !* " to which he replied with an ironical bow: " *Tu l'as voulu, George Daudin !* "

At last, after the usual outburst of politeness and amiability, which appears on the faces of a bored assembly on the point of breaking up, after sudden handshakings and friendly smiles, the weary guests and weary hosts separated.

Solomin, who had been given almost the best bedroom on the second floor, with English toilette accessories and a bathroom attached, went in to Nejdanov.

The latter began by thanking him heartily for having agreed to stay.

" I know it's a sacrifice on your part——"

" Not at all," Solomin said hastily. " There was no sort of sacrifice required. Besides I couldn't refuse *you.*"

" Why not? "

" Because I've taken a great liking to you."

Nejdanov was surprised and glad at the same time, while Solomin pressed his hand. Then he seated himself astride on a chair, lighted a cigar, and leaning both his elbows against the back, began:

" Now tell me what's the matter."

Nejdanov also seated himself astride on a chair in front of Solomin, but did not light a cigar.

" So you want to know what's the matter. . . . The fact is, I want to run away from here."

" Am I to understand that you want to leave this house? As far as I can see there is nothing to prevent you."

" Not leave it, but run away from it."

" Why? Do they want to detain you? Perhaps you've taken some money in advance . . . If so, you've only to say the word and I should be delighted——"

" I'm afraid you don't understand me, my dear Solomin. " I said run away and not leave, because I'm not going away alone."

Solomin raised his head.

" With whom then? "

" With the girl you've seen here to-day."

" With her! She has a very nice face. Are you in love with one another? Or have you simply decided to go away together because you don't like being here? "

" We love each other."

" Ah! " Solomin was silent for a while. " Is she related to the people here? "

" Yes. But she fully shares our convictions and is prepared for anything."

Solomin smiled.

" And you, Nejdanov, are you prepared? "

Nejdanov frowned slightly.

" Why ask? You will see when the time comes."

" I do not doubt you, Nejdanov. I only asked because it seemed to me that besides yourself nobody else was prepared."

" And Markelov? "

194

" Why, of course, Markelov! But then, he was born prepared."

At this moment some one knocked at the door gently, but hastily, and opened it without waiting for an answer. It was Mariana. She immediately came up to Solomin.

" I feel sure," she began, " that you are not surprised at seeing me here at this time of night. He " (Mariana pointed to Nejdanov) " has no doubt told you everything. Give me your hand, please, and believe me an honest girl is standing before you."

" I am convinced of that," Solomin said seriously.

He had risen from his chair as soon as Mariana had appeared. " I had already noticed you at table and was struck by the frank expression of your eyes. Nejdanov told me about your intentions. But may I ask why you want to run away."

" What a question! The cause with which I am fully in sympathy . . . don't be surprised. Nejdanov has kept nothing from me. . . . The great work is about to begin . . . and am I to remain in this house, where everything is deceit and falsehood? People I love will be exposed to danger, and I——"

Solomin stopped her by a wave of the hand.

" Calm yourself. Sit down, please, and you sit down too, Nejdanov. Let us all sit down. Listen to me! If you have no other reason than the one you have mentioned, then there's no need for you to run away as yet. The work will not begin so soon as you seem to anticipate. A little more prudent consideration is needed in this matter. It's no good plunging in too soon, believe me."

Mariana sat down and wrapped herself up in a large plaid, which she had thrown over her shoulders.

" But I can't stay here any longer! I am being insulted by everybody. Only to-day that idiot Anna Zaharovna said before Kolia, alluding to my father, that a bad tree does not bring forth good fruit! Kolia was even surprised, and asked what it meant. Not to speak of Valentina Mihailovna!"

Solomin stopped her again, this time with a smile.

Mariana felt that he was laughing at her a little, but this smile could not have offended any one.

" But, my dear lady, I don't know who Anna Zaharovna is, nor what tree you are talking about. A foolish woman says some foolish things to you and you can't endure it! How will you live in that case? The whole world is composed of fools. Your reason is not good enough. Have you any other? "

" I am convinced," Nejdanov interposed in a hollow voice, " that Mr. Sipiagin will turn me out of the house to-morrow of his own accord. Some one must have told him. He treats me . . . in the most contemptuous manner."

Solomin turned to Nejdanov.

" If that's the case, then why run away? "

Nejdanov did not know what to say.

" But I've already told you——," he began.

" He said that," Mariana put in, " because I am going with him."

Solomin looked at her and shook his head good-naturedly.

" In that case, my dear lady, I say again, that if you want to leave here because you think the revolution is about to break out——"

" That was precisely why we asked you to come," Mariana interrupted him; " we wanted to find out exactly how matters stood."

" If that's your reason for going," Solomin continued, " I repeat once more, you can stay at home for some time to come yet, but if you want to run away because you love each other and can't be united otherwise, then——"

" Well? What then? "

" Then I must first congratulate you and, if need be, give you all the help in my power. I may say, my dear lady, that I took a liking to you both at first sight and love you as brother and sister."

Mariana and Nejdanov both went up to him on the right and left and each clasped a hand.

"Only tell us what to do," Mariana implored. "Supposing the revolution is still far off, there must be preparatory work to be done, a thing impossible in this house, in the midst of these surroundings. We should so gladly go together. . . . Show us what we can do; tell us where to go. . . . Send us anywhere you like! You will send us, won't you? "

" Where to? "

" To the people. . . . Where can one go if not among the people? "

" Into the forest," Nejdanov thought, calling to mind Paklin's words.

Solomin looked intently at Mariana.

" Do you want to know the people? "

" Yes; that is, we not only want to get to know them, but we want to work . . . to toil for them."

" Very well. I promise you that you shall get to know them. I will give you the opportunity of doing as you wish. And you, Nejdanov, are you ready to go for her . . . and for them? "

" Of course I am," he said hastily. " Juggernaut," another word of Paklin's, flashed across his mind. " Here it comes thundering along, the huge chariot. . . . I can hear the crash and rumble of its wheels."

" Very well," Solomin repeated pensively. " But when do you want to go away? "

" To-morrow, if possible," Mariana observed.

" Very good. But where? "

" Sh, sh——" Nejdanov whispered. " Some one is walking along the corridor."

They were all silent for a time.

" But where do you want to go to? " Solomin asked again, lowering his voice.

197

" We don't know," Mariana replied.

Solomin glanced at Nejdanov, but the latter merely shook his head.

Solomin stretched out his hand and carefully snuffed the candle.

" I tell you what, my children," he said at last, " come to me at the factory. It's not beautiful there, but safe, at any rate. I will hide you. I have a little spare room there. Nobody will find you. If only you get there, we won't give you up. You might think that there are far too many people about, but that's one of its good points. Where there is a crowd it's easy to hide. Will you come? Will you? "

" How can we thank you enough! " Nejdanov exclaimed, whilst Mariana, who was at first a little taken aback by the idea of the factory, added quickly:

" Of course, of course! How good of you! But you won't leave us there long, will you? You will send us on, won't you? "

" That will depend entirely on yourselves. . . . If you should want to get married that could also be arranged at the factory. I have a neighbour there close by—a cousin of mine, a priest, and very friendly. He would marry you with the greatest of pleasure."

Mariana smiled to herself, whilst Nejdanov again pressed Solomin's hand.

" But I say, won't your employer, the owner of the factory, be annoyed about it. Won't he make it unpleasant for you? " he asked after a pause.

Solomin looked askance at Nejdanov.

" Oh, don't bother about me! It's quite unnecessary. So long as things at the factory go on all right it's all the same to my employer. You need neither of you fear the least unpleasantness. And you need not be afraid of the workpeople either. Only let me know what time to expect you."

Nejdanov and Mariana exchanged glances.

"The day after to-morrow, early in the morning, or the day after that. We can't wait any longer. As likely as not they'll tell me to go to-morrow."

"Well then," Solomin said, rising from his chair. "I'll wait for you every morning. I won't leave the place for the rest of the week. Every precaution will be taken."

Mariana drew near to him (she was on her way to the door). "Good-bye, my dear kind Vassily Fedotitch . . . that is your name, isn't it?"

"That's right."

"Good-bye till we meet again. And thank you so much!"

"Good-bye, good night!"

"Good-bye, Nejdanov; till to-morrow," she added, and went out quickly.

The young men remained for some time motionless, and both were silent.

"Nejdanov . . ." Solomin began at last, and stopped. "Nejdanov . . ." he began a second time, "tell me about this girl . . . tell me everything you can. What has her life been until now? Who is she? Why is she here?"

Nejdanov told Solomin briefly what he knew about her.

"Nejdanov," he said at last, "you must take great care of her, because . . . if . . . anything . . . were to happen, you would be very much to blame. Good-bye."

He went out, while Nejdanov stood still for a time in the middle of the room, and muttering, "Oh dear! It's better not to think!" threw himself face downwards on the bed.

When Mariana returned to her room she found a note on the table containing the following:

"I am sorry for you. You are ruining yourself. Think what you are doing. Into what abysses are you throwing yourself with your eyes shut. For whom and for what? —V."

There was a peculiarly fine fresh scent in the room; evidently Valentina Mihailovna had only just left it. Mariana took a pen and wrote underneath: "You need not be sorry

199

for me. God knows which of us two is more in need of pity. I only know that I wouldn't like to be in your place for worlds.—M." She put the note on the table, not doubting that it would fall into Valentina Mihailovna's hand.

On the following morning, Solomin, after seeing Nejdanov and definitely declining to undertake the management of Sipiagin's factory, set out for home. He mused all the way home, a thing that rarely occurred with him; the motion of the carriage usually had a drowsy effect on him. He thought of Mariana and of Nejdanov; it seemed to him that if he had been in love —he, Solomin—he would have had quite a different air, would have looked and spoken differently. " But," he thought, " such a thing has never happened to me, so I can't tell what sort of an air I would have." He recalled an Irish girl whom he had once seen in a shop behind a counter; recalled her wonderful black hair, blue eyes, and thick lashes, and how she had looked at him with a sad, wistful expression, and how he had paced up and down the street before her window for a long time, how excited he had been, and had kept asking himself if he should try and get to know her. He was in London at the time, where he had been sent by his employer with a sum of money to make various purchases. He very nearly decided to remain in London and send back the money, so strong was the impression produced on him by the beautiful Polly. (He had got to know her name, one of the other girls had called her by it.) He had mastered himself, however, and went back to his employer. Polly was more beautiful than Mariana, but Mariana had the same sad, wistful expression in her eyes . . . and Mariana was a Russian.

" But what am I doing? " Solomin exclaimed in an undertone, " bothering about other men's brides! " and he shook back the collar of his coat, as if he wanted to shake off all superfluous thoughts. Just then he drove up to the factory and caught sight of the faithful Pavel in the doorway of his little dwelling.

XXVI

Solomin's refusal greatly offended Sipiagin; so much so, that he suddenly found that this home-bred Stevenson was not such a wonderful engineer after all, and that though he was not perhaps a complete poser, yet gave himself airs like the plebeian he was. "All these Russians when they imagine they know a thing become insufferable! *Au fond* Kollomietzev was right!" Under the influence of such hostile and irritable sensations, the statesman—*en herbe*—was even more unsympathetic and distant in his intercourse with Nejdanov. He told Kolia that he need not take lessons that day and that he must try to be more independent in future. He did not, however, dismiss the tutor himself as the latter had expected, but continued to ignore him. But Valentina Mihailovna did not ignore Mariana. A dreadful scene took place between them.

About two hours before dinner they suddenly found themselves alone in the drawing-room. They both felt that the inevitable moment for the battle had arrived and, after a moment's hesitation, instinctively drew near to one another. Valentina Mihailovna was slightly smiling, Mariana pressed her lips firmly together; both were pale. When walking across the room, Valentina Mihailovna looked uneasily to the right and left and tore off a geranium leaf. Mariana's eyes were fixed straight on the smiling face coming towards her. Madame Sipiagina was the first to stop, and drumming her finger-tips on the back of a chair began in a free and easy tone:

"Mariana Vikentievna, it seems that we have entered upon a correspondence with one another. . . . Living under the same roof as we do it strikes me as being rather strange. And you know I am not very fond of strange things."

201

"I did not begin the correspondence, Valentina Mihailovna."

"That is true. As it happens, I am to blame in that. Only I could not think of any other means of arousing in you a feeling . . . how shall I say? A feeling——"

"You can speak quite plainly, Valentina Mihailovna. You need not be afraid of offending me."

"A feeling . . . of propriety."

Valentina Mihailovna ceased; nothing but the drumming of her fingers could be heard in the room.

"In what way do you think I have failed to observe the rules of propriety?" Mariana asked.

Valentina Mihailovna shrugged her shoulders.

"*Ma chère, vous n'êtes plus un enfant*—I think you know what I mean. Do you suppose that your behaviour could have remained a secret to me, to Anna Zaharovna, to the whole household in fact? However, I must say you are not over-particular about secrecy. You simply acted in bravado. Only Boris Andraevitch does not know what you have done. . . . But he is occupied with far more serious and important matters. Apart from him, everybody else knows, everybody!"

Mariana's pallor increased.

"I must ask you to express yourself more clearly, Valentina Mihailovna. What is it you are displeased about?"

"*L'insolente!*" Madame Sipiagina thought, but contained herself.

"Do you want to know why I am displeased with you, Mariana? Then I must tell you that I disapprove of your prolonged interviews with a young man who is very much beneath you in birth, breeding, and social position. I am displeased . . . no! this word is far too mild—I am shocked at your late . . . your night visits to this young man! And where does it happen? Under my own roof! Perhaps you see nothing wrong in it and think that it has nothing to do with me, that I should be silent and thereby screen

202

your disgraceful conduct. As an honourable woman . . .
oui, mademoiselle, je l'ai été, je le suis, et je le serai toujours !
I can't help being horrified at such proceedings! "

Valentina Mihailovna threw herself into an arm-chair as
if overcome by her indignation. Mariana smiled for the first
time.

" I do not doubt your honour, past, present, and to come,"
she began; " and I mean this quite sincerely. Your indignation is needless. I have brought no shame on your house.
The young man whom you alluded to . . . yes, I have
certainly . . . fallen in love with him."

" You love Mr. Nejdanov? "

" Yes, I love him."

Valentina Mihailovna sat up straight in her chair.

"But, Mariana! he's only a student, of no birth, no family,
and he is younger than you are! " (These words were pronounced not without a certain spiteful pleasure.) "What
earthly good can come of it? What do you see in him?
He is only an empty-headed boy."

" That was not always your opinion of him, Valentina
Mihailovna."

" For heaven's sake leave me out of the question, my
dear! . . . *Pas tant d'esprit que ça, je vous prie.* The thing
concerns you and your future. Just consider for a moment.
What sort of a match is this for you? "

" I must confess, Valentina Mihailovna, that I did not
look at it in that light."

" What? What did you say? What am I to think?
Let us assume that you followed the dictates of your heart,
but then it must end in marriage some time or other."

" I don't know . . . I had not thought of that."

" You had not thought of that? You must be mad! "

Mariana turned away.

" Let us make an end of this conversation, Valentina
Mihailovna. It won't lead to anything. In any case we
won't understand each other."

203

Valentina Mihailovna started up.

" I can't, I won't put an end to this conversation! It's far too serious. . . . I am responsible for you before . . ." Valentina Mihailovna was going to say God, but hesitated and added, " before the whole world! I can't be silent when I hear such utter madness! And why can't I understand you, pray? What insufferable pride these young people have nowadays! On the contrary, I understand you only too well . . . I can see that you are infected with these new ideas, which will only be your ruin. It will be too late to turn back then."

" May be; but believe me, even if we perish, we will not so much as stretch out a finger that you might save us ! "

" Pride again! This awful pride! But listen, Mariana, listen to me," she added, suddenly changing her tone. She wanted to draw Mariana nearer to herself, but the latter stepped back a pace. " *Ecoutez-moi, je vous en conjure !* After all, I am not so old nor so stupid that it should be impossible for us to understand each other! *Je ne suis pas une encroûtée.* I was even considered a republican as a girl . . . no less than you. Listen, I won't pretend that I ever had any motherly feeling towards you . . . and it is not in your nature to complain of that. . . . But I always felt, and feel now, that I owed certain duties towards you, and I have always endeavoured to fulfil them. Perhaps the match I had in my mind for you, for which both Boris Andraevitch and I would have been ready to make any sacrifice . . . may not have been fully in accordance with your ideas . . . but in the bottom of my heart——"

Mariana looked at Valentina Mihailovna, at her wonderful eyes, her slightly painted lips, at her white hands, the parted fingers adorned with rings, which the elegant lady so energetically pressed against the bodice of her silk dress. . . . Suddenly she interrupted her.

" Did you say a match, Valentina Mihailovna? Do you

call that heartless, vulgar friend of yours, Mr. Kollomietzev, ' a match? ' "

Valentina Mihailovna took her fingers from her bodice.

"Yes, Mariana Vikentievna! I am speaking of that cultured, excellent young man, Mr. Kollomietzev, who would make a wife happy and whom only a mad-woman could refuse! Yes, only a mad-woman!"

"What can I do, *ma tante*? It seems that I am mad!"

" Have you anything serious against him? "

" Nothing whatever. I simply despise him."

Valentina Mihailovna shook her head impatiently and dropped into her chair again.

"Let us leave him. *Retournons à nos moutons.* And so you love Mr. Nejdanov? "

"Yes."

"And do you intend to continue your interviews with him? "

"Yes."

" But supposing I forbid it? "

" I won't listen to you."

Valentina Mihailovna sprang up from her chair.

"What! You won't listen to me! I see. . . . And that is said to me by a girl who has known nothing but kindness from me, whom I have brought up in my own house, that is said to me . . . said to me——"

" By the daughter of a disgraced father," Mariana put in, sternly. " Go on, don't be on ceremonies! "

" *Ce n'est pas moi qui vous le fait dire, mademoiselle!* In any case, *that* is nothing to be proud of! A girl who lives at my expense——"

"Don't throw that in my face, Valentina Mihailovna! It would cost you more to keep a French governess for Kolia. . . . It is I who give him French lessons! "

Valentina Mihailovna raised a hand holding a scented cambric pocket-handkerchief with a large white monogram

205

embroidered in one corner and tried to say something, but Mariana continued passionately:

" You would have been right, a thousand times right, if, instead of counting up all your petty benefits and sacrifices, you could have been in a position to say ' the girl I loved ' . . . but you are too honest to lie about that! " Mariana trembled feverishly. " You have always hated me. And even now you are glad in the bottom of your heart—that same heart you have just mentioned—glad that I am justifying your constant predictions, covering myself with shame and scandal—you are only annoyed because part of this shame is bound to fall on your virtuous, aristocratic house! "

" You are insulting me," Valentina Mihailovna whispered. " Be kind enough to leave the room! "

But Mariana could no longer contain herself. " Your household, you said, all your household, Anna Zaharovna and everybody knows of my behaviour! And every one is horrified and indignant. . . . But am I asking anything of you, of all these people? Do you think I care for their good opinion? Do you think that eating your bread has been sweet? I would prefer the greatest poverty to this luxury. There is a gulf between me and your house, an interminable gulf that cannot be crossed. You are an intelligent woman, don't you feel it too? And if you hate me, what do you think I feel towards you? We won't go into unnecessary details, it's too obvious."

" *Sortez, sortez, vous dis-je* . . ." Valentina Mihailovna repeated, stamping her pretty little foot.

Mariana took a few steps towards the door.

" I will rid you of my presence directly, only do you know what, Valentina Mihailovna? They say that in Racine's *Bajazet* even Rachel's *sortez !* was not effective, and you don't come anywhere near her! Then, what was it you said . . . *Je suis une honnête femme, je l'ai été et le serai toujours ?* But I am convinced that I am far more honest than you are! Good-bye! "

Mariana went out quickly and Valentina Mihailovna sprang up from her chair. She wanted to scream, to cry, but did not know what to scream about, and the tears would not come at her bidding.

So she fanned herself with her pocket-handkerchief, but the strong scent of it affected her nerves still more. She felt miserable, insulted. . . . She was conscious of a certain amount of truth in what she had just heard, but how could any one be so unjust to her? " Am I really so bad? " she thought, and looked at herself in a mirror hanging opposite between two windows. The looking-glass reflected a charming face, somewhat excited, the colour coming and going, but still a fascinating face, with wonderful soft, velvety eyes. . . . " I? I am bad? " she thought again. . . . " With such eyes? "

But at this moment her husband entered the room and she again covered her face with her pocket-handkerchief.

" What is the matter with you? " he asked anxiously. " What is the matter, Valia? " (He had invented this pet name, but only allowed himself to use it when they were quite alone, particularly in the country.)

At first she declared that there was nothing the matter, but ended by turning round in her chair in a very charming and touching manner and, flinging her arms round his shoulders (he stood bending over her) and hiding her face in the slit of his waistcoat, told him everything. Without any hypocrisy or any interested motive on her part, she tried to excuse Mariana as much as she could, putting all the blame on her extreme youth, her passionate temperament, and the defects of her early education. In the same way she also, without any hidden motive, blamed herself a great deal, saying, " With a daughter of mine this would never have happened! I would have looked after her quite differently! " Sipiagin listened to her indulgently, sympathetically, but with a severe expression on his face. He continued standing in a stooping position without moving his head so long as she held her arms round his shoulders; he called her an angel, kissed her on the forehead, declared that he now knew what course he must pursue as head of the house, and went out, carrying himself like an energetic humane man, who was conscious of having to perform an unpleasant but necessary duty.

At eight o'clock, after dinner, Nejdanov was sitting in his room writing to his friend Silin.

" MY DEAR VLADIMIR,—I write to you at a critical moment of my life. I have been dismissed from this house, I am going away from here. That in itself would be nothing —I am not going alone. The girl I wrote to you about is coming with me. We are drawn together by the similarity of our fate in life, by our loneliness, convictions, aspirations, and, above all, by our mutual love. Yes, we love each other. I am convinced that I could not experience the passion of love in any other form than that which presents itself to me now. But I should not be speaking the truth if I were to say that I had no mysterious fear, no misgivings at heart. . . . Everything in front of us is enveloped in darkness and we are plunging into that darkness. I need not tell you what we are going for and what we have chosen to do. Mariana and I are not in search of happiness or vain delight; we want to enter the fight together, side by side, supporting each other. Our aim is clear to us, but we do not know the roads that lead to it. Shall we find, if not help and sympathy, at any rate the opportunity to work? Mariana is a wonderfully honest girl. Should we be fated to perish, I will not blame myself for having enticed her away, because now no other life is possible for her. But, Vladimir, Vladimir! I feel so miserable. . . . I am torn by doubt, not in my feelings towards her, of course, but . . . I do not know! And it is too late to turn back. Stretch out your hands to us from afar, and wish us patience, the power of self-sacrifice, and love . . . most of all love. And ye, Russian people, unknown to us, but beloved by us with all the force of our beings, with our hearts' blood, receive us in your midst, be kind to us, and teach us what we may expect from you. Good-bye, Vladimir, good-bye!"

Having finished these few lines Nejdanov set out for the village.

The following night before daybreak he stood on the out-skirts of the birch grove, not far from Sipiagin's garden. A little further on behind the tangled branches of a nut-bush stood a peasant cart harnessed to a pair of unbridled horses. Inside, under the seat of plaited rope, a little grey old peasant was lying asleep on a bundle of hay, covered up to the ears with an old patched coat. Nejdanov kept looking eagerly at the road, at the clumps of laburnums at the bottom of the garden; the still grey night lay around, the little stars did their best to outshine one another and were lost in the vast expanse of sky. To the east the rounded edges of the spreading clouds were tinged with a faint flush of dawn. Suddenly Nejdanov trembled and became alert. Something squeaked near by, the opening of a gate was heard; a tiny feminine creature, wrapped up in a shawl with a bundle slung over her bare arm, walked slowly out of the deep shadow of the laburnums into the dusty road, and crossing over as if on tip-toe, turned towards the grove. Nejdanov rushed towards her.

" Mariana? " he whispered.

" It's I! " came a soft reply from under the shawl.

" This way, come with me," Nejdanov responded, seizing her awkwardly by the bare arm, holding the bundle.

She trembled as if with cold. He led her up to the cart and woke the peasant. The latter jumped up quickly, instantly took his seat on the box, put his arms into the coat sleeves, and seized the rope that served as reins. The horses moved; he encouraged them cautiously in a voice still hoarse from a heavy sleep. Nejdanov placed Mariana on the seat, first spreading out his cloak for her to sit on, wrapped her feet in a rug, as the hay was rather damp, and sitting down beside her, gave the order to start. The peasant pulled the reins, the horses came out of the grove, snorting and shaking themselves, and bumping and rattling its small wheels the cart rolled out on to the road. Nejdanov had his arm round Mariana's waist, whilst she, raising the shawl with her cold fingers and turning her smiling face towards him, exclaimed:

" How beautifully fresh the air is, Aliosha! "

" Yes," the peasant replied, " there'll be a heavy dew! "

There was already such a heavy dew that the axles of the cart wheels as they caught in the tall grass along the road-side shook off whole showers of tiny drops and the grass looked silver-grey.

Mariana again trembled from the cold.

" How cold it is! " she said gaily. " But freedom, Aliosha, freedom! "

XXVII

SOLOMIN rushed out to the factory gates as soon as he was informed that some sort of gentleman with a lady, who had arrived in a cart, were asking for him. Without a word of greeting to his visitors, merely nodding his head to them several times, he told the peasant to drive into the yard, and asking him to stop before his own little dwelling, helped Mariana out of the cart. Nejdanov jumped out after her. Solomin conducted them both through a long dark passage, up a narrow, crooked little staircase at the back of the house, up to the second floor. He opened a door and they all went into a tiny neat little room with two windows.

" I'm so glad you've come! " Solomin exclaimed, with his habitual smile, which now seemed even broader and brighter than usual.

" Here are your rooms. This one and another adjoining it. Not much to look at, but never mind, one can live here and there's no one to spy on you. Just under your window there is what my employer calls a flower garden, but which I should call a kitchen garden. It lies right up against the wall and there are hedges to right and left. A quiet little spot. Well, how are you, my dear lady? And how are you, Nejdanov? "

He shook hands with them both. They stood motionless, not taking off their things, and with silent, half-bewildered, half-joyful emotion gazed straight in front of them.

" Well? Why don't you take your things off? " Solomin asked. " Have you much luggage? "

Mariana held up her little bundle.

" I have only this."

" I have a portmanteau and a bag, which I left in the cart. I'll go and——"

"Don't bother, don't bother." Solomin opened the door. "Pavel!" he shouted down the dark staircase, "run and fetch the things from the cart!"

"All right!" answered the never-failing Pavel.

Solomin turned to Mariana, who had taken off her shawl and was unfastening her cloak.

"Did everything go off happily?" he asked.

"Quite . . . not a soul saw us. I left a letter for Madame Sipiagina. Vassily Fedotitch, I didn't bring any clothes with me, because you're going to send us . . ." (Mariana wanted to say to the people, but hesitated). "They wouldn't have been of any use in any case. I have money to buy what is necessary."

"We'll see to that later on. . . . Ah!" he exclaimed, pointing to Pavel who was at that moment coming in together with Nejdanov and the luggage from the cart, "I can recommend you my best friend here. You may rely on him absolutely, as you would on me. Have you told Tatiana about the samovar?" he added in an undertone.

"It will soon be ready," Pavel replied; "and cream and everything."

"Tatiana is Pavel's wife and just as reliable as he is," Solomin continued. "Until you get used to things, my dear lady, she will look after you."

Mariana flung her cloak on to a couch covered with leather, which was standing in a corner of the room.

"Will you please call me Mariana, Vassily Fedotitch; I don't want to be a lady, neither do I want servants. . . . I did not go away from there to be waited on. Don't look at my dress—I hadn't any other. I must change all that now."

Her dress of fine brown cloth was very simple, but made by a St. Petersburg dressmaker. It fitted beautifully round her waist and shoulders and had altogether a fashionable air.

"Well, not a servant if you like, but a help, in the American fashion. But you must have some tea. It's early yet, but you are both tired, no doubt. I have to be at the factory now on business, but will look in later on. If you want anything ask Pavel or Tatiana."

Mariana held out both her hands to him quickly.

"How can we thank you enough, Vassily Fedotitch?" She looked at him with emotion. Solomin stroked one of her hands gently. "I should say it's not worth thanking for, but that wouldn't be true. I had better say that your thanks give me the greatest of pleasure. So we are quits. Good morning. Come along, Pavel."

Mariana and Nejdanov were left alone.

She rushed up to him and looked at him with the same expression with which she had looked at Solomin, only with even greater delight, emotion, radiance: "Oh, my dear!" she exclaimed. "We are beginning a new life . . . at last! At last! You can't believe how this poor little room, where we are to spend a few days, seems sweet and charming compared to those hateful palaces! Are you glad?"

Nejdanov took her hands and pressed them against his breast.

"I am happy, Mariana, to begin this new life with you! You will be my guiding star, my support, my strength——"

"Dear, darling Aliosha! But stop—we must wash and tidy ourselves a little. I will go into my room . . . and you . . . stay here. I won't be a minute——"

Mariana went into the other room and shut the door. A minute later she opened it half-way and, putting her head through, said: "Isn't Solomin nice!" Then she shut the door again and the key turned in the lock.

Nejdanov went up to the window and looked out into the garden. . . . One old, very old, apple tree particularly attracted his attention. He shook himself, stretched, opened his portmanteau, but took nothing out of it; he became lost in thought. . . .

A quarter of an hour later Mariana returned with a beaming, freshly-washed face, brimming over with gaiety, and a few minutes later Tatiana, Pavel's wife, appeared with the samovar, tea things, rolls, and cream.

In striking contrast to her gipsy-like husband she was a typical Russian, buxom, with masses of flaxen hair, which she wore in a thick plait twisted round a horn comb. She had coarse, though pleasant features, good-natured grey eyes, and was dressed in a very neat though somewhat faded print dress. Her hands were clean and well-shaped, though large. She bowed composedly, greeted them in a firm, clear accent without any sing-song about it, and set to work arranging the tea things.

Mariana went up to her.

" Let me help you, Tatiana. Only give me a napkin."

" Don't bother, miss, we are used to it. Vassily Fedotitch told me to. If you want anything please let us know. We shall be delighted to do anything we can."

" Please don't call me miss, Tatiana. I am dressed like a lady, but I am . . . I am quite——"

Tatiana's penetrating glance disconcerted Mariana; she ceased.

" And what are you then? " Tatiana asked in her steady voice.

" If you really want to know . . . I am certainly a lady by birth. But I want to get rid of all that. I want to become like all simple women."

" Oh, I see! You want to become simplified, like so many do nowadays."

" What did you say, Tatiana? To become simplified? "

" Yes, that's a word that has sprung up among us. To become simplified means to be like the common people. Teaching the people is all very well in its way, but it must be a difficult task, very difficult! I hope you'll get on."

" To become simplified! " Mariana repeated. " Do you hear, Aliosha, you and I have now become simplified! "

" Is he your husband or your brother? " Tatiana asked,

carefully washing the cups with her large, skilful hands as she looked from one to the other with a kindly smile.

" No," Mariana replied; " he is neither my husband nor my brother."

Tatiana raised her head.

" Then you are just living together freely? That also happens very often now. At one time it was to be met with only among nonconformists, but nowadays other folks do it too. Where there is God's blessing you can live in peace without the priest's aid. We have some living like that at the factory. Not the worst of folk either."

" What nice words you use, Tatiana! ' Living together freely ' . . . I like that. I'll tell you what I want to ask of you, Tatiana. I want to make or buy a dress, something like yours, only a little plainer. Then I want shoes and stockings and a kerchief—everything like you have. I've got some money."

" That's quite easy, miss. . . . There, there, don't be cross. I won't call you miss if you don't like it. But what am I to call you? "

" Call me Mariana."

" And what is your father's Christian name? "

" Why do you want my father's name? Call me simply Mariana, as I call you Tatiana."

" I don't like to somehow. You had better tell me."

" As you like. My father's name was Vikent. And what was your father's? "

" He was called Osip."

" Then I shall call you Tatiana Osipovna."

" And I'll call you Mariana Vikentievna. That will be splendid."

" Won't you take a cup of tea with us, Tatiana Osipovna? "

" For once I will, Mariana Vikentievna, although Egoritch will scold me afterwards."

" Who is Egoritch? "

" Pavel, my husband."

" Sit down, Tatiana Osipovna."

" Thank you, Mariana Vikentievna."

Tatiana sat down and began sipping her tea and nibbling pieces of sugar. She kept turning the lump of sugar round in her fingers, screwing up her eye on the side on which she bit it. Mariana entered into conversation with her and she replied quite at her ease, asked questions in her turn, and volunteered various pieces of information. She simply worshipped Solomin and put her husband only second to him. She did not, however, care for the factory life.

" It's neither town nor country here. I wouldn't stop an hour if it were not for Vassily Fedotitch! "

Mariana listened to her attentively, whilst Nejdanov, sitting a little to one side, watched her and wondered at her interest. For Mariana it was all so new, but it seemed to him that he had seen crowds of women like Tatiana and spoken to them hundreds of times.

" Do you know, Tatiana Osipovna? " Mariana began at last; " you think that we want to teach the people, but we want to serve them."

" Serve them? Teach them; that's the best thing you can do for them. Look at me, for instance. When I married Egoritch I didn't so much as know how to read and write. Now I've learnt, thanks to Vassily Fedotitch. He didn't teach me himself, he paid an old man to do it. It was he who taught me. You see I'm still young, although I'm grown up."

Mariana was silent.

" I wanted to learn some sort of trade, Tatiana Osipovna," Mariana began; " we must talk about that later on. I'm not good at sewing, but if I could learn to cook, then I could go out as a cook."

Tatiana became thoughtful.

" Why a cook? Only rich people and merchants keep cooks; the poor do their own cooking. And to cook at a mess for workmen . . . why you couldn't do that! "

216

VIRGIN SOIL

" But I could live in a rich man's house and get to know
poor people. How else can I get to know them? I shall
not always have such an opportunity as I have with you."

Tatiana turned her empty cup up-side down on the
saucer.

" It's a difficult matter," she said at last with a sigh,
" and can't be settled so easily. I'll do what I can, but I'm
not very clever. We must talk it over with Egoritch. He's
clever if you like! Reads all sorts of books and has everything at his fingers' ends." At this point she glanced at
Mariana who was rolling up a cigarette.

" You'll excuse me, Mariana Vikentievna, but if you really
want to become simplified you must give that up." She
pointed to the cigarette. " If you want to be a cook, that
would never do. Every one would see at once that you are
a lady."

Mariana threw the cigarette out of the window.

" I won't smoke any more. . . . It's quite easy to give
that up. Women of the people don't smoke, so I suppose I
ought not to."

" That's quite true, Mariana Vikentievna. Our men
indulge in it, but not the women. And here's Vassily
Fedotitch coming to see you. Those are his steps. You ask
him. He'll arrange everything for you in the best possible
way."

Solomin's voice was heard at the door.

" Can I come in? "

" Come in, come in! " Mariana called out.

" It's an English habit of mine," Solomin observed as he
came in. " Well, and how are you getting on? Not home-
sick yet, eh? I see you're having tea with Tatiana. You
listen to her, she's a sensible person. My employer is coming
to-day. It's rather a nuisance. He's staying to dinner.
But it can't be helped. He's the master."

" What sort of a man is he? " Nejdanov asked, coming
out of his corner.

217

" Oh, he's not bad . . . knows what he's about. One of the new generation. He's very polite, wears cuffs, and has his eyes about him no less than the old sort. He would skin a flint with his own hands and say, ' Turn to this side a little, please . . . there is still a living spot here . . . I must clean it! ' He's nice enough to me, because I'm necessary to him. I just looked in to say that I may not get a chance of seeing you again to-day. Dinner will be brought to you here and please don't show yourselves in the yard. Do you think the Sipiagins will make a search for you, Mariana? Will they make a hunt? "

" I don't think so," Mariana replied.

" And I think they will," Nejdanov remarked.

" It doesn't matter either way," Solomin continued. " You must be a little careful at first, but in a short time you can do as you like."

" Yes; only there's one thing," Nejdanov observed, " Markelov must know where I am; he must be informed."

" But why? "

" I am afraid it must be done—for the cause. He must always know my whereabouts. I've given my word. But he's quite safe, you know! "

" Very well. We can send Pavel."

" And will my clothes be ready for me? "

" Your special costume you mean? Why, of course . . . the same masquerade. It's not expensive at any rate. Good-bye. You must be tired. Come, Tatiana."

Mariana and Nejdanov were left alone again.

XXVIII

FIRST they clasped each other's hands, then Mariana offered to help him tidy his room. She immediately began unpacking his portmanteau and bag, declining his offer of help on the ground that she must get used to work and wished to do it all herself. She hung his clothes on nails which she discovered in the table drawer and knocked into the wall with the back of a hairbrush for want of a hammer. Then she arranged his linen in a little old chest of drawers standing in between the two windows.

" What is this? " she asked suddenly. " Why, it's a revolver. Is it loaded? What do you want it for? "

" It is not loaded . . . but you had better give it to me. You want to know why I have it? How can one get on without a revolver in our calling? "

She laughed and went on with her work, shaking each thing out separately and beating it with her hand; she even stood two pairs of boots under the sofa; the few books, packet of papers, and tiny copy-book of verses she placed triumphantly upon a three-cornered table, calling it a writing and work table, whilst the other, a round one, she called a dining and tea table. Then she took up the copy-book of verses in both hands and, raising it on a level with her face, looked over the edge at Nejdanov and said with a smile:

" We will read this together when we have some time to spare, won't we? "

" Give it to me! I'll burn it! " Nejdanov burst out. " That's all it's fit for! "

" Then why did you take it with you? No, I won't let you burn it. However, authors are always threatening to burn their things, but they never do. I will put it in my room."

Nejdanov was just about to protest when Mariana rushed into the next room with the copy-book and came back without it.

She sat down beside him, but instantly got up again. " You have not yet been in my room; would you like to see it? It's quite as nice as yours. Come and look."

Nejdanov rose and followed her. Her room, as she called it, was somewhat smaller than his, but the furniture was altogether smarter and newer. Some flowers in a crystal vase stood on the window-sill and there was an iron bedstead in a corner.

" Isn't Solomin a darling!" Mariana exclaimed. " But we mustn't get too spoilt. I don't suppose we shall often have rooms like these. Do you know what I've been thinking? It would be rather nice if we could get a place together so that we need not part! It will probably be difficult," she added after a pause; " but we must think of it. But all the same, you won't go back to St. Petersburg, will you? "

" What should I do in St. Petersburg? Attend lectures at the university or give lessons? That's no use to me now."

" We must ask Solomin," Mariana observed. " He will know best."

They went back to the other room and sat down beside each other again. They praised Solomin, Tatiana, Pavel; spoke of the Sipiagins and how their former life had receded from them far into the distance, as if enveloped in a mist; then they clasped each other's hand again, exchanged tender glances; wondered what class they had better go among first, and how to behave so that people should not suspect them.

Nejdanov declared that the less they thought about that, and the more naturally they behaved, the better.

" Of course! We want to become simple, as Tatiana says."

" I didn't mean it in that sense," Nejdanov began; " I meant that we must not be self-conscious."

Mariana suddenly burst out laughing

" Do you remember, Aliosha, how I said that we had both become simplified? "

Nejdanov also laughed, repeated " simplified," and began musing. Mariana too became pensive.

" Aliosha! " she exclaimed.

" What is it? "

" It seems to me that we are both a little uncomfortable. Young—*des nouveaux mariés*," she explained, " when away on their honeymoon no doubt feel as we do. They are happy . . . all is well with them—but they feel uncomfortable."

Nejdanov gave a forced smile.

" You know very well, Mariana, that we are not young . . . in that sense."

Mariana rose from her chair and stood before him.

" That depends on yourself."

" How? "

" Aliosha, you know, dear, that when you tell me, as a man of honour . . . and I will believe you because I know you are honourable; when you tell me that you love me with that love . . . the love that gives one person the right over another's life, when you tell me that—I am yours."

Nejdanov blushed and turned away a little.

" When I tell you that. . . ."

" Yes, then! But you see, Aliosha, you don't say that to me now. . . . Oh yes, Aliosha, you are truly an honourable man. Enough of this! Let us talk of more serious things."

" But I do love you, Mariana! "

" I don't doubt that . . . and shall wait. But there, I have not quite finished arranging your writing table. Here is something wrapped up, something hard."

Nejdanov sprang up from his chair.

" Don't touch that, Mariana. . . . Leave it alone, please! "

Mariana looked at him over her shoulder and raised her eyebrows in amazement.

" Is it a mystery? A secret? Have you a secret? "

" Yes . . . yes . . ." Nejdanov stammered out, and added by way of explanation, " it's a portrait."

The word escaped him unawares. The packet Mariana held in her hand was her own portrait, which Markelov had given Nejdanov.

" A portrait? " she drawled out.   " Is it a woman's? "

She handed him the packet, which he took so clumsily that it slipped out of his hand and fell open.

" Why . . . it's my portrait! " Mariana exclaimed quickly. " I suppose I may look at my own portrait." She took it out of Nejdanov's hand.

" Did you do it? "

" No . . . I didn't."

" Who then?   Markelov? "

" Yes, you've guessed right."

" Then how did it come to be in your possession? "

" He gave it to me."

" When? "

Nejdanov told her when and under what circumstances. Whilst he was speaking Mariana glanced from him to the portrait. The same thought flashed across both their minds. " If *he* were in this room, then *he* would have the right to demand . . ." But neither Mariana nor Nejdanov gave expression to this thought in words, perhaps because each was conscious what was in the other's mind.

Mariana quietly wrapped the portrait up again in its paper and put it on the table.

" What a good man he is! " she murmured.   " I wonder where he is now? "

" Why, at home of course.   To-morrow or the day after I must go and see him about some books and pamphlets.

He promised to give me some, but evidently forgot to do so before I left."

" And do you think, Aliosha, that when he gave you this portrait he renounced everything . . . absolutely everything? "

" I think so."

" Do you think you will find him at home? "

" Of course."

" Ah! " Mariana lowered her eyes and dropped her hands at her sides. " But here comes Tatiana with our dinner," she exclaimed suddenly. " Isn't she a dear! "

Tatiana appeared with the knives and forks, serviettes, plates and dishes. Whilst laying the table she related all the news about the factory. " The master came from Moscow by rail and started running from floor to floor like a madman. Of course he doesn't understand anything and does it only for show; to set an example so to speak. Vassily Fedotitch treats him like a child. The master wanted to make some unpleasantness, but Vassily Fedotitch soon shut him up. ' I'll throw it up this minute,' he said, so he soon began to sing small. They are having dinner now. The master brought some one with him. A Moscow swell who does nothing but admire everything. He must be very rich, I think, by the way he holds his tongue and shakes his head. And so stout, very stout! A real swell! No wonder there's a saying that ' Moscow lies at the foot of Russia and everything rolls down to her.' "

" How you notice everything! " Mariana exclaimed.

" Yes, I do rather," Tatiana observed. " Well, here is your dinner. Come and have it and I'll sit and look at you for a little while."

Mariana and Nejdanov sat down to table, whilst Tatiana sat down on the window-sill and rested her cheek in her hand.

" I watch you . . ." she observed. " And what dear, young, tender creatures you are. You're so nice to look at that it quite makes my heart ache. Ah, my dear! You are taking a heavier burden on your shoulders than you can bear. It's people like you that the tsar's folk are ready to put into prison."

"Nothing of the kind. Don't frighten us," Nejdanov remarked. "You know the old saying, ' As you make your bed so you must lie on it.' "

"Yes, I know. But the beds are so narrow nowadays that you can't get out of them! "

" Have you any children? " Mariana asked to change the subject.

"Yes, I have a boy. He goes to school now. I had a girl too, but she's gone, the little bird! An accident happened to her. She fell under a wheel. If only it had killed her at once! But no, she suffered a long while. Since then I've become more tender-hearted. Before I was as wild and hard as a tree! "

" Why, did you not love your Pavel? '

" But that's not the same. Only a girl's feelings. And you—do you love *him* ? "

" Of course I do."

" Very much? "

" Ever so much."

" Really? . . ." Tatiana looked from one to the other, but said nothing more.

" I'll tell you what I would like. Could you get me some coarse, strong wool? I want to knit some stockings . . . plain ones."

Tatiana promised to have everything done, and clearing the table, went out of the room with her firm, quiet step.

" Well, what shall we do now? " Mariana asked, turning to Nejdanov, and without waiting for a reply, continued, " Since our real work does not begin until to-morrow, let us devote this evening to literature. Would you like to? We can read your poems. I will be a severe critic, I promise you."

224

VIRGIN SOIL

It took Nejdanov a long time before he consented, but he gave in at last and began reading aloud out of his copybook. Mariana sat close to him and gazed into his face as he read. She had been right; she turned out to be a very severe critic. Very few of the verses pleased her. She preferred the purely lyrical, short ones, to the didactic, as she expressed it. Nejdanov did not read well. He had not the courage to attempt any style, and at the same time wanted to avoid a dry tone. It turned out neither the one thing nor the other. Mariana interrupted him suddenly by asking if he knew Dobrolubov's beautiful poem,[1] which begins, " To die for me no terror holds." She read it to him —also not very well—in a somewhat childish manner.

Nejdanov thought that it was too sad and too bitter. He could not have written a poem like that, he added, as he had no fears of any one weeping over his grave . . . there would be no tears.

" There will be if I outlive you," Mariana observed slowly, and lifting her eyes to the ceiling she asked, in a whisper, as if speaking to herself:

" How did he do the portrait of me? From memory? "

Nejdanov turned to her quickly.

" Yes, from memory."

Mariana was surprised at his reply. It seemed to her

[1] To die for me no terror holds,
Yet one fear presses on my mind,
That death should on me helpless play
A satire of the bitter kind.

For much I fear that o'er my corse
The scalding tears of friends shall flow,
And that, too late, they should with zeal
Fresh flowers upon my body throw.

That fate sardonic should recall
The ones I loved to my cold side,
And make me lying in the ground,
The object of love once denied.

That all my aching heart's desires,
So vainly sought for from my birth,
Should crowd unbidden, smiling kind
Above my body's mound of earth.

that she merely thought the question. "It is really wonderful . . ." she continued in the same tone of voice. "Why, he can't draw at all. What was I talking about?" she added aloud. "Oh yes, it was about Dobrolubov's poems. One ought to write poems like Pushkin's, or even like Dobrolubov's. It is not poetry exactly, but something nearly as good."

"And poems like mine one should not write at all. Isn't that so?" Nejdanov asked.

"Poems like yours please your friends, not because they are good, but because *you* are a good man and they are like you."

Nejdanov smiled.

"You have completely buried them and me with them!"

Mariana slapped his hand and called him naughty. Soon after she announced that she was tired and wanted to go to bed.

"By the way," she added, shaking back her short thick curls, "do you know that I have a hundred and thirty roubles? And how much have you?"

"Ninety-eight."

"Oh, then we are rich . . . for simplified folk. Well, good night, till to-morrow."

She went out, but in a minute or two her door opened slightly and he heard her say, "Good night!" then more softly another "Good night!" and the key turned in the lock.

Nejdanov sank on to the sofa and covered his face with his hands. Then he got up quickly, went to her door and knocked.

"What is it?" was heard from within.

"Not till to-morrow, Mariana . . . not till to-morrow!"

"Till to-morrow," she replied softly.

XXIX

EARLY the next morning Nejdanov again knocked at Mariana's door.

"It is I," he replied in answer to her "Who's that?" "Can you come out to me?"

"In a minute."

She came out and uttered a cry of alarm. At first she did not recognise him. He had on a long-skirted, shabby, yellowish nankin coat, with small buttons and a high waist; his hair was dressed in the Russian fashion with a parting straight down the middle; he had a blue kerchief round his neck, in his hand he held a cap with a broken peak, on his feet a pair of dirty leather boots.

"Heavens!" Mariana exclaimed. "How ugly you look!" and thereupon threw her arms round him and kissed him quickly. "But why did you get yourself up like this? You look like some sort of shopkeeper, or pedlar, or a retired servant. Why this long coat? Why not simply like a peasant?"

"Why?" Nejdanov began. He certainly did look like some sort of fishmonger in that garb, was conscious of it himself, and was annoyed and embarrassed at heart. He felt uncomfortable, and not knowing what to do with his hands, kept patting himself on the breast with the fingers outspread, as though he were brushing himself.

"Because as a peasant I should have been recognised at once Pavel says, and that in this costume I look as if I had been born to it . . . which is not very flattering to my vanity, by the way."

"Are you going to begin at once?" Mariana asked eagerly.

"Yes, I shall try, though in reality——"

227

" You are lucky! " Mariana interrupted him.

" This Pavel is a wonderful fellow," Nejdanov continued.
" He can see through and through you in a second, and will
suddenly screw up his face as if he knew nothing, and would
not interfere with anything for the world. He works for
the cause himself, yet laughs at it the whole time. He
brought me the books from Markelov; he knows him and
calls him Sergai Mihailovitch; and as for Solomin, he would
go through fire and water for him."

" And so would Tatiana," Mariana observed. " Why are
people so devoted to him? "

Nejdanov did not reply.

" What sort of books did Pavel bring you? " Mariana
asked.

" Oh, nothing new. ' The Story of the Four Brothers,'
and then the ordinary, well-known ones, which are far better
I think."

Mariana looked round uneasily.

" I wonder what has become of Tatiana? She promised
to come early."

" Here I am! " Tatiana exclaimed, coming in with a bundle
in her hand. She had heard Mariana's exclamation from
behind the door.

" There's plenty of time. See what I've brought you! "
Mariana flew towards her.

" Have you brought it? "

Tatiana patted the bundle.

" Everything is here, quite ready. You have only to put
the things on and go out to astonish the world."

" Come along, come along, Tatiana Osipovna, you are a
dear——"

Mariana led her off to her own room.

Left alone, Nejdanov walked up and down the room once
or twice with a peculiarly shuffling gait (he imagined that
all shopkeepers walked like that), then he carefully sniffed
at this sleeves, the inside of his cap, made a grimace, looked

228

at himself in the little looking-glass hanging in between the windows, and shook his head; he certainly did not look very prepossessing. "So much the better," he thought. Then he took several pamphlets, thrust them into his side pocket, and began to practise speaking like a shopkeeper. "That sounds like it," he thought, "but after all there is no need of acting, my get-up is convincing enough." Just then he recollected a German exile, who had to make his escape right across Russia with only a poor knowledge of the language. But thanks to a merchant's cap which he had bought in a provincial town, he was taken everywhere for a merchant and had successfully made his way across the frontier.

At this moment Solomin entered.

"I say!" he exclaimed. "Arrayed in all your war paint? Excuse me, my dear fellow, but in that garb one can hardly speak to you respectfully."

"Please don't. I had long meant to ask you——"

"But it's early as yet. It doesn't matter if you only want to get used to it, only you must not go out yet. My employer is still here. He's in bed."

"I'll go out later on," Nejdanov responded. "I'll explore the neighbourhood a little, until further orders come."

"Capital! But I tell you what, Alexai. . . . I may call you Alexai, may I not?"

"Certainly, or Lexy if you like," Nejdanov added with a smile.

"No; there is no need to over-do things. Listen. Good counsel is better than money, as the saying goes. I see that you have pamphlets. Distribute them wherever you like, only not in the factory on any account!"

"Why not?"

"In the first place, because it won't be safe for you; in the second, because I promised the owner not to do that sort of thing here. You see the place is his after all, and then something has already been done . . . a school and

229

so on. You might do more harm than good. Further than that, you may do as you like, I shall not hinder you. But you must not interfere with my workpeople."

" Caution is always useful," Nejdanov remarked with a sarcastic smile.

Solomin smiled his characteristic broad smile.

" Yes, my dear Alexai, it's always useful. But what do I see? Where are we? "

The last words referred to Mariana, who at that moment appeared in the doorway of her room in a print dress that had been washed a great many times, with a yellow kerchief over her shoulders and a red one on her head. Tatiana stood behind her, smiling good-naturedly. Mariana seemed younger and brighter in her simple garment and looked far better than Nejdanov in his long-skirted coat.

"Vassily Fedotitch, don't laugh, please," Mariana implored, turning as red as a poppy.

" There's a nice couple! " Tatiana exclaimed, clapping her hands. " But you, my dear, don't be angry, you look well enough, but beside my little dove you're nowhere."

" And, really, she is charming," Nejdanov thought; " oh, how I love her! "

" Look now," Tatiana continued, " she insisted on changing rings with me. She has given me a golden ring and taken my silver one."

" Girls of the people do not wear gold rings," Mariana observed.

Tatiana sighed.

" I'll take good care of it, my dear; don't be afraid."

" Well, sit down, sit down both of you," Solomin began; he had been standing all the while with his head bent a little to one side, gazing at Mariana. " In olden days, if you remember, people always sat down before starting on a journey. And you have both a long and wearisome one before you."

Mariana, still crimson, sat down, then Nejdanov and Solomin, and last of all Tatiana took her seat on a thick block of wood. Solomin looked at each of them in turn.

> " Let us step back a pace,
> Let us step back a bit,
> To see with what grace
> And how nicely we sit,"

he said with a frown. Suddenly he burst out laughing, but so good-naturedly that no one was in the least offended, on the contrary, they all began to feel merry too. Only Nejdanov rose suddenly.

" I must go now," he said; " this is all very nice, but rather like a farce. Don't be uneasy," he added, turning to Solomin. " I shall not interfere with your people. I'll try my tongue on the folk round about and will tell you all about it when I come back, Mariana, if there is anything to tell. Wish me luck! "

" Why not have a cup of tea first? " Tatiana remarked.

" No thanks. If I want any I can go into an eating-house or into a public house."

Tatiana shook her head.

" Good-bye, good-bye . . . good luck to you! " Nejdanov added, entering upon his rôle of small shopkeeper. But before he had reached the door Pavel thrust his head in from the passage under his very nose, and handing him a thin, long staff, cut out all the way down like a screw, he said:

" Take this, Alexai Dmitritch, and lean on it as you walk. And the farther you hold it away from yourself the better it will look."

Nejdanov took the staff without a word and went out. Tatiana wanted to go out too, but Mariana stopped her.

" Wait a minute, Tatiana Osipovna. I want you."

" I'll be back directly with the samovar. Your friend has gone off without tea, he was in such a mighty hurry. But that is no reason why you should not have any. Later on things will be clearer."

Tatiana went out and Solomin also rose. Mariana was

standing with her back to him, but when at last she turned towards him, rather surprised that he had not said a single word, she saw in his face, in his eyes that were fixed on her, an expression she had not seen there before; an expression of inquiry, anxiety, almost of curiosity. She became confused and blushed again. Solomin, too, was ashamed of what she had read in his face and began talking louder than was his wont.

" Well, well, Mariana, and so you have made a beginning."

" What sort of beginning, Vassily Fedotitch? Do you call this a beginning? Alexai was right. It's as if we were acting a farce."

Solomin sat down again.

" But, Mariana . . . what did you picture the beginning to be like? Not standing behind the barricades waving a flag and shouting, ' Hurrah for the republic! ' Besides, that is not a woman's work. Now, to-day you will begin teaching some Lukeria something good for her, and a difficult matter it will be, because you won't understand your Lukeria and she won't understand you, and on top of it she will imagine that what you are teaching is of no earthly use to her. In two or three weeks you will try your hand on another Lukeria, and meanwhile you will be washing a baby here, teaching another the alphabet, or handing some sick man his medicine. That will be your beginning."

" But sisters of mercy do that, Vassily Fedotitch! What is the use of all this, then? " Mariana pointed to herself and round about with a vague gesture. " I dreamt of something else."

" Did you want to sacrifice yourself? "

Mariana's eyes glistened.

" Yes, yes, yes! "

" And Nejdanov? "

Mariana shrugged her shoulders.

" What of Nejdanov? We shall go together . . . or I will go alone."

Solomin looked at her intently.

" Do you know, Mariana . . . excuse the coarse expression . . . but, to my mind, combing the scurfy head of a gutter child is a sacrifice; a great sacrifice of which not many people are capable."

" I would not shirk that, Vassily Fedotitch."

" I know you would not. You are capable of doing that and will do it, until something else turns up."

" But for that sort of thing I must learn of Tatiana!"

" You could not do better. You will be washing pots and plucking chickens. . . . And, who knows, maybe you will save your country in that way!"

" You are laughing at me, Vassily Fedotitch."

Solomin shook his head slowly.

" My dear Mariana, believe me, I am not laughing at you. What I said was the simple truth. You are already, all you Russian women, more capable and higher than we men."

Mariana raised her eyes.

" I would like to live up to your idea of us, Solomin . . . and then I should be ready to die."

Solomin stood up.

" No, it is better to live! That's the main thing. By the way, would you like to know what is happening at the Sipiagins? Won't they do anything? You have only to drop Pavel a hint and he will find out everything in a twinkling."

Mariana was surprised.

" What a wonderful person he is!"

" Yes, he certainly is wonderful. And should you want to marry Alexai, he will arrange that too with Zosim, the priest. You remember I told you about him. But perhaps it is not necessary as yet, eh?"

" No, not yet."

" Very well." Solomin went up to the door dividing the two rooms, Mariana's and Nejdanov's, and examined the lock.

" What are you doing? " Mariana asked.

" Does it lock all right? "

" Yes," Mariana whispered.

Solomin turned to her. She did not raise her eyes.

" Then there is no need to bother about the Sipiagins,"
he continued gaily, " is there? "

Solomin was about to go out.

" Vassily Fedotitch . . ."

" Yes. . . ."

" Why is it you are so talkative with me when you are
usually so silent? You can't imagine what pleasure it gives
me."

" Why? " Solomin took both her soft little hands in his
big hard ones. " Why, did you ask? Well, I suppose it
must be because I love you so much. Good-bye."

He went out. Mariana stood pensive looking after him.
In a little while she went to find Tatiana who had not yet
brought the samovar. She had tea with her, washed some
pots, plucked a chicken, and even combed out some boy's
tangled head of hair.

Before dinner she returned to her own rooms and soon
afterwards Nejdanov arrived.

He came in tired and covered with dust and dropped on
to the sofa. She immediately sat down beside him.

" Well, tell me what happened."

" You remember the two lines," he responded in a weary
voice:

> " It would have been so funny
> Were it not so sad."

" Do you remember? "

" Of course I do."

" Well, these lines apply admirably to my first expedition,
excepting that it was more funny than sad. I've come to
the conclusion that there is nothing easier than to act a part.
No one dreamed of suspecting me. There was one thing,
however, that I had not thought of. You must be prepared

234

with some sort of yarn beforehand, or else when any one asks you where you've come from and why you've come, you don't know what to say. But, however, even that is not so important. You've only to stand a drink and lie as much as you like."

" And you? Did you lie? "

" Of course I did, as much as I could. And then I've discovered that absolutely every one you come across is discontented, only no one cares to find out the remedy for this discontent. I made a very poor show at propaganda, only succeeded in leaving a couple of pamphlets in a room and shoving a third into a cart. What may come of them the Lord only knows! I ran across four men whom I offered some pamphlets. The first asked if it was a religious book and refused to take it; the second could not read, but took it home to his children for the sake of the picture on the cover; the third seemed hopeful at first, but ended by abusing me soundly and also not taking it; the fourth took a little book, thanked me very much, but I doubt if he understood a single word I said to him. Besides that, a dog bit my leg, a peasant woman threatened me with a poker from the door of her hut, shouting, ' Ugh! you pig! You Moscow rascals! There's no end to you! ' and then a soldier shouted after me, ' Hi, there! We'll make mince-meat of you! ' and he got drunk at my expense! "

" Well, and what else? "

" What else? I've got a blister on my foot; one of my boots is horribly large. And now I'm as hungry as a wolf and my head is splitting from the vodka."

" Why, did you drink much? "

" No, only a little to set the example, but I've been in five public-houses. I can't endure this beastliness, vodka. Goodness knows why our people drink it. If one must drink this stuff in order to become simplified, then I had rather be excused! "

" And so no one suspected you? "

"No one, with the exception, perhaps, of a bar-man, a stout individual with pale eyes, who did look at me somewhat suspiciously. I overheard him saying to his wife, "Keep an eye on that carroty-haired one with the squint.' (I was not aware until that moment that I had a squint.) 'There's something wrong about him. See how he's sticking over his vodka.' What he meant by 'sticking' exactly, I didn't understand, but it could hardly have been to my credit. It reminded me of the *mauvais ton* in Gogol's *Revisor*, do you remember? Perhaps because I tried to pour my vodka under the table. Oh dear! It is difficult for an æsthetic creature like me to come in contact with real life."

"Never mind. Better luck next time," Mariana said consolingly. "But I am glad you see the humorous side of this, your first attempt. You were not really bored, were you?"

"No, it was rather amusing. But I know that I shall think it all over now and it will make me miserable."

"But I won't let you think about it! I will tell you everything I did. Dinner will be here in a minute. By the way, I must tell you that I washed the saucepan Tatiana cooked the soup in. . . . I'll tell you everything, every little detail."

And so she did. Nejdanov listened and could not take his eyes off her. She stopped several times to ask why he looked at her so intently, but he was silent.

After dinner she offered to read Spielhagen aloud to him, but had scarcely got through one page when he got up suddenly and fell at her feet. She stood up; he flung both his arms round her knees and began uttering passionate, disconnected, and despairing words. He wanted to die, he knew he would soon die. . . . She did not stir, did not resist. She calmly submitted to his passionate embraces, and calmly, even affectionately, glanced down upon him. She laid both her hands on his head, feverishly pressed to the fold of her dress, but her calmness had a more powerful effect on him

236

than if she had repulsed him. He got up murmuring: " Forgive me, Mariana, for to-day and for yesterday. Tell me again that you are prepared to wait until I am worthy of your love, and forgive me."

" I gave you my word. I never change."

" Thank you, dear. Good-bye."

Nejdanov went out and Mariana locked the door of her room.

XXX

A FORTNIGHT later, in the same room, Nejdanov sat bending over his three-legged table, writing to his friend Silin by the dim light of a tallow candle. (It was long past midnight. Muddy garments lay scattered on the sofa, on the floor, just where they had been thrown off. A fine drizzly rain pattered against the window-panes and a strong, warm wind moaned about the roof of the house.)

MY DEAR VLADIMIR,—I am writing to you without giving my address and will send this letter by a messenger to a distant posting-station as my being here is a secret, and to disclose it might mean the ruin not of myself alone. It is enough for you to know that for the last two weeks I have been living in a large factory together with Mariana. We ran away from the Sipiagins on the day on which I last wrote to you. A friend has given us shelter here. For convenience' sake I will call him Vassily. He is the chief here and an excellent man. Our stay is only of a temporary nature; we will move on when the time for action comes. But, however, judging by events so far, the time is hardly likely ever to come! Vladimir, I am horribly miserable. I must tell you before everything that although Mariana and I ran away together, we have so far been living like brother and sister. She loves me and told me she would be mine if I feel I have the right to ask it of her.

Vladimir, I do not feel that I have the right! She trusts me, believes in my honour—I cannot deceive her. I know that I never loved nor will ever love any one more than her (of that I am convinced), but for all that, how can I unite her fate for ever with mine? A living being to a corpse?

Well, if not a complete corpse, at any rate, a half-dead creature. Where would one's conscience be? I can hear you say that if passion was strong enough the conscience would be silent. But that is just the point; I am a corpse, an honest, well-meaning corpse if you like, but a corpse nevertheless. Please do not say that I always exaggerate. Everything I have told you is absolutely true. Mariana is very reserved and is at present wrapped up in her activities in which she believes, and I?

Well, enough of love and personal happiness and all that. It is now a fortnight since I have been going among " the people," and really it would be impossible to imagine anything more stupid than they are. Of course the fault lies probably more in me than in the work itself. I am not a fanatic. I am not one of those who regenerate themselves by contact with the people and do not lay them on my aching bosom like a flannel bandage—I want to influence them. But how? How can it be done? When I am among them I find myself listening all the time, taking things in, but when it comes to saying anything—I am at a loss for a word! I feel that I am no good, a bad actor in a part that does not suit him. Conscientiousness or scepticism are absolutely of no use, nor is a pitiful sort of humour directed against oneself. It is worse than useless! I find it disgusting to look at the filthy rags I carry about on me, the masquerade as Vassily calls it! They say you must first learn the language of the people, their habits and customs, but rubbish, rubbish, rubbish, I say! You have only to *believe* in what you say and say what you like! I once happened to hear a sectarian prophet delivering a sermon. Goodness only knows what arrant nonsense he talked, a sort of gorgeous mix-up of ecclesiastical learning, interspersed with peasant expressions, not even in decent Russian, but in some outlandish dialect, but he took one by storm with his enthusiasm—went straight to the heart. There he stood with flashing eyes, the voice deep and firm, with clenched fist—as though he were made of iron! No one

239

understood what he was saying, but every one bowed down before him and followed him. But when I begin to speak, I seem like a culprit begging for forgiveness. I ought to join the sectarians, although their wisdom is not great . . . but they have faith, faith! Mariana too has faith. She works from morning till night with Tatiana—a peasant woman here, as good as can be and not by any means stupid; she says, by the way, that we want to become simplified and calls us simple souls. Mariana is about working with this woman from morning till night, scarcely sitting down for a moment, just like a regular ant! She is delighted that her hands are turning red and rough, and in the midst of these humble occupations is looking forward to the scaffold! She has even attempted to discard shoes; went out somewhere barefoot and came back barefoot. I heard her washing her feet for a long time afterwards and then saw her come out, treading cautiously; they were evidently sore, poor thing, but her face was radiant with smiles as though she had found a treasure or been illuminated by the sun. Yes, Mariana is a brick! But when I try to talk to her of my feelings, a certain shame comes over me somehow, as though I were violating something that was not my own, and then that glance . . . Oh, that awful devoted, irresistible glance! " Take me," it seems to say, " *but remember.* . . ." Enough of this! Is there not something higher and better in this world? In other words, put on your filthy coat and go among the people. . . . Oh, yes, I am just going.

How I loathe this irritability, sensitiveness, impressionableness, fastidiousness, inherited from my aristocratic father! What right had he to bring me into this world, endowed with qualities quite unsuited to the sphere in which I must live? To create a bird and throw it in the water? An æsthetic amidst filth! A democrat, a lover of the people, yet the very smell of their filthy vodka makes me feel sick!

But it's too bad blaming my father. He was not responsible for my becoming a democrat.

VIRGIN SOIL

Yes, Vladimir, I am in a bad plight. Grey, depressing thoughts are continually haunting me. Can it be, you will be asking me, that I have not met with anything consoling, any good living personality, however ignorant he might not be? How shall I tell you? I have run across some one— a decent clever chap, but unfortunately, however hard I may try to get nearer him, he has no need of either me or my pamphlets—that is the root of the matter! Pavel, a factory hand here (he is Vassily's right hand, a clever fellow with his head screwed on the right way, a future " head," I think I wrote to you about him), well this Pavel has a friend, a peasant called Elizar, also a smart chap, as free and courage-ous as one would wish, but as soon as we get together there seems a dead wall between us! his face spells one big " No! " Then there was another man I ran across—he was a rather quarrelsome type by the way. " Don't you try to get round me, sir," he said. " What I want to know is would you give up your land now, or not? " " But I'm not a gentleman," I remonstrated. " Bless you! " he ex-claimed, " you a common man and no more sense than that! Leave me alone, please! "

Another thing I've noticed is that if any one listens to you readily and takes your pamphlets at once, he is sure to be of an undesirable, brainless sort. Or you may chance upon some frightfully talkative individual who can do nothing but keep on repeating some favourite expression. One such nearly drove me mad; everything with him was " produc-tion." No matter what you said to him he came out with his " production," damn him! Just one more remark. Do you remember some time ago there used to be a great deal of talk about " superfluous " people, Hamlets? Such " super-fluous people " are now to be met with among the peasants! They have their own characteristics of course and are for the most part inclined to consumption. They are interesting types and come to us readily, but as far as the cause is con-cerned they are ineffective, like all other Hamlets. Well,

241

what can one do? Start a secret printing press? There are pamphlets enough as it is, some that say, " Cross yourself and take up the hatchet," and others that say simply, " Take up the hatchet " without the crossing. Or should one write novels of peasant life with plenty of padding? They wouldn't get published, you know. Perhaps it might be better to take up the hatchet after all? But against whom, with whom, and what for? So that our state soldier may shoot us down with the state rifle? It would only be a complicated form of suicide! It would be better to make an end of your-self—you would at any rate know when and how, and choose the spot to aim at.

I am beginning to think that if some war were to break out, some people's war—I would go and take part in it, not so as to free others (free others whilst one's own are groaning under the yoke!!), but to make an end of myself. . . .

Our friend Vassily, who gave us shelter here, is a lucky man. He belongs to our camp, but is so calm and quiet. He doesn't want to hurry over things. I should have quar-relled with another, but I can't with him. The secret lies not in his convictions, but in the man himself. Vassily has a character that you can't kindle, but he's all right nevertheless. He is with us a good deal, with Mariana. What surprises me is that although I love her and she loves me (I see you smiling at this, but the fact remains!) we have nothing to talk about, whilst she is constantly discussing and arguing with him and listening too. I am not jealous of him; he is trying to find a place for her somewhere, at any rate, she keeps on asking him to do so, but it makes me feel bitter to look at them both. And would you believe it—I have only to drop a hint about marrying and she would agree at once and the priest Zosim would put in an appearance, " Isaiah, rejoice! " and the rest of it. But this would not make it any easier for me and *nothing would be changed by it*. . . . What-ever you do, there is no way out of it! Life has cut me short, my dear Vladimir, as our little drunken tailor used

242

to say, you remember, when he used to complain about his wife.

I have a feeling that it can't go on somehow, that something is preparing. . . .

Have I not again and again said that the time has come for action? Well, so here we are in the thick of it.

I can't remember if I told you anything about another friend of mine—a relative of the Sipiagins. He will get himself into such a mess that it won't be easy for him to get out of it.

I quite meant finishing this letter and am still going on. It seems to me that nothing matters and yet I scribble verses. I don't read them to Mariana and she is not very anxious to hear them, but you have sometimes praised my poor attempts and most of all you'll keep them to yourself. I have been struck by a common phenomenon in Russia. . . . But, however, let the verses speak for themselves—

SLEEP

After long absence I return to my native land,
Finding no striking change there.
The same dead, senseless stagnation; crumbling houses, crumbling walls,
And the same filth, dirt, poverty, and misery.
Unchanged the servile glance, now insolent, now dejected.
Free have our people become, and the free arm
Hangs as before like a whip unused.
All, all as before. In one thing only may we equal
Europe, Asia, and the World!
Never before has such a fearful sleep oppressed our land.

All are asleep, on all sides are they;
Through town and country, in carts and in sledges,
By day or night, sitting or standing,
The merchant and the official, and the sentinel at his post
In biting snow and burning heat—all sleep.
The judged ones doze, and the judge snores,
And peasants plough and reap like dead men,
Father, mother, children; all are asleep.
He who beats, and he who is beaten.
Alone the tavern of the tsar ne'er closes a relentless eye.
So, grasping tight in hand the bottle,
His brow at the Pole and his heel in the Caucasus,
Holy Russia, our fatherland, lies in eternal sleep.

I am sorry, Vladimir. I never meant to write you such a melancholy letter without a few cheering words at the end. (You will no doubt tumble across some defects in the lines!) When shall I write to you again? Shall I ever write? But whatever happens to me I am sure you will never forget,

Your devoted friend,

A. N.

P.S.—Our people are asleep. . . . But I have a feeling that if anything does wake them, it will not be what *we* think. . . .

After writing the last line, Nejdanov flung down the pen. " Well, now you must try and sleep and forget all this nonsense, scribbler! " he exclaimed, and lay down on the bed. But it was long before he fell asleep.

The next morning Mariana woke him passing through his room on her way to Tatiana. He had scarcely dressed when she came back. She seemed excited, her face expressing delight and anxiety at the same time.

" Do you know, Aliosha, they say that in the province of T., quite near here, it has already begun! "

" What? What has begun? Who said so? "

" Pavel. They say the peasants are rising, refusing to pay taxes, collecting in mobs."

" Have you heard that yourself? "

" Tatiana told me. But here is Pavel himself. You had better ask him."

Pavel came in and confirmed what Mariana had said.

" There is certainly some disturbance in T.," he began, shaking his beard and screwing up his bright black eyes. " Sergai Mihailovitch must have had a hand in it. He hasn't been home for five days."

Nejdanov took his cap.

" Where are you off to? " Mariana asked.

" Why there of course," he replied, not raising his eyes and frowning, " I am going to T."

244

" Then I will come with you. You'll take me, won't you?
Just let me get a shawl."

" It's not a woman's work," Nejdanov said irritably with
his eyes still fixed on the floor.

" No, no! You do well to go, or Markelov would think
you a coward . . . but I'm coming with you."

" I am not a coward," Nejdanov observed gloomily.

" I meant to say that he would have thought us both
cowards. I am coming with you."

Mariana went into her own room to get a shawl, whilst
Pavel gave an inward ha, ha, and quickly vanished. He ran
to warn Solomin.

Mariana had not yet appeared, when Solomin came into
Nejdanov's room. The latter was standing with his face to
the window, his forehead resting on the palm of his hand and
his elbow on the window-pane. Solomin touched him on
the shoulder. He turned round quickly; dishevelled and
unwashed, Nejdanov had a strange wild look. Solomin, too,
had changed during the last days. His face was yellow and
drawn and his upper front teeth showed slightly—he, too,
seemed agitated as far as it was possible for his well-balanced
temperament to be so.

" Markelov could not control himself after all," he began.
" This may turn out badly both for him and for others."

" I want to go and see what's going on there," Nejdanov
observed.

" And I too," Mariana added as she appeared in the doorway.

Solomin turned to her quickly.

" I would not advise you to go, Mariana. You may give
yourself away—and us, without meaning to and without
the slightest necessity. Let Nejdanov go and see how the
land lies, if he wants to—and the sooner he's back the better!
But why should you go? "

" I don't want to be parted from him."

" You will be in his way."

Mariana looked at Nejdanov. He was standing motionless with a set sullen expression on his face.

" But supposing there should be danger? " she asked.

Solomin smiled.

"Don't be afraid . . . when there's danger I will let you go."

Mariana took off her shawl without a word and sat down. Solomin then turned to Nejdanov.

" It would be a good thing for you to look about a little, Alexai. I dare say they exaggerate. Only do be careful. But, however, you will not be going alone. Come back as quickly as you can. Will you promise? Nejdanov? Will you promise? "

" Yes."

" For certain? "

" I suppose so, since everybody here obeys you, including Mariana."

Nejdanov went out without saying good-bye. Pavel appeared from somewhere out of the darkness and ran down the stairs before him with a great clatter of his hob-nailed boots. Was *he* then to accompany Nejdanov?

Solomin sat down beside Mariana.

" You heard Nejdanov's last word? "

" Yes. He is annoyed that I listen to you more than to him. But it's quite true. I love *him* and listen to you. He is dear to me . . . and you are near to me.

Solomin stroked her hand gently.

" This is a very unpleasant business," he observed at last. " If Markelov is mixed up in it then he's a lost man."

Mariana shuddered.

" Lost? "

" Yes. He doesn't do things by halves—and won't hide things for the sake of others."

" Lost! " Mariana whispered again as the tears rolled down her cheeks. " Oh, Vassily Fedotitch! I feel so sorry for him.

But what makes you think that he won't succeed? Why must he inevitably be lost? "

" Because in such enterprises the first always perish even if they come off victorious. And in this thing not only the first and second, but the tenth and twentieth will perish——"

" Then we shall never live to see it? "

" What you have in your mind—never. We shall never see it with our eyes; with these living eyes of ours. But with our spiritual . . . but that is another matter. We may see it in that way now; there is nothing to hinder us."

" Then why do you——"

" What? "

" Why do you follow this road? "

" Because there is no other. I mean that my aims are the same as Markelov's—but our paths are different."

" Poor Sergai Mihailovitch! " Mariana exclaimed sadly. Solomin passed his hand cautiously over hers.

" There, there, we know nothing as yet. We'll see what news Pavel brings back. In our calling one must be brave. The English have a proverb ' Never say die.' A very good proverb, I think, much better than our Russian, ' When trouble knocks, open the gates wide! ' We mustn't meet trouble half way."

Solomin stood up.

" And the place you were going to find me? " Mariana asked suddenly. The tears were still shining on her cheeks, but there was no sadness in her eyes. Solomin sat down again.

" Are you in such a great hurry to get away from here? "

" Oh, no! only I wanted to do something useful."

" You are useful here, Mariana. Don't leave us yet, wait a little longer. What is it? " Solomin asked of Tatiana who was just coming in.

" Some sort of female is asking for Alexai Dmitritch," Tatiana replied, laughing and gesticulating with her hands.

" I said that there was no such person living here, that we did not know him at all, when she——"

" Who is she? "

" Why the female of course. She wrote her name on this piece of paper and asked me to bring it here and let her in, saying that if Alexai Dmitritch was really not at home, she could wait for him."

On the paper was written in large letters " Mashurina."

" Show her in," Solomin said. " You don't mind my asking her in here, Mariana, do you? She is also one of us."

" Not at all."

A few moments later Mashurina appeared in the doorway, in the same dress in which we saw her at the beginning of the first chapter.

XXXI

" Is Nejdanov not at home? " she asked, then catching
sight of Solomin, came up to him and extended her hand.

" How do you do, Solomin? " She threw a side-glance
at Mariana.

" He will be back directly," Solomin said. " But tell me
how you came to know——"

" Markelov told me. Besides several people in the town
already know that he's here."

" Really? "

" Yes. Somebody must have let it out. Besides Nejdanov
has been recognised."

" For all the dressing up! " Solomin muttered to himself.
" Allow me to introduce you," he said aloud, " Miss Sinitska,
Miss Mashurina! Won't you sit down? "

Mashurina nodded her head slightly and sat down.

" I have a letter for Nejdanov and a message for you,
Solomin."

" What message? And from whom? "

" From some one who is well known to you. . . . Well,
is everything ready here? "

" Nothing whatever."

Mashurina opened her tiny eyes as wide as she could.

" Nothing? "

" Nothing."

" Absolutely nothing? "

" Absolutely nothing."

" Is that what I am to say? "

" Exactly."

Mashurina became thoughtful and pulled a cigarette out
of her pocket.

" Can I have a light? "

" Here is a match."

Mashurina lighted her cigarette.

" They expected something different," she began, " Altogether different from what you have here. However, that is your affair. I am not going to stay long. I only want to see Nejdanov and give him the letter."

" Where are you going to? "

" A long way from here." (She was going to Geneva, but did not want Solomin to know as she did not quite trust him, and besides a stranger was present. Mashurina, who scarcely knew a word of German, was being sent to Geneva to hand over to a person absolutely unknown to her a piece of cardboard with a vine-branch sketched on it and two hundred and seventy-nine roubles.)

" And where is Ostrodumov? Is he with you? "

" No, but he's quite near. Got stuck on the way. He'll be here when he's wanted. Pemien can look after himself. There is no need to worry about him."

" How did you get here? "

" In a cart of course. How else could I have come? Give me another match, please."

Solomin gave her a light.

" Vassily Fedotitch! " A voice called out suddenly from the other side of the door. " Can you come out? "

" Who is it? What do you want? "

" Do come, please," the voice repeated insistently. " Some new workmen have come. They're trying to explain something, and Pavel Egoritch is not there."

Solomin excused himself and went out. Mashurina fixed her gaze on Mariana and stared at her for so long that the latter began to feel uncomfortable.

" Excuse me," Mashurina exclaimed suddenly in her hard abrupt voice, " I am a plain woman and don't know how to put these things. Don't be angry with me. You need not tell me if you don't wish to. Are you the girl who ran away from the Sipiagins? "

" Yes," Mariana replied, a little surprised.

" With Nejdanov?

" Yes."

" Please give me your hand . . . and forgive me. You must be good since he loves you."

Mariana pressed Mashurina's hand.

" Have you known him long? "

" I knew him in St. Petersburg. That was what made me talk to you. Sergai Mihailovitch has also told me——"

" Oh Markelov! Is it long since you've seen him?

" No, not long. But he's gone away now."

" Where to? "

" Where he was ordered."

Mariana sighed.

" Oh, Miss Mashurina, I fear for him."

" In the first place, I'm not miss. You ought to cast off such manners. In the second, you say . . . ' I fear,' and that you must also cast aside. If you do not fear for yourself, you will leave off fearing for others. You must not think of yourself, nor fear for yourself. I dare say it's easy for me to talk like that. I am ugly, whilst you are beautiful. It must be so much harder for you." (Mariana looked down and turned away.) " Sergai Mihailovitch told me. . . . He knew I had a letter for Nejdanov. . . . ' Don't go to the factory,' he said, ' don't take the letter. It will upset everything there. Leave them alone! They are both happy. . . . Don't interfere with them! ' I should be glad not to inter- fere, but what shall I do about the letter? "

" Give it to him by all means," Mariana put in. " How awfully good Sergai Mihailovitch is! Will they kill him, Mashurina . . . or send him to Siberia? "

" Well, what then? Don't people come back from Siberia? And as for losing one's life; it is not all honey alike to everybody. To some it is sweet, to others bitter. His life has not been over-sweet."

Mashurina gave Mariana a fixed searching look.

251

" How beautiful you are! " she exclaimed, " just like a bird! I don't think Alexai is coming. . . . I'll give you the letter. It's no use waiting any longer."

" I will give it him, you may be sure."

Mashurina rested her cheek in her hand and for a long, long time did not speak.

" Tell me," she began, " forgive me for asking . . . do you love him? "

" Yes."

Mashurina shook her heavy head.

" There is no need to ask if he loves you. However, I had better be going, otherwise I shall be late. Tell him that I was here . . . give him my kind regards. Tell him Mashurina was here. You won't forget my name, will you? Mashurina. And the letter . . . but stay, where have I put it? "

Mashurina stood up, turned round as though she were rummaging in her pockets for the letter, and quickly raising a small piece of folded paper to her lips, swallowed it. " Oh, dear me! What have I done with it? Have I lost it? I must have dropped it. Dear me! Supposing some one should find it! I can't find it anywhere. It's turned out exactly as Sergai Mihailovitch wanted after all! "

" Look again," Mariana whispered.

Mashurina waved her hand.

" It's no good. I've lost it."

Mariana came up to her.

" Well, then, kiss me."

Mashurina suddenly put her arms about Mariana and pressed her to her bosom with more than a woman's strength.

" I would not have done this for anybody," she said, a lump rising in her throat, " against my conscience . . . the first time! Tell him to be more careful. . . . And you too. Be cautious. It will soon be very dangerous for everybody here, very dangerous. You had better both go away, whilst there's still time. . . . Good-bye! " she added loudly with some severity. " Just one more thing . . . tell him . . . no, it's not necessary. It's nothing."

Mashurina went out, banging the door behind her, whilst Mariana stood perplexed in the middle of the room.

" What does it all mean? " she exclaimed at last. " This woman loves him more than I do! What did she want to convey by her hints? And why did Solomin disappear so suddenly, and why didn't he come back again? "

She began pacing up and down the room. A curious sensation of fear, annoyance, and amazement took possession of her. Why did she not go with Nejdanov? Solomin had persuaded her not to . . . but where is Solomin? And what is going on around? Of course Mashurina did not give her the letter because of her love for Nejdanov. But how could she decide to disregard orders? Did she want to appear magnanimous? What right had she? And why was *she*, Mariana, so touched by her act? An unattractive woman interests herself in a young man. . . . What is there extraordinary about it? And why should Mashurina assume that Mariana's attachment to Nejdanov is stronger than the feelings of duty? And did Mariana ask for such a sacrifice? And what could the letter have contained? A call for speedy action? Well, and what then?

And Markelov? He is in danger . . . and what are we doing? Markelov spares us both, gives us the opportunity of being happy, does not part us. . . . What makes him do it? Is it also magnaminity . . . or contempt?

And did we run away from that hateful house merely to live like turtle doves?

Thus Mariana pondered, whilst the feeling of agitation and annoyance grew stronger and stronger within her. Her pride was hurt. Why had every one forsaken her? *Every one*. This stout woman had called her a bird, a beauty . . . why not quite plainly a doll? And why did Nejdanov not go alone, but with Pavel? It's just as if he needed some one to look after him! And what are really Solomin's convictions? It's quite clear that he's not a revolutionist! And could any one really think that he does not treat the whole thing seriously?

These were the thoughts that whirled round, chasing one another and becoming entangled in Mariana's feverish brain. Pressing her lips closely together and folding her arms like a man, she sat down by the window at last and remained immovable, straight up in her chair, all alertness and intensity, ready to spring up any moment. She had no desire to go to Tatiana and work; she wanted to wait alone. And she sat waiting obstinately, almost angrily. From time to time her mood seemed strange and incomprehensible even to herself. . . . Never mind. " Am I jealous? " flashed across her mind, but remembering poor Mashurina's figure she shrugged her shoulders and dismissed the idea.

Mariana had been waiting for a long time when suddenly she heard the sound of two persons' footsteps coming up the stairs. She fixed her eyes on the door . . . the steps drew nearer. The door opened and Nejdanov, supported under the arm by Pavel, appeared in the doorway. He was deadly pale, without a cap, his dishevelled hair hung in wet tufts over his forehead, he stared vacantly straight in front of him. Pavel helped him across the room (Nejdanov's legs were weak and shaky) and made him sit down on the couch.

Mariana sprang up from her seat.

" What is the meaning of this? What's the matter with him? Is he ill? "

As he settled Nejdanov, Pavel answered her with a smile, looking at her over his shoulder.

" You needn't worry. He'll soon be all right. It's only because he's not used to it."

" What's the matter? " Mariana persisted.

" He's only a little tipsy. Been drinking on an empty stomach; that's all."

Mariana bent over Nejdanov. He was half lying on the

couch, his head sunk on his breast, his eyes closed. He smelt of vodka; he was quite drunk.

" Alexai! " escaped her lips.

He raised his heavy eye-lids with difficulty and tried to smile.

" Well, Mariana! " he stammered out, " you've always talked of sim-plif-ication . . . so here I am quite simplified. Because the people are always drunk . . . and so . . ."

He ceased, then muttered something indistinctly to himself, closed his eyes, and fell asleep. Pavel stretched him carefully on the couch.

" Don't worry, Mariana Vikentievna," he repeated. " He'll sleep an hour or two and wake up as fresh as can be."

Mariana wanted to ask how this had happened, but her questions would have detained Pavel and she wanted to be alone . . . she did not wish Pavel to see him in this disgusting state before her. She walked away to the window whilst Pavel, who instantly understood her, carefully covered Nejdanov's legs with the skirts of his coat, put a pillow under his head, and observing once again, " It's nothing," went out on tip-toe.

Mariana looked round. Nejdanov's head was buried in the pillow and on his pale face there was an expression of fixed intensity as on the face of one dangerously ill.

" I wonder how it happened? " she thought.

XXXII

It happened like this.

Sitting down beside Pavel in the cart, Nejdanov fell into a state of great excitement. As soon as they rolled out of the court-yard on to the high road leading to T. he began shouting out the most absurd things to the peasants he met on the way. " Why are you asleep? Rouse yourself! The time has come! Down with the taxes! Down with the landlords! "

Some of the peasants stared at him in amazement, others passed on without taking any notice of him, thinking that he was drunk; one even said when he got home that he had met a Frenchman on the way who was jabbering away at something he did not understand. Nejdanov had common sense enough to know that what he was doing was unutterably stupid and absurd had he not got himself up to such a pitch of excitement that he was no longer able to discriminate between sense and nonsense. Pavel tried to quieten him, saying that it was impossible to go on like that; that they were quite near a large village, the first on the borders of T., and that there they could look round. . . . But Nejdanov would not calm down, and at the same time his face bore a sad, almost despairing, expression. Their horse was an energetic, round little thing, with a clipped mane on its scraggy neck. It tugged at the reins, and its strong little legs flew as fast as they could, just as if it were conscious of bearing important people to the scene of action. Just before they reached the village, Nejdanov saw a group of about eight peasants standing by the side of the road at the closed doors of a granary. He instantly jumped out of the cart, rushed up to them, and began shouting at them, thumping

his fists and gesticulating for about five minutes. The words
" For Freedom! March on! Put the shoulder to the
wheel!" could be distinguished from among the rest of his
confused words.

The peasants, who had met before the granary for the
purpose of discussing how to fill it once more—if only to show
that they were doing something (it was the communal
granary and consequently empty)—fixed their eyes on Nejdanov and seemed to listen to him with the greatest attention, but they had evidently not understood a word he had
said, for no sooner was his back turned, shouting for the
last time " Freedom! " as he rushed away, when one of them,
the most sagacious of the lot, shook his head saying, " What
a severe one! " " He must be an officer," another remarked,
to which the wise one said: " We know all about that—he
doesn't talk for nothing. We'll have to pay the piper."

" Heavens! what nonsense this all is! " Nejdanov thought
to himself, as he sat down next to Pavel in the cart. " But
then none of us know how to get at the people—perhaps
this is the right way after all! Who knows? Go on! Does
your heart ache? Let it! "

They found themselves in the main street of the village
in the middle of which a number of people were gathered
together before a tavern. Nejdanov, paying no heed to Pavel,
who was trying to hold him back, leapt down from the cart
with a cry of " Brothers! " The crowd made way for him
and he again began preaching, looking neither to right nor
left, as if furious and weeping at the same time. But things
turned out quite differently than with his former attempt
at the barn. An enormous fellow with a clean-shaven,
vicious face, in a short greasy coat, high boots, and a sheep-
skin cap, came up to him and clapped him on the shoulder.

" All right! my fine fellow! " he bawled out in a wheezy
voice; " but wait a bit! good deeds must be rewarded. Come
along in here. It'll be much better talking in there." He
pulled Nejdanov into the tavern, the others streamed in

after them. "Michaitch!" the fellow shouted, "twopenny-
worth! My favourite drink! I want to treat a friend. Who
he is, what's his family, and where he's from, only the devil
knows! Drink!" he said, turning to Nejdanov and handing
him a heavy, full glass, wet all over on the outside, as though
perspiring, "drink, if you really have any feeling for us!"
"Drink!" came a chorus of voices. Nejdanov, who seemed
as if in a fever, seized the glass and with a cry of "I drink
to you, children!" drank it off at a gulp. Ugh! He drank
it off with the same desperate heroism with which he would
have flung himself in storming a battery or on a line of
bayonets. But what was happening to him? Something
seemed to have struck his spine, his legs, burnt his throat,
his chest, his stomach, made the tears come into his eyes.
A shudder of disgust passed all over him. He began shouting
at the top of his voice to drown the throbbing in his head.
The dark tavern room suddenly became hot and thick and
suffocating—and people, people everywhere! Nejdanov
began talking, talking incessantly, shouting furiously, in
exasperation, shaking broad rough hands, kissing prickly
beards. . . . The enormous fellow in the greasy coat kissed
him too, nearly breaking his ribs. This fellow turned out
to be a perfect fiend. "I'll wring the neck," he shouted, "I'll
wring the neck of any one who dares to offend our brother!
And what's more, I'll make mincemeat of him too . . .
I'll make him cry out! That's nothing to me. I was a
butcher and know how to do such jobs!" At this he held
up an enormous fist covered with freckles. Some one again
shouted, "Drink!" and Nejdanov again swallowed a glass
of the filthy poison. But this second time was truly awful!
Blunt hooks seemed to be tearing him to pieces inside. His
head was in a whirl, green circles swam before his eyes. A
hubbub arouse . . . O horror! a third glass. Was it
possible he emptied that too? He seemed to be surrounded
by purple noses, dusty heads of hair, tanned necks covered
with nets of wrinkles. Rough hands seized him. "Go on!"
they bawled out in angry voices, "talk away! The day

258

814.

before yesterday another stranger talked like that. Go on
. . ." The earth seemed reeling under Nejdanov's feet, his
voice sounded strange to his own ears as though coming from
a long way off. . . . Was it death or what?

And suddenly he felt the fresh air blowing about his face,
no more pushing and shoving, no more stench of spirits,
sheep-skin, tar, nor leather. . . . He was again sitting
beside Pavel in the cart, struggling at first and shouting,
"Where are you off to? Stop! I haven't had time to tell
them anything—I must explain . . ." and then added,
"and what are your own ideas on the subject, you sly-
boots?"

"It would certainly be well if there were no gentry and the
land belonged to us, of course," Pavel replied, "but there's
been no such order from the government." He quietly
turned the horse's head and, suddenly lashing it on the back
with the reins, set off at full gallop, away from this din and
uproar, back to the factory.

Nejdanov sat dozing, rocked by the motion of the cart,
whilst the wind played pleasantly about his face and kept
back gloomy depressing thoughts.

He was annoyed that he had not been allowed to say all
that he had wanted to say. . . . Again the wind caressed
his overheated face.

And then—a momentary glimpse of Mariana—a burning
sense of shame—and sleep, deep, sound sleep. . . .

Pavel told Solomin all this afterwards, not hiding the fact
that he did not attempt to prevent Nejdanov from drinking
—otherwise he could not have got him out of the whirl. The
others would not have let him go.

"When he seemed to be getting very feeble, I asked them
to let him off, and they agreed to, on condition that I gave
them a shilling, so I gave it them."

"You acted quite rightly," Solomin said, approvingly.

Nejdanov slept, whilst Mariana sat at the window looking
out into the garden. Strange to say the angry, almost
wicked, thoughts that had been tormenting her until Najdenov

and Pavel arrived had completely disappeared. Nejdanov himself was not in the least repulsive or disgusting to her; she was only sorry for him. She knew quite well that he was not a debauchee, a drunkard, and was wondering what she would say to him when he woke up; something friendly and affectionate to minimise the first sting of conscience and shame. "I must try and get him to tell me himself how it all happened," she thought.

She was not disturbed, but depressed—hopelessly depressed. It seemed as if a breath of the real atmosphere of the world towards which she was striving had blown on her suddenly, making her shudder at its coarseness and darkness. What Moloch was this to which she was going to sacrifice herself?

But no! It could not be! This was merely an incident, it would soon pass over. A momentary impression that had struck her so forcibly because it had happened so unexpectedly. She got up, walked over to the couch on which Nejdanov was lying, took out her pocket-handkerchief and wiped his pale forehead, which was painfully drawn, even in sleep, and smoothed back his hair. . . .

She pitied him as a mother pities her suffering child. But it was somewhat painful for her to look at him, so she went quietly into her own room, leaving the door unlocked.

She did not attempt to take any work in her hand. She sat down and thoughts began crowding in upon her. She felt how the time was slipping away, how one minute flew after another, and the sensation was even pleasant to her. Her heart beat fast and again she seemed to be waiting for something.

What has become of Solomin?

The door creaked softly and Tatiana came into the room.

"What do you want?" Mariana asked with a shade of annoyance.

"Mariana Vikentievna," Tatiana began in an undertone, "don't worry, my dear. Such things happen every day. Besides, the Lord be thanked——"

"I am not worrying at all, Tatiana Osipovna," Mariana

interrupted her. "Alexai Dmitritch is a little indisposed, nothing very serious!"

"That's all right! I wondered why you didn't come, and thought there might be something the matter with you. But still I wouldn't have come in to you. It's always best not to interfere. But some one has come— a little lame man, the Lord knows who he is—and demands to see Alexai Dmitritch! I wonder what for? This morning that female came for him and now this little cripple. 'If Alexai Dmitritch is not at home,' he says, 'then I must see Vassily Fedotitch! I won't go away without seeing him. It's on a very urgent matter.' We wanted to get rid of him, as we did of that woman, told him Vassily Fedotitch was not at home, but he is determined to see him even if he has to wait until midnight. There he is walking about in the yard. Come and have a look at him through the little window in the corridor. Perhaps you'll recognise him."

Mariana followed Tatiana out into the corridor, and on passing Nejdanov was again struck by that painful frown on his forehead and passed her pocket-handkerchief over it a second time.

Through the dusty little window she caught a glimpse of the visitor whom Tatiana had spoken of. He was unknown to her. At this moment Solomin appeared from a corner of the house.

The little cripple rushed up to him and extended his hand. Solomin pressed it. He was obviously acquainted with him. They both disappeared. . . . Soon their footsteps were heard coming up the stairs. They were coming to see her. . . .

Mariana fled into her own room and remained standing in the middle of it, hardly able to breathe. She was mortally afraid . . . but of what? She did not know herself.

Solomin's head appeared through the door.

"Mariana Vikentievna, can I come in? I have brought some one whom it's absolutely necessary for you to see."

Mariana merely nodded her head in reply and behind Solomin in walked—Paklin.

XXXIII

" I am a friend of your husband's," he said, bowing very low, as if anxious to conceal his frightened face, " and also of Vassily Fedotitch. I hear Alexai Dmitritch is asleep and not very well. Unfortunately, I have brought bad news. I have already told Vassily Fedotitch something about it and am afraid decisive measures will have to be taken.

Paklin's voice broke continually, like that of a man who was tortured by thirst. The items of news he had to com- municate were certainly very unpleasant ones. Some peasants had seized Markelov and brought him to the town. The stupid clerk had betrayed Golushkin, who was now under arrest. He in his turn was betraying everything and everybody, wanted to go over to the Orthodox Church, had offered to present a portrait of the Bishop Filaret to the public school, and had already given five thousand roubles to be distributed among crippled soldiers. There was not a shadow of a doubt that he had informed against Nejdanov; the police might make a raid upon the factory any moment. Vassily Fedotitch was also in danger. " As for myself," Paklin added, " I am surprised that I'm still allowed to roam at large, although it's true that I've never really interested myself in practical politics or taken part in any schemes. I have taken advantage of this oversight on the part of the police to put you on your guard and find out what had best be done to avoid any unpleasantness."

Mariana listened to Paklin to the end. She did not seem alarmed; on the other hand she was quite calm. But some- thing must really be done! She fixed her eyes on Solomin.

He was also composed; only around his lips there was the faintest movement of the muscles; but it was not his habitual smile.

Solomin understood the meaning of Mariana's glance; she waited for him to say what had best be done.

" It's a very awkward business," he began; " I don't think it would do Nejdanov any harm to go into hiding for a time. But, by the way, how did you get to know that he was here, Mr. Paklin? "

Paklin gave a wave of the hand.

" A certain individual told me. He had seen him preaching about the neighbourhood and had followed him, though with no evil intent. He is a sympathiser. Excuse me," he added, turning to Mariana, " is it true that our friend Nejdanov has been very . . . very careless? "

" It's no good blaming him now," Solomin began again. " What a pity we can't talk things over with him now, but by to-morrow he will be all right again. The police don't do things as quickly as you seem to imagine. You will have to go away with him, Mariana Vikentievna."

" Certainly," she said resolutely, a lump rising in her throat.

" Yes," Solomin said, " we must think it over, consider ways and means."

" May I make a suggestion? " Paklin began. " It entered my head as I was coming along here. I must tell you, by the way, that I dismissed the cabman from the town a mile away from here."

" What is your suggestion? " Solomin asked.

" Let me have some horses at once and I'll gallop off to the Sipiagins."

" To the Sipiagins! " Mariana exclaimed. " Why? "

" You will see."

" But do you know them? "

" Not at all! But listen. Do think over my suggestion thoroughly. It seems to me a brilliant one. Markelov is Sipiagin's brother-in-law, his wife's brother, isn't that so? Would this gentleman really make no attempt to save him? And as for Nejdanov himself, granting that Mr. Sipiagin is most awfully angry with him, still he has become a relation of his by marrying you. And the danger hanging over our friend——"

" I am not married," Mariana observed.

Paklin started.

" What? Haven't managed it all this time! Well, never mind," he added, " one can pretend a little. All the same, you will get married directly. There seems nothing else to be done! Take into consideration the fact that up till now Sipiagin has not persecuted you, which shows him to be a man capable of a certain amount of generosity. I see that you don't like the expression—well, a certain amount of pride. Why should we not take advantage of it? Consider for yourself! "

Mariana raised her head and passed her hand through her hair.

" You can take advantage of whatever you like for Markelov, Mr. Paklin . . . or for yourself, but Alexai and I do not desire the protection or patronage of Mr. Sipiagin. We did not leave his house only to go knocking at his door as beggars. The pride and generosity of Mr. Sipiagin and his wife have nothing whatever to do with us! "

" Such sentiments are extremely praiseworthy," Paklin replied (" How utterly crushed! " he thought to himself), " though, on the other hand, if you think of it. . . . However, I am ready to obey you. I will exert myself only on Markelov's account, our good Markelov! I must say, however, that he is not his blood relation, but only related to him through his wife—whilst you——"

" Mr Paklin, I beg of you! "

" I'm sorry. . . . Only I can't tell you how disappointing it is—Sipiagin is a very influential man."

" Have you no fears for yourself? " Solomin asked.

Paklin drew himself up.

" There are moments when one must not think of oneself! " he said proudly. And he was thinking of himself all

264

the while. Poor little man! he wanted to run away as fast as he could. On the strength of the service rendered him, Sipiagin might, if need be, speak a word in his favour. For he too—say what he would—was implicated, he had listened and had chattered a little himself.

" I don't think your suggestion is a bad one," Solomin observed at last, " although there is not much hope of success. At any rate there is no harm in trying."

" Of course not. Supposing they pitch me out by the scruff of the neck, what harm will it do? "

" That won't matter very much " (" *Merci*," Paklin thought to himself). " What is the time? " Solomin asked. " Five o'clock. We mustn't dawdle. You shall have the horses directly. Pavel! "

But instead of Pavel, Nejdanov appeared in the doorway. He staggered and steadied himself on the doorpost. He opened his mouth feebly, looked round with his glassy eyes, comprehending nothing. Paklin was the first to approach him.

" Aliosha! " he exclaimed, " don't you know me? "

Nejdanov stared at him, blinking slowly.

" Paklin? " he said at last.

" Yes, it is I. Aren't you well? "

" No . . . I'm not well. But why are you here? "

" Why? " . . . But at this moment Mariana stealthily touched Paklin on the elbow. He turned round and saw that she was making signs to him. " Oh, yes! " he muttered. " Yes. . . . You see, Aliosha," he added aloud, " I've come here upon a very important matter and must go away at once. Solomin will tell you all about it—and Mariana—Mariana Vikentievna. They both fully approve of what I am going to do. The thing concerns us all. No, no," he put in hastily in response to a look and gesture from Mariana. " The thing concerns Markelov; our mutual friend Markelov; it concerns him alone. But I must say good-bye now. Every minute is precious. Good-bye, Aliosha. . . . We'll see each

265

other again some time. Vassily Fedotitch, can you come with me to see about the horses? "

" Certainly. Mariana, I wanted to ask you to be firm, but that is not necessary. You're a brick! "

" Yes, yes," Paklin chimed in, " you are just like a Roman maiden in Cato's time! Cato of Utica! We must be off, Vassily Fedotitch, come along! "

" There's plenty of time," Solomin observed with a faint smile. Nejdanov stood on one side to allow them room to pass out, but there was the same vacant expression in his eyes. After they had gone he took a step or two forward and sat down on a chair facing Mariana.

" Alexai," she began, " everything has been found out. Markelov has been seized by the very peasants he was trying to better, and is now under arrest in this town, and so is the merchant with whom you dined once. I dare say the police will soon be here for us too. Paklin has gone to Sipiagin."

" Why? " Nejdanov asked in a scarcely audible whisper. But there was a keen look in his eyes—his face assumed it's habitual expression. The stupor had left him instantly.

" To try and find out if he would be willing to intercede."

Nejdanov sat up straight.

" For us? "

" No, for Markelov. He wanted to ask him to intercede for us too . . . but I wouldn't let him. Have I done well, Alexai? "

" Have you done well? " Nejdanov asked and without rising from his chair, stretched out his arms to her. " Have you done well? " he repeated, drawing her close to him, and pressing his face against her waist, suddenly burst into tears.

" What is the matter? What is the matter with you? " Mariana exclaimed. And as on the day when he had fallen on his knees before her, trembling and breathless in a torrent of passion, she laid both her hands on his trembling head. But what she felt now was quite different from what she had felt then. Then she had given herself up to him—had submitted

266

to him and only waited to hear what he would say next, but now she pitied him and only wondered what she could do to calm him.

" What is the matter with you? " she repeated. " Why are you crying? Not because you came home in a somewhat . . . strange condition? It can't be! Or are you sorry for Markelov—afraid for me, for yourself? Or is it for our lost hopes? You did not really expect that everything would go off smoothly! "

Nejdanov suddenly lifted his head.

" It's not that, Mariana," he said, mastering his sobs by an effort, " I am not afraid for either of us . . . but . . . I am sorry——"

" For whom? "

" For you, Mariana! I am sorry that you should have united your fate with a man who is not worthy of you."

" Why not? "

" If only because he can be crying at a moment as this! "

" It is not you but your nerves that are crying! "

" You can't separate me from my nerves! But listen, Mariana, look me in the face; can you tell me now that you do not regret——"

" What? "

" That you ran away with me."

" No! "

" And would you go with me further? Anywhere? "

" Yes! "

" Really? Mariana . . . really? "

" Yes. I have given you my word, and so long as you remain the man I love—I shall not take it back."

Nejdanov remained sitting on the chair, Mariana standing before him. His arms were about her waist, her's were resting on his shoulders.

" Yes, no," Nejdanov thought . . . " when I last held her in my arms like this, her body was at least motionless, but now I can feel it—against her will, perhaps—shrink away from me gently! "

He loosened his arms and Mariana did in fact move away from him a little.

" If that's so," he said aloud, " if we must run away from here before the police find us . . . I think it wouldn't be a bad thing if we were to get married. We may not find another such accommodating priest as Father Zosim! "

" I am quite ready," Mariana observed.

Nejdanov gave her a searching glance.

" A Roman maiden! " he exclaimed with a sarcastic half-smile. " What a feeling of duty! "

Mariana shrugged her shoulders.

" We must tell Solomin."

" Yes . . . Solomin . . ." Nejdanov drawled out. " But he is also in danger. The police would arrest him too. It seems to me that he also took part in things and knew even more than we did."

" I don't know about that," Mariana observed. " He never speaks of himself! "

" Not as I do! " Nejdanov thought. " That was what she meant to imply. Solomin . . . Solomin! " he added after a pause. "Do you know, Mariana, I should not be at all sorry if you had linked your fate for ever with a man like Solomin . . . or with Solomin himself."

Mariana gave Nejdanov a penetrating glance in her turn. " You had no right to say that," she observed at last.

" I had no right! In what sense am I to take that? Does it mean that you love me, or that I ought not to touch upon this question generally speaking? "

" You had no right," Mariana repeated.

Nejdanov lowered his head.

" Mariana! " he exclaimed in a slightly different tone of voice.

" Yes? "

" If I were to ask you now . . . now . . . you know what.

268

. . . But no, I will not ask anything of you . . . good-bye."

He got up and went out; Mariana did not detain him.

Nejdanov sat down on the couch and covered his face with his hands. He was afraid of his own thoughts and tried to stop thinking. He felt that some sort of dark, underground hand had clutched at the very root of his being and would not let him go. He knew that the dear, sweet creature he had left in the next room would not come out to him and he dared not go to her. What for? What would he say to her?

Firm, rapid footsteps made him open his eyes. Solomin passed through his room, knocked at Mariana's door, and went in.

" Honour where honour is due! " Nejdanov whispered bitterly.

269

XXXIV

It was already ten o'clock in the evening; in the drawing-room of the Arjanov house Sipiagin, his wife, and Kollomiet-zev were sitting over a game at cards when a footman entered and announced that an unknown gentleman, a certain Mr. Paklin, wished to see Boris Andraevitch upon a very urgent business.

"So late!" Valentina Mihailovna exclaimed, surprised.

"What?" Boris Andraevitch asked, screwing up his hand-some nose; "what did you say the gentleman's name was?"

"Mr. Paklin, sir."

"Paklin!" Kollomietzev exclaimed; "a real country name. Paklin . . . Solomin . . . *De vrais noms ruraux, hein?*"

"Did you say," Boris Andraevitch continued, still turned towards the footman with his nose screwed up, "that the business was an urgent one?"

"The gentleman said so, sir."

"H'm. . . . No doubt some beggar or intriguer."

"Or both," Kollomietzev chimed in.

"Very likely. Ask him into my study." Boris Andrae-vitch got up. "*Pardon, ma bonne.* Have a game of écarté till I come back, unless you would like to wait for me. I won't be long."

"*Nous causerons.* . . . *Allez!*" Kollomietzev said.

When Sipiagin entered his study and caught sight of Paklin's poor, feeble little figure meekly leaning up against the door between the wall and the fireplace, he was seized by that truly ministerial sensation of haughty compassion and fastidious condescension so characteristic of the St. Peters-burg bureaucrat. "Heavens! What a miserable little wretch!" he thought; "and lame too, I believe!"

270

"Sit down, please," he said aloud, making use of some of his most benevolent baritone notes and throwing back his head, sat down before his guest did. "You are no doubt tired from the journey. Sit down, please, and tell me about this important matter that has brought you so late."

"Your excellency," Paklin began, cautiously dropping into an arm-chair, "I have taken the liberty of coming to you——"

"Just a minute, please," Sipiagin interrupted him, "I think I've seen you before. I never forget faces. But er . . . er . . . really . . . where have I seen you?"

"You are not mistaken, your excellency. I had the honour of meeting you in St. Petersburg at a certain person's who . . . who has since . . . unfortunately . . . incurred your displeasure——"

Sipiagin jumped up from his chair.

"Why, at Mr. Nejdanov's? I remember now. You haven't come from him by the way, have you?"

"Not at all, your excellency; on the contrary . . . I——"

Sipiagin sat down again.

"That's good. For had you come on his account I should have asked you to leave the house at once. I cannot allow any mediator between myself and Mr. Nejdanov. Mr. Nejdanov has insulted me in a way which cannot be forgotten. . . . I am above any feelings of revenge, but I don't wish to know anything of him, nor of the girl—more depraved in mind than in heart" (Sipiagin had repeated this phrase at least thirty times since Mariana ran away), "who could bring herself to abandon a home that had sheltered her to become the mistress of a nameless adventurer! It is enough for them that I am content to forget them."

At this last word Sipiagin waved his wrist into space.

"I forget them, my dear sir!"

"Your excellency, I have already told you that I did not come from them in particular, but I may inform your excellency that they are legally married. . . ." (" It's all the same," Paklin thought; " I said that I would lie and so here I am. Never mind! ")

Sipiagin moved his head from left to right on the back of his chair.

" It does not interest me in the least, sir. It only makes one foolish marriage the more in the world—that's all. But what is this urgent matter to which I am indebted for the pleasure of your visit? "

" Ugh! you cursed director of a department! " Paklin thought, " I'll soon make you pull a different face! Your wife's brother," he said aloud, " Mr. Markelov, has been seized by the peasants whom he had been inciting to rebellion and is now under arrest in the governor's house."

Sipiagin jumped up a second time.

" What . . . what did you say? " he blurted out, not at all in his accustomed ministerial baritones, but in an extremely undignified manner.

" I said that your brother-in-law has been seized and is in chains. As soon as I heard of it, I procured horses and came straight away to tell you. I thought that I might be rendering a service to you and to the unfortunate man whom you may be able to save! "

" I am extremely grateful to you," Sipiagin said in the same feeble tone of voice, and violently pressing a bell, shaped like a mushroom, he filled the whole house with its clear metallic ring. " I am extremely grateful to you," he repeated more sharply, " but I must tell you that a man who can bring himself to trample under foot all laws, human and divine, were he a hundred times related to me—is in my eyes not unfortunate; he is a criminal! "

A footman came in quickly.

" Your orders, sir? "

" The carriage! the carriage and four horses this minute! I am going to town. Philip and Stepan are to come with me! " The footman disappeared   " Yes, sir, my brother-in-

272

law is a criminal! I am going to town not to save him! Oh, no!"

" But, your excellency——"

" Such are my principles, my dear sir, and I beg you not to annoy me by your objections!"

Sipiagin began pacing up and down the room, whilst Paklin stared with all his might. " Ugh! you devil!" he thought, " I heard that you were a liberal, but you're just like a hungry lion!"

The door was flung open and Valentina Mihailovna came into the room with hurried steps, followed by Kollòmietzev.

" What is the matter, Boris? Why have you ordered the carriage? Are you going to town? What has happened? "

Sipiagin went up to his wife and took her by the arm, between the elbow and wrist. " *Il faut vous armer de courage, ma chère.* Your brother has been arrested."

" My brother? Sergai? What for? "

He has been preaching socialism to the peasants." (Kollomietzev gave a faint little scream.) " Yes! preaching revolutionary ideas, making propaganda! They seized him— and gave him up. He is now under arrest in the town."

" Madman! But who told you? "

" This Mr. . . . Mr. . . . what's his name? Mr. Konopatin brought the news."

Valentina Mihailovna glanced at Paklin; the latter bowed dejectedly. (" What a glorious woman!" he thought. Even in such difficult moments . . . alas! how susceptible Paklin was to feminine beauty!)

" And you want to go to town at this hour? "

" I think the governor will still be up."

" I always said it would end like this," Kollomietzev put in. " It couldn't have been otherwise! But what dears our peasants are really! *Pardon, madame, c'est votre frère ! Mais la vérité avant tout !* "

" Do you really intend going to town, Boria? " Valentina Mihailovna asked.

" I feel absolutely certain," Kollomietzev continued, " that that *tutor*, Mr. Nejdanov, is mixed up in this. *J'en mettrais ma main au feu.* It's all one gang! Haven't they seized him? Don't you know? "

Sipiagin waved his wrist again.

" I don't know—and don't want to know! By the way," he added, turning to his wife, " *il paraît qu'il sont mariés.*"

" Who said so? That same gentleman? " Valentina Mihailovna looked at Paklin again, this time with half-closed eyes.

" Yes."

" In that case," Kollomietzev put in, " he must know where they are. Do you know where they are? Do you know? Eh? Do you know? "

Kollomietzev took to walking up and down in front of Paklin as if to cut off his way, although the latter had not betrayed the slightest inclination of wanting to run away. " Why don't you speak? Answer me! Do you know, eh? Do you know? "

" Even if I knew," Paklin began, annoyed; his wrath had risen up in him at last and his eyes flashed fire: " even if I knew I would not tell you."

" Oh . . . oh . . ." Kollomietzev muttered. " Do you hear? Do you hear? This one too—this one too is of their gang! "

" The carriage is ready! " a footman announced loudly.

Sipiagin with a quick graceful movement seized his hat, but Valentina Mihailovna was so insistent in her persuasions for him to put off the journey until the morning and brought so many convincing arguments to bear—such as: that it was pitch dark outside, that everybody in town would be asleep, that he would only upset his nerves and might catch cold—that Sipiagin at length came to agree with her.

" I obey! " he exclaimed, and with the same graceful gesture, not so rapid this time, replaced his hat on the table.

" I shall not want the carriage now," he said to the footman,

" but see that it's ready at six o'clock in the morning! Do
you hear? You can go now! But stay! See that the
gentleman's carriage is sent off and the driver paid! What?
Did you say anything, Mr. Konopatin? I am going to take
you to town with me to-morrow, Mr. Konopatin! What
did you say? I can't hear. . . . Do you take vodka?
Give Mr. Konopatin some vodka! No? You don't drink?
In that case . . . Feodor! take the gentleman into the
green room! Good-night, Mr. Kono——"

Paklin lost all patience.

" Paklin! " he shouted, " my name is Paklin! "

" Oh, yes . . . it makes no difference. A bit alike, you
know. What a powerful voice you have for your spare
build! Till to-morrow, Mr. Paklin. . . . Have I got it
right this time? *Siméon, vous viendrez avec nous ?* "

" *Je crois bien !* "

Paklin was conducted into the green room and locked in.
He distinctly heard the key turned in the English lock as he
got into bed. He scolded himself severely for his " brilliant
idea " and slept very badly.

He was awakened early the next morning at half-past five
and given coffee. As he drank it a footman with striped
shoulder-knots stood over him with the tray in his hand,
shifting from one leg to the other as though he were saying,
" Hurry up! the gentlemen are waiting! " He was taken
downstairs. The carriage was already waiting at the door.
Kollomietzev's open carriage was also there. Sipiagin
appeared on the steps in a cloak made of camel's hair with
a round collar. Such cloaks had long ago ceased to be worn
except by a certain important dignitary whom Sipiagin
pandered to and wished to imitate. On important official
occasions he invariably put on this cloak.

Sipiagin greeted Paklin affably, and with an energetic
movement of the hand pointed to the carriage and asked him
to take his seat. " Mr. Paklin, you are coming with me,
Mr. Paklin! Put your bag on the box, Mr. Paklin! I am

taking Mr. Paklin," he said, emphasising the word " Paklin "
with special stress on the letter *a*. "You have an awful name
like that and get insulted when people change it for you—so
here you are then! Take your fill of it! Mr. Paklin!
Paklin!" The unfortunate name rang out clearly in the
cool morning air. It was so keen as to make Kollomietzev,
who came out after Sipiagin, exclaim several times in French:
" Brrr! brrr! brrr!" He wrapped his cloak more closely
about him and seated himself in his elegant carriage with the
hood thrown back. (Had his poor friend Michael Obrenovitch, the Servian prince, seen it, he would certainly have
bought one like it at Binder's. . . . " *Vous savez Binder,
le grand carrossier des Champs Elysées ?* ")

Valentina Mihailovna, still in her night garments, peeped
out from behind the half-open shutters of her bedroom.
Sipiagin waved his hand to her from the carriage.

" Are you quite comfortable, Mr. Paklin? Go on!"

" *Je vous recommande mon frère, épargnez-le !*" Valentina
Mihailovna said.

" *Soyez tranquille !*" Kollomietzev exclaimed, glancing up
at her quickly from under the brim of his travelling cap—
one of his own special design with a cockade in it—" *C'est
surtout l'autre, qu'il faut pincer !*"

" Go on!" Sipiagin exclaimed again. "You are not cold,
Mr. Paklin? Go on!"

The two carriages rolled away.

For about ten minutes neither Sipiagin nor Paklin pronounced a single word. The unfortunate Sila, in his shabby
little coat and crumpled cap, looked even more wretched
than usual in contrast to the rich background of dark blue
silk with which the carriage was upholstered. He looked
round in silence at the delicate pale blue blinds, which flew
up instantly at the mere press of a button, at the soft white
sheep-skin rug at their feet, at the mahogany box in front
with a movable desk for letters and even a shelf for books.
(Boris Andraevitch never worked in his carriage, but he liked

people to think that he did, after the manner of Thiers, who always worked when travelling.) Paklin felt shy. Sipiagin glanced at him once or twice over his clean-shaven cheek, and with a pompous deliberation pulled out of a side-pocket a silver cigar-case with a curly monogram and a Slavonic band and offered him . . . really offered him a cigar, holding it gently between the second and third fingers of a hand neatly clad in an English glove of yellow dogskin.

" I don't smoke," Paklin muttered.

" Really! " Sipiagin exclaimed and lighted the cigar himself, an excellent regalia.

" I must tell you . . . my dear Mr. Paklin," he began, puffing gracefully at his cigar and sending out delicate rings of delicious smoke, " that I am . . . really . . . very grateful to you. I might have . . . seemed . . . a little severe . . . last night . . . which does not really . . . do justice to my character . . . believe me." (Sipiagin purposely hesitated over his speech.) " But just put yourself in my place, Mr. Paklin! " (Sipiagin rolled the cigar from one corner of his mouth to the other.) " The position I occupy places me . . . so to speak . . . before the public eye, and suddenly, without any warning . . . my wife's brother . . . compromises himself . . . and me, in this impossible way! Well, Mr. Paklin? But perhaps you think that it's nothing?"

" I am far from thinking that, your excellency."

" You don't happen to know exactly why . . . and where he was arrested? "

" I heard that he was arrested in T. district."

" Who told you so? "

" A certain person."

" Of course it could hardly have been a bird. But who was this person? "

" An assistant . . . of the director of the governor's office——"

" What's his name? "

" The director's? "

" No, the assistant's."

" His name is . . . Ulyashevitch. He is a very honest man, your excellency. As soon as I heard of the affair, I hastened to tell you."

" Yes, yes. I am very grateful to you indeed. But what utter madness! downright madness! Don't you think so, Mr. Paklin? "

" Utter madness! " Paklin exclaimed, while the perspiration rolled down his back in a hot stream. " It just shows," he continued, " the folly of not understanding the peasant. Mr. Markelov, so far as I know him, has a very kind and generous heart, but he has no conception of what the Russian peasant is really like." (Paklin glanced at Sipiagin who sat slightly turned towards him, gazing at him with a cold, though not unfriendly, light in his eyes.) " The Russian peasant can never be induced to revolt except by taking advantage of that devotion of his to some high authority, some tsar. Some sort of legend must be invented—you remember Dmitrius the pretender—some sort of royal sign must be shown him, branded on the breast."

" Just like Pugatchev," Sipiagin interrupted him in a tone of voice which seemed to imply that he had not yet forgotten his history and that it was really not necessary for Paklin to go on. " What madness! what madness! " he added, and became wrapped in the contemplation of the rings of smoke as they rose quickly one after another from the end of his cigar.

" Your excellency," Paklin began apologetically, " I have just said that I didn't smoke . . . but it was not true. I do smoke and your cigar smells so nice——"

" Eh? What? " Sigiapin asked as if waking up; and without giving Paklin time to repeat his request, he proved in the most unmistakable manner that he had heard every word, and had merely asked his questions for the sake of dignity, by offering him his cigar-case.

Paklin took a cigar gratefully and lighted it with care.

"Here's a good opportunity," he thought, but Sipiagin had anticipated him.

"I remember your saying . . ." he began carelessly, stopping to look at his cigar and pulling his hat lower over his forehead, "you spoke . . . of . . . of that friend of yours, who married my . . . niece. Do you ever see them? They've settled not far from here, eh?"

("Take care! be on your guard, Sila!" Paklin thought.)

"I have only seen them once, your excellency. They are living . . . certainly . . . not very far from here."

"You quite understand, I hope," Sipiagin continued in the same tone, "that I can take no further serious interest—as I explained to you—either in that frivolous girl or in your friend. Heaven knows that I have no prejudices, but really, you will agree with me, this is too much! So foolish, you know. However, I suppose they were more drawn together by politics . . ." ("politics!" he repeated, shrugging his shoulders) "than by any other feeling!"

"I think so too, your excellency!"

"Yes, Mr. Nejdanov was certainly revolutionary. To do him justice he made no secret of his opinions."

"Nejdanov," Paklin ventured, "may have been carried away, but his heart——"

"Is good," Sipiagin put in; "I know, like Markelov's. They all have good hearts. He has no doubt also been mixed up in this affair . . . and will be implicated. . . . I suppose I shall have to intercede for him too!"

Paklin clasped his hands to his breast.

"Oh, your excellency! Extend your protection to him! He fully . . . deserves . . . your sympathy."

Sipiagin snorted.

"You think so?"

"At any rate if not for him . . . for your niece's sake; for his wife!" ("Heavens! What lies I'm telling," Paklin thought.)

Sipiagin half-closed his eyes.

279

" I see that you're a very devoted friend. That's a very good quality, very praiseworthy, young man. And so you said they lived in this neighbourhood? "

" Yes, your excellency; in a large establishment——" Here Paklin bit his tongue.

" Why, of course, at Solomin's! that's where they are! However, I knew it all along. I've been told so, I've already been informed." (Mr. Sipiagin did not know this in the least, and no one had told him, but recollecting Solomin's visit and their midnight interview, he promptly threw out this bait, which caught Paklin at once.)

" Since you know that," he began and bit his tongue a second time. . . . But it was already too late. A single glance at Sipiagin made him realise that he had been playing with him as a cat plays with a mouse.

" I must say, your excellency," the unfortunate Paklin stammered out; " I must say, that I really know nothing——"

" But I ask you no questions! Really! What do you take me and yourself for? " Sipiagin asked haughtily, and promptly withdrew into his ministerial heights.

And Paklin again felt himself a mean little ensnared creature. Until that moment he had kept the cigar in the corner of his mouth away from Sipiagin and puffed at it quietly, blowing the smoke to one side; now he took it out of his mouth and ceased smoking altogether.

" My God! " he groaned inwardly, whilst the perspiration streamed down his back more and more, " what have I done? I have betrayed everything and everybody. . . . I have been duped, been bought over by a good cigar! ! I am a traitor! What shall I do now to help matters? O God! "

But there was nothing to be done. Sipiagin dozed off in a haughty, dignified, ministerial manner, enveloped in his stately cloak.

XXXV

THE governor of S. was one of those good-natured, happy-go-lucky, worldly generals who, endowed with wonderfully clean, snow-white bodies and souls to match, of good breeding and education, are turned out of a mill where they are never ground down to becoming the "shepherds of the people." Nevertheless they prove themselves capable of a tolerable amount of administrative ability; do little work, but are for ever sighing after St. Petersburg and paying court to all the pretty women of the place. These are men who in some unaccountable way become useful to their province and manage to leave pleasant memories behind them. The governor had only just got out of bed, and was comfortably seated before his dressing-table in his night-shirt and silk dressing-gown, bathing his face and neck with eau-de-cologne after having removed a whole collection of charms and coins dangling from it, when he was informed of the arrival of Sipiagin and Kollomietzev upon some urgent business. He was very familiar with Sipiagin, having known him from childhood and constantly run across him in St. Petersburg drawing-rooms, and lately he had begun to ejaculate a respectful " Ah! " every time his name occurred to him— as if he saw in him a future statesman. Kollomietzev he did not know so well and respected less in consequence of various unpleasant complaints that had been made against him; however, he looked upon him as a man *qui fera chemin* in any case.

He ordered his guests to be shown into his study, where he soon joined them, as he was, in his silk dressing-gown, and not so much as excusing himself for receiving them in such an unofficial costume, shook hands with them heartily.

281

Only Sipiagin and Kollomietzev appeared in the governor's study; Paklin remained in the drawing-room. On getting out of the carriage he had tried to slip away, muttering that he had some business at home, but Sipiagin had detained him with a polite firmness (Kollomietzev had rushed up to him and whispered in his ear: " *Ne le lâcher pas ! Tonnerre de tonnerres !* ") and taken him in. He had not, however, taken him to the study, but had asked him, with the same polite firmness, to wait in the drawing-room until he was wanted. Even here Paklin had hoped to escape, but a robust gendarme at Kollomietzev's instruction appeared in the doorway; so Paklin remained.

" I dare say you've guessed what has brought me to you, *Voldemar*," Sipiagin began.

" No, my dear, no, I can't," the amiable Epicurean replied, while a smile of welcome played about his rosy cheeks, showing a glimpse of shiny teeth, half hidden by his silky moustache.

" What? Don't you know about Markelov? "

" What do you mean? What Markelov? " the governor repeated with the same joyful expression on his face. He did not remember, in the first place, that the man who was arrested yesterday was called Markelov, and, in the second, he had quite forgotten that Sipiagin's wife had a brother of that name. " But why are you standing, Boris? Sit down. Would you like some tea? "

Sipiagin's mind was far from tea.

When at last he explained why they had both appeared, the governor uttered an exclamation of pain and struck himself on the forehead, while his face assumed a sympathetic expression.

" Dear me! what a misfortune! And he's here now— to-day. . . . You know we never keep *that sort* with us for more than one night at the outside, but the chief of police is out of town, so your brother-in-law has been detained. He is to be sent on to-morrow. Dear me! what a dreadful

282

thing! What your wife must have gone through! What would you like me to do? "

" I would like to have an interview with him here, if it is not against the law."

" My dear boy! laws are not made for men like you. I do feel so sorry for you. . . . *C'est affreux, tu sais !* "

He gave a peculiar ring. An adjutant appeared.

" My dear baron, do please make some arrangement there. . . ." He told him what he wanted and the baron vanished. " Only think, *mon cher ami*, the peasants nearly killed him. They tied his hands behind him, flung him in a cart, and brought him here! And he's not in the least bit angry or indignant with them you know! He was so calm altogether that I was amazed! But you will see for yourself. *C'est un fanatique tranquille.*"

" *Ce sont les pires,*" Kollomietzev remarked sarcastically.

The governor looked up at him from under his eyebrows.

" By the way, I must have a word with you, Simion Petrovitch."

" Yes; what about? "

" I don't like things at all——"

" What things? "

" You know that peasant who owed you money and came here to complain——"

" Well? "

" He's hanged himself."

" When? "

" It's of no consequence when; but it's an ugly affair."

Kollomietzev merely shrugged his shoulders and moved away to the window with a graceful swing of the body. At this moment the adjutant brought in Markelov.

The governor had been right; he was unnaturally calm. Even his habitual moroseness had given place to an expression of weary indifference, which did not change when he caught sight of his brother-in-law. Only in the glance which he threw on the German adjutant, who was escorting him, there was a momentary flash of the old hatred he felt towards such people. His coat had been torn in several places and hurriedly stitched up with coarse thread; his forehead, eyebrows, and the bridge of his nose were covered with small scars caked with clotted blood. He had not washed, but had combed his hair.

"Sergai Mihailovitch!" Sipiagin began excitedly, taking a step or two towards him and extending his right hand, only so that he might touch him or stop him if he made a movement in advance, "Sergai Mihailovitch! I am not here to tell you of our amazement, our deep distress—you can have no doubt of that! You *wanted* to ruin yourself and have done so! But I've come to tell you . . . that . . . that . . . to give you the chance of hearing sound common-sense through the voice of honour and friendship. You can still migitate your lot and, believe me, I will do all in my power to help you, as the honoured head of this province can bear witness!" At this point Sipiagin raised his voice. "A real penitence of your wrongs and a full confession without reserve which will be duly presented in the proper quarters——"

"Your excellency," Markelov exclaimed suddenly, turning towards the governor—the very sound of his voice was calm, though it was a little hoarse; "I thought that you wanted to see me in order to cross-examine me again, but if I have been brought here solely by Mr. Sipiagin's wish, then please order me to be taken back again. We cannot understand one another. All he says is so much Greek to me."

"Greek, eh!" Kollomietzev shrieked. 'And to set peasants rioting, is that Greek too? Is that Greek too, eh?"

"What have you here, your excellency? A landowner of the secret police? And how zealous he is!" Markelov remarked, a faint smile of pleasure playing about his pale lips.

Kollomietzev stamped and raged, but the governor stopped him.

284

" It serves you right, Simion Petrovitch. You shouldn't interfere in what is not your business."

" Not my business . . . not my business. . . . It seems to me that it's the business of every nobleman——"

Markelov scanned Kollomietzev coldly and slowly, as if for the last time and then turned to Sipiagin.

" If you really want to know my views, my dear brother-in-law, here they are. I admit that the peasants had a right to arrest me and give me up if they disapproved of what I preached to them. They were free to do what they wanted. I came to them, not they to me. As for the government—if it does send me to Siberia, I'll go without grumbling, although I don't consider myself guilty. The government does its work, defends itself. Are you satisfied?"

Sipiagin wrung his hands in despair.

" Satisfied! ! What a word! That's not the point, and it is not for us to judge the doings of the government. The question, my dear Sergai, is whether you feel " (Sipiagin had decided to touch the tender strings) " the utter unreasonableness, senselessness, of your undertaking and are prepared to repent; and whether I can answer for you at all, my dear Sergai."

Markelov frowned.

" I have said all I have to say and don't want to repeat it."

" But don't you repent? Don't you repent? "

" Oh, leave me alone with your repentence! You want to steal into my very soul? Leave that, at any rate, to me."

Sipiagin shrugged his shoulders.

" You were always like that; never would listen to common-sense. You have a splendid chance of getting out of this quietly, honourably——"

" Quietly, honourably," Markelov repeated savagely. " We know those words. They are always flung at a man when he's wanted to do something mean! That is what these fine phrases are for! "

"We sympathise with you," Sipiagin continued reproachfully, "and you hate us."

"Fine sympathy! To Siberia and hard labour with us; that is your sympathy. Oh, let me alone! let me alone! for Heaven's sake!"

Markelov lowered his head.

He was agitated at heart, though externally calm. He was most of all tortured by the fact that he had been betrayed —and by whom? By Eremy of Goloplok! That same Eremy whom he had trusted so much! That Mendely the sulky had not followed him, had really not surprised him. Mendely was drunk and was consequently afraid. But Eremy! For Markelov, Eremy stood in some way as the personification of the whole Russian people, and Eremy had deceived him! Had he been mistaken about the thing he was striving for? Was Kisliakov a liar? And were Vassily Nikolaevitch's orders all stupid? And all the articles, books, works of socialists and thinkers, every letter of which had seemed to him invincible truth, were they all nonsense too? Was it really so? And the beautiful simile of the abcess awaiting the prick of the lancet—was that, too, nothing more than a phrase? " No! no!" he whispered to himself, and the colour spread faintly over his bronze-coloured face; "no! All these things are true, true . . . only I am to blame. I did not know how to do things, did not put things in the right way! I ought simply to have given orders, and if any one had tried to hinder, or object—put a bullet through his head! there is nothing else to be done! He who is against us has no right to live. Don't they kill spies like dogs, worse than dogs? "

All the details of his capture rose up in Markelov's mind. First the silence, the leers, then the shrieks from the back of the crowd . . . some one coming up sideways as if bowing to him, then that sudden rush, when he was knocked down. His own cries of " What are you doing, my boys? " and their shouts, " A belt! A belt! tie him up! " Then the rattling of his bones . . . unspeakable rage . . . filth in his mouth, his nostrils. . . . "Shove him in the cart! shove him in the cart!" some one roared with laughter. . . .

"I didn't go about it in the right way. . . ." That was the thing that most tormented him. That he had fallen under the wheel was his personal misfortune and had nothing to do with the cause—it was possible to bear that . . . but Eremy! Eremy!!

Whilst Markelov was standing with his head sunk on his breast, Sipiagin drew the governor aside and began talking to him in undertones. He flourished two fingers across his forehead, as though he would suggest that the unfortunate man was not quite right in his head, in order to arouse if not sympathy, at any rate indulgence towards the madman. The governor shrugged his shoulders, opened and shut his eyes, regretted his inability to do anything, but made some sort of promise in the end. "*Tous les égards . . . certainement, tous les égards,*" the soft, pleasant words flowed through his scented moustache. "But you know the law, my boy!"

"Of course I do!" Sipiagin responded with a sort of submissive severity.

Whilst they were talking in the corner, Kollomietzev could scarcely stand still in one spot. He walked up and down, hummed and hawed, showed every sign of impatience. At last he went up to Sipiagin, saying hastily, "*Vous oublier l'autre!*"

"Oh, yes!" Sipiagin exclaimed loudly. "*Merci de me l'avoir rappelé.* Your excellency," he said, turning to the governor (he purposely addressed his friend Voldemar in this formal way, so as not to compromise the prestige of authority in Markelov's presence), "I must draw your attention to the fact that my brother-in-law's mad attempt has certain ramifications, and one of these branches, that is to say, one of the suspected persons, is to be found not very far from here, in this town. I've brought another with me," he added in a whisper, " he's in the drawing-room. Have him brought in here."

" What a man! " the governor thought with admiration, gazing respectfully at Sipiagin. He gave the order and a minute later Sila Paklin stood before him.

Paklin bowed very low to the governor as he came in, but catching sight of Markelov before he had time to raise himself, remained as he was, half bent down, fidgetting with his cap. Markelov looked at him vacantly, but could hardly have recognised him, as he withdrew into his own thoughts.

" Is this the branch? " the governor asked, pointing to Paklin with a long white finger adorned with a turquoise ring.

" Oh, no! " Sipiagin exclaimed with a slight smile. " However, who knows! " he added after a moment's thought. " Your excellency," he said aloud, " the gentleman before you is Mr. Paklin. He comes from St. Petersburg and is a close friend of a certain person who for a time held the position of tutor in my house and who ran away, taking with him a certain young girl who, I blush to say, is my niece."

" Ah! *oui, oui*," the governor mumbled, shaking his head, " I heard the story. . . . The princess told me——"

Sipiagin raised his voice.

" That person is a certain Mr. Nejdanov, whom I strongly suspect of dangerous ideas and theories——"

" *Un rouge à tous crins,*" Kollomietzev put in.

" Yes, dangerous ideas and theories," Sipiagin repeated more emphatically. " He must certainly know something about this propaganda. He is . . . in hiding, as I have been informed by Mr. Paklin, in the merchant Falyaeva's factory——"

At these words Markelov threw another glance at Paklin and gave a slow, indifferent smile.

" Excuse me, excuse me, your excellency," Paklin cried, " and you, Mr. Sipiagin, I never . . . never——"

"Did you say the merchant Falyaeva?" the governor asked, turning to Sipiagin and merely shaking his fingers in Paklin's direction, as much as to say, "Gently, my good man, gently." "What is coming over our respectable, bearded merchants? Only yesterday one was arrested in connection with this affair. You may have heard of him—Golushkin, a very rich man. But he's harmless enough. He won't make revolutions; he's grovelling on his knees already."

"The merchant Falyaeva has nothing whatever to do with it," Sipiagin began; "I know nothing of his ideas; I was only talking of his factory where Mr. Nejdanov is to be found at this very moment, as Mr. Paklin says——"

"I said nothing of the kind!" Paklin cried; "you said it yourself!"

"Excuse me, Mr. Paklin," Sipiagin pronounced with the same relentless precision, "I admire that feeling of friendship which prompts you to deny it." ("A regular Guizot, upon my word!" the governor thought to himself.) "But take example by me. Do you suppose that the feeling of kinship is less strong in me than your feeling of friendship? But there is another feeling, my dear sir, yet stronger still, which guides all our deeds and actions, and that is duty!"

"*Le sentiment du devoir*," Kollomietzev explained.

Markelov took both the speakers in at a glance.

"Your excellency!" he exclaimed, "I ask you a second time; please have me removed out of sight of these babblers."

But there the governor lost patience a little.

"Mr. Markelov!" he pronounced severely, "I would advise you, in your present position, to be a little more careful of your tongue, and to show a little more respect to your elders, especially when they give expression to such patriotic sentiments as those you have just heard from the lips of your *beau-frère!* I shall be delighted, my dear Boris," he added, turning to Sipiagin, "to tell the minister of your noble action. But with whom is this Nejdanov staying at the factory?"

Sipiagin frowned.

" With a certain Mr. Solomin, the chief engineer there, Mr. Paklin says."

It seemed to afford Sipiagin some peculiar pleasure in tormenting poor Sila. He made him pay dearly for the cigar he had given him and the playful familiarity of his behaviour.

" This Solomin," Kollomietzev put in, " is an out-and-out radical and republican. It would be a good thing if your excellency were to turn your attention to him too."

" Do you know these gentlemen . . . Solomin, and what's his name . . . Nejdanov? " the governor asked Markelov, somewhat authoritatively.

Markelov distended his nostrils malignantly.

" Do you know Confucius and Titus Livius, your excellency? "

The governor turned away.

" *Il n'y a pas moyen de causer avec cette homme,*" he said, shrugging his shoulders. " Baron, come here, please."

The adjutant went up to him quickly and Paklin seized the opportunity of limping over to Sipiagin.

" What are you doing? " he asked in a whisper. " Why do you want to ruin your niece? Why, she's with him, with Nejdanov! "

" I am not ruining any one, my dear sir," Sipiagin said loudly, " I am only doing what my conscience bids me do, and——"

" And what your wife, my sister, bids you do; you dare not stand up against her! " Markelov exclaimed just as loudly.

Sipiagin took no notice of the remark; it was too much beneath him!

" Listen," Paklin continued, trembling all over with agitation, or may be from timidity; there was a malignant light in his eyes and the tears were nearly choking him— tears of pity for *them* and rage at himself; " listen, I told

290

you she was married—it wasn't true, I lied! but they must get married—and if you prevent it, if the police get there—there will be a stain on your conscience which you'll never be able to wipe out—and you——"

"If what you have just told me be true," Sipiagin interrupted him still more loudly, "then it can only hasten the measures which I think necessary to take in this matter; and as for the purity of my conscience, I beg you not to trouble about that, my dear sir."

"It's been polished," Markelov put in again; "there is a coat of St. Petersburg varnish upon it; no amount of washing will make it come clean. You may whisper as much as you like, Mr. Paklin, but you won't get anything out of it!"

At this point the governor considered it necessary to interfere.

"I think that you have said enough, gentlemen," he began, "and I'll ask you, my dear baron, to take Mr. Markelov away. *N'est ce pas*, Boris, you don't want him any further——"

Sipiagin made a gesture with his hands.

"I said everything I could think of!"

"Very well, baron!"

The adjutant came up to Markelov, clinked his spurs, made a horizontal movement of the hand, as if to request Markelov to make a move; the latter turned and walked out. Paklin, only in imagination it is true, but with bitter sympathy and pity, shook him by the hand.

"We'll send some of our men to the factory," the governor continued; "but you know, Boris, I thought this gentleman" (he moved his chin in Paklin's direction) "told you something about your niece . . . I understood that she was there at the factory. Then how——"

"It's impossible to arrest her in any case," Sipiagin remarked thoughtfully; "perhaps she will think better of it and return. I'll write her a note, if I may."

"Do please. You may be quite sure . . . *nons coffrerous*

le quidam . . . mais nous sommes galants avec les dames . . . et avec celle-là donc ! "

" But you've made no arrangements about this Solomin," Kollomietzev exclaimed plaintively. He had been on the alert all the while, trying to catch what the governor and Sipiagin were saying. " I assure you he's the principal ringleader ! I have a wonderful instinct about these things ! "

" *Pas trop de zèle*, my dear Simion Petrovitch," the governor remarked with a smile. " You remember Talleyrand ! If it is really as you say the fellow won't escape us. You had better think of your——" the governor put his hand to his throat significantly. " By the way," he said, turning to Sipiagin, " *et ce gaillard-là* " (he moved his chin in Paklin's direction). " *Qu'en ferons nous ?* He does not appear very dangerous."

" Let him go," Sipiagin said in an undertone, and added in German, " *Lass' den Lumpen laufen !* "

He imagined for some reason that he was quoting from Goethe's *Götz von Berlichingen*.

" You can go, sir ! " the governor said aloud. " We do not require you any longer. Good day."

Paklin bowed to the company in general and went out into the street completely crushed and humiliated. Heavens ! this contempt had utterly broken him.

" Good God ! What am I ? A coward, a traitor ? " he thought, in unutterable despair. " Oh, no, no ! I am an honest man, gentlemen ! I have still some manhood left ! "

But who was this familiar figure sitting on the governor's step and looking at him with a dejected, reproachful glance ? It was Markelov's old servant. He had evidently come to town for his master, and would not for a moment leave the door of his prison. But why did he look so reproachfully at Paklin ? He had not betrayed Markelov !

" And why did I go poking my nose into things that did not concern me ? Why could I not sit quietly at home ? And now it will be said and written that Paklin betrayed

292

them—betrayed his friends to the enemy!" He recalled
the look Markelov had given him and his last words, " Whisper as much as you like, Mr. Paklin, but you won't get anything out of it!" and then these sad, aged, dejected eyes!
he thought in desperation. And as it says in the scriptures,
he " wept bitterly " as he turned his steps towards the oasis,
to Fomishka and Fimishka and Snandulia.

XXXVI

WHEN Mariana came out of her room that morning she noticed Nejdanov sitting on the couch fully dressed. His head was resting against one arm, whilst the other lay weak and helpless on his knee. She went up to him.

" Good-morning, Alexai. Why, you haven't undressed? Haven't you slept? How pale you are! "

His heavy eyelids rose slowly.

" No, I haven't."

" Aren't you well, or is it the after-effects of yesterday? "

Nejdanov shook his head.

" I couldn't sleep after Solomin went into your room."

" When? "

" Last night."

" Alexai! are you jealous? A new idea! What a time to be jealous in! Why, he was only with me a quarter of an hour. We talked about his cousin, the priest, and discussed arrangements for our marriage."

" I know that he was only with you a short time. I saw him come out. And I'm not jealous, oh no! But still I couldn't fall asleep after that."

" But why? "

Nejdanov was silent.

" I kept thinking . . . thinking . . . thinking! "

" Of what? "

" Oh, of you . . . of him . . . and of myself."

" And what came of all your thinking? "

" Shall I tell you? "

" Yes, tell me."

" It seemed to me that I stood in your way—in his . . . and in my own."

" Mine? His? It's easy to see what you mean by that, though you declare you're not jealous, but your own? "

" Mariana, there are two men in me and one doesn't let the other live. So I thought it might be better if both ceased to live."

" Please don't, Alexai. Why do you want to torment yourself and me? We ought to be considering ways and means of getting away. They won't leave us in peace you know."

Nejdanov took her hand caressingly.

" Sit down beside me, Mariana, and let us talk things over like comrades while there is still time. Give me your hand. It would be a good thing for us to have an explanation, though they say that all explanations only lead to further muddle. But you are kind and intelligent and are sure to understand, even the things that I am unable to express. Come, sit down."

Nejdanov's voice was soft, and a peculiarly affectionate tenderness shone in his eyes as he looked entreatingly at Mariana.

She sat down beside him readily and took his hand.

" Thanks, dearest. I won't keep you long. I thought out all the things I wanted to say to you last night. Don't think I was too much upset by yesterday's occurrence. I was no doubt extremely ridiculous and rather disgusting, but I know you didn't think anything bad of me—you know me. I am not telling the truth exactly when I say that I wasn't upset—I was horribly upset, not because I was brought home drunk, but because I was convinced of my utter inefficiency. Not because I could not drink like a real Russian—but in everything! everything! Mariana, I must tell you that I no longer believe in the cause that united us and on the strength of which we ran away together. To tell the truth, I had already lost faith when your enthusiasm set me on fire again. I don't believe in it! I can't believe in it! "

He put his disengaged hand over his eyes and ceased for a while. Mariana did not utter a single word and sat looking downwards. She felt that he had told her nothing new.

" I always thought," Nejdanov continued, taking his hand away from his eyes, but not looking at Mariana again, " that I believed in the cause itself, but had no faith in myself, in my own strength, my own capacities. I used to think that my abilities did not come up to my convictions. . . . But you can't separate these things. And what's the use of deceiving oneself? No—I don't believe in the *cause itself*. And you, Mariana, do you believe in it? "

Mariana sat up straight and raised her head.

" Yes, I do, Alexai. I believe in it with all the strength of my soul, and will devote my whole life to it, to the last breath! "

Nejdanov turned towards her and looked at her enviously, with a tender light in his eyes.

" I knew you would answer like that. So you see there is nothing for us to do together; you have severed our tie with one blow."

Mariana was silent.

" Take Solomin, for instance," Nejdanov began again, " though he does not believe——"

" What do you mean? "

" It's quite true. He does not believe . . . but that is not necessary for him; he is moving steadily onwards. A man walking along a road in a town does not question the existence of the town—he just goes his way. That is Solomin. That is all that's needed. But I . . . I can't go ahead, don't want to turn back, and am sick of staying where I am. How dare I ask any one to be my companion? You know the old proverb, ' With two people to carry the pole, the burden will be easier.' But if you let go your end— what becomes of the other? "

" Alexai," Mariana began irresolutely, " I think you exaggerate. Do we not love each other? "

296

Nejdanov gave a deep sigh.

" Mariana . . . I bow down before you . . . you pity me, and each of us has implicit faith in the other's honesty—that is our position. But there is no love between us."

" Stop, Alexai! what are you saying? The police may come for us to-day . . . we must go away together and not part——"

"And get Father Zosim to marry us at Solomin's suggestion. I know that you merely look upon our marriage as a kind of passport—a means of avoiding any difficulties with the police . . . but still it will bind us to some extent; necessitate our living together and all that. Besides it always presupposes a desire to live together."

" What do you mean, Alexai? You don't intend staying here? "

" N-n-no," Nejdanov said hesitatingly. The word " yes " nearly escaped his lips, but he recollected himself in time.

" Then you are going to a different place—not where I am going? "

Nejdanov pressed her hand which still lay in his own.

" It would indeed be vile to leave you without a supporter, without a protector, but I won't do that, as bad as I may be. You shall have a protector—rest assured."

Mariana bent down towards him and, putting her face close against his, looked anxiously into his eyes, as though trying to penetrate to his very soul.

" What is the matter, Alexai? What have you on your mind? Tell me . . . you frighten me. Your words are so strange and enigmatical. . . . And your face! I have never seen your face like that! "

Nejdanov put her from him gently and kissed her hand tenderly. This time she made no resistance and did not laugh, but sat still looking at him anxiously.

" Don't be alarmed, dear. There is nothing strange in it. They say Markelov was beaten by the peasants; he felt their blows—they crushed his ribs. They did not beat me, they

297

even drank with me—drank my health—but they crushed my soul more completely than they did Markelov's ribs. I was born out of joint, wanted to set myself right, and have made matters worse. That is what you notice in my face."

"Alexai," Mariana said slowly, "it would be very wrong of you not to be frank with me."

He clenched his hands.

"Mariana, my whole being is laid bare before you, and whatever I might do, I tell you beforehand, nothing will really surprise you; nothing whatever!"

Mariana wanted to ask him what he meant, but at that moment Solomin entered the room.

His movements were sharper and more rapid than usual. His eyes were half closed, his lips compressed, the whole of his face wore a drier, harder, somewhat rougher expression.

"My dear friends," he began, "I must ask you not to waste time, but prepare yourselves as soon as possible. You must be ready in an hour. You have to go through the marriage ceremony. There is no news of Paklin. His horses were detained for a time at Arjanov and then sent back. He has been kept there. They've no doubt brought him to town by this time. I don't think he would betray us, but he might let things out unwittingly. Besides, they might have guessed from the horses. My cousin has been informed of your coming. Pavel will go with you. He will be a witness."

"And you . . . and you?" Nejdanov asked. "Aren't you going? I see you're dressed for the road," he added, indicating Solomin's high boots with his eyes.

"Oh, I only put them on . . . because it's rather muddy outside."

"But you won't be held responsible for us, will you?"

"I hardly think so . . . in any case . . . that's my affair. So you'll be ready in an hour. Mariana, I believe Tatiana wants to see you. She has something prepared for you."

"Oh, yes! I wanted to see her too. . . ." Mariana turned to the door.

A peculiar expression of fear, despair, spread itself over Nejdanov's face.

"Mariana, you're not going?" he asked in a frightened tone of voice.

She stood still.

"I'll be back in half an hour. It won't take me long to pack."

"Come here, close to me, Mariana——"

"Certainly, but what for?"

"I wanted to have one more look at you." He looked at her intently. Good-bye, good-bye, Mariana!"

She seemed bewildered.

"Why . . . what nonsense I'm talking! You'll be back in half an hour, won't you, eh?"

"Of course——"

"Never mind; forgive me, dear. My brain is in a whirl from lack of sleep. I must begin . . . packing, too."

Mariana went out of the room and Solomin was about to follow her when Nejdanov stopped him.

"Solomin!"

"What is it?"

"Give me your hand. I must thank you for your kindness and hospitality."

Solomin smiled.

"What an idea!" He extended his hand.

"There's another thing I wished to say," Nejdanov continued. "Supposing anything were to happen to me, may I hope that you won't abandon Mariana?"

"Your future wife?"

"Yes . . . Mariana!"

"I don't think anything is likely to happen to you, but you may set your mind at rest. Mariana is just as dear to me as she is to you."

"Oh, I knew it . . . knew it, knew it! I'm so glad! thanks. So in an hour?"

"In an hour."

"I shall be ready. Good-bye, my friend!"

Solomin went out and caught Mariana up on the staircase. He had intended saying something to her about Nejdanov, but refrained from doing so. And Mariana guessed that he wished to say something about him and that he could not. She, too, was silent.

XXXVII

DIRECTLY Solomin had gone, Nejdanov jumped up from the couch, walked up and down the room several times, then stood still in the middle in a sort of stony indecision. Suddenly he threw off his " masquerade " costume, kicked it into a corner of the room, and put on his own clothes. He then went up to the little three-legged table, pulled out of a drawer two sealed letters and some other object which he thrust into his pocket; the letters he left on the table. Then he crouched down before the stove and opened the little door. A whole heap of ashes lay inside. This was all that remained of Nejdanov's papers, of his sacred book of verses . . . He had burned them all in the night. Leaning against one side of the stove was Mariana's portrait that Markelov had given him. He had evidently not had the heart to burn that too! He took it out carefully and put in on the table beside the two letters.

Then, with a quick resolute movement, he put on his cap and walked towards the door. But suddenly he stopped, turned back, and went into Mariana's room. There, he stood still for a moment, gazed round, then approaching her narrow little bed, bent down and with one stifled sob pressed his lips to the foot of the bed. He then jumped up, thrust his cap over his forehead, and rushed out. Without meeting any one in the corridor, on the stairs, or down below, he darted out into the garden. It was a grey day, with a low-hanging sky and a damp breeze that blew in waves over the tops of the grass and made the trees rustle. A whiff of coal, tar, and tallow was borne along from the yard, but the noise and rattling in the factory was fainter than usual at that time of day. Nejdanov looked round sharply to see if any one was about and made straight for the old apple tree that had first attracted his attention when he had looked out of the little window of his room on the day of his arrival. The whole of its trunk was evergrown with dry moss, its bare, rugged branches, sparsely covered with reddish leaves, rose crookedly, like some old arms held up in supplication. Nejdanov stepped firmly on to the dark soil beneath the tree and pulled out the object he had taken from the table drawer. He looked up intently at the windows of the little house. " If somebody were to see me now, perhaps I wouldn't do it," he thought. But no human being was to be seen anywhere—every one seemed dead or turned away from him, leaving him to the mercy of fate. Only the muffled hum and roar of the factory betrayed any signs of life; and overhead a fine, keen, chilly rain began falling.

Nejdanov gazed up through the crooked branches of the tree under which he was standing at the grey, cloudy sky looking down upon him so unfeelingly. He yawned and lay down. " There's nothing else to be done. I can't go back to St. Petersburg, to prison," he thought. A kind of pleasant heaviness spread all over his body. . . . He threw away his cap, took up the revolver, and pulled the trigger. . . . Something struck him instantly, but with no very great violence. . . . He was lying on his back trying to make out what had happened to him and how it was that he had just seen Tatiana. He tried to call her . . . but a peculiar numbness had taken possession of him and curious dark green spots were whirling about all over him—in his eyes, over his head, in his brain—and some frightfully heavy, dull weight seemed to press him to the earth for ever.

Nejdanov did really get a glimpse of Tatiana. At the moment when he pulled the trigger she had looked out of a window and caught sight of him standing under the tree. She had hardly time to ask herself what he was doing there in the rain without a hat, when he rolled to the ground like a sheaf of corn. She did not hear the shot—it was very

faint—but instantly felt that something was amiss and rushed
out into the garden. . . . She came up to Nejdanov breathless.

" Alexai Dmitritch! What is the matter with you? "

But a darkness had already descended upon him. Tatiana
bent over and noticed blood. . . .

" Pavel! " she shouted at the top of her voice, " Pavel! "

A minute or two later, Mariana, Solomin, Pavel, and two
workmen were in the garden. They lifted him instantly,
carried him into the house, and laid him on the same couch
on which he had passed his last night.

He lay on his back with half-closed eyes, his face blue all
over. There was a rattling in his throat, and every now and
again he gave a choking sob. Life had not yet left him.
Mariana and Solomin were standing on either side of him,
almost as pale as he was himself. They both felt crushed,
stunned, especially Mariana—but they were not surprised.
" How did we not foresee this? " they asked themselves,
but it seemed to them that they had foreseen it all along.
When he said to Mariana, " Whatever I do, I tell you beforehand, nothing will really surprise you," and when he had
spoken of the two men in him that would not let each other
live, had she not felt a kind of vague presentiment? Then
why had she ignored it? Why was it she did not now dare
to look at Solomin, as though he were her accomplice . . .
as though he, too, were conscience-stricken? Why was it
that her unutterable, despairing pity for Nejdanov was
mixed with a feeling of horror, dread, and shame? Perhaps
she could have saved him? Why are they both standing
there, not daring to pronounce a word, hardly daring to
breathe—waiting . . . for what? Oh, God! "

Solomin sent for a doctor, though there was no hope.
Tatiana bathed Nejdanov's head with cold water and vinegar
and laid a cold sponge on the small, dark wound, now free
from blood. Suddenly the rattling in Nejdanov's throat
ceased and he stirred a little.

303

" He is coming to himself," Solomin whispered.

Mariana dropped down on her knees before him. Nejdanov glanced at her . . . up till then his eyes had borne that fixed, far-away look of the dying.

" I am . . . still alive," he pronounced scarcely audible. " I couldn't even do this properly. . . . I am detaining . . . you."

" Aliosha! " Mariana sobbed out.

" It won't . . . be long. . . . Do you . . . remember . . . Mariana . . . my poem? . . . Surround me with flowers. . . . But where . . . are the . . . flowers? . . . Never mind . . . so long as you . . . are here. There . . . in . . . my letter. . . ."

He suddenly shuddered.

" Ah! here it comes. . . . Take . . . each other's . . . hands . . . before me . . . quickly . . . take. . . ."

Solomin seized Mariana's hand. Her head lay on the couch, face downwards, close to the wound. Solomin, dark as night, held himself severely erect.

" That's right . . . that's. . . ."

Nejdanov broke out into sobs again—strange unusual sobs. . . . His breast rose, his sides heaved. . . .

He tried to lay his hand on their united ones, but it fell back dead.

" He is passing away," Tatiana whispered as she stood at the door, and began crossing herself.

His sobs grew briefer, fewer. . . . He still searched round for Mariana with his eyes, but a menacing white film was spreading over them. . . .

" That's right," were his last words.

He had breathed his last . . . and the clasped hands of Mariana and Solomin still lay upon his breast.

The following are the contents of the two letters he had left. One consisting only of a few lines, was addressed to Silin:

" Good-bye, my dear friend, good-bye! When this

reaches you, I shall be no more. Don't ask why or where-
fore, and don't grieve; be sure that I am better off now.
Take up our immortal Pushkin and read over the description
of the death of Lensky in 'Yevgenia Onegin.' Do you
remember? The windows are white-washed. The mistress
has gone—that's all. There is nothing more for me to say.
Were I to say all I wanted to, it would take up too much
time. But I could not leave this world without telling you,
or you might have gone on thinking of me as living and I
should have put a stain upon our friendship. Good-bye;
live well.—Your friend, A. N."

The other letter, somewhat longer, was addressed to
Solomin and Mariana. It began thus:

" My Dear Children " (immediately after these words
there was a break, as if something had been scratched or
smeared out, as if tears had fallen upon it),—" It may seem
strange to you that I should address you in this way—I am
almost a child myself and you, Solomin, are older than I am.
But I am about to die—and standing as I do at the end of
my life, I look upon myself as an old man. I have wronged
you both, especially you, Mariana, by causing you so much
grief and pain (I know you will grieve, Mariana) and giving
you so much anxiety. But what could I do? I could think
of no other way out. I could not *simplify* myself, so the only
thing left for me to do was to blot myself out altogether.
Mariana, I would have been a burden to you and to myself.
You are generous, you would have borne the burden gladly,
as a new sacrifice, but I have no right to demand such a
sacrifice of you—you have a higher and better work before
you. My children, let me unite you as it were from the
grave. You will live happily together. Mariana, I know
you will come to love Solomin—and he . . . he loved you
from the moment he first saw you at the Sipiagins. It was
no secret to me, although we ran away a few days later. Ah!
that glorious morning! how exquisite and fresh and young

305

it was! It comes back to me now as a token, a symbol of your life together—your life and his—and I by the merest chance happened to be in his place. But enough! I don't want to complain, I only want to justify myself. Some very sorrowful moments are in store for you to-morrow. But what could I do? There was no other alternative. Good-bye, Mariana, my dear good girl! Good-bye, Solomin! I leave her in your charge. Be happy together; live for the sake of others. And you, Mariana, think of me only when you are happy. Think of me as a man who had also some good in him, but for whom it was better to die than to live. Did I really love you? I don't know, dear friend. But I do know that I never loved any one more than you, and that it would have been more terrible for me to die had I not that feeling for you to carry away with me to the grave. Mariana, if you ever come across a Miss Mashurina—Solomin knows her, and by the way, I think you've met her too—tell her that I thought of her with gratitude just before the end. She will understand. But I must tear myself away at last. I looked out of the window just now and saw a lovely star amidst the swiftly moving clouds. No matter how quickly they chased one another, they could not hide it from view. That star reminded me of you, Mariana. At this moment you are asleep in the next room, unsuspecting. . . . I went to your door, listened, and fancied I heard your pure, calm breathing. . . . Good-bye! good-bye! good-bye, my children, my friends!—Yours, A.

"Dear me! how is it that in my final letter I made no mention of our great cause? I suppose lying is of no use when you're on the point of death. Forgive this postscript, Mariana. . . . The falsehood lies in me, not in the thing in which you believe! One more word. You might have thought perhaps, Mariana, that I put an end to myself merely because I was afraid of going to prison, but believe me that is not true. There is nothing terrible about going to prison in itself, but being shut up there for a cause in which you have no faith is unthinkable. It was not fear of prison that drove me to this, Mariana. Good-bye! good-bye! my dear, pure girl."

Mariana and Solomin each read the letter in turn. She then put her own portrait and the two letters into her pocket and remained standing motionless.

" Let us go, Mariana; everything is ready. We must fulfil his wish," Solomin said to her.

Mariana drew near to Nejdanov and pressed her lips against his forehead which was already turning cold.

" Come," she said, turning to Solomin. They went out, hand in hand.

When the police arrived at the factory, a few hours later, they found Nejdanov's corpse. Tatiana had laid out the body, put a white pillow under his head, crossed his arms, and even placed a bunch of flowers on a little table beside him. Pavel, who had been given all the needful instructions, received the police officers with the greatest respect and as great a contempt, so that those worthies were not quite sure whether to thank or arrest him. He gave them all the details of the suicide, regaled them with Swiss cheese and Madeira, but as for the whereabouts of Vassily Fedotitch and the young lady, he knew nothing of that. He was most effusive in his assurances that Vassily Fedotitch was never away for long at a time on account of his work, that he was sure to be back either to-day or to-morrow, and that he would let them know as soon as he arrived. They might depend on him!

So the officers went away no wiser than they had come, leaving a guard in charge of the body and promising to send a coroner.

XXXVIII

Two days after these events a cart drove up the court-yard
of the worthy Father Zosim containing a man and woman
who are already known to the reader. The following day
they were legally married. Soon afterwards they disappeared, and the good father never regretted what he had
done. Solomin had left a letter in Pavel's charge, addressed
to the proprietor of the factory, giving a full statement of the
condition of the business (it turned out most flourishing) and
asking for three months' leave. The letter was dated two
days before Nejdanov's death, from which might be gathered
that Solomin had considered it necessary even then to go
away with him and Mariana and hide for a time. Nothing
was revealed by the inquiry held over the suicide. The body
was buried. Sipiagin gave up searching for his niece.

Nine months later Markelov was tried. At the trial he
was just as calm as he had been at the governor's. He
carried himself with dignity, but was rather depressed. His
habitual hardness had toned down somewhat, not from any
cowardice; a nobler element had been at work. He did not
defend himself, did not regret what he had done, blamed no
one, and mentioned no names. His emaciated face with the
lustreless eyes retained but one expression: submission to
his fate and firmness. His brief, direct, truthful answers
aroused in his very judges a feeling akin to pity. Even the
peasants who had seized him and were giving evidence against
him shared this feeling and spoke of him as a good, simple-
hearted gentleman. But his guilt could not possibly be
passed over; he could not escape punishment, and he himself seemed to look upon it as his due. Of his few accom-
plices, Mashurina disappeared for a time. Ostrodumov was

killed by a shopkeeper he was inciting to revolt, who had struck him an "awkward" blow. Golushkin, in consideration of his penitence (he was nearly frightened out of his wits), was let off lightly. Kisliakov was kept under arrest for about a month, after which he was released and even allowed to continue "galloping" from province of province. Nejdanov died, Solomin was under suspicion, but for lack of sufficient evidence was left in peace. (He did not, however, avoid trial and appeared when wanted.) Mariana was not even mentioned; Paklin came off splendidly; indeed no notice was taken of him.

A year and a half had gone by—it was the winter of 1870. In St. Petersburg—the very same St. Petersburg where the chamberlain Sipiagin, now a privy councillor, was beginning to play such an important part; where his wife patronised the arts, gave musical evenings, and founded charitable cookshops; where Kollomietzev was considered one of the most hopeful members of the ministerial department—a little man was limping along one of the streets of the Vassily island, attired in a shabby coat with a catskin collar. This was no other than our old friend Paklin. He had changed a great deal since we last saw him. On his temples a few strands of silvery hair peeped out from under his fur cap. A tall, stout woman, closely muffled in a dark cloth coat, was coming towards him on the pavement. Paklin looked at her indifferently and passed on. Suddenly he stopped, threw up his arms as though struck by something, turned back quickly, and overtaking her peeped under her hat.

" Mashurina! " he exclaimed in an undertone.

The lady looked at him haughtily and walked on without saying a word.

" Dear Mashurina, I recognised you at once," Paklin continued, hobbling along beside her; " don't be afraid, I won't give you away! I am so glad to see you! I'm Paklin, Sila Paklin, you know, Nejdanov's friend. Do come home with me. I live quite near here. Do come! "

" *Io sono contessa Rocca di Santo Fiume !* " the lady said softly, but in a wonderfully pure Russian accent.

" Contessa! nonsense! Do come in and let us talk about old times——"

" Where do you live? " the Italian countess asked suddenly in Russian. " I'm in a hurry."

" In this very street; in that grey three-storied house over there. It's so nice of you not to have snubbed me! Give me your hand, come on. Have you been here long? How do you come to be a countess? Have you married an Italian count? "

Mashurina had not married an Italian count. She had been provided with a passport made out in the name of a certain Countess Rocca di Santo Fiume, who had died a short time ago, and had come quite calmly to Russia, though she did not know a single word of Italian and had the most typical of Russian faces.

Paklin brought her to his humble little lodging. His humpbacked sister who shared it with him came out to greet them from behind the partition dividing the kitchen from the passage.

" Here, Snapotchka," he said, " let me introduce you to a great friend of mine. We should like some tea as soon as you can get it."

Mashurina, who would on no account have come had not Paklin mentioned Nejdanov, bowed, then taking off her hat and passing her masculine hand through her closely cropped hair, sat down in silence. She had scarcely changed at all; even her dress was the same she had worn two years ago; only her eyes wore a fixed, sad expression, giving a pathetic look to her usually hard face. Snandulia went out for the samovar, whilst Paklin sat down opposite Mashurina and stroked her knee sympathetically. His head dropped on his breast, he could not speak from choking, and the tears glistened in his eyes. Mashurina sat erect and motionless, gazing severely to one side.

" Those were times! " Paklin began at last. " As I look at you everything comes back to me, the living and the dead. Even my little poll-parrots are no more. . . . I don't think you knew them, by the way. They both died on the same day, as I always predicted they would. And Nejdanov . . . poor Nejdanov! I suppose you know——"

" Yes, I know," Mashurina interrupted him, still looking away.

" And do you know about Ostrodumov too? "

Mashurina merely nodded her head. She wanted him to go on talking about Nejdanov, but could not bring herself to ask him. He understood her, however.

" I was told that he mentioned you in the letter he left. Was it true? "

" Yes," Mashurina replied after a pause.

" What a splendid chap he was! He didn't fall into the right rut somehow. He was about as fitted to be a revolutionist as I am! Do you know what he really was? The idealist of realism. Do you understand me? "

Mashurina flung him a rapid glance. She did not understand him and did not want to understand him. It seemed to her impertinent that he should compare himself to Nejdanov. " Let him brag! " she thought, though he was not bragging at all, but rather depreciating himself, according to his own ideas.

" Some fellow called Silin sought me out; Nejdanov, it seems, had left a letter for him too. Well, he wanted to know if Alexai had left any papers, but we hunted through all his things and found nothing. He must have burned everything, even his poems. Did you know that he wrote verses? I'm sorry they were destroyed; there must have been some good things among them. They all vanished with him— became lost in the general whirl, dead and gone for ever. Nothing was left except the memories of his friends—until they, too, vanish in their turn! "

Paklin ceased.

"Do you remember the Sipiagins?" he began again; "those respectable, patronising, loathsome swells are now at the very height of power and glory." Mashurina, of course, did not remember the Sipiagins, but Paklin hated them so much that he could not keep from abusing them on every possible occasion. "They say there's such a high tone in their house! they're always talking about virtue! It's a bad sign, I think. Reminds me rather of an over-scented sick room. There must be some bad smell to conceal. Poor Alexai! It was they who ruined him!"

"And what is Solomin doing?" Mashurina asked. She had suddenly ceased wishing to hear Paklin talk about *him*.

"Solomin!" Paklin exclaimed. "He's a clever chap! turned out well too. He's left the old factory and taken all the best men with him. There was one fellow there called Pavel—could do anything; he's taken him along too. They say he has a small factory of his own now, somewhere near Perm, run on co-operative lines. He's all right! he'll stick to anything he undertakes. Got some grit in him! His strength lies in the fact that he doesn't attempt to cure all the social ills with one blow. What a rum set we are to be sure, we Russians! We sit down quietly and wait for something or some one to come along and cure us all at once; heal all our wounds, pull out all our diseases, like a bad tooth. But who or what is to work this magic spell, Darwinism, the land, the Archbishop Perepentiev, a foreign war, we don't know and don't care, but we must have our tooth pulled out for us! It's nothing but mere idleness, sluggishness, want of thinking. Solomin, on the other hand, is different; he doesn't go in for pulling teeth—he knows what he's about!"

Mashurina gave an impatient wave of the hand, as though she wished to dismiss the subject.

"And that girl," she began, "I forget her name . . . the one who ran away with Nejdanov—what became of her?"

"Mariana? She's Solomin's wife now. They married

312

over a year ago. It was merely for the sake of formality at first, but now they say she really is his wife."

Mashurina gave another impatient gesture. There was a time when she was jealous of Mariana, but now she was indignant with her for having been false to Nejdanov's memory.

" I suppose they have a baby by now," she said in an off-handed tone.

" I really don't know. But where are you off to? " Paklin asked, seeing that she had taken up her hat. " Do stay a little longer; my sister will bring us some tea directly."

It was not so much that he wanted Mashurina to stay, as that he could not let an opportunity slip by of giving utterance to what had accumulated and was boiling over in his breast. Since his return to St. Petersburg he had seen very little of people, especially of the younger generation. The Nejdanov affair had scared him; he grew more cautious, avoided society, and the young generation on their side looked upon him with suspicion. Once some one had even called him a traitor to his face.

As he was not fond of associating with the elder generation, it sometimes fell to his lot to be silent for weeks. To his sister he could not speak out freely, not because he considered her too stupid to understand him—oh, no! he had the highest opinion of her intelligence—but as soon as he began letting off some of his pet fireworks she would look at him with those sad reproachful eyes of hers, making him feel quite ashamed. And really, how is a man to go through life without letting off just a few squibs every now and again? So life in St. Petersburg became insupportable to Paklin and he longed to remove to Moscow. Speculations of all sorts, ideas, fancies, and sarcasms were stored up in him, like water in a closed mill. The floodgates could not be opened and the water grew stagnant. With the appearance of Mashurina the gates opened wide, and all his pent-up ideas came pouring out with a rush. He talked about

313

St. Petersburg, St. Petersburg life, the whole of Russia. No
one was spared! Mashurina was very little interested in all
this, but she did not contradict or interrupt, and that was
all he wanted of her.

"Yes," he began, "a fine time we are living in, I can
assure you! Society in a state of absolute stagnation; every
one bored to death! As for literature it's been reduced
to a complete vacuum swept clean! Take criticism for
example. If a promising young critic has to say, 'It's natural
for a hen to lay eggs,' it takes him at least twenty whole pages
to expound this mighty truth, and even then he doesn't
quite manage it! They're as puffed up as feather-beds,
these fine gentlemen, as soft-soapy as can be, and are always
in raptures over the merest commonplaces! As for science,
ha, ha, ha! we too have our learned *Kant!*[1] on the collars
of our engineers! And it's no better in art! You go to a
concert and listen to our national singer Agremantsky.
Every one is raving about him. But he has no more voice
than a cat! Even Skoropikin, you know, our immortal
Aristarchus, rings his praises. 'Here is something,' he
declares, 'quite unlike Western art!' Then he raves about
our insignificant painters too! 'At one time, I bowed down
before Europe and the Italians,' he says, 'but I've heard
Rossini and seen Raphael and confess was not at all impressed.' And our young men just go about repeating what
he says and feel quite satisfied with themselves. And meanwhile the people are dying of hunger, crushed down by taxes.
The only reform that has been accomplished is that the men
have taken to wearing caps and the women have left off
their head-dresses! And the poverty! the drunkenness! the
usury!"

But at this point Mashurina yawned and Paklin saw that
he must change the subject.

"You haven't told me yet," he said, turning to her, "where
you've been these two years, when you came back, what

[1] The word *kant* in Russian means a kind of braid or piping.

you've been doing with yourself, and how you managed to turn into an Italian countess——"

" There is no need for you to know all that," she put in. " It can hardly have any interest for you now. You see, you are no longer of our camp."

Paklin felt a pang and gave a forced laugh to hide his confusion.

" As you please," he said; " I know I'm regarded as out-of-date by the present generation, and really I can hardly count myself . . . of those ranks——" He did not finish the sentence. " Here comes Snapotchka with the tea. Take a cup with us and stay a little longer. Perhaps I may tell you something of interest to you."

Mashurina took a cup of tea and began sipping it with a lump of sugar in her mouth.

Paklin laughed heartily.

" It's a good thing the police are not here to see an Italian countess——"

" Rocca di Santo Fiume," Mashurina put in solemnly, sipping the hot tea.

" Contessa Rocca di Santo Fiume! " Paklin repeated after her; " and drinking her tea in the typical Russian way! That's rather suspicious, you know! The police would be on the alert in an instant."

" Some fellow in uniform bothered me when I was abroad," Mashurina remarked. " He kept on asking so many questions until I couldn't stand it any longer. ' Leave me alone, for heaven's sake! ' I said to him at last."

" In Italian? "

" Oh no, in Russian."

" And what did he do? "

" Went away, of course."

" Bravo! " Paklin exclaimed. " Well, countess, have another cup. There is just one other thing I wanted to say to you. It seemed to me that you expressed yourself rather contemptuously of Solomin. But I tell you that people like

315

him are the real men! It's difficult to understand them at
first, but, believe me, they're the real men. The future is in
their hands. They are not heroes, not even 'heroes of
labour' as some crank of an American, or Englishman,
called them in a book he wrote for the edification of us
heathens, but they are robust, strong, dull men of the people.
They are exactly what we want just now. You have only
to look at Solomin. A head as clear as the day and a body
as strong as an ox. Isn't that a wonder in itself? Why,
any man with us in Russia who has had any brains, or feelings, or a conscience, has always been a physical wreck.
Solomin's heart aches just as ours does; he hates the same
things that we hate, but his nerves are of iron and his body
is under his full control. He's a splendid man, I tell you!
Why, think of it! here is a man with ideals, and no nonsense
about him; educated and from the people, simple, yet all
there. . . . What more do you want?

" It's of no consequence," Paklin continued, working himself up more and more, without noticing that Mashurina had
long ago ceased listening to him and was looking away somewhere, " it's of no consequence that Russia is now full of all
sorts of queer people, fanatics, officials, generals plain and
decorated, Epicureans, imitators, all manner of cranks. I
once knew a lady, a certain Havrona Prishtekov, who, one
fine day, suddenly turned a legitimist and assured everybody
that when she died they had only to open her body and
the name of Henry V. would be found engraven on her
heart! All these people do not count, my dear lady; our true
salvation lies with the Solomins, the dull, plain, but wise
Solomins! Remember that I say this to you in the winter
of 1870, when Germany is preparing to crush France——"

" Silishka," Snandulia's soft voice was heard from behind
Paklin, " I think in your speculations about the future you
have quite forgotten our religion and its influence. And
besides," she added hastily, " Miss Mashurina is not listening
to you. You had much better offer her some more tea."

316

Paklin pulled himself up.

" Why, of course . . . do have some more tea."

But Mashurina fixed her dark eyes upon him and said pensively:

" You don't happen to have any letter of Nejdanov's . . . or his photograph? "

" I have a photograph and quite a good one too. I believe it's in the table drawer. I'll get it in a minute."

He began rummaging about in the drawer, whilst Snandulia went up to Mashurina and with a long, intent look full of sympathy, clasped her hand like a comrade.

" Here it is! " Paklin exclaimed and handed her the photograph.

Mashurina thrust it into her pocket quickly, scarcely glancing at it, and without a word of thanks, flushing bright red, she put on her hat and made for the door.

" Are you going? " Paklin asked. " Where do you live? You might tell me that at any rate."

" Wherever I happen to be."

" I understand. You don't want me to know. Tell me at least, are you still working under Vassily Nikolaevitch? "

" What does it matter to you? "

" Or some one else, perhaps Sidor Sidoritch? "

Mashurina did not reply.

" Or is your director some anonymous person? "

Mashurina had already stepped across the threshold.

" Perhaps it is some one anonymous! "

She slammed the door.

Paklin stood for a long time motionless before this closed door.

" Anonymous Russia! " he said at last.

This book, designed by
William B. Taylor
is a production of
Edito-Service S.A., Geneva

Printed in Switzerland